**"You c...**
**me ...**

Von Steigerwal... the Mauser you used at Omdurman?"

Churchill shook his head as he straightened his shabby coat. "That is long gone. I took the one you're holding from a man I killed. Killed today, I mean."

"A German?"

Churchill nodded. "The officer of the guard. He was inspecting us—inspecting me, at the time. I happened to say something that interested him, he stayed to talk, and I was able to surprise him. May I omit the details?"

"Until later. Yes. We have no time to talk. We're going back. I am still an S.S. officer. I still believe you to be an English traitor. I am borrowing you for a day or two—I require your service. They won't be able to prevent us without revealing that you escaped them." Von Steigerwald gave Churchill a smile that was charming and not at all cruel. "As you did yourself in speaking with me. They may shoot us. I think it's much more likely that they'll simply let us go, hoping I'll return you without ever learning your identity."

"And in America . . . ?"

"In America, Donovan wants you, not Kuhn. Not the Bund. Donovan knows you."

Slowly, Churchill nodded. "We met in . . . in forty-one, I think it was. Forty would've been an election year, and Roosevelt was already looking shaky in July—"

They were walking fast already, with Churchill a polite half-step behind; and Von Steigerwald no longer listened.

—From "Donovan Sent Us"
By Gene Wolfe

# OTHER EARTHS

EDITED BY
## Nick Gevers
## and Jay Lake

**DAW BOOKS, INC.**
DONALD A. WOLLHEIM, FOUNDER
375 Hudson Street, New York, NY 10014

ELIZABETH R. WOLLHEIM
SHEILA E. GILBERT
PUBLISHERS
http://www.dawbooks.com

First Printing, April 2009
1  2  3  4  5  6  7  8  9

# ACKNOWLEDGMENTS

# Table of Contents

# INTRODUCTION

## Nick Gevers and Jay Lake

In a sense, all fiction is alternate history. Did Odysseus rule in Ithaca? Where is Jack Aubrey in the recorded naval annals of the Napoleonic period? Did Rabbit Angstrom really play high school basketball? These characters are people that never were—that is what makes them part of fiction, after all.

Works that meet a relatively formal definition of alternate history have been with us since at least the nineteenth century. Aside from occasional fascinating literary sallies by the likes of Nathaniel Hawthorne and Benjamin Disraeli, most early counterfactual fictions were jingoistic wish-fulfillments or utopian whimsies, followed somewhat later by academic *gedankenexperimenten*. With the evolution of modern science fiction, alternate history came along for the ride, enriching the genre with visions of altered actualities to complement those of distant planets and turbulent futures.

Today alternate history is in its own right a major subgenre of speculative fiction. There are superstars such as Harry Turtledove and Eric Flint, more experimental efforts from Esther Friesner, Kim Stanley Robinson, and Christopher Priest, and continued incursions from literature by way of writers such as Peter Ackroyd and Philip Roth. Alternate history even has its own award, the Sidewise, named in honor of the seminal Murray Leinster short story "Sidewise in Time."

The award is administered by the estimable Steven H. Silver, whose dedication to the form is legendary.

Alternate history is alive and well and living on bookshelves worldwide. So why this anthology? Because, rightly or wrongly, alternate history has come to form a ghetto of its own within speculative fiction. A very large portion of the alternate history canon is concerned with militaria, fiction about soldiers and the wars they fight. This is as if an entire symphony orchestra were represented only by the brass section; however grand, the brass quickly becomes monotonous playing on its own.

We solicited work from among the best writers in the field. Some are masters of the genre, with the sort of deep thought and brilliant voice that makes a book such as this eminently rewarding. Others are newer players becoming well known for their achievements in urban fantasy, new weird, and all the other movements and subgenres of the past decade or two.

We felt that the form would benefit from being challenged by these sharply innovative voices. These are writers who can produce fascinating work in striking out across the countries of the mind where Lincoln was just a country lawyer, Ralph Vaughan Williams was only a soldier, and Bugsy Siegel was a Knight Templar. Even better, they can take us to places where the shift of history was something else entirely—a faery queen on England's throne, stars missing from the summer sky, an endless spiral of time along the shores of the Mekong. In short, this book is intended to be a showcase of what can be done by some of the most brilliant minds writing today, many working in a form not normally their own.

Like a microcosm of speculative fiction, alternate history's name is legion, for it is many, with a multitude of potentials. This collection brings new names and new ideas to this old and honorable field. With luck, it will bring new readers as well.

# THIS PEACEABLE LAND; OR, THE UNBEARABLE VISION OF HARRIET BEECHER STOWE

### Robert Charles Wilson

"It's worth your life to go up there," the tavernkeeper's wife said. "What do you want to go up there for, anyway?"

"The property is for sale," I said.

"Property!" The landlady of the roadside tavern nearly spat out the word. "There's nothing up there but sand hills and saggy old sheds. That, and a family of crazy colored people. Someone claims they sold you that? You ought to check with the bank, Mister, see about getting your money back."

She smiled at her own joke, showing tobacco-stained teeth. In this part of the country there were spittoons in every taproom and Bull Durham advertisements on every wall. It was 1895. It was August. It was hot, and we were in the South.

I was only posing as an investor. I had no money in all the baggage I was carrying—very little, anyhow. I had photographic equipment instead.

"You go up those hills," the tavernkeeper's wife said more soberly, "you carry a gun, and you keep it handy. I mean that."

I had no gun.

I wasn't worried about what I might find up in the pine barrens.

I was worried about what I would tell my daughter.

I paid the lady for the meal she had served me and for a second meal she had put up in a neat small box. I asked her whether a room was available for the night. There was. We discussed the arrangements and came to an agreement. Then I went out to where Percy was waiting in the carriage.

"You'll have to sleep outside," I said. "But I got this for you." I gave him the wrapped dinner. "And the landlady says she'll bring you a box breakfast in the morning, as long as there's nobody around to see her."

Percy nodded. None of this came as a surprise to him. He knew where he was, and who he was, and what was expected of him. "And then," he said, "we'll drive up to the place, weather permitting."

To Percy it was always "the place"—each place we found.

Storm clouds had dallied along this river valley all the hot day, but no rain had come. If it came tonight, and if it was torrential, the dirt roads would quickly become useless creeks of mud. We would be stuck here for days.

And Percy would get wet, sleeping in the carriage as he did. But he preferred the carriage to the stable where our horses were put up. The carriage was covered with rubberized cloth, and there was a big sheet of mosquito netting he stretched over the open places during the night. But a truly stiff rain was bound to get in the cracks and make him miserable.

Percy Camber was an educated black man. He wrote columns and articles for the *Tocsin*, a Negro paper published out of Windsor, Canada. Three years ago a Boston press had put out a book he'd written, though he admitted the sales had been slight.

I wondered what the landlady would say if I told her Percy was a book writer. Most likely she would have denied the possibility of an educated black man. Except perhaps as a circus act, like that Barnum horse that counts to ten with its hoof.

"Make sure your gear is ready first thing," Percy said, keeping his voice low although there was nobody else about—this was a poor tavern on a poor road in an undeveloped county. "And don't drink too much tonight, Tom, if you can help it."

"That's sound advice," I agreed, by way of not pledging an answer. "Oh, and the keeper's wife tells me we ought to carry a gun. Wild men up there, she says."

"I don't go armed."

"Nor do I."

"Then I guess we'll be prey for the wild men," said Percy, smiling.

The room where I spent the night was not fancy, which made me feel better about leaving my employer to sleep out-of-doors. It was debatable which of us was better off. The carriage seat where Percy curled up was not infested with fleas, as was the mattress on which I lay. Percy customarily slept on a folded jacket, while my pillow was a sugar sack stuffed with corn huskings, which rattled beneath my ear as if the beetles inside were putting on a musical show.

I slept a little, woke up, scratched myself, lit the lamp, took a drink.

I will not drink, I told myself as I poured the liquor. I will not drink "to excess." I will not become drunk. I will only calm the noise in my head.

My companion in this campaign was a bottle of rye whiskey. Mister Whiskey Bottle, unfortunately, was only half full and not up to the task assigned him. I drank but kept on thinking unwelcome thoughts, while the night simmered and creaked with insect noises.

"Why do you have to go away for so long?" Elsebeth asked me.

In this incarnation she wore a white dress. It looked like her christening dress. She was thirteen years old.

"Taking pictures," I told her. "Same as always."

"Why can't you take pictures at the portrait studio?"

"These are different pictures, Elsie. The kind you have to travel for."

Her flawless young face took on an accusatory cast. "Mama says you're stirring up old trouble. She says you're poking into things nobody wants to hear about any more, much less see photographs of."

"She may be right. But I'm being paid money, and money buys pretty dresses, among other good things."

"Why make such trouble, though? Why do you want to make people feel bad?"

Elsie was a phantom. I blinked her away. These were questions she had not yet actually posed, though our last conversation, before I left Detroit, had come uncomfortably close. But they were questions I would sooner or later have to answer.

I slept very little, despite the drink. I woke up before dawn.

I inventoried my photographic equipment by lamplight, just to make sure everything was ready.

It had not rained during the night. I settled up with the landlady and removed my baggage from the room. Percy had already hitched the horses to the carriage. The sky was drab under high cloud, the sun a spot of light like a candle flame burning through a linen handkerchief.

The landlady's husband was nowhere to be seen. He had gone down to Crib Lake for supplies, she said, as she packed up two box lunches, cold cuts of beef with pickles and bread, which I had requested of her. She had two adult sons living with her, one of whom I had met in the stables, and she felt safe enough, she told me, even with her husband absent. "But we're a long way from anywhere," she added, "and the traffic along this road has been light ever since—well, ever since the Lodge closed down. I wasn't kidding about those sand hills, Mister. Be careful up there."

"We mean to be back by nightfall," I said.

\*   \*   \*

My daughter Elsebeth had met Percy Camber just once, when he came to the house in Detroit to discuss his plans with me. Elsie had been meticulously polite to him. Percy had offered her his hand, and she, wide-eyed, had taken it. "You're very neatly dressed," she had said.

She was not used to well-dressed black men. The only blacks Elsebeth had seen were the day laborers who gathered on the wharves. Detroit housed a small community of Negroes who had come north with the decline of slavery, before Congress passed the Labor Protection Act. They did "the jobs white men won't do," for wages to which white men would not submit.

"You're very prettily dressed yourself," Percy Camber said, ignoring the unintended insult.

Maggie, my wife, had simply refused to see him.

"I'm not some radical old Congregationalist," she told me, "eager to socialize with every tawny Moor who comes down the pike. That's your side of the family, Tom, not mine."

True enough. Maggie's people were Episcopalians who had prospered in Michigan since before it was a state—sturdy, reliable folks. They ran a string of warehouses that catered to the lake trade. My father was a disappointed Whig who had spent a single term in the Massachusetts legislature pursuing the chimera of Free Education before he died at an early age, and my mother's bookshelves still groaned under the weight of faded tomes on the subjects of Enlightened Marriage and Women's Suffrage. I came from a genteel family of radical tendencies and modest means. I was never sure Maggie's people understood that poverty and gentility could truly coexist.

"Maggie's indisposed today," I had told Percy, who may or may not have believed me, and then we had settled down to the business of planning our three-month tour of the South, according to the map he had made.

"There ought to be photographs," Percy said, "before it's all gone."

We traveled several miles from the tavern, sweating in the airless heat of the morning, following directions Percy had deduced from bills-of-transfer, railway records, and old advertisements placed in the Richmond and Atlanta papers.

The locality to which we were headed had been called Pilgassi Acres. It had been chartered as a business by two brothers, Marcus and Benjamin Pilgassi of South Carolina, in 1879, and it had operated for five years before the Ritter Inquiry shut it down.

There were no existing photographs of Pilgassi Acres, or any of the institutions like it, unless the Ritter Inquiry had commissioned them. And the Final Report of the Ritter Inquiry had been sealed from the public by consent of Congress, not to be reopened until some time in the twentieth century.

Percy Camber intended to shed some light into that officially ordained darkness.

He sat with me on the driver's board of the carriage as I coaxed the team over the rutted and runneled trail. This had once been a wider road, much used, but it had been bypassed by a Federal turnpike in 1887. Since then nature and the seasons had mauled it, so the ride was tedious and slow. We subdued the boredom by swapping stories: Percy of his home in Canada, me of my time in the army.

Percy "talked white." That was the verdict Elsebeth had passed after meeting him. It was a condescending thing to say, excusable only from the lips of a child, but I knew what she meant. Percy was two generations out of slavery. If I closed my eyes and listened to his voice, I could imagine that I had been hired by some soft-spoken Harvard graduate. He was articulate, even for a newspaper man. And we had learned, over the course of this lengthy expedition, to make allowances for our differences. We had some common ground. We were both the offspring of radical parents, for example. The "madness of the fifties" had touched us both, in different ways.

"You suppose we'll find anything substantial at the end of this road?" Percy asked.

"The landlady mentioned some old sheds."

"Sheds would be acceptable," Percy said, his weariness showing. "It's been a long haul for you, Tom. And not much substantial work. Maybe this time?"

"Maybe."

"Documents, oral accounts, that's all useful, but a photograph—just one, just to show that something remains—well, that would be important."

"I'll photograph any old shed you like, Percy, if it pleases you." Though on this trip I had seen more open fields—long since burned over and regrown— than anything worthy of being immortalized. Places edited from history. Absences constructed as carefully as architecture. I had no reason to think Pilgassi Acres would be different.

Percy seldom spoke out loud about the deeper purpose of his quest or the book he was currently writing. Fair enough, I thought; it was a sensitive subject. Like the way I don't talk much about Cuba, though I had served a year and a half there under Lee. The spot is too tender to touch.

These hills were low and covered with stunted pines and other rude vegetation. The road soon grew even more rough, but we began to encounter evidence of a prior human presence. A few fenceposts. Scraps of rusted barbwire. The traces of an old narrow-gauge railbed. Then we passed under a wooden sign suspended between two lodgepoles on which the words *PILGASSI ACRES* in an ornate script were still legible, though the seasons had bleached the letters to ghosts.

There was also the remains of a wire fence, tangled over with brambles.

"Stop here," Percy said.

"Might be more ahead," I suggested.

"This is already more than we've seen elsewhere. I want a picture of that sign."

"I can't guarantee it'll be legible," I said, given the way the sun was striking it, and the faint color of the letters, pale as chalk on the white wood.

"Well, try," Percy said shortly.

So I set up my equipment and did that. For the first time in a long while, I felt as though I was earning my keep.

The first book Percy had written was called *Every Measure Short of War*, and it was a history of Abolitionism from the Negro point of view.

The one he was writing now was to be called *Where Are the Three Million?*

I made a dozen or so exposures and put my gear back in the carriage. Percy took the reins this time and urged the horses farther up the trail. Scrub grass and runt pines closed in on both sides of us, and I found myself watching the undergrowth for motion. The landlady's warning had come back to haunt me.

But the woods were empty. An old stray dog paced us for a few minutes, then fell behind.

My mother had once corresponded with Mrs. Harriet Beecher Stowe, who was a well-known abolitionist at one time, though the name is now mostly forgotten. Percy had contacted my parents in order to obtain copies of that correspondence, which he had quoted in an article for the *Tocsin*.

My mother, of course, was flattered, and she continued her correspondence with Percy on an occasional basis. In one of his replies Percy happened to remark that he was looking for a reliable photographer to hire for the new project he had in mind. My mother, of course, sent him to me. Perhaps she thought she was doing me a favor.

Thus it was not money but conscience that had propelled me on this journey. Conscience, that crabbed and ecclesiastical nag, which inevitably spoke, whether I heeded it or not, in a voice much like my mother's.

The remains of Pilgassi Acres became visible as we rounded a final bend, and I was frankly astonished that so much of it remained intact. Percy Camber drew in his breath.

Here were the administrators' quarters (a small building with pretensions to the colonial style), as well as five huge barnlike buildings and fragments of paving stones and mortared brick where more substantial structures had been demolished.

All silent, all empty. No glass in the small windows. A breeze like the breath from a hard-coal stove seeped around the buildings and tousled the meadow weeds that lapped at them. There was the smell of old wood that had stood in the sunlight for a long time. There was, beneath that, the smell of something less pleasant, like an abandoned latrine doused with lime and left to simmer in the heat.

Percy was working to conceal his excitement. He pretended to be casual, but I could see that every muscle in him had gone tense.

"Your camera, Tom," he said, as if the scene were in some danger of evaporating before our eyes.

"You don't want to explore the place a little first?"

"Not yet. I want to capture it as we see it now—from a distance, all the buildings all together."

And I did that. The sun, though masked by light high clouds, was a feverish nuisance over my right shoulder.

I thought of my daughter Elsebeth. She would see these pictures some day. "What place is this?" she would ask.

But what would I say in return?

Any answer I could think of amounted to drilling a hole in her innocence and pouring poison in.

*Every Measure Short of War*, the title of Percy's first book, implied that there might have been one—a war over Abolition, that is, a war between the states. My mother agreed. "Though it was not the North that would have brought it on," she insisted. (A conversation we had had on the eve of my marriage to Maggie.) "People forget how sullen the South was in the years before the Douglas Compromise. How fierce in the defense of slavery. Their 'Peculiar Institution'! Strange, isn't it, how people cling most desperately to a thing when it becomes least useful to them?"

My mother's dream, and Mrs. Stowe's, for that matter, had never been achieved. No Abolition by federal statute had ever been legislated. Slavery had simply become unprofitable, as its milder opponents and apologists used to insist it inevitably would. Scientific farming killed it. Crop rotation killed it. Deep plowing killed it, mechanized harvesters killed it, soil fertilization killed it.

Embarrassment killed it, once Southern farmers began to take seriously the condescension and disapproval of the European powers whose textile and tobacco markets they craved. Organized labor killed it.

Ultimately, the expense and absurdity of maintaining human beings as farm chattel killed it.

A few slaves were still held under permissive state laws (in Virginia and South Carolina, for example), but they tended to be the pets of the old planter aristocracy—kept, as pets might be kept, because the children of the household had grown fond of them and objected to their eviction.

I walked with Percy Camber through the abandoned administration building at Pilgassi Acres. It had been stripped of everything—all furniture, every document, any scrap that might have testified to its human utility. Even the wallpaper had peeled or rotted away. One well-placed lightning strike would have burned the whole thing to the ground.

Its decomposing stairs were too hazardous to attempt. Animals had covered the floorboards with dung, and birds lofted out of every room we opened.

Our progress could have been charted by the uprisings of the swallows and the indignation of the owls.

"It's just an empty building," I said to Percy, who had been silent throughout the visit, his features knotted and tense.

"Empty of what, though?" he asked.

I took a few more exposures on the outside. The crumbling pillars. The worm-tunneled verandah casting a sinister shade. A chimney leaning sideways like a drunken man.

I did not believe, could not bring myself to believe, that a war within the boundaries of the Union could ever have been fought, though historians still worry about that question like a loose tooth. If the years after '55 had been less prosperous, if Douglas had not been elected President, if the terrorist John Brown had not been tried in a Northern court and hanged on a Northern gallows . . . *if, if,* and *if, ad infinitum.*

All nonsense, it seemed to me. Whatever Harriet Beecher Stowe might have dreamed, whatever Percy Camber might have uncovered, this was fundamentally a peaceable land.

*This is a peaceable land*, I imagined myself telling my daughter Elsebeth; but my imagination would extend itself no farther.

"Now the barracks," Percy said.

It had been even hotter in the administration building than it was outside, and Percy's clothes were drenched through. So were mine. "You mean those barns?"

"Barracks," Percy repeated.

Barracks or barns—they were a little of both, as it turned out. The one we inspected was a cavernous wooden box, held up by mildew and inertia. Percy wanted photographs of the rusted iron brackets that had supported rows of wooden platforms—a few of these remained—on which men and women had once slept. There were a great many of these brackets, and I estimated that a single barracks-barn might have housed as many as two hundred persons in its day. An even larger number if mattresses had been laid on the floors.

I took the pictures he wanted by the light that came through fallen boards. The air in the barn was stale, despite all the holes in the walls, and it was a relief to finish my work and step out into the relentless, dull sunshine.

The presence of so many people must have necessitated a dining hall, a communal kitchen, sanitary facilities at Pilgassi Acres. Those structures had not survived except as barren patches among the weeds. Dig down a little—Percy had learned this technique in his research—and you would find a layer of charcoal for each burned building or outhouse. Not every structure in Pilgassi Acres had survived the years, but each had left its subtle mark.

One of the five barns was not like the others, and I made this observation to Percy Camber as soon as I noticed it. "The rest of these barracks, the doors and windows are open to the breeze. The far one in the north quarter has been boarded up—d'you see?"

"That's the one we should inspect next, then," Percy said.

We were on our way there when the first bullet struck.

My mother had always been an embarrassment to me, with her faded enthusiasms, her Bible verses and Congregationalist poetry, her missionary zeal on behalf of people whose lives were so tangential to mine that I could barely imagine them.

She didn't like it when I volunteered for Cuba in 1880. It wasn't a proper war, she said. She said it was yet another concession to the South, to the aristocracy's greed for expansion toward the equator. "A war engineered at the Virginia Military Institute," she called it, "fought for no good reason."

But it blended Northerners and Southerners on a

neutral field of battle, where we were all just American soldiers. It was the glue that repaired many ancient sectional rifts. Out of it emerged great leaders, like old Robert E. Lee, who transcended regional loyalties (though when he spoke of "America," I often suspected he used the word as a synonym for "Virginia"), and his son, also a talented commander. In Cuba we all wore a common uniform, and we all learned, rich and poor, North and South, to duck the Spaniards' bullets.

The bullet hit a shed wall just above Percy Camber's skull. Splinters flew through the air like a cloud of mosquitoes. The sound of the gunshot arrived a split second later, damped by the humid afternoon to a harmless-sounding *pop*. The rifleman was some distance away. But he was accurate.

I dropped to the ground—or, rather, discovered that I had already dropped to the ground, obeying an instinct swifter than reason.

Percy, who had never been to war, lacked that ingrained impulse. I'm not sure he understood what had happened. He stood there in the rising heat, bewildered.

"Get down," I said.

"What is it, Tom?"

"Your doom, if you don't get down. *Get down!*"

He understood then. But it was as if the excitement had loosened all the strings of his body. He couldn't decide which way to fold. He was the picture of confusion.

Then a second bullet struck him in the shoulder.

"Liberty Lodges," they had been called at first.

I mean the places like Pilgassi Acres, back when they were allowed to flourish.

They were a response to a difficult time. Slavery had died, but the slaves had not. That was the dilemma of the South. Black men without skills, along with their families and countless unaccompanied children, crowded the roads—more of them every day, as "free-labor cotton" became a rallying cry for progressive French and English buyers.

Who were Marcus and Benjamin Pilgassi? Probably nothing more than a pair of Richmond investors jumping on a bandwagon. The Liberty Lodges bore no onus then. The appeal of the business was explicit: Don't put your slaves on the road and risk prosecution or fines for "abandonment of property." We will take your aging and unprofitable chattel and house them. The men will be kept separate from the women to prevent any reckless reproduction. They will live out their lives with their basic needs attended to for an annual fee only a fraction of what it would cost to keep them privately.

What the Pilgassi brothers (and businessmen like them) did not say directly—but implied in every line of their advertisements—was that the Liberty Lodge movement aimed to achieve an absolute and irreversible decline in the Negro population in the South.

In time, Percy had told me, the clients of these businesses came to include entire state governments, which had tired of the expense and notoriety incurred by the existence of temporary camps in which tens of thousands of "intramural refugees" could neither be fed economically nor be allowed to starve. It had been less onerous for them to subsidize the Lodges, which tended to be built in isolated places, away from casual observation.

Percy's grandfather had escaped slavery in the 1830s and settled in Boston, where he picked up enough education to make himself prominent in the Abolition movement. Percy's father, an ordained minister, had spoken at Lyman Beecher's famous church, in the days before he founded the journal that became the *Tocsin*.

Percy had taken up the moral burden of his forebears in a way I had not, but there was still a similarity between us. We were the children of crusaders. We had inherited their disappointments and drunk the lees of their bitterness.

I was not a medical man, but I had witnessed bullet wounds in Cuba. Percy had been shot in the shoulder. He lay on the ground with his eyes open, blinking, his left hand pressed against the wound. I pried his hand away so that I could examine his injury.

The wound was bleeding badly, but the blood did not spurt out, a good sign. I took a handkerchief from my pocket, folded it and pressed it against the hole.

"Am I dying?" Percy asked. "I don't feel like I'm dying."

"You're not all that badly hurt or you wouldn't be talking. You need attention, though."

A third shot rang out. I couldn't tell where the bullet went.

"And we need to get under cover," I added.

The nearest building was the boarded-up barracks. I told Percy to hold the handkerchief in place. His right arm didn't seem to work correctly, perhaps because the bullet had damaged some bundle of muscles or nerves. But I got him crouching, and we hurried toward shelter.

We came into the shadow of the building and stumbled to the side of it away from the direction from which the shots had come. Grasshoppers buzzed out of the weeds in fierce brown flurries, some of them lighting on our clothes. There was the sound of dry thunder down the valley. This barracks had a door—a wooden door on a rail, large enough to admit dozens of people at once. But it was closed, and there was a brass latch and a padlock on it.

So we had no real shelter—just some shade and a moment's peace.

I used the time to put a fresh handkerchief on Percy's wound and to bind it with a strip of cloth torn from my own shirt.

"Thank you," Percy said breathlessly.

"Welcome. The problem now is how to get back to

the carriage." We had no weapons, and we could hardly withstand a siege, no matter where we hid. Our only hope was escape, and I could not see any likely way of achieving it.

Then the question became moot, for the man who had tried to kill us came around the corner of the barracks.

"Why do you want to make these pictures?" Elsie asked yet again, from a dim cavern at the back of my mind.

In an adjoining chamber of my skull a different voice reminded me that I wanted a drink, a strong one, immediately.

The ancient Greeks (I imagined myself telling Elsebeth) believed that vision is a force that flies out from the eyes when directed by the human will. They were wrong. There is no force or will in vision. There is only light. Light direct or light reflected. Light, which behaves in predictable ways. Put a prism in front of it, and it breaks into colors. Open a shuttered lens, and some fraction of it can be trapped in nitrocellulose or collodion as neatly as a bug in a killing jar.

A man with a camera is like a naturalist, I told Elsebeth. Where one man might catch butterflies, another catches wasps.

I did not make these pictures.

I only caught them.

The man with the rifle stood five or six yards away at the corner of the barracks. He was a black man in threadbare coveralls. He was sweating in the heat. For a while there was silence, the three of us blinking at each other.

Then, "I didn't mean to shoot him," the black man said.

"Then you shouldn't have aimed a rifle at him and pulled the trigger," I said back, recklessly.

Our assailant made no immediate response. He seemed to be thinking this over. Grasshoppers lit on the cuffs of his ragged pants. His head was large, his hair cut crudely close to the skull. His eyes were narrow and suspicious. He was barefoot.

"It was not my intention to hurt anyone," he said again. "I was shooting from a distance, sir."

By this time Percy had managed to sit up. He seemed less afraid of the rifleman than he ought to have been. Less afraid, at any rate, than I was. "What *did* you intend?"

He gave his attention to Percy. "To warn you away, is all."

"Away from what?"

"This building."

"Why? What's in this building?"

"My son."

The "three million" in Percy's title were the men, women and children of African descent held in bondage in the South in the year 1860. For obvious reasons, the number is approximate. Percy always tried to be conservative in his estimates, for he did not want to be vulnerable to accusations of sensationalizing history.

Given that number to begin with, what Percy had done was to tally up census polls, where they existed, alongside the archived reports of various state and local governments, tax and business statements, Federal surveys, rail records, etc., over the years between then and now.

What befell the three million?

A great many—as many as one third—emigrated North, before changes in the law made that difficult. Some of those who migrated continued on up to Canada. Others made lives for themselves in the big cities, insofar as they were allowed to. A smaller number were taken up against their will and shipped to certain inhospitable "colonies" in Africa, until the excesses and horrors of repatriation became notorious and the whole enterprise was outlawed.

Some found a place among the freemen of New Orleans or worked boats, largely unmolested, along the Gulf Coast. A great many went West, where they

were received with varying degrees of hostility. Five
thousand "irredeemably criminal" black prisoners were
taken from Southern jails and deposited in a Utah
desert, where they died not long after.

Certain jobs remained open to black men and
women—as servants, rail porters, and so forth—and
many did well enough in these professions.

But add the numbers, Percy said, even with a generous allowance for error, and it still comes up shy of
the requisite three million.

How many were delivered into the Liberty Lodges?
No one can answer that question with any certainty,
at least not until the evidence sealed by the Ritter
Inquiry is opened to the public. Percy's estimate was
somewhere in the neighborhood of 50,000. But as I
said, he tended to be conservative in his figures.

"We were warned there was a family of wild men
up here," I said.

"I'm no wilder than I have to be," the gunman said.
"I didn't ask you to come visit."

"You hurt Percy bad enough, whether you're wild
or not. Look at him. He needs a medic."

"I see him all right, sir."

"Then, unless you mean to shoot us both to death,
will you help me get him back to our carriage?"

There was another lengthy pause.

"I don't like to do that," the black man said finally.
"There won't be any end to the trouble. But I don't
suppose I have a choice, except, as you say, sir, to kill
you. And that I cannot bring myself to do."

He said these words calmly enough, but he had a
way of forming his vowels, and pronouncing them
deep in his throat, that defies transcription. It was like
listening to a volcano rumble.

"Take his right arm, then," I said. "I'll get on his
left. The carriage is beyond that ridge."

"I know where your carriage is. But, sir, I won't
put down this rifle. I don't think that would be wise.
You can help him yourself."

I went to where Percy sat and began to lift him up.

Percy startled me by saying, "No, Tom, I don't want to go to the carriage."

"What do you mean?" the assailant asked, before I could pose the same question.

"Do you have a name?" Percy asked him.

"Ephraim," the man said, reluctantly.

"Ephraim, my name is Percy Camber. What did you mean when you said your son was inside this barracks?"

"I don't like to tell you that," Ephraim said, shifting his gaze between Percy and me.

"Percy," I said, "you need a doctor. We're wasting time."

He looked at me sharply. "I'll live a while longer. Let me talk to Ephraim, please, Tom."

"Stand off there where I can see you, sir," Ephraim directed. "I know this man needs a doctor. I'm not stupid. This won't take long."

I concluded from all this that the family of wild Negroes the landlady had warned me about was real and that they were living in the sealed barn.

Why they should want to inhabit such a place I could not say.

I stood apart while Percy, wounded as he was, held a hushed conversation with Ephraim, who had shot him.

I understood that they could talk more freely without me as an auditor. I was a white man. It was true that I worked for Percy, but that fact would not have been obvious to Ephraim any more than it had been obvious to the dozens of hotelkeepers who had assumed without asking that I was the master, and Percy the servant. My closeness to Percy was unique and all but invisible.

After a while Ephraim allowed me to gather up my photographic gear, which had been scattered in the crisis.

I had been fascinated by photography even as a child. It had seemed like such patent magic! The magic of stopped time, places and persons rescued from their ephemeral natures. My parents had given me books containing photographs of Indian elephants, of the pyramids of Egypt, of the natural wonders of Florida.

I put my gear together and waited for Percy to finish his talk with the armed lunatic who had shot him.

The high cloud that had polluted the sky all morning had dissipated during the afternoon. The air was still scaldingly hot, but it was a touch less humid. A certain brittle clarity had set in. The light was hard, crystalline. A fine light for photography, though it was beginning to grow long.

"Percy," I called out.

"What is it, Tom?"

"We have to leave now, before the sun gets any lower. It's a long journey to Crib Lake." There was a doctor at Crib Lake. I remembered seeing his shingle when we passed through that town. Some rural bonesetter, probably, a doughty relic of the mustard-plaster era. But better than no doctor at all.

Percy's voice sounded weak; but what he said was, "We're not finished here yet."

"What do you mean, not finished?"

"We've been invited inside," he said. "To see Ephraim's son."

Some bird, perhaps a mourning dove, called out from the gathering shadows among the trees where the meadow ended.

I did not want to meet Ephraim's son. There was a dreadful aspect to the whole affair. If Ephraim's son was in the barn, why had he not come out at the sound of gunshots and voices? (Ephraim, as far as I could tell, was an old man, and his son wasn't likely to be an infant.) Why, for that matter, was the barracks closed and locked? To keep the world away from Ephraim's son? Or to keep Ephraim's son away from the world?

"What is his name?" I asked. "This son of yours."

"Jordan," he said.

I had married Maggie not long after I got back from

Cuba. I had been trying to set up my photography business at the time. I was far from wealthy, and what resources I had I had put into my business. But there was a vogue among young women of the better type for manly veterans. I was manly enough, I suppose, or at least presentable, and I was authentically a veteran. I met Maggie when she came to my shop to sit for a portrait. I escorted her to dinner. Maggie was fond of me; and I was fond of Maggie, in part because she had no political convictions or fierce unorthodox ideals. She took the world as she found it.

Elsebeth came along a year or so after the wedding. It was a difficult birth. I remember the sound of Maggie's screams. I remember Elsebeth as a newborn, bloody in a towel, handed to me by the doctor. I wiped the remnant blood and fluid from her tiny body. She had been unspeakably beautiful.

Ephraim wore the key to the barn on a string around his neck. He applied it to the massive lock, still giving me suspicious glances. He kept his rifle in the crook of his arm as he did this. He slid the huge door open. Inside, the barn was dark. The air that wafted out was a degree or two cooler than outside, and it carried a sour tang, as of long-rotten hay or clover.

Ephraim did not call out to his son, and there was no sound inside the abandoned barracks.

Had Ephraim once held his newborn son in his arms, as I had held Elsebeth?

The last of the Liberty Lodges were closed down in 1888. Scandal had swirled around them for years, but no sweeping legal action had been taken. In part this was because the Lodges were not a monolithic enterprise; a hundred independent companies held title to them. In part it was because various state legislatures were afraid of disclosing their own involvement. The Lodges had not proved as profitable as their founders expected; the plans had not anticipated, for instance, all the ancillary costs of keeping human beings confined in what amounted to a jail (guards, walls, fences, discipline, etc.) for life. But the *utility* of the Lodges was undisputed, and several states had quietly subsidized them. A "full accounting," as Percy called it, would have tainted every government south of the Mason Dixon Line and not a few above it. Old wounds might have been reopened.

The Ritter Inquiry was called by Congress when the abuses inherent in the Lodge system began to come to light, inch by inch. By that time, though, there had been many other scandals, many other inquests, and the public had grown weary of all such issues. Newspapers, apart from papers like the *Tocsin*, hardly touched the story. The Inquiry sealed its own evidence, the surviving Lodges were hastily dismantled, and the general population (apart from a handful of aged reformers) paid no significant attention.

"Why dredge up all that ugliness?" Maggie had asked me.

*Nobody wants to see those pictures*, Elsebeth whispered.

Nobody but a few old scolds.

It was too dark in the immense barracks to be certain, but it seemed to me there was nobody inside but the three of us.

"I came here with Jordan in '78," Ephraim said. "Jordan was twelve years old at the time. I don't know what happened to his mama. We got separated at the Federal camp on the Kansas border. Jordan and I were housed in different buildings."

He looked around, his eyes abstracted, and seemed to see more than an old and ruined barracks. Perhaps he could see in the dark—it was dark in here, the only light coming through the fractionally open door. All I could see was a board floor, immaculately swept, picked out in that wedge of sun. All else was shadow.

He found an old crate for Percy to sit on. The crate was the only thing like furniture I could see. There was nothing to suggest a family resided here apart from the neatness, the sealed entrances and windows, the absence of bird dung. I began to feel impatient.

"You said your son was here," I prompted him.

"Oh, yes, sir. Jordan's here."

"Where? I don't see him."

Percy shot me an angry look.

"He's everywhere in here," the madman said.

Oh, I thought, it's not Jordan, then, it's the spirit of Jordan, or some conceit like that. This barn is a shrine the man has been keeping. I had the unpleasant idea that Jordan's body might be tucked away in one of its shadowed corners, dry and lifeless as an old Egyptian king.

"Or at least," Ephraim said, "from about eight foot down."

He found and lit a lantern.

One evening in the midst of our journey through the South I had got drunk and shared with Percy, too ebulliently, my idea that we were really very much alike.

This was in Atlanta, in one of the hotels that provides separate quarters for colored servants traveling with their employers. That was good because it meant Percy could sleep in relative comfort. I had snuck down to his room, which was little more than a cubicle, and I had brought a bottle with me, although Percy refused to share it. He was an abstinent man.

I talked freely about my mother's fervent abolitionism and how it had hovered over my childhood like a storm cloud stitched with lightning. I told Percy how we were both the children of idealists, and so forth.

He listened patiently, but at the end, when I had finally run down, or my jaw was too weary to continue, he rummaged through the papers he carried with him and drew out a letter that had been written to him by Mrs. Harriet Beecher Stowe.

Mrs. Stowe is best remembered for her work on behalf of the China Inland Mission, but she came from an abolitionist family. Her father was the first president of the famous Lane Theological Seminary. At one point in her life she had attempted a novel meant to expose the evils of slavery, but she could not find a publisher.

Percy handed me the woman's letter.

*I have received your book "Every Measure Short of War,"* the letter began, *and it brings back terrible memories and forebodings. I remember all too distinctly what it meant to love my country in those troubled years and to tremble at the coming day of wrath.*

"You want me to read this?" I asked drunkenly.

"Just that next part," Percy said.

*Perhaps because of your book, Mr. Camber,* Mrs. Stowe wrote, *or because of the memories it aroused, I suffered an unbearable dream last night. It was about that war. I mean the war that was so much discussed but that never took place, the war from which both North and South stepped back as from the brink of a terrible abyss.*

*In my dream that precipice loomed again, and this time there was no Stephen Douglas to call us away with concessions and compromises and his disgusting deference to the Slave Aristocracy. In my dream, the war took place. And it was an awful war, Mr. Camber. It seemed to flow before my eyes in a series of bloody tableaux. A half a million dead. Battlefields too awful to contemplate, North and South. Industries crippled, both the print and the cotton presses silenced, thriving cities reduced to smoldering ruins—all this I saw, or knew, as one sees or knows in dreams.*

*But that was not the unbearable part of it.*

*Let me say that I have known death altogether too intimately. I have suffered the loss of children. I love peace just as fervently as I despise injustice. I would not wish grief or heartbreak on any mother of any section of this country, or any other country. And yet—!*

*And yet, in light of what I have inferred from recent numbers of your newspaper, and from the letters you have written me, and from what old friends and ac-*

*quaintances have said or written about the camps, the deportations, the Lodges, etc.,—because of all that, a part of me wishes that that war had indeed been fought if only because it might have ended slavery. Ended it cleanly, I mean, with a sane and straightforward libera-tion, or even a liberation partial and incomplete—a dec-laration, at least, of the immorality and unacceptablity of human bondage—anything but this sickening decline by extinction, this surreptitious (as you so bitterly de-scribe it) "cleansing."*

*I suppose this makes me sound like a monster, a sort of female John Brown, confusing righteousness with violence and murder with redemption.*

*I am not such a monster. I confess a certain admira-tion for those who, like President Douglas, worked so very hard to prevent the apocalypse of which I dreamed last night, even if I distrust their motives and condemn their means. The instinct for peace is the most honor-able of all Christian impulses. My conscience rebels at a single death, much less one million.*

*But if a war could have ended slavery . . . would I have wished it? Welcomed it?*

*What is unbearable, Mr. Camber, is that I don't know that I can answer my own horrifying question either honestly or decently. And so I have to ask: Can you?*

I puzzled it out. Then I gave Percy a blank stare. "Why are you showing me this?"

"We're alike in many ways, as you say, Tom. But not all ways. Not all ways. Mrs. Stowe asks an interest-ing question. Answering it isn't easy. I don't know your mind, but fundamentally, Tom, despite all the sympathies between us, the fact is, I suspect that in the end you might give the *wrong* answer to that question—and I expect you think the same of me."

There was another difference, which I did not men-tion to Percy, and that was that every time I remarked on our similarities, I could hear my wife's scornful voice saying (as she had said when I first shared the idea of this project with her), "Oh, Tom, don't be ridiculous. You're nothing like that Percy Camber. That's your mother talking—all that abolitionist guilt she burdened you with. As if you need to prove you haven't betrayed the *cause*, whatever the *cause* is, exactly."

Maggie failed to change my mind, though what she said was true.

"From about eight feet down," Ephraim said cryptically, lifting the lantern.

Eight feet is as high an average man can reach without standing on something. Between eight feet and the floor is the span of a man's reach.

"You see, sir," Ephraim said, "my son and I were held in separate barracks. The idea behind that was that a man might be less eager to escape if it meant leaving behind a son or father or uncle. The overseers said, if you run, your people will suffer for it. But when my chance come I took it. I don't know if that's a sin. I think about it often." He walked toward the nearest wall, the lantern breaking up the darkness as it swayed in his grip. "This barracks here was my son's barracks."

"Were there many escapes?" Percy asked.

I began to see that something might have been written on the wall, though at first it looked more like an *idea* of writing: a text as crabbed and indecipherable as the scratchings of the Persians or the Medes.

"Yes, many," Ephraim said, "though not many successful. At first there was fewer guards on the gates. They built the walls up, too, over time. Problem is, you get away, where is there to go? Even if you get past these sandy hills, the country's not welcoming. And the guards had rifles, sir, the guards had dogs."

"But you got away, Ephraim."

"Not far away. When I escaped it was very near the last days of Pilgassi Acres." (He pronounced it *Pigassi*, with a reflexive curl of contempt on his lips.) "Company men coming in from Richmond to the overseer's house, you could hear the shouting some nights. Rations went from meat twice a week to a handful of cornmeal a day and green bacon on Sundays. They fired the little Dutch doctor who used to tend to us. Sickness come to us. They let the old ones die in place, took the bodies away to bury or burn. Pretty soon we knew what was meant to happen next. They could not keep us, sir, nor could they set us free."

"That was when you escaped?"

"Very near the end, sir, yes, that's when. I did not want to go without Jordan. But if I waited, I knew I'd be too weak to run. I told myself I could live in the woods and get stronger, that I would come back for Jordan when I was more myself."

He held the lantern close to the board wall of this abandoned barracks.

Percy was suffering more from his wound now than he had seemed to when he received it, and he grimaced as I helped him follow Ephraim. We stood close to the wild man and his circle of light, though not too close—I was still conscious of his rifle and of his willingness to use it, even if he was not in a killing mood right now.

The writing on the wall consisted of names. Hundreds of names. They chased each other around the whole of the barn in tight horizontal bands.

"I expect the overseers would have let us starve if they had the time. But they were afraid federal men would come digging around. There ought to be nothing of us left to find, I think was the reasoning. By that time the cholera had taken many of us anyhow, weak and hungry as we were, and the rest . . . well, death is a house, Mr. Camber, with many doorways. This is my son's name right here."

*Jordan Nash* was picked out by the yellow lantern light.

"Dear God," said Percy Camber, softly.

"I don't think God come into it, sir."

"Did he write his own name?"

"Oh, yes, sir. A Northern lady taught us both to

read, back in the Missouri camp. I had a Bible and a
copybook from her. I still read that Bible to this day.
Jordan was proud of his letters." Ephraim turned to
me as if I, not Percy, had asked the question: "Most
of these men couldn't write nor read. Jordan didn't
just write his own name. He wrote *all* these names.
Each and every one. A new man came in, he would
ask the name and put it down as best he could. The
list grew as we came and went. Many years' worth,
sir. All the prisoners talked about it, how he did that.
He had no pencil or chalk, you know. He made a kind
of pen or brush by chewing down sapling twigs to
soften their ends. Ink he made all kind of ways. He
was very clever about that. Riverbottom clay, soot,
blood even. In the autumns the work crews drawing
water from the river might find mushrooms which turn
black when you picked them, and they brought them
back to Jordan—those made fine ink, he said."

The pride in Ephraim's voice was unmistakable. He
marched along the wall with his lantern held high so
we could see his son's work in all its complexity. All
those names, written in the space between a man's
reach and the floor. The letters were meticulously
formed, the lines as level as the sea. Some of the
names were whole names, some were single names,
some were the kind of whimsical names given to house
servants. They all ran together, to conserve space, so
that in places you had to guess whether the names
represented one person or two.

. . . *John Kincaid Tom Abel Fortune Bob Swift Pom-
pey Atticus Joseph Wilson Elijah Elijah Jim Jim's Son
Rufus Moses Deerborn Moses Raffity* . . .

"I don't know altogether why he did it," Ephraim
said. "I think it made him feel better to see the men's
names written down. Just so somebody might know
we passed this way, he said."

Jordan lived in this barracks from eight foot down.
And so did shockingly many others.

"This is why you shot at us," Percy whispered, a
kind of awe or dread constricting his throat.

"I make it seem dangerous up here, yes, sir, so that nobody won't come back and take it down or burn it. And yet I suppose they will sooner or later whether I scare anybody or not. Or if not that, then the weather will wear it down. I keep it best I can against the rain, sir. I don't let birds or animals inside. Or even the daylight, sir, because the daylight fades things, that ink of Jordan's is sensitive to it. All be gone one day, I suppose, but I will be too, bye and bye, and yourselves as well, of course."

"Perhaps we can make it last a little longer," Percy said.

Of course I knew what he meant.

"I'll need light," I said.

The fierce, hot light of the fading day.

Ephraim was anxious to help, once Percy explained the notion to him. He threw open the barracks door. He took down the wood he had tacked over the south-facing windows. There were still iron bars in the window frames.

In the corners the light was not adequate despite our best efforts. Ephraim said he had a sheet of polished tin he used for a mirror, which might help reflect the sunlight in. He went to his encampment to get it. By that time he trusted us enough to leave us alone for a short time.

Once again I suggested escape, but Percy refused to leave. So I kept about my work.

There were only so many exposures I could make, and I wanted the names to be legible. In the end I could not capture everything. But I did my best.

Ephraim told us about the end of Pilgassi Acres. He had been nearby, hidden half starving in a grove of dwarf pines, when he heard the initial volley of gunshots. It was the first of many over the several hours that followed. Gunfire in waves, and then the cries of the dying. By that sound he knew he would never see his son Jordan again.

Trenches were dug in the ground. Smoke from the chimneys lay over the low country for days. But the owners had been hasty to finish their work, Ephraim said. They had not bothered to burn the empty barracks before they rode off in their trucks and carriages.

Ever since that time Ephraim had sheltered in the barn of a poor white farmer who was sympathetic to him. Ephraim trapped game in exchange for this modest shelter. Eventually the farmer lent him his rifle so that Ephraim could bring back an occasional deer as well as rabbits and birds. The farmer didn't talk much, Ephraim said, but there were age-browned copies of Garrison's *Liberator* stored in the barn; and Ephraim read these with interest, and improved his vocabulary and his understanding of the world.

Hardly anyone came up to Pilgassi Acres nowadays except hunters following game trails. He scared them off with his rifle if they got too close to Jordan's barracks.

There was no point leaving the barracks after dark, since we could not travel in the carriage until sunrise. Percy's condition worsened during the night. He came down with a fever, and as he shivered, his wound began to seep. I made him as comfortable as possible with blankets from the carriage, and Ephraim brought him water in a cracked clay jug.

Percy was lucid, but his ideas began to run in whimsical directions as midnight passed. He insisted that I take Mrs. Stowe's letter from where he kept it in his satchel and read it aloud by lamplight. It was this letter, he said, that had been the genesis of the book he was writing now, about the three million. He wanted to know what Ephraim would make of it.

I kept my voice neutral as I read, so that Mrs. Stowe's stark words might speak for themselves.

"That is a decent white woman," Ephraim said when he had heard the letter and given it some thought. "A Christian woman. She reminds me of the woman that taught me and Jordan to read. But I don't know what she's so troubled about, Mr. Camber. This idea there was no war. I suppose there wasn't, if by war you mean the children of white men fighting the children of white men. But, sir, I have seen the guns, sir, and I have seen them used, sir, all my life—*all* my life. And in my father's time and before him. Isn't that war? And if it *is* war, how can she say war was avoided? There were many casualties, sir, though their names are not generally recorded; many graves, though not marked; and many battlefields, though not admitted to the history books."

"I will pass that thought on to Mrs. Stowe," Percy whispered, smiling in his discomfort, "although she's very old now and might not live to receive it."

And I decided I would pass it on to Elsebeth, my daughter.

I packed up my gear very carefully, come morning. *This is Jordan's name*, I imagined myself telling Elsie, pointing to a picture in a book, the book Percy Camber would write.

This photograph, I would tell her, represents light cast in a dark place. Like an old cellar gone musty for lack of sun. Sunlight has a cleansing property, I would tell her. See: I caught a little of it here.

I supposed there was enough of her grandmother in her that Elsebeth might understand.

I began to feel hopeful about the prospect.

Ephraim was less talkative in the morning light. I helped poor shivering Percy into the carriage. I told Ephraim my mother had once published a poem in the *Liberator*, years ago. I couldn't remember which issue.

"I may not have seen that number," Ephraim said. "But I'm sure it was a fine poem."

I drove Percy to the doctor in Crib Lake. The doctor was an old man with pinch-nose glasses and dirty fingernails. I told him I had shot my servant accidentally, while hunting. The doctor said he did not usually work on colored men, but an extra ten dollars on top of his fee changed his mind.

He told me there was a good chance Percy would pull through, if the fever didn't worsen.

I thanked him, and I went off to buy myself a drink.

# THE GOAT VARIATIONS

## Jeff VanderMeer

It would have been hot and humid in September in that city, and the Secret Service would have gone in first, before him, to scan for hostile minds, even though it was just a middle school in a county he'd won in the elections, far away from the fighting. He would have emerged from the third black armored vehicle, blinking and looking bewildered as he got his bearings in the sudden sunlight. His aide and the personal bodyguards, who had grown up protecting him, would have surrounded him by his first step onto the asphalt of the driveway. They would have entered the school through the front, stopping under the sign for photos and a few words with the principal, the television cameras recording it all from a safe distance.

He would already be thinking past the event, to the next, and how to prop up sagging public approval ratings, due both to the conflict and his recent "indecision," which he knew was more analogous to "sickness." He would be thinking about, or around, the secret cavern beneath the Pentagon and the pale, almost grublike face of the adept in his tank. He would already be thinking about the machine.

By the end of the photo op, the sweat itches on his forehead, trickles into his eyes, burns sour in his mouth, but he has to ignore it for the cameras. He's turning a new word he learned from a Czech diplomat over and over in his mind. *Ossuary.* A word that sounds free and soaring but just means a pile of skulls. The latest satellite photos from the battlefield states of Kansas, Nebraska, and Idaho make him think of the word. The evangelicals have been eschewing god-missiles for more personal methods of vengeance, even as they tie down federal armies in an endless guerilla war. Sometimes he feels as though he's presiding over a pile of skulls.

The smile on his face has frozen into a rictus as he realizes there's something wrong with the sun; there's a red dot in its center, and it's eating away at the yellow, bringing a hint of green with it. He can tell he's the only one who can see it, can sense the pulsing, nervous worry on the face of his aide.

He almost says "ossuary" aloud, but then, as sun-spots wander across his eyes, they are bringing him down a corridor to the classroom where he will meet with the students and tell them a story. They walk past the open doors to the cafeteria—row on row of sagging wooden tables propped up by rusted metal legs; and he experiences a flare of anger. Why *this* school, with the infrastructure crumbling away? The overpowering stale smell of macaroni and cheese and meatloaf nauseates him.

All the while, he engages in small talk with the entourage of teachers trailing in his wake, almost all overweight middle-aged women with circles under their eyes and sagging flesh on their arms. Many of them are black. He smiles into their shiny, receptive faces and remembers the hired help in the mansion growing up. Some of his best friends were black until he took up politics.

For a second, as he looks down, marveling at their snouts and beaks and muzzles, their smiles melt away and he's surrounded by a pack of animals.

His aide mutters to him through clenched teeth, and two seconds later he realizes the words were, "Stop staring at them so much." There have always been times when meeting too many people at once has made him feel as if he's somewhere strange, all the mannerisms and gesticulations and varying tones of voice shimmering into babble. But it's only lately that people's faces have changed into a menagerie if he looks at them too long.

They'd briefed him on the secret rooms and the possibility of the machine even before giving him the latest intel on China's occupation of Japan and Taiwan. Only three hours into his presidency, an armored car had taken him to the Pentagon, away from his wife and the beginnings of the inauguration party. He'd told his vice president to meet the press while he was gone, even though he was now convinced the old man had dementia.

Once inside the Pentagon, they'd entered a green-lit steel elevator that went down for so long he thought for a moment it was broken. It was just him, his aide, a black-ops commander who didn't give his name, and a small, haggard man who wore an old gray suit over a faded white dress shirt, with no tie.

The elevators had opened to a rush of stale, cool air, like being under a mountain. Beneath the dark green glow of overhead lamps, he could see rows and rows of transparent, bathtub-shaped deprivation vats. In each floated one dreaming adept, skin wrinkled and robbed of color by the exposure to the chemicals that preserved and pacified them. Every shaven head was attached to wires and electrodes, every mouth attached to a breathing tube. Catheters took care of waste.

The stale air soon faded as they walked silent down the rows, replaced by a smell like turpentine mixed with honeysuckle. Sometimes the hands of the adepts twitched, like dogs running in their sleep.

A vast, slow, repeating sound registered in his awareness. Only after several minutes did he realize it was the sound of the adepts as they moved in their vats, each sending a ripple of water that wouldn't have registered if not for its repetition in thousands of other vats. The room seemed to go on forever, into the far distance of a horizon tinged at its extremity by a darkening that hinted of blood.

His sense of disgust, even revulsion, grew as the little man ran out ahead of them, navigated a path to the control center, a hundred yards in and to the left, its blank, luminous blue glass set a story up and jutting out over the vats like some infernal crane. And still he could not speak, did not know what to say. The atmosphere was a strange combination of morgue, cathedral, and torture chamber. He felt a compulsion, if he spoke, to whisper.

The briefing papers he'd read on the ride over had told him just about everything. For years, adepts had been screened out at birth and, depending on the secret orders peculiar to each administration, either euthanized or imprisoned in remote overseas detention camps. Those that managed to escape detection until adulthood had no rights if caught, not even the rights given to illegal immigrants. The Founding Fathers had been very clear on that in the Constitution.

He had always assumed that adults when caught were eliminated or also sent to the camps. Some might call it the last vestige of a Puritanical brutality, but most citizens despised the invasion of privacy an adept represented or were more worried about how the separatist evangelicals had turned the homeland into a nation of West and East Coasts, with no middle.

But now he knew where his predecessor had been storing the bodies. He just didn't yet know why.

In the control center, they showed him the images being mined from the depths of the adepts' REM sleep. They ranged from montages as incomprehensible as the experimental films he'd seen in college to single shots of dead people to grassy hills littered with wildflowers. Ecstasy, grief, madness, peace. Anything imaginable came through in the adepts' endless sleep.

"Only ten people in the world know every aspect of this project, and three of them are dead, Mr. President," the black-ops commander told him.

Down below, he could see the little man, blue-tinted, going from vat to vat, checking readings.

"We experimented until we found the right combination of drugs to augment their sight. One particular formula, culled from South American mushrooms mostly, worked best. Suddenly, we began to get more coherent and varied images. Very different from before."

He felt numb. He had no sympathy for the men and women curled up in the vats below him—an adept's grenade had killed his father in mid-campaign a decade before, launching his own reluctant career in politics—but, still, he felt numb.

"Are any of them dangerous?" he asked the black-ops commander.

"They're all dangerous, Mr. President," the black-ops commander told him. "Every last one."

"When did this start?"

"With a secret order from your predecessor, Mr. President. Before, we just disappeared them or sent them to work camps in the Alaskas."

"Why did he do it?"

Even then, he would realize later, a strange music was growing in his head, a distant sound fast approaching.

"He did it, Mr. President, or said he did it, as a way of getting intel on the Heartland separatists."

Understandable, if extreme. The separatists and the fact that the federal armies had become bogged down fighting them in the Heartland were the main reasons his predecessor's party no longer controlled the executive, judicial, or legislative branches. And no one had ever succeeded in placing a mole within evangelical ranks.

The scenes continued to cascade over the monitors in a rapid-fire nonsense rhythm.

"What do you do with the images?"

"They're sent to a team of experts for interpretation, Mr. President. These experts are not told where the images come from."

"What do these adepts see that is so important?"

The black-ops commander grimaced at the tone of rebuke. "The future, Mr. President. It's early days, but we believe they see the future."

"And have you gained much in the way of intel?"

The black-ops commander looked at his feet. "No, not yet, we haven't. And we don't know why. The images are jumbled. Some might even be from our past or present. But we have managed to figure out one thing, which is why you've been brought here so quickly: Something will happen later this year, in September."

"Something?"

Down below, the little man had stopped his purposeful wandering and gazed into one of the vats as if mesmerized.

"Something cataclysmic, Mr. President. Across the channels. Across all of the adepts. It's quite clear. Every adept has a different version of what that something is. And we don't know *exactly* when, but in September."

He had a thousand more questions, but at that moment one of the military's top scientific researchers entered the control room to show them the schematics for the machine—the machine they'd found in the mind of one particular adept.

The time machine.

The teachers are telling him about the weather, and he's pretending to care as he continues to notice the florescent lighting as yellow as the skin that forms on old butter, the cracks in the dull beige walls, the faded construction paper of old projects taped to those walls, drooping down toward a tired, washed-out green carpet that's paper-thin under foot.

It's the kind of event that he's never really understood the point of, even as he understands the *reason* for it. To prove that he's still fit for office. To prove that the country, most of it, is free of war and division. To prove he cares about kids, even though this particular school is falling apart. Why this class, why today, is what he really doesn't understand, with so many world crises—like China's imperialism, like Iraq as the only bulwark against Russian influence in the Middle East. Or a vice president he now knows may be too old and delusional to be anything other than an embarrassment, and a cabinet he let his family's political cronies bully him into appointing, and a secret cavern that has infected his thoughts, infected his mind.

And that leads to memories of his father and of the awful silence into which they told him, as he sat coked up and hungover that morning on the pastel couch in some sleazy apartment, how it had happened while his father was working an audience in Atlanta.

All of this has made him realize that there's only one way to survive the presidency: to just let go of the reality of the world in favor of whatever reality he wants or needs, no matter how selfish.

The teachers are turning into animals again, and he can't seem to stop it from happening.

The time machine had appeared as an image on their monitors from an adept named Peter in vat 1023, and because they couldn't figure out the context— weapon? camera? something new?—they had to wake Peter up and have a conversation with him.

*A time machine*, he told them.

A time machine?

*A machine that travels through time,* he'd clarified.

And they'd believed him or, if not believed him, dared to hope he was right. That what Peter had seen while deprived of anything but his own brain, like some deep-sea fish, like something constantly turning inward and then turning inward again, had been a time machine.

If they didn't build it and they found out later that it might have worked and could have helped them avert or change what was fated to happen in September . . . Well, who could live with that thought?

That day, three hours after being sworn in, he had

had to give the order to build a time machine, and quickly.

*"Something bad will happen in September. Something bad. Across the channels. Something awful."*

"What?" he kept asking, and the answer was always the same: *"We don't know."*

They kept telling him that the adepts didn't seem to convey literal information as much as impressions and visions of the future, filtered through dreamscapes. As if the drugs they'd perfected, which had changed the way the adepts dreamed, both improved and destroyed focus.

In the end, he had decided to build the machine and to defend against almost everything they could think of or divine from the images: any attack against the still thriving New York financial district or the monument to the Queen Mother in the New York harbor; the random god-missiles of the Christian jihadists of the Heartland, who still hadn't managed to unlock the nuclear codes in the occupied states; and even the lingering cesspool that was Los Angeles after the viruses and riots.

But they still did not really know.

He's good at talking to people when it's not a prepared speech, good at letting his mind be elsewhere while he talks to a series of masks from behind his own mask. The prepared speeches are different because he's expected to *inhabit* them, and he's never fully inhabited anything, any role, in his life.

They round the corner and enter the classroom and are greeted by thirty children in plastic one-piece desk chairs, looking solemn, and the teacher standing in front of a beat-up battlewagon of a desk, overflowing with papers.

Behind her, posters they'd made for him, or someone had made to look as though the children made them, most showing him with the crown on his head. But also a blackboard, which amazes him. So anachronistic, and he's always hated the sound of chalk on a blackboard. Hated the smell of glue and the sour food-sweat of unwashed kids. It's all so squalid and tired and oddly close to the atmosphere in the underground cavern, the smell the adepts give off as they thrash in slow motion in their vats, silently screaming out images of September oblivion.

The children look up at him when he enters the room as if they're watching something far away and half wondrous, half monstrous.

He stands there and talks to them for a while first, trying to ignore the window in the back of the classroom that wants to show him a scene that shouldn't have been there. He says the kinds of things he's said to kids for years while on the campaign trail, running for ever-greater office; he has said these things for so many years that it's become a sawdust litany meant to convince *him* of his charm, his wit, his competence. Later, he won't remember what he said or what they said back. It's not important.

But he's thought about the implications in bed at night, lying there while his wife reads, her pale, freckled shoulder like a wall above him. He could stand in a classroom and say nothing, and still they would be fascinated with him, like a talisman, like a golden statue. No one had ever told him that sometimes you don't have to inhabit the presidency—sometimes, it inhabits you.

He'd wondered at the time of his coronation if he'd feel different. He'd wondered how the parliament members would receive him, given the split between the popular vote and the legislative vote. But nothing had happened. The parliament members had clapped, some longer than others, and he'd been sworn in, duly noting the absence of the rogue Scottish delegation. The Crown of the Americas had briefly touched his head, like an "iron kiss from the mouth of God," as his predecessor had put it, and then it was gone again, under glass, and he was back to being the secular president, not some sort of divine king.

Then they'd taken him to the Pentagon, hurtled him

half a mile underground, and he'd felt like a man who wins a prize only to find out it's worthless. *Ossuary.* He'd expected clandestine spy programs, secret weapons, special powers. But he hadn't expected the faces in the vats or the machine.

Before they built the time machine, he had insisted on meeting Peter in an interrogation room near the vats. He felt strongly about this, about looking into the eyes of the man he had almost decided to trust.

"Are you sure this will work?" he asked Peter, even as he found the question irrelevant, ridiculous. No matter what Peter said, no matter how impossible his scientists said it was, how it subverted known science, he was going to do it. The curiosity was too strong. The effort to get to this point had been too great, even if it had been his predecessor's effort.

Peter's eyes were bright with a kind of fever. His face was the palest white possible, and he stank of the chemicals. They'd put him in a white jumpsuit to cover his nakedness.

"It'll work. I pulled it out of another place. It was a true-sight. A true-seeing. I don't know how it works, but it works. It'll work, it'll work, and then," he turned toward the black one-way glass at the far end of the room, hands in restraints behind his back, "I'll be free?"

There was a blankness to Peter's face that he refused to acknowledge. A sense of something being held back, of something not quite right. Later, he would wonder why he hadn't trusted that instinct.

"What exactly is the machine for? Exactly. Not just . . . time travel. Tell me something more specific."

The scientist accompanying them smiled. He had a withered, narrow face and a firm chin, and he wore a jumpsuit that matched Peter's, with a black belt at the waist that held the holster for an even blacker semiautomatic pistol. He smelled strongly of a sickly sweet cologne, as if he were hiding some essential putrefaction.

"Mr. President," he said, "Peter is not a scientist. And we cannot peer into his mind. We can only see the images his mind projects. Until we build it, we will not know exactly how it works."

And then, when it was built, and they took him to it, he didn't know what to make of it. He didn't think they did, either—they were gathered around it in their protective suits like apes trying to figure out an internal combustion engine.

"Don't look directly into it," the scientist beside him advised. "Those who have experience a kind of . . . disorientation."

Unlike the apes examining it, the two of them stood behind three feet of protective, blast-proof glass, and yet both of them had moved to the back of the viewing room—as far away from the artifact as possible.

The machine consisted of a square housing made of irregular-looking gray metal, caulked on the interior with what looked like rotted beef; and in the center of this assemblage there was an eye of green light. In the middle of the eye was a piercing red dot. The machine was about the size of a microwave oven.

When he saw it, he shuddered; he could not tell at first if the eye was organic or a metallic lens. The effect of the machine on his mind was of a thousand maggots inching their way across the top of a television set turned on but not receiving a station.

He couldn't stop looking, as if the scientist's warning had made it impossible not to look. A crawling sensation spread across his scalp, his arms, his hands, his legs.

"How does it work?" he asked the scientist.

"We still don't know."

"Does the adept know?"

"Not really. He just told us not to look into it directly."

"Is it from the future?"

"That is the most logical guess."

To him, it didn't look real. It looked either like

something from another planet or something a psychotic child would put together before turning to more violent pursuits.

"Where else could it be from?"

The scientist didn't reply, and anger began to override his fear. He continued to look directly into the eye, even as it made him feel sick.

"Well, what do you know?"

"That it shouldn't work. As we put the pieces together . . . we all thought . . . we all thought it was more like witchcraft than science. Forgive me, Mr. President."

He gave the scientist a look that the scientist couldn't meet. Had he meant the gravity of the insult? Had he meant to imply their efforts were as blasphemous as the adept's second sight?

"And now? What do you think now?"

"It's awake, alive. But we don't see how it's . . ."

"It's what?"

"Breathing, Mr. President. A machine shouldn't breathe."

"How does it take anyone into the future, do you think?"

The temperature in the room seemed to have gone up. He was sweating. The eye of the thing, impossibly alien, bored into him. Was it changing color?

"We think it doesn't physically send anyone into the future. That's the problem. We think it might somehow . . . create a localized phenomenon."

He sighed. "Just say what you mean."

The pulsing red dot. The shifting green. Looking at him. Looking into him.

"We think it might not allow physical travel, just mental travel."

In that instant, he saw adept Peter's pale face again, and he felt a weakness in his stomach; and even though there was so much protection between him and the machine, he turned to the scientist and said, "Get me out of here."

Only it was too late.

The sickness, the shifting had started the next day, and he couldn't tell anyone about it, not even his wife, or they would have removed him from office. The Constitution was quite clear about what to do with "witches and warlocks."

At this point, his aide would hand him the book. They'd have gone through a dozen books before choosing that one. It is the only one with nothing in it anyone could object to; nothing in it of substance, nothing, his people thought, that the still-free press could use to damage him. There was just a goat in the book, a goat having adventures. It was written by a constitutionalist, an outspoken supporter of coronation and expansion.

As he takes the book, he realizes, mildly surprised, that he has already become used to the smell of sweating children (he has none of his own) and the classroom grunge. The students who attend the school all experience it differently from him, their minds editing out all of the sensory perceptions he's still receiving. The mess. The depressed quality of the infrastructure. But what if you couldn't edit it out? And what if the stakes were much, much higher? (*Ossuary*. It sounded like a combination of "osprey" and "sanctuary.")

So then they would sit him down at a ridiculously small chair, almost as small as the ones used by the students, but somehow he would feel smaller in it despite that, as if he were back in college, surrounded by people both smarter and more dedicated than him, as if he were posing and being told he's not as good: an imposter.

But it's still just a children's book, after all, and at least there's air conditioning kicking in, and the kids really seem to want him to read the book, as if they haven't heard it a thousand times before, and he feeds off the look in their eyes—*the President of North America and the Britains is telling us a story*—and so he begins to read.

He enjoys the storytelling. Nothing he does with the

book can hurt him. Nothing about it has weight. Still, he has to keep the pale face of the adept out of his voice, and the Russian problem, and the Chinese problem, and the full extent of military operations in the Heartland. (There are cameras, after all.)

It's September 11, 2001, and something terrible is going to happen, and he doesn't know what it is.

That's when his aide interrupts his reading, comes up to him with a fake smile and serious eyes, and whispers in his ear.

Whispers in his ear, and the sound is like a buzzing, and the buzzing is numinous, all encompassing. The breath on his ear is a tiny curse, an infernal itch. There's a sudden rush of blood to his brain as he hears the words, and his aide withdraws. He can hardly move, is seeing light where there shouldn't be light. The words drop heavy into his ear, as if they have weight.

And he receives them and keeps receiving them, and he knows what they mean, eventually; he knows what they mean throughout his body.

The aide says, his voice flecked with relief, "Mr. President, our scientists have solved it. It's not time travel or far-sight. It's alternate universes. The adepts have been staring into alternate universes. What happens there in September may not happen here. That's why they've had such trouble with the intel. The machine isn't a time machine."

Except, as soon as the aide opens his mouth, the words become a trigger, a catalyst, and it's too late for him. A door is opening wider than ever before. The machine has already infected him.

There are variations. A long row of them, detonating in his mind, trying to destroy him. A strange, sad song is creeping up inside him, and he can't stop that, either.

>>>He's sitting in the chair, wearing a black military uniform with medals on it. He's much fitter, the clothes tight to emphasize his muscle tone. But his

face is contorted around the hole of a festering local-ized virus, charcoal and green and viscous. He doesn't wear an eye patch because he wants his people to see how he fights the disease. His left arm is made of metal. His tongue is not his own, colonized the way his nation has been colonized, waging a war against bio-research gone wrong, and the rebels who welcome it, who want to tear down anything remotely human, themselves no longer recognizable as human.

His aide comes up and whispers that the rebels have detonated a bio-mass bomb in New York City, which is now stewing in a broth of fungus and mutation: the nearly instantaneous transformation of an entire metropolis into something living but alien, the rate of change become strange and accelerated in a world where this was always true, the age of industrialization slowing it, if only for a moment.

"There are no people left in New York City," his aide says. "What are your orders?"

He hadn't expected this, not so soon, and it takes him seven minutes to recover from the news of the death of millions. Seven minutes to turn to his aide and say, "Call in a nuclear strike."

>>> . . . and his aide comes up to him and whispers in his ear, "It's time to go now. They've moved up another meeting. Wrap it up." Health insurance is on the agenda today, along with Social Security. Some-thing will get done about that and the environment this year or he'll die trying . . .

>>>He's sitting in the chair reading the book, and he's gaunt, eyes feverish, military personnel sur-rounding him. There's one camera with them, army TV, and the students are all in camouflage. The elec-tricity flickers on and off. The schoolroom has rein-forced metal and concrete all around it. The event is propaganda being packaged and pumped out to those still watching in places where the enemy hasn't jammed the satellites. He's fighting a war against an escaped,

human-created, rapidly reproducing intelligent species prototype that looks like a chimpanzee crossed with a Doberman. The scattered remnants of the hated adept underclass have made common cause with the animals, disrupting communications.

His aide whispers in his ear that Atlanta has fallen, with over sixty thousand troops and civilians massacred in pitched battles all over the city. There's no safe air corridor back to the capital. In fact, the capital seems to be under attack as well.

"What should we do?"

He returns to reading the book. Nothing he can do in the next seven minutes will make any difference to the outcome. He knows what they have to do, but he's too tired to contemplate it just yet. They will have to head to the Heartland and make peace with the Ecstatics and their god-missiles. It's either that or render entire stretches of North America uninhabitable from nukes, and he's not that desperate yet.

He begins to review the ten commandments of the Ecstatics in his mind, one by one, like rosary beads.

>>>He's in mid-sentence when the aide hurries over and begins to whisper in his ear—just as the first of the god-missiles strikes and the fire washes over and through him, not even time to scream, and he's nothing any more, not even an ossuary.

>>>He's in a chair, wearing a suit with a sweat-stained white shirt and he's tired, his voice as he reads thin and raspy. Five days and nights of negotiations between the rival factions of the New Southern Confederacy following a month of genocide between blacks and whites from Arkansas to Georgia: too few resources, too many natural disasters, and no jobs, the whole system breaking down, although Los Angeles is still trying to pretend the world isn't coming to an end, even as jets are falling out the sky. Except, that's why he's in the classroom: *pretending*. Pretending neighbor hasn't set upon neighbor for thirty days, ex-

cept with guns, not machetes. Bands of teenagers shooting people in the stomach, the head, and laughing. Extremist talk radio urging them on. A million people dead. Maybe more.

His aide comes up and whispers in his ear: "The truce has fallen apart. They're killing each other again. And not just in the South. In the North, along political lines."

He sits there because he's run out of answers. He thinks: *In another time, another place, I would have been a great president.*

>>>He's sitting in the classroom, in the small chair, in comfortable clothes, reading the goat story. There are no god-missiles here, no viruses, no invasion. The Chinese and Russians are only on the cusp of being a threat. Adepts here have no real far-sight, or are not believed, and roam free. Los Angeles is a thriving money generator, not a husked-out shadow.

No, the real threat here, besides pollution, is that he's mentally ill, although no one around him seems to know it. This pale, vacuous replica has a head full of worms, insecurity, and pure, naked, selfish need. He rules a country called the United States, squandering its resources, compromising its ability to function with greed and corruption.

When the aide comes up and whispers in his ear to tell him that terrorists have flown two planes into buildings in New York City, there's blood behind his eyes, as well as a deafening silence, and a sudden leap from people falling from the burning buildings to endless war in the Middle East, bodies broken in blood and bullets and bombs. The future torques into secret trials, torture, rape, and hundreds of thousands of civilians dead, two million people displaced, a country bankrupted and defenseless, ruled ultimately by martial law and generals.

He sits there for seven minutes because he really has no idea what to do.

\*     \*     \*

. . . and *his* fate is to exist in a reality where towers do not explode in September, where Islamic fundamentalists are the least of his worries.

There is only one present, only one future now, and he's back in it, driving it. Seven minutes have elapsed, with a graveyard in his head. Seven minutes, and he's gradually aware that in that span he's read the goat story twice and then sat there for thirty seconds, silent.

Now he smiles, says a few reassuring words, just as his aide has decided to come up and rescue him from the yawning chasm. He's living in a place where they'll never find him, those children, where there's a torrent of blood, and a sky dark with planes and helicopters, and men blown to bits by the roadside. Cities burn, and the screaming of the living is as loud as the screaming of the dying.

He rises from his chair, and his aide claps, encouraging the students to clap, and they do, bewildered by this man about whom reporters will say later, "He doesn't seem quite all there."

An endless line of presidents rises from the chair with him, the weight almost too much. He can see each clearly in his head. He can see what they're doing and who they're doing it to.

Saying his goodbyes is like learning how to walk again, while a nightmare plays out in the background. He knows as they lead him down the corridor that he'll have to learn to live with it, like and unlike a man learning to live with a missing limb: a multitude of phantom limbs that do not belong, that he cannot control, but are always there. And he'll never be able to explain it to anyone. He'll be as alone and yet as haunted as a person can be. The wall between him and his wife will be more unbearable than ever.

He thinks of Peter's pale, wrinkled, yearning face, and he knows two things: He's going to make them release the man, put him on a plane somewhere beyond his country's influence, and then he's going to have them destroy the machine and end the adept project. Beyond that, he knows nothing and everything.

Then he's back in the wretched, glorious sunlight of a real, an ordinary day, and so are all of his reflections and shadows. Mimicking him. Forever.

# THE UNBLINKING EYE

## Stephen Baxter

Under an empty night sky, the Inca ship stood proud before the old Roman bridge of Londres.

Jenny and Alphonse, both sixteen years old, pressed their way through grimy mobs of Londres. As night closed in, they had slipped away from the dreary ceremonial rehearsals at Saint Paul's. They couldn't resist escaping to mingle with the excited Festival crowds.

And, of course, they had been drawn here, to the *Viracocha*, the most spectacular sight of all.

Beside the Inca ship's dazzling lines, even the domes, spires and pylons of the Festival, erected to mark the anniversary of the Frankish Conquest in this year of Our Lord Christus Ra 1966, looked shabby indeed. Her towering hull was made entirely of metal, clinkered in some seamless way that gave it flexibility, and the sails were llama wool, colored as brilliantly as the Inca clothes that had been the talk of the Paris fashion houses this season.

Jenny Cook was from a family of shipowners, and the very sight excited her. "Looking at her, you can believe she has sailed from the other side of the world, even from the south—"

"That's blasphemy," Alphonse snapped. But he remembered himself and shrugged. What had been blasphemy a year ago, before the first Inca ships had come sailing north around the west coast of Africa, was common knowledge now, and the old reflexes did not apply.

Jenny said, "Surely on such a craft those sails are only for show, or for trim. There must be some mighty engine buried in her guts—but where are the smoke stacks?"

The prince said gloomily, "Well, you and I are going to have months to find that out, Jenny. And where you see a pretty ship," he said darkly, "I see a statement of power." Jenny was to be among the party of friends and tutors who would accompany sixteen-year-old Prince Alphonse during his years-long stay in Cuzco, capital of the Inca. Alphonse had a sense of adventure, even of fun. But as the second son of the Emperor Charlemagne XXXII, he saw the world differently from Jenny.

She protested, "Oh, you're too suspicious, Alphonse. Why, they say there are whole continents out there we know nothing about! Why should the Inca care about the Frankish empire?"

"Perhaps they have conceived an ambition to own us as we own you Anglais."

Jenny prickled. However, she had learned some diplomacy in her time at court. "Well, I can't agree with you, and that's that," she said.

Suddenly a flight of Inca air machines swept over like soaring silver birds, following the line of the river, their lights blazing against the darkling night. The crowds ducked and gasped, some of them crossing themselves in awe. After all, the *Viracocha* was only a ship, and the empires of Europe had ships. But none of them, not even the Ottomans, had machines that could fly.

"You see?" Alphonse muttered. "What is that but a naked demonstration of Inca might? And I'll tell you something, those metal birds don't scare me half as much as other tools I've seen. Such as a box that can talk to other boxes a world away—they call it a farspeaker—I don't pretend to understand how it works. They gave one to my father's office so I can

talk to him from Cuzco. What else have they got that
they haven't shown us? . . . Well, come on," he said,
plucking her arm. "We're going to be late for Atahualpa's ceremony."

Jenny followed reluctantly.

She watched the flying machines until they had
passed out of sight, heading west up the river. When
their lights had gone the night sky was revealed,
cloudless and moonless, utterly dark, with no planets
visible, an infinite emptiness. As if in response, the
gas lanterns of Londres burned brighter, defiant.

The Inca caravan was drawn up before the face of
Saint Paul's. As grandees passed into the building, at-
tendants fed the llamas that had borne the colorful
litters. You never saw the Inca use a wheel; they relied
entirely on these haughty, exotic beasts.

Inside the cathedral, Jenny and Alphonse found
their places hurriedly.

The procession passed grandly through the cramped
candlelit aisles, led by servants who carried the Orb of
the Unblinking Eye. These were followed by George
Darwin, archbishop of Londres, who chattered ner-
vously to Atahualpa, commander of the *Viracocha* and
emissary of Huayna Capac XIII, Emperor of the Inca.
In the long tail of the procession were representatives
from all the great empires of Europe: the Danes, the
Germans, the Muscovites, even the Ottomans, grandly
bejeweled Muslims in this Christian church. They
marched to the gentle playing of Galilean lutes, an
ensemble supplied by the Germans. It was remarkable
to think, Jenny reflected, that if the Inca had come
sailing out of the south three hundred years ago, they
would have been met by ambassadors from much the
same combination of powers. Though there had always been border disputes and even wars, the political
map of Europe had changed little since the Ottoman
capture of Vienna had marked the westernmost march
of Islam.

But the Inca towered over the European nobility.

They wore woollen suits dyed scarlet and electric blue, colors brighter than the cathedral's stained glass. And they all wore facemasks as defense against the "herd diseases" they insultingly claimed infested Europe. The effect was to make these imposing figures even more enigmatic, for the only expression you could see was in their black eyes.

Jenny, at Alphonse's side and mixed in with some of the Inca party, was only a few rows back from Atahualpa and Darwin, and she could clearly hear every word they said.

"My own family has a long association with this old church," the bishop said. "My ancestor Charles Darwin was a country parson who, dedicated to his theology, rose to become dean here. The Anglais built the first Christian church on this site in the year of Christus Ra 604. After the Conquest the emperors were most generous in endowing this magnificent building in our humble, remote city . . ."

As the interpreter translated this, Atahualpa murmured some reply in Quechua, and the two of them laughed softly.

One of the Inca party walking beside Jenny was a boy about her age. He wore an Inca costume like the rest but without a face mask. He whispered in passable Frankish, "The emissary's being a bit rude about your church. He says it's a sandstone heap he wouldn't use to stable his llamas."

"Charming," Jenny whispered back.

"Well, you haven't seen his llamas."

Jenny had to cover her face to keep from giggling. She got a glare from Alphonse and recovered her composure.

"Sorry," said the boy. He was dark skinned, with a mop of short-cut, tightly curled black hair. The spiral tattoo on his left cheek made him look a little severe, until he smiled, showing bright teeth. "My name's— well, it's complicated, and the Inca never get it right. You can call me Dreamer."

"Hello, Dreamer," she whispered. "I'm Jenny Cook."

"Pretty name."

Jenny raised her eyebrows. "Oh, is it really? You're not Inca, are you?"

"No, I just travel with them. They like to move us around, their subject peoples. I'm from the South Land . . ."

But she didn't know where that was, and the party had paused before the great altar where the emissary and the archbishop were talking again, and Jenny and Dreamer fell silent.

Atahualpa said to Darwin, "I am intrigued by the god of this church. Christus Ra? He is a god who is two gods."

"In a sense." Darwin spoke rapidly of the career of Christ. The Romans had conquered Egypt but had suffered a sort of reverse religious takeover; their pantheon had seemed flimsy before the power and sheer logic of the Egyptians' faith in their sun god. The sun was the only point of stability in a sky populated by chaotic planets, mankind's only defense against the infinite dark. Who could argue against its worship? Centuries after Christ's execution His cult was adopted as the empire's official religion, and the bishops and theologians had made a formal identification of Christ with Ra, a unity that had outlasted the empire itself.

Atahualpa expressed mild interest in this. He said the worship of the sun was a global phenomenon. The Incas' own sun god was called Inti. Perhaps Inti and Christ-Ra were mere manifestations of the same primal figure.

The procession moved on.

" 'Cook'," Dreamer whispered. He was more interested in Jenny than in theology. "That's a funny sort of name. Not Frankish, is it?"

"I don't know. I think it has an Anglais root. My family are Anglais, from the north of Grand Bretagne."

"You must be rich. You've got to be either royal or rich to be in this procession, right?"

She smiled. "Rich enough. I'm at court as part of my

education. My grandfathers have been in the coal trade since our ancestor founded the business two hundred years ago. He was called James Cook. My father's called James too. It's a mucky business but lucrative."

"I'll bet. Those Watt engines I see everywhere eat enough coal, don't they?"

"So what do your family do?"

He said simply, "We serve the Inca."

The procession reached a chapel dedicated to Isaac Newton, the renowned alchemist and theologian who had developed a conclusive proof of the age of the Earth. Here they prayed to their gods, the Inca prostrating themselves before Inti, and the Christians kneeling to Christ.

And the Inca servants came forward with their Orb of the Unblinking Eye. It was a sphere of some translucent white material, half as tall as a man; the servants carried it in a rope netting and set it down on a wooden cradle before the statue of Newton himself.

Atahualpa turned and faced the procession. He may have smiled; his facemask creased. He said through his interpreter: "Once it was our practice to plant our temples in the chapels of those we sought to vanquish. Now I place this gift from my emperor, this symbol of our greatest god, in the finest church in this province." And, Jenny knew, other Inca parties were handing over similar orbs in all the great capitals of Europe. "Once we would move peoples about, whole populations, to cut them away from their roots and so control them. Now we welcome the children of your princes and merchants, while leaving our own children in your cities, so that we may each learn the culture and the ways of the other." He gestured to Alphonse.

The prince bowed, but he muttered through his teeth, "*And* get hold of a nice set of hostages."

"Hush," Jenny murmured.

Atahualpa said, "Let this globe shine for all eternity as a symbol of our friendship, united under the Unblinking Eye of the One Sun." He clapped his hands.

And the orb lit up, casting a steady pearl-like glow

over the grimy statuary of the chapel. The Europeans applauded helplessly.

Jenny stared, amazed. She could see no power supply, no tank of gas; and the light didn't flicker like the flame of a candle or a lamp but burned as steady as the sun itself.

With the ceremony over, the procession began to break up. Jenny turned to the boy, Dreamer. "Are you sailing on the *Viracocha*?"

"Oh, yes. You'll be seeing a lot more of me. The emissary has one more appointment, a ride on a Watt-engine train to some place called Bataille—"

"That's where the Frankish army defeated the Anglais back in 1066."

"Yes. And then we sail."

"And then we sail," Jenny said, fearful, excited, gazing into the dark, playful eyes of this boy from the other side of the world, a boy whose land didn't even exist in her imagination.

Alphonse glared at them, brooding.

The dignitaries were still talking, with stiff politeness. Atahualpa seemed intrigued by Newton's determination of the Earth's age. "And how did this Newton achieve his result? A study of the rocks, of living things, of the sky? I did not know such sciences were so advanced here."

But when Archbishop Darwin explained that Newton's calculations had been based on records of births and deaths in a holy book, and that his conclusion was that the Earth was only a few thousand years old, Atahualpa's laughter was gusty, echoing from the walls of the cramped chapel.

Alphonse's party, with Jenny and other companions and with Archbishop Darwin attached as a moral guardian, boarded the Inca ship.

The *Viracocha*, Jenny learned, was named after a creator god and cultural hero of the Inca. It was as extraordinary inside as out, a floating palace of wide corridors and vast staterooms that glowed with a steady pearl light. Jenny was quite surprised when crew members went barreling up and down the corridors on wheeled carts. The Inca embraced the wheel's obvious advantages, but for ceremonial occasions they walked or rode their animals, as their ancestors had done long before their age of exploration. The wheeled carts, like the ubiquitous lights, had no obvious power source, no boiler or steam stack.

The Frankish and Anglais were allowed to stay on deck as the great woollen sails were unfurled and the ship pulled away from Londres, which sprawled over its banks in heaps of smoky industry. Jenny looked for her family's ships in the docks; she was going to be away from home for years, and the parting from her mother had been tearful.

But before the ship had left the Thames estuary the guests were ordered below deck, and the hatches were locked and sealed. There weren't even any windows in the ship's sleek hull. Their Inca hosts wanted to save a remarkable surprise for them, they said, a surprise revealed to every crew who crossed the equator, but not until then.

And they were all, even Alphonse, put through a program of inoculation, injected with various potions and their bodies bathed with a prickly light. The Inca doctors said this was to weed out their "herd diseases." All the Europeans resented this, though Darwin marveled at the medical technology on display.

At least you could see the Incas' faces, however, now that they had discarded their masks. They were a proud-looking people with jet black hair, dark skin, and noses that would have been called Roman in Europe. None of the crew was particularly friendly. They wouldn't speak Frankish or Anglais, and they looked on the Europeans with a kind of amused contempt. This infuriated Alphonse, for he was used to looking on others in precisely that way.

Still, the ship's sights were spectacular. Jenny was shown the great smelly hold where the llamas were kept during the journey. And she was shown around an engine room. Jenny's family ran steam scows, and she had expected Watt engines, heavy, clunky, soot-coated iron monsters. The *Viracocha*'s engine room was a pristine white-walled hall inhabited by sleek metal shapes. The air was filled with a soft humming, and there was a sharp smell in the air that reminded her of the seashore. These smooth sculptures didn't even look like engines to Jenny, and whatever principle they worked on had nothing to do with steam, evidently. So much for her father's fond hopes of selling coal to the mighty Inca empire!

Despite such marvels, Jenny chafed at her confinement below decks. What made it worse was that she saw little of her friends. Alphonse was whisked off to a program of study of Inca culture and science, mediated by Darwin. And in his free time he monopolized Dreamer for private language classes; he wanted to learn as much Quechua as he could manage, for he did not trust the Inca.

This irritated Jenny more than she was prepared to admit, for the times she relished most of all were the snatched moments she spent with Dreamer.

One free evening Dreamer took her to the navigation bay. The walls were covered with charts, curves that might have shown the trajectory of the sun and moon across the sky, and other diagrams showing various aspects of a misty-gold spiral shape that meant nothing to Jenny. There was a globe that drew her eye; glowing, painted, it was covered with unfamiliar shapes, but one strip of blue looked just like a map of the Mediterranean.

The most wondrous object in the room was a kind of loom, rank upon rank of knotted string that stretched from floor to ceiling and wall to wall—but unlike a loom it was extended in depth as well. As she peered into this array, she saw metal fingers pluck blindly at the strings, making the knots slide this way and that.

Dreamer watched her, as she watched the string. "I'm starting to think Alphonse is using the language classes as an excuse to keep me away from you. Perhaps the prince wants you for himself. Who wouldn't desire such beauty?"

Jenny pulled her face at this gross flattery. "Tell me what this loom is for."

"The Inca have always represented their numbers and words on quipus, bits of knotted string. Even after they learned writing from their Aztec neighbors, whom they encountered at the start of the Sunrise."

"The Sunrise?"

"That is their modest name for their program of expansion across the world. Jenny, this is a machine for figuring numbers. The Inca use it to calculate their journeys across the world's oceans. But it can perform any sum you like."

"My father would like one of these to figure his tax return."

Dreamer laughed.

She said, "But everybody knows that you can't navigate at night, when the sun goes down, and the only beacons in the sky are the moon and planets, which career unpredictably all over the place. How, then, do the Inca find their way?" For the Europeans this was the greatest mystery about the Inca. Even the greatest seamen of the past, the Vikings, had barely had the courage to probe away from the shore.

Dreamer glanced at the strange charts on the wall. "Look, they made us promise not to tell any of you about—well, certain matters, before the Inca deem you ready. But there's something here I do want to show you." He led her across the room to the globe.

That blue shape was undoubtedly the Mediterranean. "It's the world," she breathed.

"Yes." He smiled. "The Inca have marked what they know of the European empires. Look, here is Grand Bretagne."

"Why, even Europe is only a peninsula dangling from the carcass of Asia."

"You know, your sense of wonder is the most attractive thing about you."

She snorted. "Really? More than my eyes and teeth

and neck, and the other bits of me you've been prais-
ing? I'll believe that when a second sun rises in the
sky. Show me where you come from—and the Inca."

Passing his hand over the globe, he made the world
spin and dip.

He showed her what lay beyond the Ottoman empire, the solemn Islamic unity that had blocked Christendom from the east for centuries: the vast expanses
of Asia, India, the sprawling empire of China, Nippon,
the Spice Islands. And he showed how Africa extended far beyond the arid northern regions held by
the Ottomans, a great pendulous continent in its own
right that sprawled, thrillingly, right across the equator.

"You can in fact reach India and the east by sailing
south around the cape of southern Africa," Dreamer
said. "Without losing sight of land, even. A man called
Columbus was the first to attempt this in 1492. But he
lacked the courage to cross the equator. Columbus
went back to the family business of trouser-making,
and Christian Europe stayed locked in."

Now he spun the globe to show her even stranger
sights: a double continent, far to the west of Europe
across the ocean, lands wholly unknown to any European. The Inca had come from a high country that
ran north to south along the spine of the southernmost
of the twin continents. "It is a place of mountains and
coast, of long, long roads, and bridges centuries old,
woven from vines, still in use . . ."

Around the year 1500, according to the Christian
calendar, the Inca's greatest emperor Huayna Capac
I, had emerged from a savage succession dispute to
take sole control of the mountain empire. And under
him, as the Inca consolidated, the great expansion
called the Sunrise had begun. At first the Inca had
used their woollen-sailed ships for trade and military
expeditions up and down their long coastlines. But
gradually they crept away from the shore.

At last, on an island that turned out to be the tip
of a grand volcanic mountain that stuck out of the
sea, they found people. "These were a primitive sort,

who sailed the oceans in canoes dug out of logs. Nevertheless, they had come out of the southeast of Asia and sailed right to the middle of the ocean, colonizing island chains as they went." The Inca, emboldened by the geographical knowledge they took from their new island subjects, set off west once more, following island chains until they reached southeast Asia. All this sparked intellectual ferment, as exploration and conquest led to a revolution in sky watching, mathematics, and the sciences of life and language.

The Inca, probing westward, at last reached Africa. And when in the early twentieth century they acquired lodestone compasses from Chinese traders, they found the courage to venture north.

Jenny stared at the South Land. There was no real detail, just a few Inca towns dotted around the coast, an interior like a blank red canvas. "Tell me about your home."

He brushed the image of the island continent with his fingertips. "It is a harsh country, I suppose. Rust-red, worn flat by time. But there is much beauty and strangeness. Animals that jump rather than run, and carry their young in pouches on their bellies. Don't laugh, it's true! My people have lived there for sixty thousand years. That's what the Inca scholars say, though how they can tell that from bits of bone and shards of stone tools *I* don't know. My people are called the Bininj-Mungguy, and we live in the north, up here, in a land we call Kakadu."

Jenny's imagination raced, and his strange words fascinated her. She drew closer to him, almost unconsciously, watching his mouth.

"We have six seasons," he said, "for our weather is not like yours. There is Gunumeleng, which is the season before the great rains, and then Gudjewg, when the rain comes, and then Banggerreng—"

She stopped up his mouth with hers.

After a week's sailing the *Viracocha* crossed the equator. Atahualpa ordered a feast to be laid for his senior officers and guests. They were brought to a stateroom that, Jenny suspected from the stairs she had to climb, lay just under the deck itself. Tonight, Atahualpa promised, his passengers would be allowed on deck for the first time since Londres, and the great secret that the Incas had been hiding would be revealed.

But by now Dreamer and Jenny had shared so many secrets that she scarcely cared.

While the Inca crew wore their customary llama-wool and cotton uniforms, George Darwin wore his clerical finery, Alphonse the powdered wig and face powder of his father's court, and Jenny a simple shift, her Sunday best. Dreamer was just one of the many representatives of provinces of the Inca's ocean-spanning empire aboard ship. They wore elaborate costumes of cloth and feather, so that they looked like a row of exotic birds, Jenny thought, sitting there in a row at the commander's table.

In some ways Dreamer's own garb was the most extraordinary. He was stripped naked save for a loincloth, his face-spiral tattoo was picked out in some yellow dye, and he had finger-painted designs on his body in chalk-white, a sprawling lizard, an outstretched hand. Jenny was jealously aware that she wasn't the only woman who kept glancing at Dreamer's muscled torso—and a few men did too.

The Inca went through their own equator-crossing ritual. This involved taking a live chicken, slitting its belly and pulling out its entrails, right there on the dinner table, while muttering antique-sounding prayers.

Bishop Darwin tried to watch this with calm appreciation. "Evidently an element of animism and the superstitious has survived in our hosts' theology," he murmured.

Alphonse didn't bother to hide his disgust. "I've had enough of these savages."

"Hush," Jenny murmured. "If you assume none of them can speak Frankish, you're a fool."

He glared defiantly, but he switched to Anglais.

"Well, I've never heard any of them utter a single word. And they assume I know a lot less Quechua than I've learned, thanks to your bare-chested friend over there. They say things in front of me that they think I won't understand—but I do."

He was only sixteen, as Jenny was; he sounded absurd, self-important. But he was a prince who had grown up in the atmosphere of the most conspiratorial and backstabbing court in all Christendom. He was attuned to detecting lies and power plays. She asked, "What sort of things?"

"About the 'problem' we pose them. We Europeans. We aren't like Dreamer's folk of the South Land, hairy-arsed savages in the desert. We have great cities; we have armies. We may not have their silver ships and flying machines, but we could put up a fight. That's the problem."

She frowned. "It's a problem only if the Inca come looking for war."

He scoffed. "Oh, come, Jenny, even an Anglais can't be so naïve. All this friendship-across-the-sea stuff is just a smoke screen. Everything they've done has been in the manner of an opening salvo: the donation of farspeakers to every palace in Europe, the planting of their Orbs of the Unblinking Eye in every city. What I can't figure out is what they intend by all this."

"Maybe Inca warriors will jump out of the Orbs and run off with the altar silver."

"You're a fool," he murmured without malice. "Like all Anglais. You and desert boy over there deserve each other. Well, I've had enough of Atahualpa's droning voice. While they're all busy here, I'm going to see what I can find out." He stood.

She hissed. "Be careful."

He ignored her. He nodded to his host. Atahualpa waved him away, uncaring.

Atahualpa had begun a conversation with Darwin on the supposed backwardness of European science and philosophy. Evidently it was a dialog that had been developing during the voyage, as the Inca tutors got to know the minds of their students. "Here is the flaw in your history as I see it," he said. "Unlike the Inca, you Europeans never mastered the science of the sky. To you all is chaos."

Jenny admired old Darwin's stoicism. With resigned good humor, he said, "Isn't that obvious? All those planets swooping around the sky—only the sun is stable, the pivot of the universe. Do you know, long before the birth of Christ-Ra a Greek philosopher called Aristotle tried to prove that the sun revolves round the Earth, rather than the other way around!"

But Atahualpa would not be deflected. "The point is that the motion of the planets is *not* chaotic, not if you look at it correctly." A bowl of the chicken's blood had been set before him. He dipped his finger in this and sketched a solar system on the tabletop, sun at the center, Earth's orbit, the neat circles of the inner planets and the wildly swooping flights of the outer.

Servants brought plates of food. There was the meat of roast rodent and duck, heaps of maize, squash, tomatoes, peanuts, and plates of a white tuber, a root vegetable unknown to Europe but tasty and filling.

"There," said Atahualpa. "Now, look, you see. Each planet follows an ellipse, with the sun at one focus. These patterns are repeated and quite predictable, though the extreme eccentricity of the outer worlds' orbits makes them hard to decipher. *We* managed it, though—although I grant you we always had one significant advantage over you, as you will learn tonight! Let me tell you how our science developed after that . . ."

He listed Inca astronomers and mathematicians, names like Huascar and Manco and Yupanqui, which meant nothing to Jenny. "After we mapped the planets' elliptical trajectories, it was the genius of Yupanqui that he was able to show *why* the worlds followed such paths, because of a single, simple law: The planets are drawn to the sun with an attraction that falls off inversely with the square of distance."

Darwin said bravely, "I am sure our scholars in Paris and Damascus would welcome—"

Atahualpa ignored him, digging into his food with his blood-stained fingers. "But Yupanqui's greatest legacy was the insight that the world is explicable: that simple, general laws can explain a range of particular instances. It is that core philosophy that we have applied to other disciplines." He gestured at the diffuse light that filled the room. "You cower from the light of the sun, and fear the lightning, and are baffled by the wandering of a lodestone. But we know that these are all aspects of a single underlying force, which we can manipulate to build the engines that drive this ship and the farspeakers that enable the emperor's voice to span continents. If *your* minds had been opened up, your science might be less of a hotchpotch. And your religion might not be so primitive."

Darwin flinched at that. "Well, it's true there has been no serious Christian heresy since Martin Luther was burned by the Inquisition—"

"If only you had not been so afraid of the sky! But then," he said, smiling, "our sky always did contain one treasure yours did not."

Jenny was growing annoyed with the Inca's patronizing treatment of Darwin, a decent man. She said now, "Commander, even before we sailed you dropped hints about some wonder in the sky we knew nothing about."

As his translator murmured in his ear, Atahualpa looked at her in surprise.

Darwin murmured, "Mademoiselle Cook, please—"

"If you're so superior, maybe you should stop playing games and *show* us this wonder—if it exists at all!"

Dreamer shook his head. "Oh, Jenny. Just wait and see."

The officers were glaring. But Atahualpa held up an indulgent hand. "I will not punish bravery, Mademoiselle Cook, and you are brave, if foolish with it. We like to keep our great surprise from our European passengers—call it an experiment—because your first reaction is always worth relishing. We were going to wait until the end of the meal, but—Pachacuti, will you see to the roof?"

Wiping his lips on a cloth, one of the officers got up from the table and went to the wall, where a small panel of buttons had been fixed. With a whir of smooth motors, the roof slid back.

Fresh salt air, a little cold, billowed over the diners. Jenny looked up. In an otherwise black sky, a slim crescent moon hung directly over her head. She had the sense that the moon was tilted on its side—a measure of how far she had traveled around the curve of the world in just a few days aboard this ship.

Atahualpa smiled, curious, perhaps cruel. "Never mind the moon, Mademoiselle Cook. Look that way." He pointed south.

She stood. And there, clearly visible over the lip of the roof, something was suspended in the sky. Not the sun or moon, not a planet—something entirely different. It was a disc of light, a swirl, with a brilliant point at its center, and a ragged spiral glow all around it. It was the emblem she had observed on the navigational displays but far more delicate—a sculpture of light, hanging in the sky.

"Oh," she gasped, awed, terrified. "It's beautiful."

Beside her, Archbishop Darwin muttered prayers and crossed himself.

She felt Dreamer's hand take hers. "I wanted to tell you," he murmured. "They forbade me . . ."

Atahualpa watched them. "What do you think you are seeing?"

Darwin said, "It looks like a hole in the sky. Into which all light is draining."

"No. In fact it's quite the opposite. It is the *source* of all light."

"And that is how you navigate," Jenny said. "By the cloud—you could pick out the point of light at the center, and measure your position on a curving Earth from that. This is your treasure—a beacon in the sky."

"You're an insightful young woman. It is only recently, in fact, that with our farseers—another technology you lack—we have been able to resolve those spiral streams to reveal their true nature."

"Which is?"

"The cloud is a sea of suns, Mademoiselle. Billions upon billions of suns, so far away they look like droplets in mist."

The Inca sky-scientists believed that the cloud was in fact a kind of factory of suns; the sun and its planets couldn't have formed in the black void across which they traveled.

"As to how we ended up here—some believe that it was a chance encounter between our sun and another. If they come close, you see, suns attract each other. Our sun was flung out of the sea, *northward*, generally speaking, off into the void. The encounter damaged the system itself; the inner planets and Earth were left in their neat circles, but the outer planets were flung onto their looping orbits. All this is entirely explicable by the laws of motion developed by Yupanqui and others." Atahualpa lifted his finely chiseled face to the milky light of the spiral. "This was billions of years back, when the world was young. Just as well; life was too primitive to have been extinguished by the tides and earthquakes. But what a sight it would have been then, the sea of suns huge in the sky, if there had been eyes to see it!"

There was a commotion outside the stateroom. "Let me go!" somebody yelled in Frankish. "Let me go!"

An officer went to the door. Alphonse was dragged in by two burly Inca holding his arms. His nose was bloodied, his face powder smeared, his powdered wig askew, but he was furious, defiant.

Archbishop Darwin bustled to the side of his charge. "This is an outrage. He is a prince of the empire!"

At a nod from the commander, Alphonse was released. He stood there massaging bruised arms. And he stared up at the spiral in the sky.

"Sir, we found him in the farspeaker room," said one of the guards. "He was tampering with the equipment." For the guests, this was slowly translated from the Quechua.

But Alphonse interrupted the translation. He said in Frankish, "Yes, I was in your farspeaker room, Atahualpa. Yes, I understand Quechua better than you thought, don't I? And I wasn't tampering with the equipment. I was sending a message to my father. Even now, I imagine, his guards will be closing in on the Orb you planted in Saint Paul's—and those elsewhere."

Darwin stared at him. "Your royal highness, I've no idea what is happening here—why you would be so discourteous to our hosts."

"Discourteous?" He glared at Atahualpa. "Ask him, then. Ask him what a sun bomb is."

Atahualpa stared back stonily.

Dreamer came forward. "Tell him the truth, Inca. He knows most of it anyhow." And one by one the other representatives of the Inca's subject races, in their beads and feathers, stepped forward to stand with Dreamer.

And so Atahualpa yielded. A sun bomb was a weapon small enough to fit into one of the Incas' Orbs of the Unblinking Eye yet powerful enough to flatten a city—a weapon that harnessed the power of the sun itself.

Jenny was shocked. "We welcomed you in Londres. Why would you plant such a thing in our city?"

"Isn't it obvious?" Alphonse answered. "Because these all-conquering Inca can't cow Franks and Germans and Ottomans with a pretty silver ship as they did these others, or you Anglais."

Atahualpa said, "A war of conquest would be long and bloody, though the outcome would be beyond doubt. We thought that if the sun bombs were planted, so that your cities were held hostage—if one of them was detonated for a demonstration, if a backward provincial city was sacrificed—"

"Like Londres," said Jenny, appalled.

"And then," Alphonse said, "you would use your farspeakers to speak to the emperors and state your demands. Well, it's not going to happen, Inca. Looks like it will be bloody after all, doesn't it?"

Darwin touched his shoulder. "You have done your empire a great service today, Prince Alphonse. But war is not yet inevitable between the people of the north and the south. Perhaps this will be a turning point in our relationship. Let us hope that wiser counsels prevail."

"We'll see," Alphonse said, staring at Atahualpa. "We'll see."

Servants bustled in, to clear dishes and set another course. The normality after the confrontation was bewildering.

Slowly tensions eased.

Jenny impulsively grabbed Dreamer's arm. They walked away from the rest.

She stared up at the sea of suns. "If we are all lost in this gulf, we ought to learn to get along."

Dreamer grunted. "You convince the emperors. I will speak to the Inca."

She imagined Earth swimming in light. "Dreamer, will we ever sail back to the sea of suns, back to where we came from?"

"Well, you never know," he said. "But the sea is farther away than you imagine, I think. I don't think you and I will live to see it."

Jenny said impulsively, "Our children might."

"Yes. Our children might. Come on. Let's get this wretched dinner over with."

The stateroom roof slid closed, hiding the sea of suns from their sight.

# CSILLA'S STORY

## *Theodora Goss*

Porch steps. Wooden steps, with a dandelion growing through a hole in the wood. A dandelion covered with white tufts.

The breeze blew away a tuft, with its brown seed attached, and a frightened voice said, "She hasn't talked since I met her at the airport." A hand touched her arm. "What's your name, child? Your real name? *Mi a néve*?" The hand withdrew, and the frightened voice continued, "Did I pronounce that correctly?"

And the other woman, the one standing on the porch steps, with two dandelion tufts caught in the fabric of her dress, said, "How long has the child been traveling, Mrs. Martin?"

Mrs. Martin said, her frightened voice growing fainter, "A week, I think. The trip to Vienna should only have taken one day, but Helga was stopped at the border, and the guards kept telling her to wait another day and then another, although she'd given them all her money, until finally she gave them her wedding ring, and they let her through." She added, her voice so faint that it seemed to float away on the breeze, "But in Vienna they had a passport ready and put her on the plane to New York . . ."

Another tuft detached itself from the dandelion. An inchworm stretched and hunched onto the bottom step.

"I tried to buy her something to eat on the train . . ."

"And the border guards never found her?" Now the woman on the porch steps had three dandelion tufts caught in her dress.

"Well, you see, the car had two bottoms, and she was lying between them."

From the corner of her eye, a ghost. No, a handkerchief fluttering down to rest on the grass. It was wrinkled, and she remembered Miss Martin sitting in the train compartment, crumpling a handkerchief in her hands.

"You mean that for three days she lay between . . ." The woman on the porch steps moved, and the tufts caught in her dress floated away over the grass. "I'm surprised the child is alive." Her voice was not frightened. There was another word for it, perhaps angry, or tired, or—the inchworm stretched and hunched up to the next step.

"I'm so terribly sorry, Mrs. Madár."

But already she was climbing the porch steps, and Miss Martin was behind her, bending to pick up the handkerchief, and the hand on her shoulder belonged to the woman on the porch, who was wearing a turban on her head, like Imre when he hid in the Turkish camp, and whose voice was neither tired nor angry as she said, "Drink this." And the pillow smelled like grass.

In one corner of the room was a spider. Her grandmother had kept a spider in one corner of the apartment, because spiderwebs caught good fortune. A house with a spider would always have good fortune in it.

"I'm glad you're awake," said Mrs. Madár. "Will you take some broth?"

It tasted like her grandmother's mushroom soup. The mushrooms were gathered by moonlight . . .

"No, child. I want you to pay attention. Can you tell me your name?"

The spider let itself down from its web and dangled in the corner. A crack ran across the ceiling, from the spiderweb to the window.

"Do you remember the train ride? Being in the airplane? Leaving Budapest?"

Outside the window she could see a tree. One of its branches tapped against the glass.

"Listen, then. I'm going to tell you a story. This happened long ago, on the shores of the Volga, a great river. Along the shores of this river grew groves of oak and alder, birch and willow. And among those groves lived the Daughters of the Moon."

### Hársfa's Story

"I wish we were dead," said Hársfa. She sat on a rock covered with moss and shaded by an oak tree. The river was green under the tree's shadow, and it flowed so slowly that she could see its branches and leaves reflected. In a hundred years, those reflections would not have changed. The oak tree would still be there.

"Hush," said Nyírfa, applying another wet leaf to Hársfa's forehead. "When you move, it begins bleeding again. And who would lead our sisters, if we were—" The words hovered in the air between them, like a dragonfly. Dead, like Tölgy. Tölgy of the light foot, like foam floating on the water. Tölgy of the wise words, as slow as the river and as filled with shining things: silver fish, stones with veins of crystal, laughter. Tölgy, the eldest and best. Lying at the center of the village with blood on her tunic, as though she were covered with leaves.

Awkwardly, because Nyírfa was still holding the leaf, Hársfa wiped her cheeks with one hand. "Where would we lead them? We've never known anywhere but here." Her fingers were pale green with blood and tears. "Why can't things be the way they were before?"

Nyírfa sat down beside her. "Hold this now."

Hársfa held the leaf to her temple. "Do you remember the milk?" Left by the villagers in hollow stones. When their mother was shining in the sky like a silver egg, all of the sisters would leave the forest to drink and dance in the pastures, among the silent sheep. Sometimes the villagers left wool, which the sisters spun on wooden spindles and wove into winter coats. In return they left walnuts and baskets woven from willow branches.

Nyírfa stared at the river. Was she also thinking of its permanence, its peace? "All I remember now is the village burning. The screams, Hársfa. And the blood. And the swords of the Horsemen." She sat so still that Hársfa was afraid she had been injured and was bearing the pain in silence. But when Hársfa touched her hand where it lay clenched on the moss, she said, "Tölgy wasn't the only one. I saw Boróka fallen, and Ibolya didn't come back with us. There, I said if you moved, it would bleed again."

"I wish we had stayed in the forest! If we hadn't been picking flax in the meadow and smelled the burning—"

Nyírfa put a hand on her shoulder. "I told you, you must stay still."

"Tölgy was wrong to lead us into the battle. The villagers could have fought the Horsemen alone. They would have lost just the same. They're not warriors, any more than we are."

"Hársfa, you don't mean that. How could we abandon them? Think of what they have given us, and some of them—are our children. Here, cry on my shoulder if you have to."

"Sometimes," said Mrs. Madár, putting a damp cloth on her forehead, "when the Daughters of the Moon danced in the pastures, one found a shepherd sleeping among his sheep. If he was handsome in the way of the village people, with black lashes fluttering against his cheeks like wings, she would wake him and lead him into the forest, where she would lie with him on a bed of ferns and mosses. If a child was born with skin that was paler than the brown skin of the villagers, with hair as green as leaves and eyes like the pools of the forest, which reflect the leaves above, it was left at the edge of the village. The villagers would care for it, because it was considered fortunate to have a grandchild of the Moon. There, it would grow to become a poet or perhaps a prophet, which were much the same thing in those days. But it could never sew, or fish, or hunt, because the touch of needle or hook or knife would burn it like fire." She felt a hand on her cheek. "Are you more comfortable now?"

"Let me wash your face a little. Is that better? We have to go back to the cave. Our sisters need us to be strong for them, Hársfa. As Tölgy would have been."

Hársfa dried her face with the edge of her tunic, leaving streaks like grass stains on the fabric, and stood. "I think I'm ready."

Suddenly, Nyírfa screamed. Hársfa saw a flash, like a fish leaping from the water—no, a sword at her sister's throat. Then Hársfa felt her own throat burning like fire from the touch of a knife. They were surrounded by Horsemen.

The Horsemen wore leather boots to the knees and leather tunics. Their coarse black hair was tied back with strips of leather. They smelled of sweat and horses. One, whose hair was braided with red wool, tied strips of leather around her wrists. He touched the wound on her head and then her hair, with a look of wonder. Then he led her, stumbling after Nyírfa, through the forest.

The village also smelled of horses and blood. Women in tunics of red wool were taking what remained from the burned houses: sacks of grain, carved bowls, beds stuffed with straw. They stared at Nyírfa and Hársfa, and one made a sign over her forehead. A child playing with a wooden spoon began to cry and hid his head in her skirts.

There was blood on the earth, churned by the

hooves of the horses. Hársfa felt her stomach turn. Would she be sick, right here before the Horsemen? The man with red wool braided into his hair touched her arm. He tapped himself on the chest and said, "Magyar." How could Nyírfa walk before her so calmly, like the river, so straight, like a fir in the Northern Mountains? Then she noticed that Nyírfa's hands were clenched so tightly that the nails must be leaving new moons on her palms. What had he said, that his name was Magyar? Afraid, she pulled away from him.

At the center of the village, horses tied to what had once been doorposts stamped and snorted. Horsemen cleaned their swords, or ate bread and dried meat, or played with bones that were marked with red lines. They shook the bones in their hands, then let them fall to the earth. Each fall of the bones was followed by laughter and exchange: knives, horsehair bridles, a ring. By a burned wall sat the villagers, their wrists and ankles bound with leather strips. They looked at Nyírfa and Hársfa with frightened eyes. How many of them were left? she wondered. Here and there, she saw a face that was paler than the others, hair that was tinged with green. She and her sisters had never known the villagers well. Perhaps, she thought, we should have known them better.

On a carved stool sat a man with a ragged scar across his face, from his left eye to the right corner of his mouth, like lightning. Magyar gestured toward Nyírfa and Hársfa, then spoke in the Horsemen's language. The bones stopped clicking and the Horsemen stared at them.

"They are brothers, Hunyor and Magyar." Hársfa turned. The man who had spoken was shorter than she was, balding and dressed in a frayed yellow tunic. "Do not be surprised. I speak many languages: Attic, Phrygian, barbaroi."

"You are not one of these Horsemen," said Nyírfa. The man chuckled and thumped his chest. "I am

Demas. Father was merchant, captured by barbaroi. I was small boy." He held out his hand at his waist, to show how small.

Hunyor rose and spoke in a voice as rough as bark. So close to him, she could see that he resembled Magyar; they both had broad foreheads and noses that curved like the beaks of hawks.

Demas replied, gesturing toward the clouds above, the forest around them. "Hunyor asks, are women with hair like leaves ghosts? I say, they are spirits of trees, daughters of Forest Goddess. My father taught me: dryads, hamadryads."

"Can you ask them what will happen to the villagers?"

Demas' face wrinkled in an anxious smile. He shook his head, as though unsure what Nyírfa had asked him. She pointed to the villagers. "Those people."

Demas spread his hands, as though the answer were evident. "Slaves."

"What about our sisters?" asked Hársfa. It was the first time she had spoken, and the sound of her voice frightened her. So many Horsemen staring, and Magyar staring at her with an intensity she did not understand. "Women like us, with hair like leaves."

"Hársfa, you're bleeding again," said Nyírfa. She raised her bound hands, but Magyar was there already. He tore a strip from the edge of his tunic, wet it from the waterskin at his waist, and cleaned Hársfa's wound, holding her chin to keep her face steady. His eyes, she noticed, were brown, and ringed with black lashes. She swayed for a moment, but when he reached out to steady her, she held on to Nyírfa.

"Hunyor says two are dead. He says, if you are daughters of Forest Goddess, then show him." Demas looked up at Nyírfa, anxiously. "You can show him?"

What was the penalty, Hársfa wondered, for failing to prove that one was a spirit of the trees? She looked at Hunyor's face, as expressionless as a rock. Then she looked at Magyar and saw the answer in his eyes. There was only one penalty among the Horsemen.

"If only our brother were here," she whispered to Nyírfa before she swayed and fell.

"Try to sit up," said Mrs. Madár. "Let me move the pillow. There." She felt the blankets being arranged around her. "Would you like me to open the window?" She heard the sash being raised, but she did not turn her head to look. A breeze blew through the open window. It smelled of rain.

"Once, the Moon looked down upon the hills of Anatolia and saw a shepherd lying in a meadow. She loved him, but the love of the Moon is dangerous to mortals, so she poured a potion made of the meadow poppies into his eyes so he would sleep for thirty years. Each of those years, she bore him a daughter, and when that daughter was weaned she placed her in a willow basket, which she set floating on the river Volga. The first of those baskets was found by women washing clothes on the riverbank, who took the child and raised her in their village. She was called Tölgy, which in English means Oak. Did you learn English in school? Did you understand Anne Martin, when she spoke to you?"

She nodded, still without looking at Mrs. Madár.

"Would you like something to drink?"

She nodded again, and Mrs. Madár poured water from a pitcher into a cup. Both were made of a thick, green glass with bubbles in it.

"The Daughters of the Moon grow quickly. When the second of those baskets floated down the river, Tölgy carried her sister Boróka into the forest, where she raised her among the groves of oak and alder, birch and willow, with foxes and owls for companions. And so with all the Daughters of the Moon. But after thirty years the shepherd woke, to find that his friends no longer remembered him, that he had lost the shining woman who came to him in dreams, and that he could no longer sleep. He spent the rest of his life consulting doctors and magicians, drinking medicines and potions, anything that would allow him to sleep

again. But he died with his eyes open. The year after
the shepherd she had loved woke, the Moon bore a
son, the White Stag, and when the stag was weaned,
she set him down on the bank of the Volga, where he
was raised by his sisters. But being a stag, it was his
nature to roam, and he often left to wander the slopes
of the Northern Mountains. Yes? I thought you said
something. Perhaps you're wondering what happened
to Nyírfa and Hársfa. Well, I'll tell you."

Hársfa lay in Nyírfa's arms. No, they were Magyar's,
and Nyírfa was standing beside her, looking up at
the sky.

"Oh, Mother," she heard Nyírfa whisper, "if your
arms tightened around us as you lowered us into the
baskets, if one tear of yours mingled with the river
before you sent us floating away from you to live
among the trees of the forest, help me now."

The clouds shifted above them, gray and white, like
floating mountains. Then something flashed in the sky,
and Nyírfa shrieked, a high, piercing sound. The Horsemen covered their ears, and even Hunyor stepped back,
startled, kicking the stool so that it toppled onto its
side. Something shrieked in response and hurled itself
from the sky, like lightning. A falcon, as gray and
white as the clouds, perched on Nyírfa's shoulder. It
turned its head, glaring at the Horsemen.

Nyírfa glared at them as fiercely, but Hársfa saw
that her hands were trembling. The falcon had dug its
claws into her shoulder, and a stain was spreading
from her shoulder down the front of her tunic. In-
stinctively, wanting to help, she reached her hands,
aching now from the leather that bound them, toward
her sister. But there was another way.

"Let me stand," she whispered to Magyar, and gestured as well as she could so he would understand.
More gently than she had expected, he helped her to
her feet, keeping one arm around her. "Oh, Mother,"
she whispered, "let me show what you gave your

daughters when you mingled your blood with that of a mortal."

She held her hands over the mud, and so low that the Horsemen heard it only because they had been still since the falcon's scream, she made the sound of wind blowing through the meadow: "Shhhhhhh . . ."

Green stems rose from the mud, developed leaves, flowered. Magyar bent down to touch the grasses that were spreading around them, the small blue flowers of flax. Then he spoke to Hunyor, and Hunyor answered. Magyar spoke again, pointing to the falcon on Nyírfa's shoulder.

Hársfa turned to Demas. "What are they saying?"

Demas stroked the grasses with wonder and said, "Magyar wants to have you for wife. He says Hunyor should take your sister. He says it is lucky, marrying daughters of goddess. Many tribes of barbaroi are coming from mountains to north. With luck, this tribe will win battles, find land."

"Many tribes?" said Nyírfa. The falcon clutched her shoulder more tightly, glaring at Hársfa with golden eyes. "Oh, my sisters, what will happen to you when those other tribes come?" She raised her hands to her face. For the first time, Hársfa realized, she looked defeated. The falcon sprang into the air and flapped its wings.

Hársfa thought of her sisters, binding their wounds in the cave by the riverbank, waiting for her and Nyírfa to return. They were not warriors. Suddenly she said, "Let our sisters come here! Demas, tell Hunyor there are many daughters of the goddess, twenty-five, maybe twenty-six more. Tell him we will bring him luck, we will call birds from the air, make his crops grow. Tell him, oh, tell him anything!"

"Hársfa, no!" said Nyírfa. "How can we live with these barbarians?"

But Demas had already spoken. Hársfa could feel Magyar's arm tighten around her. Hunyor stood silent while the Horsemen waited for his decision. Hársfa heard the falcon shriek high above them. She looked up and watched him circle once over the village, then fly off toward the west.

Hunyor walked to Nyírfa and stood before her, then held out his hands. Slowly, reluctantly, she put her hands in his. He spoke, a single word, then untied the leather from her wrists. Nyírfa pointed to the villagers. "Them too," she said. "Untie them too."

Magyar clutched Hársfa's shoulder and shouted with triumph. He turned to Demas and said—

"This is your tribe," Demas translated. "This is your home." And through her tears, Hársfa saw that the Horsemen were untying the villagers' hands.

"So Nyírfa and Hársfa married Hunyor and Magyar. They learned the language of their husbands, and took names in that language. Nyírfa became Tünde, and Hársfa became Csilla. Be careful, you'll spill your water. Is your name Tünde, then?"

She shook her head.

"Csilla? Welcome to my house, Csilla. You've been very brave, like a Daughter of the Moon."

Csilla put the cup on the table beside the bed. "What happened then?" Her voice sounded hoarse, like a rusted lock.

"The Daughters of the Moon married Horsemen, except for Ibolya, who became a healer, collecting and studying the plants of the countries they traveled through. They traveled west, following the falcon's flight, which the Horsemen had taken for an omen. Finally, they settled in the lands about the river Danube. Their children played with the children of the tribe, and those children's pale faces, their hair as green as the leaves of the forest, were seen as signs of luck, the blessing of the Forest Goddess. But they could not touch metal, and they would not eat meat. So the tribesmen called them the Tündér, after Tünde who had married Hunyor, which means the Fairy Folk, and always regarded them as different from themselves."

\*   \*   \*

A sparrow was singing in the linden tree outside the window. Csilla could identify the tree by its heart-shaped leaves. Her father had taught her the shapes of all the leaves . . . But she did not want to think about her father.

Sunlight had dried the rain. The linden was in flower, and its scent filled the room. She was sitting up in bed, leaning against the pillows, listening to the sparrow. How cool the pillows were, how clear the sunlight.

She whistled, a tune like the sparrow's song, and it stopped to listen to her, then hopped down to the windowsill, and onto the table, and onto the finger she held out for it.

"Like Tünde," said Mrs. Madár, standing in the doorway. The sparrow, startled, whistled and flew out the window. "Do you think you can eat some cucumber salad?"

Csilla nodded.

"I made it with just a bit of sour cream."

"My grandmother always said it was best with sour cream," said Csilla.

"Well, I'm glad to hear I made it like your grandmother! Here, take these." Mrs. Madár handed her a napkin folded around two slices of brown bread, a wooden bowl filled with cucumber salad, and a wooden spoon. She sat down beside the bed in a carved wooden chair.

When Csilla had eaten the cucumber salad and both slices of bread, Mrs. Madár said, "Can you talk about it now?"

Csilla shook the breadcrumbs from her napkin onto the table and whistled. The sparrow flew through the window and landed on the table. He picked up as many of the crumbs as he could, tilted his head to look at her, then flew off again.

"He'll be back," said Mrs. Madár. "I think he has a family. There's a nest in the linden tree, and several days ago I saw brown heads poking out of it. I think

there's a Mrs. Sparrow and some young sparrows waiting for him." She paused, then said, "Csilla—"

"My father sent me away! And I had to lie in the
bottom of a car, and that woman only let me out at
night, and I thought I was going to die. And then on
the airplane and in the train I wished I had died. I
wish I were dead now." Csilla covered her face with
her hands. The tears that she had not cried, not since
her father had told her, "You have to leave
Budapest—as quickly as possible, Csillike," came now.
She shook with them, violently, like a tree in a storm.
Then, suddenly, she felt a wave of nausea, and the
bread and cucumber salad were no longer sitting quietly in her stomach—

"That's all right," said Mrs. Madár. "I can wash the
blanket. But you have to stay quiet, very quiet for a
while. You're still sick from the metal in the car.
Helga tried to protect you as well as she could with
blankets, but remember that you breathed in metal
for three days. It will be a while before you feel well
again." She took the blanket from the bed and put it
in a heap on the floor.

"I could have helped him!" said Csilla, wiping her
mouth with the napkin, ashamed of herself. "I was
helping him. Why did he have to send me away?"

She could feel Mrs. Madár's hand on her arm. "I'm
sure he sent you away because he loved you."

Csilla turned to look at her, furious. "How do you
know! You don't know anything about him, or me!
Who are you, anyway? Who are all of you, you and
Helga and that woman who brought me here, who
squeaks like a mouse?"

Mrs. Madár reached up and unwrapped the turban
around her head. Her hair fell down around her.
Green as leaves.

"Oh," said Csilla. For a moment, she could not
speak. Then she said, "Not even my grandmother's
hair was as green as yours, and my father says she
had more Tündér blood in her than anyone in Hun-

gary. That's where it comes from, doesn't it? From the Daughters of the Moon?"

"Yes," said Mrs. Madár. "My hair and yours, although you don't have quite as much of the Tündér blood as your grandmother. Your mother was not one of the Tündér, was she?"

"No," said Csilla. "She died when I was only a baby. And then my grandmother died last year, and now Papa . . ."

"Hush," said Mrs. Madár. "Remember, you have to stay quiet so you can get well. Let me put this blanket in the tub to soak—and the napkin, while I'm at it. I'll be back in a moment."

When she returned, Csilla was still sitting on the bed, staring out the window. "I've brought you more water," she said, handing Csilla the green cup. She paused, then added, "We'll have to talk about what happened—soon. But for now, why don't I tell you another story?" She waited for a moment for Csilla to answer, but Csilla was silent. So she began, "The Daughters of the Moon died, eventually. They had mortal blood in them, as well as the blood of the Moon, and they were not eternal. But their children, the Tündér, lived peacefully among the farms and villages of Hungary, until the church decided that they were children of the Devil . . ."

Reluctantly, Csilla wiped her eyes with her hands and settled back against the pillows to listen.

*Erzsébet's Story*

"Erzsike!"

"Shhh," said Erzsébet, putting one finger to her lips. She leaned closer to the chapel door, which was open just enough to let a sliver of torchlight fall on the stones of the courtyard. "I think it's the landgravine."

"You're supposed to be in bed already," said Márta, but her voice was low, and she too leaned closer to hear what the landgravine was saying.

"I have sent for Ludwig. He would prefer to stay at the university, but I've told him it's time he assumed his father's position. How peaceful the landgrave looks, as though he were sleeping. A pity if, as you tell me, his soul is suffering the torments of hellfire."

"That, I'm afraid, is the penalty for excommunication."

Poor old landgrave. Erzsébet had seen him earlier that day lying in the chapel beneath a pall of crimson velvet, looking more peaceful than he had ever looked while alive. How could the landgravine speak that way about him? And who was that other voice?

"I don't know who the landgravine's talking to," she whispered. "It doesn't sound like anyone in the castle."

"For his science, as he called it, he risked his immortal soul," said the landgravine. "I think you will find me quite different from my husband, Father Conrad. I have no interest in old women who gather weeds by moonlight, and I value an alliance with the church."

"Then I take it the Inquisition can resume its activities in Thuringia?"

"I don't think it's in either of our interests to have Thuringia isolated from the Empire."

"No," whispered Márta, "he hasn't come to the Wartburg for many years. But I'll remember the sound of his voice until the day I die. That's the Inquisitor."

Erzsébet remembered the landgrave muttering, over his pots of agrimony and rue, about "that damned superstitious nonsense, the Inquisition." Then he would finish watering his pots, make notes on a sheet of vellum, and sit with her in the sunlight of the herbarium. "Someday," he would say, "we will understand the properties of plants and draw out their essences. And then, my dear, we will cure the illnesses that have bedeviled mankind since we were banished from Eden." Finally she would read to him from his Aristotle, while he fell asleep on a bench.

"And when will you celebrate the marriage between Ludwig and Princess Elizabeth?" asked the Inquisitor.

"Perhaps you could marry them yourself, Father Conrad? It would lighten our grief, following the landgrave's funeral with a wedding. My husband was foolish, delaying her marriage to Herman until he thought she was old enough. We almost lost her dowry, until the king agreed to an engagement with Ludwig. Well, she's certainly old enough now, older than when I married. And no time should be lost, now that the king has left for Palestine. If he dies, Ludwig will have as good a claim to the throne as anyone else, I think. Oh, my poor Herman! Such a fine boy, Father. You should have seen him riding across the fields, whipping his pony into a lather. What a king of Hungary he would have made!"

"We must never regret the will of God, Landgravine. I remember hearing that the landgrave had some excellent Tokay?"

"They're coming this way!" said Erzsébet.

"Hush," said Márta, pulling her back by her sleeve, into the shadows beyond the torchlight.

The landgravine emerged from the chapel, followed by a man in a Franciscan habit. She stood in the courtyard, the torchlight from the open door flickering over her yellow hair, which was coiled in elaborate braids on either side of a cap sewn with pearls that had come all the way from Paris. "I'm glad we've had this little talk, Father. I think we will be useful to one another." She smiled as sweetly as the Virgin in the chapel window.

"I hate her!" said Erzsébet when the landgravine, followed by the Inquisitor, had disappeared across the courtyard. "I've always hated her. I looked out the window and saw her walking across the courtyard, so I thought she was going into the chapel. And I came down to ask her if I could go back to Hungary. She never liked me anyway, and I thought she would send me home, now that the landgrave is dead. But she wants me to marry that stupid son of hers, that Ludwig." She hit the chapel wall with her hand and felt a cold pain run through her arm. "Márta, I haven't even seen him since I was a child! All I remember is that he used to collect bugs. He once put a caterpillar in my hair."

"Erzsike!" said Márta, catching her hand and examining it with care. "Erzsike, you're speaking too loudly."

"You know, I bet he'll be just like Herman. Did you know that Herman used to call me a witch? He said my face was as white as the moon, and people with moon faces should be burned. Márta, do you think I'm ugly?"

"Erzsike, remember the windows."

"I don't care." Then, looking up at the shuttered windows, darker patches on the dark walls of the castle, Erzsébet said, "Yes, I do care. Márta, I'm going to run away, tonight. Don't tell me not to, because I won't listen. If I can reach Erfurt, perhaps I can stay at the Abbey and send a letter to the king—" she hesitated, then said, "—I mean, to Papa." She looked down at the stones of the courtyard. "It's been so long since he sent me away. Do you think he will recognize me, after all these years?"

Márta said, "I won't try to stop you, Erzsike, because I'm going with you. Do you really think you can run away from the strongest castle in Germany by yourself? Now go to your room and fetch your cloak and your bottle of ointment."

"My ointment? Funny Márta, to care about my complexion at a time like this!" Erzsébet almost laughed, but she remembered the windows.

"I'll pack some food. Meet me in the scullery." Márta sighed. "Oh, that I should see this time come again!" Then, more briskly and in her ordinary voice, she said, "Tell me, child, do you have any money?"

"I know this story," said Csilla. "My grandmother told it to me. King András sent Princess Erzsébet to Thuringia. She was supposed to marry the landgrave's oldest son, Herman." She remembered listening, in the kitchen of their apartment in Budapest, while her grandmother rolled the gingerbread dough.

"Remember this story, Csillike," her grandmother had said. "It's one of the most important stories to remember, almost as important as the Daughters of the Moon. That's why I tell it to you again and again, so you will remember it when you need it most."

When the gingerbread was in the oven, her grandmother had said, "Now you tell it back to me." Csilla had repeated it, again and again. She had named one of the gingerbread men Herman, and while her grandmother had sat by the stove, listening and correcting her if she made any mistakes, she had slowly eaten Herman, starting with the feet.

"The king thought she would be safer there, especially after what had happened to the queen. But Herman died, so she couldn't marry him any more. And then . . ."

"Yes?" said Mrs. Madár. "What happened to Princess Erzsébet?"

Moonlight glimmered through the branches. Erzsébet tried to avoid tripping over shadows on the path: rocks, or perhaps roots. In summer, the landgravine would go with her ladies to the forest. They would sit by a stream, gossiping and listening to one of the traveling minstrels that came to the Wartburg during the summer months, strumming his lute and singing about the landgravine's hair. The landgravine, dressed rather implausibly as Flora, would lean back against her cushions with the satisfied smile that Erzsébet always found so unsettling. She remembered the forest as a series of sunlit glades. This was not the same forest. There was a constant rustling and scurrying in the bushes around her. She smelled fallen leaves, and mushrooms and the cold smell that meant winter was coming.

She clutched Márta's cloak. "Are you sure this is the right way to Erfurt?"

The rustling and scurrying stopped, and the forest waited, unaccustomed to this new sound.

"We can ask the travelers ahead. I see a fire through the trees. Come on, Erszike."

"I thought we were trying to avoid other travelers . . ." But Márta was already ahead of her, walking toward the fire.

Hurrying to catch up, Erzsébet stumbled over a shadow that turned out to be a rock. When she found her footing again and looked around her, she was standing in a clearing. The travelers were sitting around a fire at its center.

Once, Erzsébet had gone to Erfurt with the land-gravine, to a fair celebrating the new windows of the Abbey, which showed the Virgin and Saint Anne. On the road through the forest she had seen merchants, their wagons filled with glass vessels from Venice, brocades and damasks from the weavers of Flanders, holy relics from Rome. As the landgravine's procession had drawn closer to the town, it had passed farmers carrying dried meat and heads of cabbage in nets. She had seen their wives and daughters walking beside them, their baskets filled with goose eggs, honeycombs dripping with brown honey, walnuts. Often the road ahead of the procession was blocked by travelers and sheep, who must be moved aside to let the landgravine pass.

These travelers were not like those she had seen going to the fair. On one side of the fire crouched a woman with white hair like a bird's nest, whose legs were so twisted that she could scarcely have walked along the forest road. Yet surely Erzsébet had seen her begging in front of the Abbey. And wasn't that the scullery girl from the castle, still in her apron? Beside the scullery girl sat a man surrounded by children, from a baby to a girl almost as old as Erzsébet who was holding the baby in her arms. They were dressed in rags, and the baby's mouth was surrounded by sores. She had seen the man before as well; he had been the Devil in the play at the fair. She had seen him afterward juggling colored balls, while the boy who sat beside him, with the dirty cap on his head, had walked on his hands. The landgravine had forbidden her to watch such a vulgar spectacle.

"Hello, sister," said Márta.

"Hello yourself," said a woman who was standing in the shadows beyond the firelight. "I see you've brought the girl."

Beside the children sat a peddler, who grinned at her without teeth. Out of his sack spilled bottles of ointment and what looked like a mandrake root. And then she noticed that the baby's curls, which at first had seemed yellow, were the color of spring leaves.

"Is that the way to talk to a princess? Where are your manners?" Márta turned to Erzsébet. "You'll have to forgive her, Erszike. My sister is a queen in her own right, although her nation does not belong to the Holy Roman Empire."

Márta had a sister? A sister dressed in gray, like the habit of a nun. A sister whose hair cascaded over her shoulders like ivy.

"Where have you brought me?" She was surprised to hear her voice, so frightened. Her eyes stung from looking around the fire. She rubbed them. The woman's hair was still green. "Is this a meeting of witches?"

"The Inquisitor would tell you so," said the woman in gray. Surely Erzsébet had seen her before. She remembered the mouth, with lines of laughter around it, and the nose, as thin and sharp as a knife. But where?

She felt Márta's arms around her, as comforting as when she was a child. "Erszike, these are the Tündér, and my sister Cecília is their queen."

Later she remembered music, although she was not sure when it had started: the music of a pipe and drum. She remembered a dance, but it was not like any dance she had learned at court—a wild dance in which she bent and turned and spun as though before a great wind. Later there was bread with raisins and walnuts baked in it and a honey wine that warmed her to her toes. All these she remembered, sleepily, when the dancing had stopped and she sat among the roots of an ancient oak, with her head on Márta's shoulder, listening to the queen of the Tündér.

"Let us examine the facts," said Cecília. Erzsébet touched a strand of her hair, which was curling over a root. It was as green as the moss on the root, and as soft as—well, ordinary hair. "Item primum: that your mother was murdered by Hungarian counts while your father was visiting the emperor's court. Afterward, they were absolved by the church, since the wound was so slight that it should not have killed an ordinary woman. Item secundum: that your father sent you to Thuringia, whose landgrave considered himself a man of science and forbade the burning of witches. Item tertium: that since your childhood, Márta has rubbed your face and hands with an ointment whose secret is known only to the Tündér. Aristotle would tell us that the conclusion is inevitable. But the evidence of the eyes is more convincing than logic. Give me your finger."

"My finger?" Erszébet stared at the thorn that Cecília was holding. Was this a meeting of witches after all? Witches stole the blood of baptized children to make their bread. Herman had told her that, when he had called her a witch.

"Let me do it, Erszike." And this was strange, because Márta had never even allowed her to sew, for fear that she would spoil her fingers. Perhaps she should run away from these witches, as she had run away from the landgravine. But she felt so sleepy, leaning her head against the trunk of the tree. How much honey wine had she drunk?

A drop of blood ran into her palm, leaving a trail behind it, like a snail moving over a stone. It was a clear and shining green. Suddenly the effect of the honey wine left her, and she understood.

"Then why don't I have green hair?"

"Your mother's hair was as green as mine," said Cecília. "Look around at our company." The children were sleeping at the edge of the firelight, the oldest girl still holding the baby in her arms. The peddler had made a pillow out of his sack. Only the man who had played the Devil still sat piping, like a plaintive bird. "Some of us are lucky. Sándor's hair is brown, and his eyes have enough brown in them that he can pass as an ordinary man. But you see his youngest, little Juli. Some of us must hide in the forest, for fear of being identified as a witch. Although the landgrave ordered that witches cannot be burned, they can be driven away. Sándor's wife, the mother of those children, was killed two summers ago by a miller's dog."

Sándor stopped his piping to throw another branch on the fire. Before he began piping again, he touched the baby's hair, ruffling it like spring grass. The beggar moved in her sleep, muttering something that sounded like a song Márta had sung to Erszébet when she was a child.

"You, Erszébet, look more like your father than your mother," Cecília continued. "With the help of Márta's ointment you can even handle metal, although it could not protect your mother from the prick of a knife. She did not die of her wounds but of poison, since metal is poison to us. How we appear depends on whether both of our parents were Tündér, and both of their parents. But all of us have the blood of the Tündér in us, what the Inquisition calls the witch blood: the blood of the Moon. Márta's father was not of the Tündér, but mine was. I could not live at the Wartburg, as she does." Cecília smiled. "Don't you recognize me, Erszébet? We've met before." She reached behind her and picked up a piece of gray cloth, then draped it over her head like a veil. "Now?"

And suddenly Erszébet remembered where she had seen that mouth. It had been praying in the Chapel of Saint Anne at the Abbey. She had watched it because she had been bored, and the alternative was to look at the landgravine. "If they knew that the Abbess of Erfurt . . ."

"Sit still," said Márta, who was still holding a hand-kerchief to her finger. "I don't want you to start bleed-ing again."

"Then there would be no one at the Abbey to help the Tündér. Old Ildiko there, who can't help singing the songs of the Tündér in her sleep, would no longer be able to beg on the Abbey steps or curl beside our kitchen fire. She would be cast into the street, and if the Inquisition found her . . ." The lines around her mouth became lines of anger. "I was born after the witch trials, but Márta remembers."

Márta looked down at her hands. "I was only a girl when the Inquisitor came to our town. My father was a baker; he had money to send me and my mother to Nürnberg. For that, he was burned in the marketplace, although his blood was as red as the priest's."

"Like my father sent me away." Erzsébet put her face in her hands.


"You think you're so smart, don't you?" said Csilla.

"What do you mean?" asked Mrs. Madár.

"Getting me to tell Erzsébet's story because you want me to talk about my father. He sent me away just like King András send Erzsébet away. Well, I think he should have kept her in Hungary!"

Mrs. Madár shook her head. She looked, Csilla thought, like the mathematics teacher at her school, when she had hopelessly muddled a multiplication problem. "Then she would have been killed, just as her mother the queen was killed. Csilla, you must understand that the Inquisition was burning anyone iden-tified as a witch. And the easiest way to be a witch was to be one of the Tündér. We have always been hiding, always fleeing, since the days of the Daughters of the Moon. Your father was working to change that. He was writing a book—"

"I know," said Csilla. "He worked on it all day long, and sometimes all night long." She would wake in the darkness and hear the sound of the typewriter. So she would put on the sweater that her grandmother had worn on days when the apartment was cold, walk down the hall to the kitchen, turn on the old stove, and boil the water for tea. When she brought it to him, he would look at her with that tired look in his eyes, her handsome Papa, and say, "Thank you, Csillike. You are my own guardian angel, aren't you?"

In the mornings, she would make his lunch so that he would eat something while she was at school, but often when she came home, she would find the bean soup cold, the brown bread gone stale. "You forgot to eat again," she would say, accusingly. "Have you been typing all day?"

"I'm so sorry, Csillike," he would answer. "I seem to have forgotten some of the details of Szent Erzsébet's story. Could you sit beside me and tell me if I have the name of the Abbess right? I promise I'll eat whatever you made me, no matter how cold it is."

"It was a book about the Tündér. He was writing down all of my grandmother's stories. I used to help him with it."

"Help him?" said Mrs. Madár. "How did you help him, Csilla?"

Csilla looked at Mrs. Madár curiously. She was leaning forward in her chair, no longer the disapproving teacher. Instead, she sounded like an eager child. "Well, not really help. I mean not with the typing or anything. But when he forgot something, or got something wrong, I told him how the stories went. My grandmother told them to me, and she made me tell them to her, so many times! I don't think I could forget them if I tried."

"Oh, my dear," said Mrs. Madár. "Don't you know why your father sent you away? He sent us a message, but messages are so difficult. They have to be—well, not exactly clear, in case the wrong person reads them. He said he was writing down his mother's stories, the whole history of the Tündér. We've never had a history, just stories, Csilla. Stories remembered by the old people, because the young had so many other things to think about, and when something was forgotten, it was forgotten forever. In Erzsébet's time the church burned everything written about the Tündér, and even now in Hungary books about the Tündér are banned. They cannot be published or sold because the state believes that we do not exist. Can you imagine what that means to us? We have been hiding and fleeing so long that the Tündér are scattered now, over Europe and here in America. Without a history, how can we know who we are, or find each other again? Your father was trying to teach us. His message—it was so difficult to understand. First we heard he was sending us a copy of his manuscript. Then Helga said he was sending us his daughter. And then there you were—"

"In my science class," said Csilla, "the teacher told us that the Tündér had a genetic defect. That we were . . . sick, not as strong as other people because we had bad genes. She said everything could be explained scientifically."

"Do you believe that?" asked Mrs. Madár.

"I don't know," said Csilla. "My father believes in the stories, and he's a professor at the university. But of course, he's a philosophy professor, and not at all practical. He can't even keep his socks mended. If the stories are real, what happened to Márta's ointment? I mean, there's nothing like that now."

"It's another thing we've lost," said Mrs. Madár. "That's why the stories are so important."

Csilla said, suddenly, "Did you know my name, when you told me about the Daughters of the Moon? Or did you really think I could be named Tünde?"

"No," said Mrs. Madár, "not exactly. But in his message your father referred to a guiding star— another thing I didn't understand at the time. Csilla— star. And so I guessed. I thought if I told you about the bravery of another Csilla, you might respond. About your father—you have to understand that he was in great danger, of going to prison or worse. But he was very brave."

"I could have been brave too," said Csilla.

"I'm sure he knew that," said Mrs. Madár. "But like the king of Hungary, he loved his daughter too much to put her in danger. And like Erzsébet, you're going to have to make a choice."

When Erzsébet could not sleep, Márta would stroke her hair and tell her about the Daughters of the Moon or how Saint István rode the White Stag. She was stroking her hair now. "Do you see why I brought you here, Erszike?"

Although she could hear the forest around her, the rustling and scurrying, and the crackles of the dying fire, she felt the stones of the Wartburg pressing against her, so that she could not breathe.

"To escape the landgravine?" But she knew, as she said it, that it was not the reason.

Cecília took her hand and looked at the spot where the thorn had pierced, which had already stopped bleeding. "To give you a choice."

Márta stroked her hair again, but now it offered no reassurance. "You could help the Tündér, Erzsike. If you stayed at the Wartburg . . ."

She had not noticed when the piping had stopped. Sándor lay by the fire with his mouth open, snoring slightly. He had taken the baby from his daughter, and it lay beside him, wrapped in his ragged coat. Green curls tumbled over the baby's eyes. Its thumb was in its mouth, and it made a sucking sound in its dreams.

Erzsébet looked down at the mark on her finger. Then she said to Cecília, "Márta and I have to get back before dawn. Will you distribute the money?"

"There's more," said Csilla, because Mrs. Madár had stopped.

"Is there?" said Mrs. Madár. "You see, I don't know the rest. We know our stories only in fragments. But your grandmother knew more of those fragments than anyone."

"Yes," said Csilla. "You're missing the most important part."

\*    \*    \*

The chapel was filled with the thump of boots sewn from embroidered leather, the shush of sleeves edged with ermine.

I am a cloud, thought Erzsébet. I am a mist, creeping across the room. I am invisible, like air . . .

"Elizabeth!" said the landgravine. "Father Conrad, this is the Princess Elizabeth." The pearls in the landgravine's hair glowed in the light that came through the stained glass window, turning her left cheek a delicate blue. "Elizabeth, surely you know enough to kiss the Inquisitor's hand?"

It happened, as Erzsébet knew it must, when she bent to kiss the wrinkled fingers, dirty under the nails and wearing an iron ring engraved with a cross. Out they tumbled, the rolls that she had stolen from breakfast, stolen for the woman who waited in a corner of the scullery, anxiously holding a child whose head was wrapped in a ragged scarf. How carefully she had wrapped them in her skirt, how carefully she had held her skirt so they would not fall out. And now they lay on the chapel floor, where boots stepped aside and skirts drew back to avoid them. What good was it being at the Wartburg, when all she could do to help the Tündér was steal rolls? Lenke, the scullery girl, could do more than she could.

"Bread?" said the landgravine. "Why do you need bread?" She watched the rolls rolling, as though she had never seen bread before.

Erzsébet felt as though she could not breathe. What should she answer?

"Speak, child," said Father Conrad. "Speak as truthfully as our Lord taught us." He smiled, a smile that he might have thought was kind. But his eyes glittered like steel.

What had Márta whispered, lying beside her at night when she could not sleep? The Tündér could call the blossom from its bud, the rabbit from its burrow, the fox from its den. They could smell the storm coming while the sky was still blue. She was one of the Tündér, but none of these skills would help her now. What good did it do her, having the blood of the Moon?

Then suddenly she heard it: soft, insistent. The cooing of doves in the courtyard. Usually they stayed in their cote beside the kitchen, where they were kept for their eggs, and for pie.

"Come," whispered Erzsébet. "Come to me." It was not much, it was probably less than nothing, but it was what she could do. Because she was one of the Tündér.

"What was that, Elizabeth?" asked the landgravine. "Speak up, child. Father Conrad can't hear you."

Then a rush of wings, and the doves, so many of them, white and brown and gray and speckled, were stepping over the chapel floor—pecking, pecking, until the very last crumb was gone.

"Surely these are the birds of God."

Erzsébet turned to see who had spoken. There was a boy standing beside her. He was tall and thin and slightly stooped, as though ashamed of his height. His eyebrows rose to a peak in the middle, which gave him a look of perpetual curiosity. Like the landgrave's, she thought, and, suddenly realizing who he was, looked down again at the floor, where the doves were still searching for more bread. She noticed that his boots were covered with mud.

"You don't remember me, Princess. Or if you do, I'm sorry for it. I seem to remember that I was a particularly unpleasant boy."

"Ludwig! I thought you weren't arriving until—well, later." The landgravine did not look particularly pleased to see her son.

"I left the university as soon as I heard that my father was ill. But I find that I have arrived only in time to pray by his body." He looked toward the chancel, where the landgrave lay beneath his crimson pall, in a cloud of incense. Erzsébet saw that although he seemed calm, his eyes were red, as though he had been weeping. He turned back to the landgravine. "Surely the princess meant this bread for the poor.

The landgrave himself would have done no less. The Word of God traveled as a dove to announce our Savior. Isn't that right, Father Conrad? I think these birds rebuke us for our impiety. Here, Princess. Give this to those who need it."

The purse jingled as he dropped it into her hands, sending the doves flying upward, while velvet sleeves fluttered to protect faces. They flew around the beams of the chapel, then out through the door and up into the blue of the sky. She clutched the purse carefully and watched as Ludwig walked up the steps to the chancel, then knelt beside the landgrave's body, with his head in his hands. She thought, He is not like Herman, and perhaps in time I could like him, just a little.

"So she married Ludwig," said Csilla, "and they lived happily until he died in the Crusades. Then she went into a convent, where she lived for the rest of her life. And the people said she could perform miracles, like curing the sick. So they called her a saint."

"Is that the end?" asked Mrs. Madár. "I'm glad you told it to me. It's not like in the official history books, is it?"

"It never is," said Csilla.

"And you know all of your grandmother's stories, like this, so complete?"

"Of course," said Csilla, wondering why Mrs. Madár should doubt her.

"Csilla," said Mrs. Madár, "I want to tell you a story that I know you have not heard. But first we must have some dinner, and then we must take a walk into the forest. Do you think that you're strong enough? It's not too far."

"I'm all right," said Csilla, although as she sat up, she felt the nausea again. But she was going to be brave, like her father.

Mrs. Madár wrapped a shawl around Csilla's shoulders. "This dress used to be Susanna Martin's. That's Mrs. Martin's daughter. You look a little like her—it was her passport we used to get you on the airplane in Vienna. It's going to be colder in the forest. Are you ready, Csilla?"

"Yes," said Csilla, although she did not know what she was supposed to be ready for.

They walked down the back steps and through what had once been a garden. It was dilapidated now. Weeds grew in the flower beds, and the pond was covered with scum. But some ancient peach trees still stood to mark where an orchard had once been. Soon the garden gave way to rhododendrons and mountain laurels, and then an oak forest, and they were walking along a path littered with oak leaves. Sunlight came down through the branches above, and the shadows of the trees stretched eastward. The sun was beginning to set. The forest was silent, except for the occasional call of a bird or the rustle of a squirrel in the treetops.

"I wonder if Erzsébet's forest was like this," said Csilla.

"Older," said Mrs. Madár. "This forest was cut seventy years ago for lumber. These are young trees. No, this reminds me of another forest." She walked on for a moment in silence. Leaves crackled under her shoes, and a twig broke with a loud snap. Then she continued, "Once, there was a girl named Margit."

*Margit's Story*

Margit wondered how long they had been sitting in the barn, surrounded by the smell of hay and horses. She thought there was only one horse in the barn—she could hear it stamping in a corner and occasionally banging its bucket against the far wall. But the sky was clouded, and moonlight came only occasionally through the barn door, which anyway was only half open. Judit would not allow them to open it further.

"I'm hungry," said Debóra.

"Hush," said Judit. "We have to stay quiet. Anyway, you ate the last sandwich hours ago."

"How do you know it was hours?" asked Margit.

"Can you see your watch?" It was so dark in the barn that she could barely see Judit's face, or Debóra's, scowling as though she were about to cry, or Magda's, silly Magda's, blowing spit bubbles that shimmered in the faint light. With her handkerchief, which smelled like cheese from the sandwiches, she wiped the trail of spit that ran down Magda's chin. Thank goodness Dénes had fallen asleep on the straw. For a moment the moon escaped from the clouds, and she saw that he was sucking his thumb. Well, let him.

She felt a hand on her arm, and then Judit was pulling her away, saying, "Stay there, Debóra, and take care of Magda."

"Listen," said Judit. "We have to have a plan. Once Debóra gets really hungry, she won't care how much noise she makes. She's been that way since she was a baby. And what about Dénes when he wakes up? At least Magda will stay quiet as long as we tell her. But we need food too, Margit. I don't know how far it is to the border, but when Father took us to Arad last year, it was more than an hour by train. We can't walk if we're hungry."

"Can we ask the farmer for food? We could tell him we were on a trip with our parents and got lost. They'd have to feed us, wouldn't they?"

"They wouldn't have to do anything, not if they saw these on our clothes." Even in the darkness, Margit could see the yellow stars sewn on Judit's and Debóra's dresses. "Why should they treat us any better than the people in Szeged?"

Margit understood the bitterness in Judit's voice. The Lengyels had lived in one of the largest houses in Szeged. Next year, Judit was supposed to graduate from high school. She had been planning to study art in Budapest, and eventually in Paris. Margit had never understood why Judit had helped her that day in the schoolyard, when Péter Nagy and his friend Tamás had pushed her down on the pavement, shouting, "Hello, Tündér! Let's see if she has scales under her clothes." She was two years younger than Judit, and her family lived in a small house on Boszorkány street. Had lived, she corrected herself. But after Judit had pummeled the boys with her school bag, shouting, "Stop it, you idiots!" they had become friends.

"I don't want to take care of Magda anymore," said Debóra. "I want to come talk with you." Her voice rose. "You never let me do anything!"

"Shut up, or I'll make you!" said Judit. "Do you know what will happen if anyone finds out we're here?"

Debóra started to cry. "I'm going to tell Papa that you were mean to me!"

"Oh, don't, Debóra," said Margit, but Judit said, "Let her. It's more quiet than when she talks. Now, we have to get these things off our clothes. We should be able to cut them off with the pocket knife."

"But won't we get in trouble?" There had been so many ways to get in trouble, recently. First, they could not listen to the radio. Then, they could not ride in motor cars, and Mama had to walk all day to visit Aunt Ilona in the country. Then they could not play in the park, or watch movies at the cinema, and finally Margit had to stay home from school. Papa stayed home too, because he could not work at the newspaper. And finally all of them, all of the Tündér in Szeged, even those who had brown hair and went to the Catholic church, had to move into the part of the city where Judit's family had moved after the police took the big house on Gutenberg Street for their headquarters. Mr. Lengyel had asked them to move in, although there were already three families sharing the house. The police had marked down who was living there: Jews, Bolsheviks, Tündér.

"Do you think we could be in any more trouble than we're already in? We ran away from the police, Margit. If anyone finds out who we are, we'll probably go to jail."

The horse whinnied in the corner, and Dénes turned on the straw. Moonlight broke through the clouds again, and Margit saw with relief that Debóra had fallen asleep beside him. Magda was rocking back and forth, crooning quietly to herself.

"We could explain that we ran only because Papa told us to. It was so quick, with the police knocking on the door, and Papa telling Aunt Ilona to take us into the alley. We didn't know what we were doing. If we tell them that we just want to be with our parents—"

"You idiot." Judit's words felt like a slap. "Don't you understand that's what your father was trying to prevent? The police were coming to take them away. They were coming to take everyone away. They've already done that in other towns. My father heard from the Rabbi."

Papa and Mama taken away. "Where? Where would they take them?" Margit was crying now too, but silently, although she felt as though she were about to break apart. In a few moments, she would be lying in fragments on the barn floor.

"I don't know," said Judit. "Nowhere good." Margit felt Judit's arms around her, and she could not help letting out a sob so loud that it made Magda jump. "Remember what happened to your Aunt Ilona."

Margit had been trying not to remember. She had been ahead of Judit, who had been carrying Dénes and leading Magda by the hem of her skirt. Aunt Ilona had been behind them. And then—a sound, like a loud crack. She had looked back to see Aunt Ilona lying on the stones that paved the alley, in a green puddle. Aunt Ilona had lived on a farm, and Margit remembered visiting with Dénes, feeding the chickens, eating apricots picked from the orchard, swimming in the river Tisza. But eventually Aunt Ilona had moved to Szeged, saying that the countryside had become too dangerous for Tündér. She had brought Magda, a farmer's daughter whose father had been afraid to keep her. That day, Margit had wanted to go back to where Aunt Ilona lay, but Judit had not let her. She had said, "Don't stop, Margit. Go through the Szomorys' garden. Hold Debóra's hand, and don't lose your school bag. It has all the food in it.

"No," said Judit, "we'll do what our fathers planned. We'll cross the border to Romania and find my uncle in Arad. As soon as it's light enough to see, we can walk across the field and into the forest. The border is to the west, so we'll just keep walking toward where the sun sets. It's too bad the map and the compass were in the other bag. If only I knew how far it was!"

"What about food?" asked Margit. She was not going to remember the green puddle. She was going to be practical, like Judit.

"We'll have to steal it."

"Hunh," said Magda. "HunhHunhHunh!"

"Hush, Magdi," said Margit, but then Judit put a hand on her arm again, as though to hush her too.

"Listen," she said. "Do you hear it?"

The engine of a motor car. She could hear it, faintly at first and then louder. Then suddenly a sound as though the motor car were coughing, right in front of the barn. Then silence.

"Damn these country roads! Sergeant, you told us you could get us to the farm."

"Yes, sir. But, sir, the roads do get like this. When it rains, sir, and it's been raining heavily—"

"And while we sit here, stuck in mud, the children are escaping."

Margit felt Judit's hand clasp hers, hard. She wanted to tell Judit that her fingers were aching, but she was too frightened to make a sound.

"So sorry, sir. I'll go to the farmhouse and wake the farmer. He'll be able to tell us if he's seen anyone."

"Is it time for breakfast?" asked Debóra. She sat up in the straw and looked around, as though expecting to see her bedroom on Gutenberg street. When she saw Dénes lying beside her and the horse champing at the edge of his bucket, she cried, "Papa!"

A voice outside said, "Did you hear that, sir?"

"Come on," whispered Judit. She let go of Margit's hand and pulled Debóra up from the straw. "There's a door in the back, I saw it when we came in. We'll have to go out that way."

Margit shook Dénes. "Wake up! It's time to wake up." He opened his eyes and looked at her the way he did when he was going to open his mouth and wail. "But you have to be very quiet, because we're going on an adventure. We're Imre and Fair Ilona, and we're taking the children of the Tündér to the mountains. We can't let the Turks hear us, or they'll capture us again. Do you understand?"

He nodded, got to his feet, and took her hand. She held the other hand out to Magda, who was always happy to follow wherever she was led.

The back door opened with a creak as Judit pushed it, and they emerged into the night. The moon shone over the fields, alternately veiled and unveiled by clouds. They waded through barley, which scratched Margit's knees so that she wished she were wearing pants. They went quickly, as quickly as they could, but there was a sea of barley ahead of them and already they were faltering, because oh, how tired they were, thought Margit, dropping Dénes' hand for a moment to scratch her itching knees. And every step seemed more difficult, pulling Dénes and Magda, both of whom lagged behind, until she felt as though she were carrying them. And Dénes was about to cry, she knew it.

She looked behind them. The barn was already filled with light, and a voice cried, "Sir, I found a handkerchief!" Which meant the voices knew they were here, and they would be caught, and their blood would form puddles among the stalks of barley. If I really were Fair Ilona, she thought, I would make the barley grow so that the Turks could not find me. But that's only a story.

"Margit," said Judit ahead of her. Even Judit was moving slowly, carrying Debóra, who was whimpering and refusing to walk. "What's that in the trees?"

There was a light among the trees at the edge of the forest. Not like the light of a lantern, but pale and still.

And then, although a dog began barking behind them, which meant that the farmer was awake, Margit stopped and stood among the barley, thinking to herself, can it be true? But Dénes said, "Look, it's the White Stag."

He shone like the moon, and he stamped his hoof on the ground as though telling them to hurry.

"I'm Imre, and the White Stag has come to save me from the Turks!" Now Dénes was dragging her forward, and all of them were running, with a breath they did not know they had. And then the forest was all around. They were following the glimmer of the stag through the trees, while the barking of the dog faded away behind them.

"Look," said Mrs. Madár. "You can see the moon."

"I haven't heard that story," said Csilla. "Is it true?"

Mrs. Madár stared at the sliver of moon, pale against the darkening sky. "Judit was my best friend."

"Were you Margit? I mean, are you Margit?" Mrs. Madár nodded. "Well, what happened? What happened to Judit and the children?"

Mrs. Madár sighed. "Judit stayed in Romania and was sent to prison—this was many years later—because her art was considered subversive. Debóra went to Israel with her uncle. She studied economics—but I have not heard from her in years. I was sent to Switzerland with Dénes and Magda, where other children of the Tündér were sent as refugees. Magda is still there, in a good home. After the war, Dénes and I were brought to America. He went to a university and became a history professor. It was his idea to bring as many of the Tündér here as we could, from the countries where they are oppressed and imprisoned. It was also his idea that your father should write a book. He's the one who will be handling the petition to have you declared a political refugee. But you'll hear more about that soon. We're almost there."

"And—" Csilla hesitated. "Did you really see the White Stag?"

"It was long ago," said Mrs. Madár. "I'm not sure I really remember. But Dénes has always believed that we did."

The first person she saw in the clearing was Anne Martin.

"I can't tell you how glad I am to hear you're doing better," said Mrs. Martin, clasping her hands in front of her. "Helga didn't realize. I mean, most of you aren't so affected by metal anymore. My husband had some Fairy in him, on his mother's side, and he could eat with a knife and fork, just like ordinary folks. You wouldn't even have known it, except he had hazel eyes. Such beautiful eyes! He died a couple of years ago, of lung cancer. No one knew about cigarettes when we were growing up. That's why I do this, you know. For him and for Susanna. She's so proud of her heritage! Really, I'm just a librarian. And of course Mrs. Madár is so persuasive. I mean the queen. Although she never lets us call her that, outside of the forest."

Mrs. Madár looked like a queen, standing in the middle of the clearing. Someone had put a crown of ivy on her head. I could be Princess Erzsébet in the forest, thought Csilla. Except that the man talking to Mrs. Madár was wearing overalls, and the people standing and talking to each other, or sitting on the stones that ringed the clearing, looked ordinary, like people she might meet in a grocery store. But one boy who was building the fire had green in his brown curls, and a girl in a school uniform looked at her with eyes as green as a cat's.

"Are they all—Tündér?" It felt strange, speaking English, and Csilla could not use the English word, as Mrs. Martin had done.

"Or related to the Tündér, though not by blood. Like me to my Henry."

"Csilla, can I speak with you for a moment?" Mrs. Madár was standing beside her.

Mrs. Martin tactfully withdrew to speak to the girl in the school uniform. Csilla wondered if that was Susanna Martin. They were about the same age, although Csilla wondered why anyone would mistake Susanna's picture for hers. They didn't look that much alike. But perhaps they would be friends?

"This is my brother, Professor Kertész." He didn't look like Csilla's idea of a professor. Her father had always worn a jacket and tie, even to the grocery store. This man's overalls had grass stains on the knees.

Professor Kertész held out his hands. Without thinking, she put her hands in his. "Csilla, I'm sorry to bring you such bad news when we've just met. Your father has been arrested."

Csilla sat down abruptly on one of the stones. Mrs. Madár knelt beside her. "Oh, my dear. I'm so terribly sorry."

A crack was opening inside her. She could feel it open, and everything was falling inside it: her grandmother's gingerbread, her father's jackets, which always needed mending, the city of Budapest. The night itself was falling into the crack, and Csilla thought, We're all going to fall in, all of the Tündér.

There were whispers around her, as the story spread. "Yes," said Professor Kertész, turning to the people around the fire. "Antal Szarvas has been arrested. This is, of course, the worst news I could have for you. But I am also sorry to say that we have been unable to locate his manuscript. We believe there were two copies, his personal copy and another that he was sending us. We searched his apartment after his arrest, but the police had already been there. We found nothing, and we do not know if the second copy was sent. I can't tell you how sad I am to have a colleague in danger. To have lost Queen Gertrúd's stories is a double blow. Translating them into English would have been the most significant work of my life."

"We haven't lost her stories," said Mrs. Madár.

From the darkness into which she had fallen, Csilla
suddenly saw what seemed to her like a flicker of light,
bringing her back to the stone she sat on, and the
forest. "My grandmother was queen of the Tündér?"

"Yes," said Mrs. Madár. "Your grandmother was
our queen. If she had told you, it would have put you
in danger."

In the blankness of her grief, Csilla thought, I wish
people would stop trying to protect me.

Mrs. Madár looked at the people around the fire,
ordinary people who looked like farmers and teachers
and librarians but were, it turned out, not ordinary at
all. "This is Csilla Szarvas, Professor Szarvas' daughter
and Queen Gertrúd's granddaughter. She knows where
the second copy of her father's manuscript is located."
Csilla heard the people around the fire whisper to
one another.

"What do you mean?" she said. "I don't know anything about a second copy. I just know about the one
he was typing."

"Csilla," said Mrs. Madár, "don't you understand?
You are the second copy—or rather the first copy,
because what he was typing was really the second.
You know all the stories that your grandmother
knew—she made sure of that. We couldn't understand
your father's message—was he sending us his daughter
or his manuscript? It turns out he was sending us
both." Mrs. Madár put her arm around Csilla's shoulder. "But don't think about that right now. Just keep
getting stronger. We'll try to help him, I promise.
Even in prison, we'll try to help him and bring him
out. We'll never stop trying."

The people around the fire were turning to each
other, talking. She heard a pipe begin, and then a
drum. But Csilla could not stand, and she could not
speak, because her father might be dead already, and
who cared about a bunch of stories that were probably, anyway, a bunch of lies? Even the White Stag.

"Csilla, there is someone I want you to meet." Mrs.
Madár squeezed her shoulder and then stepped aside.

The woman who stood before her was so small, no taller than Csilla herself, and so slender. Her bones were like the bones of birds. She was so pale, like white stones at the bottom of a stream. Her skin was wrinkled, all over her cheeks and around her eyes. She looked infinitely old, but the hair that hung over her shoulders was as green as grass.

"Drink this," she said in an accent so strange, so ancient, that it seemed to echo from a thousand years in the past. As the honey wine burned her throat, Csilla felt the crack in her chest . . . not close, but ease.

"Csilla," said Mrs. Madár, "I told you that the Daughters of the Moon were dead. That is what we would like the world to believe—the Tündér have been feared enough, and an almost-immortal ancestress might convince even the twentieth century that we are the witches we were once thought to be. But this is Ibolya, the last of the Daughters of the Moon."

"Welcome, child," said Ibolya. Her voice sounded like the whisper of leaves overhead. "You have lost so much, we have all lost so much. That is why you must help us find ourselves again." She turned to Mrs. Madár. "Show her, Queen. Show her what we are doing here, in this new land."

"Denés," said Mrs. Madár to her brother, "I think we can begin."

It was a song Csilla's grandmother had never taught her, and it sounded as ancient as Ibolya herself. Mrs. Madár sang the first verse, then Professor Kertész joined in, then the others, one by one, until even Mrs. Martin was singing. Csilla watched firelight flicker on the singers' faces.

First came a doe, with its fawn. They looked at the firelight and the circle of singers before slipping away again into the forest. Then came a fox with a mouse, its dinner, hanging from its jaws. Then a porcupine curled into a ball by the base of a stone, like a small stone itself. An owl swooped over the fire, adding its cry before it flew off into the forest. And the forest around them was growing. Csilla could feel it, the thickening of trees, the flowing of their sap. The ferns uncurling fronds, sending their spores floating into the air. Moss climbing the tree trunks, covering the scars where there had once been saws.

Ibolya put her hand on Csilla's shoulder. It felt as light as a dry leaf. "Someday, this forest will be like those I knew in my youth, so long ago, and the Tündér will care for it. Perhaps this new world will be better for us than the old. And perhaps we will restore what has been damaged. That is what we are, my child. That is what is means to be Tündér." Then the Daughter of the Moon slipped silently into the trees, so that for a moment Csilla wondered if she had actually been there. But she was still holding the cup of honey wine in her hand.

One by one, the singers stopped, and she could hear the forest around her, the sounds and silence of the night.

"Csilla," said Professor Kertész from the other side of the fire, "will you tell us one of your grandmother's stories?"

No, she started to say. What did the stories matter? All they did was show how often the Tündér had lost. How often they had hidden, slept on straw, begged for scraps of food. But the stories had mattered to her grandmother and to her father, and they mattered to everyone here. She could see it in their faces, all the faces in the firelight looking at her, waiting. Susanna Martin nodded, as though to say, go on, I know you can.

"Shortly before István was to be crowned king of Hungary," said Csilla, "one of his huntsmen came to him and said, 'I have been hunting in the forest and have seen a marvel: a stag as white as snow.' So István determined that he would hunt the stag. He set out in the morning with his retinue, but he soon lost them and rode on through the forest alone. At noon, when he was growing hungry, he came to a glade, at the center of which stood a woman with skin like milk and hair as green as the leaves of an oak tree. 'Lady,' he said . . ."

Around her, the forest listened.

# WINTERBORN

## Liz Williams

We watched as the drowned woman walked through the palace of Coldgate. Her hair was a sodden mass; her skin as white as birch bark, mottled with blue shadows. Damp footprints appeared behind her, and swiftly vanished again.

"She isn't the first," Oldmark said to me.

"So you said in your letter." That's why they'd come to me, after all, and I had to confess it was flattering. It's not easy building up a reputation in a city as big as London, crammed with weather-readers, wind-listeners, earth-healers. And river-speakers. Not easy, especially if you are a woman, and young.

You'd think having a queen on the throne, in this year of our Lady Sixteen Hundred and Two, would make a difference. But then again, Aeve wasn't entirely human, and perhaps that made a greater one.

"You see, Mistress Dane—" Oldmark broke off. For a courtier, he seemed to have some difficulty in expressing himself.

"You may call me Mistress Isis, if you wish. We're to be working together, after all. And I've seen the drowned before, you know. Part of my job is to find the bodies of those who have been unfortunate enough to meet their deaths in the river."

"I suppose you work principally with the Thames?"

"Yes, but also with the Wye, the Tyne . . . And I

grew up on the banks of the Severn, near the Welsh border at Lydd's Ney. That was where I first found I could river-read."

*Midnight in summer, the soft stars above, and a child staring at a woman standing on the river shore, her hair weed green, the ghost of water swirling round her. "My name is Severna." A genius loci, a spirit of place, a goddess, once, when the Romans were here. And she told me what I was and what I would be able to do. Later, I came to Oxford, then London, moving eastward as the power of Aeve's throne grew, with triumphs over the Spanish, the French.*

"Do you think this is to do with the Thames?" Oldmark asked. The woman was gliding through the wall. A moist stain showed briefly in her wake, and then there was nothing.

"I'm not sure." Some mages pretend to know everything, all bombast and certainty, even if they couldn't tell you whether it was day or night. This would not, I knew, be the right tack to take at Aeve's court: the queen had half-faery blood, could smell out a lie as easily as if it were a rat under the floorboards. She hadn't kept her throne for ninety years for nothing. It was hard to explain to Oldmark, but this did not feel like the genius loci of the Thames: Thamesis, that bearded, weedy, silty presence, a spirit old when the first hunters had come to his shores, before history began.

"Can you find out?"

"I believe so. Tell me, Lord Oldmark, what is the lowest point of Coldgate?"

Oldmark thought for a moment. "It would be the cellars, where we keep the ale. They say the foundations date from the days of the Romans. I do not know whether that is true, but certainly there are a great many steps leading down to the cellar . . ."

"Please take me there, Lord Oldmark, and I will see what is to be seen."

He was right about the steps. I counted forty, leading in an arc down into the musty depths of the cellar.

The floor was made of flags, a glossy gray stone. The cellar smelled of wine, of moss, of rivers. Oldmark left me in a small pool of light cast by a candle; when he had gone, I blew the candle out and stood alone in the dark.

At once, the drowned were all around me, sensing my presence as they might sense the spirit of water. I felt a chill breath on my face. Damp fingers trailed through my hair.

"Hush now," I said, softly so as not to frighten them. "I don't mean you harm." The spirits of the water-dead are rarely hostile, tending rather to a fluid sadness, and they must be treated gently.

One of the spirits floated into view, releasing her own phosphorescence, a green-pale glow. A girl, only a little younger than myself, with a purple mark around one eye.

"Who are you?" I asked. I put ritual weight behind my words, speaking in the Tongue of Water rather than my native English. "Why are you here?"

At the sound of the Tongue, her face grew still and slack, and I felt a little guilt at that. "My name is Sarah Mew. I was told to go with the others and wait for the boat."

"Which boat is that, Sarah?" Had she been left on the shore, been taken by the waves? But she answered, "The boat that is coming. The one that leads the fleet."

"Sarah, you must tell me what you mean. Which fleet?" It struck me that, for all her mention of the future, she might still have been speaking of the past: one of the interminable skirmishes with the Spanish navy off the shores of Albion, for instance.

"The fleet that is coming," she whispered. Her drowned face contorted with the effort of speech: she was enspelled, I saw, and my own magic was trying to counter that which had been placed upon her. And that other magic was stronger. I felt it sweep through the cellar like a tide, washing her away. She spun through the dark air and through the wall, no more than flotsam, and was gone. I was alone in the cold chamber.

I went slowly back up the stairs and found Oldmark. He was standing disconsolately by a window, staring out at the rain streaking down the leaded panes.

"Mistress Dane! Is everything well?"

"I am well, Lord Oldmark, but I'm afraid that I have some bad news. I have spoken with the drowned. They tell me of a fleet that is coming, a fleet of ships, and from the magic that was placed upon the spirit with whom I spoke, we face considerable danger. This was not an ordinary spell. It swept my magic away; only now is it beginning to creep back." This was true. I could feel it starting to seep into my soul again, refreshing its parched ground.

Oldmark blanched. "Danger! From which quarter?"

"I could not say." This, on the other hand, was not true. In that moment when the tide had caught the spirit in its grasp, I'd sensed something distinctive, familiar—a mossy greenness, a sudden dank and earthy taste in the air. The magic of Aeve's cousin and mortal enemy, the Queen-under-the-Hill.

Faery magic, then. No surprises there. But Aeve would not be pleased.

The queen wanted me to find out more about the fleet. This time, she spoke to me herself. I was granted audience in the great hall of Coldgate, myself on bended knee, head bowed, Oldmark fidgeting off to one side, and the queen—in the quick glimpses I got of her—sitting upright on the carved stone throne, her skin the whiteness of the stone itself, lending her a statue's look. Her hair was the pure blood-red of faery, her gaze a slanted green. She did not look to be a hundred years old, but then, in terms of her own family, she was little more than a girl.

"You look afraid," she said, when I hesitated in the course of my explanation. "Are you?"

I saw no reason to lie. "Yes," I told her. "I am afraid of the magic of under-hill." *Of your relatives.*

Old magic, root-and-briar magic, coiling and twining and dragging you down into earth and dreams . . . I'd chosen the river rush, after all, or been chosen by it. I wanted something clear and clean.

"You are wise, then," Queen Aeve said. "Tell me. Can you find out more, or are you too afraid?"

"I am afraid, but I will do as you ask."

I felt, rather than saw, her smile.

"You'll be rewarded," was all that she said, but she did not say how.

If you want knowledge, of magic as well as rivers, you need to go to the source. The Thames rises near Oxford, the city where my mother was born, and in its early stages it is called the Isis: hence, my name. I took my mare from the royal stables at dawn the next day and rode west, setting a hard pace across the chalk hills and the beech groves, until we saw cream-gold towers in the distance and Oxford lay before us.

They'd let me study here, a great favor, since I am a woman. Not officially, of course, but *sub rosa*, lessons taken in a shadowy cell at the back of the Bodleian library. I had been granted this as a result of my grandfather, cleric and scholar, endower of a college that was already three hundred years old. I had learned a great deal about rivers, about the sea, in this landlocked, placid city in the middle of the wheat-pale hills.

Now I skirted the city bounds, stopped at an inn overnight, and continued west until I came to a stone by the side of the road that showed the way to Seven Springs. The grotto lies high at the Cotswold edge, river-birth carving limestone into palaces and caverns. When I arrived, early on the morning of the second day, there was no one there. A light mist was spiraling up through the branches. Beech mast and acorns crackled under my boots, and the cave-mouth lay before me, so enveloped in the white exposed roots of the beech that it was hard to tell where wood ended and stone began.

I was glad to be alone, but it also made me afraid.

Not good, I thought, to be up here in the hills, the kingdom of faery. The goddess would protect me, or so I believed, but who ever really knew? I remembered walking along the Severn shore, looking westward to the black line of the Queen's Forest and beyond that the dusk-blue hills of Wales and the line of fortress castles, magic-warded. The court of the Queen-under-the-Hill lay behind that iron band. Aeve's cousin, Aeve's rival, and a long enmity between the two thrones of Albion, one dark, one—or so Aeve claimed—the province of the Light.

Sometimes even a dim light can illuminate, if the shadows are dark enough.

Time to face my own darkness. I lit a candle and stepped inside. Water-breath, and presence: not the green deep presence of Thamesis himself, but the Riverine Isis, delicate, a cat-soft whisper in the shadows.

"My Lady?" No reply, but I didn't expect one, not straight away.

I walked deeper into the temple, as far as the first spring, and held the candle out over black water. I could see my own face reflected in the dark mirror of its depths: I did not look like myself, but older, the woman I would one day be. And behind that, overlaid, was another face that was not myself at all.

Reflected flame flickered. I said, "I spoke to a ghost, and she told me of a fleet. There was magic in it, from Under-Hill. I need to know where the fleet will come from."

No answer. I stared into wet fire, beginning to think that this, too, would be withheld. Then the lips of my reflection moved, although I myself had finished speaking.

"Watch for the Lowlander," the reflection said. "Watch for the midnight moon."

"Who is the Lowlander?" I asked, though I thought I already knew: the Dutch considered that they had a claim to the throne of Albion; there had been incursions, and almost certainly there were spies.

The face was silent and still. A ripple of water,

caused by a breeze that I did not feel on my skin, eddied across the surface of the black pool. The chamber grew colder; I was gazing back at myself alone. Though the candle still flickered in my hand, in the water, the flame was no longer to be seen.

I made an offering of cyclamen to the wall shrine, placing the white flowers before the black face of the Riverine Isis, and walked out into the day. The sun was rising, gilding the mist and causing the trees to drip. An insubstantial landscape, luminous, half-real. I rode back to London, thinking of the Dutch.

The queen was of the same mind as myself, Oldmark told me. A Holland spy had been arrested in the grounds of Lydgate Palace only a week before. There had been a diplomatic incident, only half-resolved, and the Dutch court was threatening to raise penalties on shipping.

"It would not surprise anyone," Oldmark said, "to learn that there is mischief afoot in that quarter."

"But why involve the dead?" I asked. "And why was there under-hill magic present?"

Oldmark looked uneasy. "I do not know. But an alliance between the Lowlands and Under-Hill would be a sorry thing. There have already been rumors that the Queen-under-the-Hill courts the Spanish, and you know that there are political connections."

I did know; I nodded. "I wish I'd been able to find out more," I said.

"I am certain that you did your best," Oldmark replied.

But that night, the drowned came over-ground.

I was roused from my sleep by distant shouts. The sound was coming from the direction of the palace gardens. Accommodated in the servants' wing as I was, it took me a little time to throw on a robe and make my way through a maze of passages to the front of the building.

They were coming out of one of the fountains, an endless procession of white-faced, green-haired spirits.

Some of them were decomposing away, just as their bodies had done: These were the ghosts of those who had lain long in the water, so long that it had seeped into their souls to rot and stain.

Oldmark appeared beside me, almost as white faced as one of the spirits.

"What are they doing?" he whispered.

"I don't know." The procession of ghosts was heading toward the water-stair, the gates that led down to Thamesis. Toward and then through, disappearing into—it must be—the river. Gesturing for Oldmark to stay where he was, I opened the French doors and ran down the steps to where the ghosts walked.

Sometimes they can't see you. To them, you are as vague and shadowy as they are to you, and perhaps as terrifying. But when I put out a hand, with the fluttering of a spell, one of the spirits turned his head.

A man in a costume I did not recognize: rough trousers and a dull tunic. Long hair straggled down his shoulders, twined with weed. Not a recent ghost, then. He spoke to me, and I did not know the language, either: something Northern and harsh. I looked over his shoulder to his fellow spirits and saw a woman in a long, draped dress, her aquiline features downcast and somber. These were ghosts from the far past of Albion, and so many of them: summoned from every well and river and spring, every shore. The reek of under-hill magic hung about them. I looked back to Coldgate and saw the gleam of gold beside Lord Oldmark. The queen had arrived.

The stream of ghosts was slowing, and soon no more crawled out of the depths of the fountain. I went slowly back into the palace.

"I have sent word to my cousin Under-Hill," Queen Aeve said. I began to curtsey but she waved me up again. "I have told her that I know of her plot with the Dutch court, that I will not tolerate it."

Lord Oldmark and I waited; neither of us wanted to be the one who asked her what she planned to do. But she went on, "I've ordered the fleet of Albion to

the mouth of the Thames, to sail for Dutch waters."
Her face twisted. "We have made mincemeat of the
Spanish. Let the Dutch see if they have better luck,
shall we? Oldmark, see that Mistress Dane is paid."
With that, she swept back into the palace.

One does not question the actions of a queen, at
least, not out loud. But Aeve was ever one for the
grand gesture. Sending the navy to chastise the Dutch,
on what was still little enough evidence, was characteristic. And the navy, though still great, was not what it
had been when Aeve first came to the throne, before
its flagship, the *Rose*, had gone down under Spanish
guns, taking Albion's Admiral Drake with her.

Oldmark turned apologetically to me, disturbing
my speculations.

"Mistress Isis, I know the queen appreciates your
help."

"I have helped little enough," I said. I was not
being modest. In fact, although I did not say so, I
felt that I had helped only in setting Queen Aeve off
upon the wrong track, a hound after a false scent. I
did not say that, either—it is not safe to compare
queens to bitches.

"Lord Oldmark, might I remain in that chamber for
a night or two more, before returning to Gloucestershire? There is an avenue of research that I should
like to pursue."

Oldmark appeared slightly surprised, but he agreed.
I returned to my room and took out the small traveling chest, setting it upon the table.

Inside the chest were the characteristic accoutre-
ments of the river-speaker: the forked hazel twig,
bound in brass, the lead and crystal compass, a collection of maps. I took the maps out of their leather
case and riffled through them. I wanted to see where
Coldgate lay.

London is a river city. Everyone thinks only of the
Thames, but the streets are built over rivers, hidden
streams, concealed rivulets. The Wandle, the Effra,
the Westbourne and the Fleet; the Falcon, the Ravens-

bourne, the Earl's Sluice, and many more. All the drowned streams that flow beneath the city to the Thames.

I was right. I'd felt it in the wine cellar, that breath of dampness, a river's ghost. The oldest map of all showed a stream running underneath Coldgate. It had been known as the Winterbourne, and at this, my heart stuttered a little, for the bournes have a magic all their own. Underground streams, which can be summoned to rise again in times of great peril.

Or in times of war.

At that moment, I thought I knew what the Queen-under-the-Hill might be trying to do.

I picked up a cloak and the hazel twig and went out into the evening. A fog had come up from the Thames and hung over the box hedges, playing around the fountain in watery coils of its own. Late November and the taste of mist in the mouth . . . Water rising, in times of war. When I reached the fountain, I held out the hazel twig. A moment, and then it twitched. From the map, the Winterbourne lay beneath. I followed it back to the wall of Coldgate, hastened back down into the cellars.

It took a lot of searching before I found the little door, hidden and dusty behind a stack of barrels. It had once been locked, but the lock was rusted, and I pulled it away. It was unlikely that what lay behind it had been deliberately concealed—the lock was there to prevent people from wandering down beneath the cellar. Steps led down, and I followed them.

I did not get far. The smell of water struck me halfway down the slippery stair, and then it was all around me—I clung to the rail, in a minute of sheer panic during which I thought I would be swept away—but it was not real. The ghost of the Winterbourne was rising, spectral water all around me. My lamp showed diffuse and dim, rocking my hand, and around it I glimpsed a shoal of eels, tails flicking as they sped along. Standing in the race of the water I felt like a ghost myself. I backed up the steps and looked down into the foaming torrent.

It wasn't just the spirit of the river that was rising. Magic was rising, too. It was all around me, tugging, curious, and I did not want to be noticed in this way. I slammed the door to the wine cellar shut with a muttered spell and went to tell Lord Oldmark to get me a boat.

Thamesside, looking back at Coldgate. We rocked on an icy current, the river slapping our little boat back and forth. Behind us, heading for Tower Bridge, one of the huge coal barges churned slowly downriver, the horse-team on the opposite bank patiently padding along toward the eastside docks.

"You had best be correct in this, Mistress Dane," the seated figure at the prow said. Aeve's voice was river-cold.

"Your Majesty, if I am not, my reputation is in any case gone, and I do not care what happens then."

The queen inclined her cowled head.

"The navy has been ordered to continue out into the North Sea," Oldmark said to me, in a low voice. "All but five ships, which are heading back to London."

"Even the navy will not be of much help, if I am right. Aeve must appeal to Thamesis, as rightful ruler of the river's city."

Oldmark nodded. "You have explained. She knows what she needs to do, if it comes to that."

*It will*, I did not say. I was sure that I was right, but arrogance is best left undisplayed. "Watch the palace," I told him.

I could sense it in the air, magic building up, as if behind a dam, with the strong mossy taste of Under-Hill. "It won't be long," I said, beneath my breath. Aeve turned, irritably, with the impatience of queens.

"Nothing is happening."

I couldn't really blame her for the irritability: It was

foggy and freezing out here in the middle of the river. I was surprised that she'd agreed to come at all. And as if prompted by my thought, the queen came to a decision.

"We will go back," Aeve said and rose.

"Wait," I said, forgetting to address her as I should, but as I spoke, Oldmark echoed me, "My Lady, *wait*."

Before us, across the black, choppy expanse of the river, Coldgate was fading. Magic was humming in the air like a beehive, so strongly that my skin prickled and burned. Aeve gasped as it struck her. Instead of the palace, its grounds, the streets that lay beyond its walls, we were facing the mouth of the now-buried Winterbourne, a ghost shore, muddy and strewn with stones. A single post rose up from the mud, tapered to a point and covered with weed: some ancient marker from the time before the Romans came to London. It shimmered, and I saw the skull that crowned it, grinning.

Aeve put out a hand, as if touching enemy magic.

"Your Majesty, be careful—" I started to say, but Aeve was already beginning the incantation I had given her, her own power rising now, the authority of the rightful ruler of Albion, calling upon her ancestors, summoning up the protection of the dead.

It was protection that was needed. A ship was coming down the mouth of the Winterbourne, a galleon with tattered sails, sides so encrusted with barnacles and shells that the ship looked more like some dredged wreck than a proper vessel. I saw the pilot standing at the wheel, a white face beneath a tricorner hat. The Lowlander. The *Dutchman*. And a ship that would sail the seas forever, unless someone not human offered another choice, an unrefusable bargain.

They say the Dutchman ruled the seas beyond death and all who sailed upon them . . . Behind his ship came others: Spanish flags flying, French, a longship with a boar's crest. Dozens of ships, all those that had gone down in the seas off the coast of Albion, the wraiths of enemy vessels, conjured by the Queen-under-the-Hill.

"Queen Aeve!" I shouted, above the sudden roar of magic and dead water. "Call on the Thames!"

And she did. She used incantations that blazed through me like flame, words that I, not of royal lineage, should not have heard, spells that are in the blood and bone of Albion's ruling house. Oldmark was crouched on the floor of the rocking boat, his hands clasped to his ears. I nearly joined him.

Then a wind stirred my hair, and I turned. The prow of a ship arched above us, an immense thing, far larger than it had been in life. Its sails billowed out, lit by a light that I could not see, as though it were catching the last rays of the sun. I had never set eyes on this ship before, and yet I knew it: the lost *Rose,* with Admiral Drake standing at the wheel.

I seized an oar. "Oldmark! Set to rowing! We have to get out of the *way.*"

Aeve was still in the prow of the rowing boat, arms outstretched, calling magic in. I didn't want to be responsible for pitching the Queen of Albion overboard into her own river, but I didn't want to be run down by even a spectral ship, either. Frantically, Oldmark and I hauled the boat around as the *Rose* glided forward.

The Dutchman's ship turned, wheeling on a tide that wasn't there. I saw the guns of the *Rose* blossom silently over my head and a watery fire erupt from the sides of the Dutchman's ship. There was the flame of a cannon behind the Dutchman's vessel; the *Rose* gave a great shudder, as if struck.

"Mistress Dane!" Oldmark cried. "Turn her! Turn her now!"

But we were too late. The *Rose* glided forward and through us, sleek as a swan. Everything went black for a moment—it's not pleasant, being run down by a ghostly galleon. My bones rang and my teeth chattered. When I could see again, the *Rose* was bearing down on the Dutchman's ship, and the magic that had drawn the ghost of the Winterbourne upward was congealing, drawing around the Dutchman's vessel to imbue it with power. Coldgate was once more visible through the shimmer of the river. The guns blazed again from the *Rose*, and this time I heard them. The Dutchman's ship gave a groaning creak and listed. We huddled in the rowing boat, Aeve damp-browed and shaking, and watched the Dutchman's ship go down.

It sank, stone-swift, as if the Thames had swallowed it. With it went the magic of Under-Hill, sucked into its wake, but the Winterbourne did not go too. Instead, I saw the course of the river turn and shift, sweeping away the post with the skull and all the spectral ships, carrying them out into the wide channel of the Thames and away toward the sea. At last the river was also gone, a foaming tide, and Coldgate loomed pale through the river mist. When the fog parted a little, I looked for the *Rose,* but it was no longer there.

Aeve proved more generous than I had expected, but then, I had saved her throne for her. I rode back to Gloucestershire and Severnside on a chilly November morning, a moneybag heavy against the flank of the mare. I felt drained, the wonder of what I had seen sitting within me as heavily as my reward, and I was thankful to see the Severn curling between its red-earth banks, with the blue hills of Wales rising beyond.

But I did not think I would be visiting those hills in the months to come, for fear of what lay beneath them. I set my heels to the sides of the mare and rode hard for home, along the river shore.

# DONOVAN SENT US

## Gene Wolfe

The plane was a JU 88 with all the proper markings, and only God knew where Donovan had gotten it. "We're over London," the man known as Paul Potter murmured. Crouching, he peered across the pilot's shoulder.

Baldur von Steigerwald (he was training himself to think of himself as that) was crouching as well. "I'm surprised there aren't more lights," he said.

"That's the Thames." Potter pointed. Far below, starlight—only starlight—gleamed on water. "Over there's where the Tower used to be." He pointed again.

"You think they might keep him there?"

"They couldn't," Potter said. "It's been blown all to hell."

Von Steigerwald said nothing.

"All London's been blown to hell. England stood alone against Germany—and England was crushed."

"The truth is awkward, Herr Potter," von Steigerwald said. "Pretty often, too awkward."

"Are you calling me a liar?"

Listening mostly to the steady throbbing of the engines, von Steigerwald shrugged.

"A damned bloody Kraut, and you call me a liar."

"I'm just another American," von Steigerwald said. "Are you?"

"We're not supposed to talk about this."

Von Steigerwald shrugged again. "You began it, *mein herr.* Here's the awkward truth. You can deny it if you want to. England, Scotland, Wales, Australia, New Zealand, India, Burma, and Northern Ireland stood—alone if you like—against Germany, Italy, Austria, and Vichy. They lost, and England was crushed. Scotland and Wales were hit almost as hard. Am I wrong?"

The JU 88 began a slow bank as Potter said, "Franco joined Germany at the end."

Von Steigerwald nodded. "You're right." He had not forgotten it, but he added, "I forgot that."

"Spain didn't bring down the house," Potter conceded.

"Get back by the doors," the pilot called over his shoulder. "Jump as soon as they're open all the way."

"You're really English, aren't you?" von Steigerwald whispered as they trotted back toward the bomb-bay doors. "You're an English Jew."

Quite properly, Potter ignored the question. "It was the Jews," he said as he watched the doors swing down. "If Roosevelt hadn't welcomed millions of European Jews into America, the American people wouldn't—" The rest was lost in the whistling wind.

It had not been millions, von Steigerwald reflected before his chute opened. It opened, and the snap of its silk cords might have been the setting of a hook. A million and a half—something like that.

He came down in Battersea Park with his chute tangled in a tree. When at last he was able to cut himself free, he knotted ornamental stones into it and threw it into the Thames. His jump suit followed it, weighted with one more. As it sunk, he paused to sniff the reek of rotting corpses—paused and shrugged.

Two of the best tailors in America had done everything possible to provide him with a black *Schutzstaffel* uniform that would look perfectly pressed after being worn under a jump suit. Shivering in the wind, he smoothed it as much as he could and got out his black leather trench coat. The black uniform cap snapped itself into shape the moment he took it out, thanks to a spring-wire skeleton. He hid the bag that had held both in some overgrown shrubbery.

The Luger in his gleaming black holster had kept its loaded magazine in place and was on safe. He paused in a moonlit clearing to admire its ivory grips and the inlaid, red-framed, black swastikas.

There seemed to be no traffic left in Battersea these days. Not at night, at least, and not even for a handsome young S.S. officer. A staff car would have been perfect, but even an army truck might do the trick.

There was nothing.

Hunched against the wind, he began to walk. The Thames bridges destroyed by the blitz had been replaced with pontoon bridges by the German Army—so his briefer had said. There would be sentries at the bridges, and those sentries might or might not know. If they did not—

Something coming! He stepped out into the road, drew his Luger, and waved both arms.

A little Morris skidded to a stop in front of him. Its front window was open, and he peered inside. "So. Ein taxi dis is? You vill carry me, ja?"

The driver shook his head vehemently. "No, gov'nor. I mean, yes, gov'nor. I'll take you anywhere you want to go, gov'nor, but it's not a cab."

"Ein two-vay radio you haff, drifer."

The driver seemed to have heard nothing.

"But no license you are haffing." Von Steigerwald chuckled evilly. "You like money, doh. Ja? I haf it. Goot occupation pounds, ja? Marks, also." He opened a rear door and slid onto the seat, only slightly impeded by his leather coat. "Where important prisoners are, you take me." He sat back. "*Macht schnell!*"

The Morris lurched forward. "Quick as a wink, gov'nor. Where is it?"

"You know, drifer." Von Steigerwald summoned all of his not inconsiderable acting ability to make his chuckle that of a Prussian sadist, and succeeded well enough that the driver's shoulders hunched. "De taxi drifers? Dey know eferyding, everywhere. Make no more troubles vor me. I vill not punish you for knowing."

"I dunno, gov'nor, and that's the honest."

Von Steigerwald's Luger was still in his right hand. Leaning forward once more, he pressed its muzzle to the driver's head and pushed off the safety. "I vill not shoot now, drifer. Not now, you are too fast drifing, ja? Ve wreck. Soon you must stop, doh. Ja? Traffic or anodder reason. Den your prain ist all ofer de vind-shield."

"G-gov'nor . . ."

"Ja?"

"My family. Timmy's only three, gov'nor."

"Longer dan you he lifs, I hope."

The Morris slowed. "The bridge, gov'nor. There's a barricade. Soldiers with guns. I'll have to stop."

"You vill not haf to start again, English pig."

"I'm takin' you there. Only I'll have to stop for 'em."

"You take me?"

"Right, gov'nor. The best I know."

"Den vhy should I shoot?" Flicking the safety on, von Steigerwald holstered his Luger.

The Morris ground to a stop before the barricade. Seeing him in the rear seat, two gray-clad soldiers snapped to attention and saluted.

He rolled down a rear window and (in flawless German) asked the corporal who had just saluted whether he wished to examine his papers, adding that he was in a hurry.

Hastily the corporal replied that the *standartenführer* might proceed at once, the barricade was raised, and the Morris lurched ahead as before.

"Vhere is dis you take me, drifer?"

"I hope you're goin' to believe me, gov'nor." The driver sounded painfully sincere. "I'm takin' you the best I know."

"So? To vhere?"

"Tube station gov'nor. The trains don't run anymore."

"Of dis I am avare."

The driver glanced over his shoulder. "If I tell you I don't know, you won't believe me, gov'nor. I don't, just the same. What I think is that they're keeping them down there."

Von Steigerwald rubbed his jaw. Did real Prussians ever do that? The driver would not know, so it hardly mattered. "Vhy you t'ink dis, drifer?"

"I've seen army trucks unloading at this station, gov'nor. Cars park there and Jerry—I mean German—officers get out of them. The driver waits, so they're not going to another station, are they?" As the little Morris slowed and stopped, the driver added, "'Course, they're not there now. It's too late."

"You haf no license vor dis taxi," von Steigerwald said. His tone was conversational. "A drifer's license you haf, doh. Gif dat to me."

"Gov'nor . . ."

"Must I shoot? Better I should spare you, drifer. I vill haf use vor you. Gif it to me."

"If I don't have that, gov'nor . . ."

"Anoder you vould get. Hand it ofer."

Reluctantly, the driver did.

"Goot. Now I gif someding." Von Steigerwald held up a bill. "You see dis vellow? Herr Himmler? He is our *Reichsführer*. Dere are numbers, besides. Dos you see also, drifer?"

The driver nodded. "Fifty quid. I can't change it, gov'nor."

"I keep your license, dis you keep. Here you vait. Ven I come out—" Von Steigerwald opened the rear door of the Morris. "You get back de license and anodder of dese."

As he descended the steps of the underground station, he wondered whether the driver really would. It would probably depend, he decided, on whether the driver realized that the fifty-pound occupation note was counterfeit.

To left and right, soiled and often defaced posters exhorted Englishmen and Englishwomen to give their all to win a war that was now lost. In one, an aproned housewife appeared to be firing a rolling pin. Yet there were lights—bright electric lights—in the station below.

It had been partitioned into offices with salvaged wood. Each cubicle was furnished with a salvaged door, and every door was shut. Gray-uniformed soldiers snapped to attention as Von Steigerwald reached the bottom of the stair and demanded to see their commandant.

He was not there, one soldier explained. Von Steigerwald ordered the soldier to fetch him, and the soldier sprinted up the stair.

When the commandant arrived, he looked tired and a trifle rumpled. Von Steigerwald did his best to salute so as to make it clear that an S.S. colonel outranked any mere general and proffered his orders, reflecting as he did that it might be possible for him to shoot the general and both sentries if the falsity of those orders was detected. Just possible, if he shot very fast indeed. Possible, but not at all likely. The burly sentry with the Schmeisser submachine gun first, the thin one who had run to get the commandant next. Last, the commandant himself. If—

The commandant returned his orders, saying that *Herr* Churchill was not at his facility.

Sharply, von Steigerwald declared that he had been told otherwise.

The commandant shook his head and repeated politely that Churchill was not there.

Where was he, then?

The commandant did not know.

Who would know?

The commandant shrugged.

The commandant was to return to bed. Von Steigerwald, who would report the entire affair to the

*Reichsführer-SS*, intended to inspect the facility. His conclusions would be included in his report.

The commandant rose.

Von Steigerwald motioned for him to sit again. He, *Standartenführer* von Steigerwald, would guide his own tour.

He would not see everything if he did, the commandant insisted; even in explosive German, the commandant sounded defeated. Sergeant Lohr would show him around. Sergeant Lohr had a flashlight.

Sergeant Lohr was the burly man with the submachine gun.

The prisoners were not held in the tunnels themselves, Lohr explained as he and von Steigerwald walked along a dark track, but in the rolling stock. There were toilets in the cars, which had been railway passenger cars before the war. If the *Standartenführer*—

"The cars were squirreled away down here to save them from German bombs," a new voice said. "The underground had been disabled, but there was sound trackage left, so why not? I take it you understand English, Colonel?"

In the near-darkness of the tunnel, the shadowy figure who had joined them was hardly more than that: a man of medium size, shabbily dressed in clothing too large for him.

"*Ja*," von Steigerwald replied. "I speak it vell. It is vor dis reason I vas sent. Und you are . . . ?"

For a moment, Lohr's flashlight played on the shabby man's face, an emaciated face whose determined jaw jutted above a wattled neck. "Lenny Spencer, Colonel. At your service."

Lohr grunted—or perhaps, growled.

"I'm a British employee, sir. A civilian employee of your army and, if I may be permitted a trifle of boldness, a man lent to you by His Majesty's occupation government. Far too many of my German friends speak little English. I interpret for them, sir. I run errands and do such humble work as my German friends judge beneath them. If I can be of any use to you, Colonel, I shall find my happiness in serving you."

Von Steigerwald stroked his chin. "Dis place you know, ja?"

The shabby man nodded. "Indeed I do, Colonel. Few, if I may say it, know the facility and its prisoners as well as I."

"Goot. Also you know Herr Churchill. He vas your leader in de var, so it must be so. He ist here. Dis I know. In Berlin he ist wanted, ja? I am to bring him. Show him to me. At vonce!"

The shabby man cowered. "Colonel, I cannot! Not with the best will in the world. He's gone."

"So?" Von Steigerwald's hand had crept to his Luger, lifting the shiny leather holster flap and resting on the ivory grip; he allowed it to remain there. "The truth you must tell now, *Herr* Schpencer. Odervise it goes hard vit you. He vas here?"

The shabby man nodded vigorously. "He was, Colonel. He was captured in a cellar in Notting Hill. So I've been informed, sir. He was brought here to recover from his wounds, or die."

"He ist dead? Dis you say? Vhy vas not dis reported?" Von Steigerwald felt that he needed a riding crop—a black riding crop with which to tap his polished boots and slash people across the face. Donovan should have thought of it.

"I don't believe he is dead, Colonel, but he is no longer here." The shabby man addressed Sergeant Lohr in halting German, asking him to confirm that Churchill was no longer there.

Sullenly, Lohr declared that he had never been there.

"Neider vun I like," von Steigerwald declared, "but you, Schpencer, I like more petter. He vas here? You see dis?"

"Yes indeed, Colonel." The shabby man had to trot to keep pace with von Steigerwald's athletic strides. "He seemed much smaller here. Much less important than he had, you know, on my wireless. He was frightened, too. Very frightened, I would say, just as I would have been myself. Pathetic at times, really. Fearful of his own fear, sir. You know the Yanks' saying? I confess I found it ironic and somewhat amusing."

"He ist gone. Zo you say. Who it is dat takes him?"

"I can't tell you that, Colonel. I wasn't here when he was taken away." The shabby man's tone was properly apologetic. "Sergeant Lohr would know."

Von Steigerwald asked Lohr, and Lohr insisted that Churchill had never been held in the facility.

This man, von Steigerwald pointed out, says otherwise.

This man, Lohr predicted, would die very soon.

Von Steigerwald's laughter echoed in the empty tunnel. "He vill shoot you, Schpencer. Better you should go to de camps, ja? Der, you might lif. A Chew you are? Say dis und I vill arrange it."

"I'd never lie to you, Colonel."

"Den tell me vhere dese cars are vhere de prisoners stay. Already ve valk far."

"Just around that bend, Colonel." The shabby man pointed, and it seemed to von Steigerwald—briefly—that there had been a distinct bulge under his coat, a hand's breadth above his waist. Whatever that bulge might be, it had been an inch or two to the left of the presumed location of the shabby man's shirt buttons.

Lohr muttered something, in which von Steigerwald caught "*Riecht wie höllisches . . .*" Von Steigerwald sniffed.

"It's the WCs," the shabby man explained. "They empty onto the tracks. The commandant had the prison cars moved down here to spare our headquarters."

"In de S.S.," von Steigerwald told him, "we haf de prisoners clean it up. Dey eat it."

"No doubt we would." The shabby man shrugged. "One becomes accustomed to the odor in time."

"I vill not. So long as dat I vill not pee here." Von Steigerwald caught sight of the stationary railroad cars as the three of them rounded the curve in the tunnel.

"Every prisoner you show to me, ja? Many times dis man Churchill I haf seen in pictures. I vill know him."

Lohr muttered something unintelligible.

Von Steigerwald rounded on him, demanding that he repeat it.

Lohr backed hurriedly away as von Steigerwald advanced shouting.

The shabby man tapped von Steigerwald's shoulder. "May I interpret, Colonel? He says—"

"*Nein!* Himself, he tells me." A competent actor, von Steigerwald shook with apparent rage.

"He said—well, it doesn't really matter now, does it? There he goes, back to headquarters."

Von Steigerwald studied the fleeing sergeant's back. "Ist goot. Him I do not like."

"Nor I." The shabby man set off in the opposite direction, toward the prison cars. "May I suggest, Colonel, that we begin at the car in which Churchill was held? It is the most distant of the eight. I can show you where we had him, and from there we can work our way back."

"Stop!" Von Steigerwald's Luger was pointed at the shabby man's back. "Up with your hands, Lenny Spencer."

The shabby man did. "You're not German."

"Walk toward that car, slowly. If you walk fast, go for that gun under your coat, or even try to turn around, I'll kill you."

Twenty halting steps brought the shabby man to the nearest coach. Von Steigerwald made him lean against it, hands raised. "Your feet are too close," he rasped when the shabby man was otherwise in position. "Move them back. Farther!"

"You might be English," the shabby man said; his tone was conversational. "Might be, but I doubt it. Canadian?"

"American."

The shabby man sighed. "That is exactly as I feared."

"You think President Kuhn has sent me because he

wants you for himself?'' Von Steigerwald pushed the
muzzle of his Luger against the nape of the shabby
man's neck, not too hard.

"I do."

Von Steigerwald's left hand jerked back the shabby
man's coat and expertly extracted a large and rather
old-fashioned pistol. "It would be out of the fire and
into the frying pan for you, even if it were true."

"I must hope so."

"You can turn around and face me now, Mr.
Churchill.'' Von Steigerwald stepped back, smiling. "Is
this the Mauser you used at Omdurman?"

Churchill shook his head as he straightened his
shabby coat. "That is long gone. I took the one you're
holding from a man I killed. Killed today, I mean."

"A German?"

Churchill nodded. "The officer of the guard. He was
inspecting us—inspecting me, at the time. I happened
to say something that interested him, he stayed to talk,
and I was able to surprise him. May I omit the details?"

"Until later. Yes. We have no time to talk. We're
going back. I am still an S.S. officer. I still believe
you to be an English traitor. I am borrowing you for
a day or two—I require your service. They won't be
able to prevent us without revealing that you escaped
them.'' Von Steigerwald gave Churchill a smile that
was charming and not at all cruel. "As you did yourself in speaking with me. They may shoot us. I think
it's much more likely that they'll simply let us go,
hoping I'll return you without ever learning your
identity."

"And in America . . . ?"

"In America, Donovan wants you, not Kuhn. Not
the Bund. Donovan knows you."

Slowly, Churchill nodded. "We met in . . . In forty-
one, I think it was. Forty would've been an election
year, and Roosevelt was already looking shaky in
July—"

They were walking fast already, with Churchill a polite half-step behind; and Von Steigerwald no longer listened.

Aboard the fishing boat he had found for them, Potter cleared away what little food remained and shut the door of the tiny cabin. "Our crew—the old man and his son—don't know who you are, Mr. Prime Minister. We'd prefer to keep it that way."

Churchill nodded.

"If you're comfortable . . . ?"

He glanced at his cigar. "I could wish for better, but I realize you did the best you could. It will be different in America, or so I hope."

Potter smiled. "It may even be different on the sub. I hope so, at least."

Churchill looked at von Steigerwald, who glanced at his watch. "Midnight. We rendezvous at three AM, if everything goes well."

Churchill grunted. "It never does."

"This went well." Potter was still smiling. "I know you two know everything, Mr. Prime Minister, but I don't. How did he get you out?"

Still in uniform, Von Steigerwald straightened his tunic and brushed away an invisible speck of lint. "He got himself out, mostly. Killed an officer. He won't tell me how."

"Killing is a brutal business." Churchill shook his head. "Even with sword or gun. With one's hands . . . He trusted me. Or trusted my age, at least. Thought I could never overpower him, or that I would lack the will to try. If it was in my weakness he trusted, he was nearly right. It was, as Wellington said of a more significant victory, a near run thing. If it was in my fear, the captain mistook foe for friend. What had I to lose? I would have been put to death, and soon. Better to perish like a Briton."

He pulled back his shabby coat to show the Mauser. "Perhaps it was seeing this. His holster covered most of it, but I could see the grip. Quite distinctive. Once upon a time, eh? Once upon a time, long before either of you saw light, I was a dashing young cavalry officer. Seeing this, I remembered."

"The Germans have pressed every kind of pistol they can find into service," von Steigerwald explained. "Even Polish and French guns."

Churchill puffed his cigar and made a face. "What I wish to know is where I tripped up. Did you recognize me? The light was so bad, and I'd starved for so long, that I thought I could risk it. No cigar, eh? No bowler. Still wearing the clothes they took me in. So how did you know?"

"That you were Churchill? From your gun. I pulled it out of your waist band and thought, by god it's a broom-handle Mauser. Churchill used one of these fifty years ago. I'd had a briefing on you, and I'd been interested in the gun. You bought it in Cairo."

Churchill nodded.

"That was when it finally struck me that Spencer was your middle name. Your byline—I read some of your books and articles—was Winston S. Churchill."

"You didn't know about Leonard, then." Churchill looked around for an ashtray and, finding none, tapped the ash from his cigar into a pocket of his shabby coat. "In full, my name is Winston Leonard Spencer Churchill. I should have been more careful about my alias. I had to think very quickly, though, and the only others I could seize on just then were John Smith and George Brown. Either, I felt, would have been less than convincing."

Potter grinned. "Very."

"In my own defense, I thought I was dealing with a German officer." Churchill turned to von Steigerwald. "This isn't what I wanted to inquire about, however. How did you know I had been lying to you?"

"I wasn't certain until I realized you were the man I'd been sent to rescue. A couple of things made me suspicious, and when I saw the bulge of your gun butt—"

"What were they?"

"Once you said 'we' in speaking of the prisoners," von Steigerwald explained. "I said that the S.S. would make the prisoners eat their excrement, and you said, 'No doubt we would.' It sounded wrong, and when I thought about it, I realized that you couldn't have been what you said you were—an Englishman working for the Germans. If you had been, they would have made you clean under the cars. Why did you confirm that you had been a prisoner when the Germans were denying they had him?"

"Ignorance. I didn't know they were. I had walked for miles along those dark tracks, trying to find a way out. I couldn't. All the tunnels ended in rubble and earth."

"Flattened by bombs?" Potter asked.

Churchill nodded. "To get out, I was going to have to go out through the German headquarters, and I could think of no practical way of doing that. Then the colonel here came, plainly a visitor since he was S.S., not army, and because he had an escort. I hoped to attach myself to him, a knowledgeable, subservient Englishman who might inform on the commandant if he could be convinced it was safe. I would persuade him to take me with him, and when he did, I would be outside. Sergeant Lohr and any Germans in the headquarters would know who I was, of course. But if they were wise—if they spoke with the commandant first, certainly—they would let me go without a word. If they prevented me, the army would be blamed for my escape; but if they held their peace and let me go, they could report quite truthfully that I had been taken away by the S.S. With luck, they might even get the credit for my recapture later."

Potter said, "That won't happen."

"I've answered your questions, Mr. Potter." Churchill looked accusingly at his smoldering cigar and set it on the edge of the little table. "Now you must answer one or two for me. The colonel here has told me that I am not being taken to President Kuhn. It relieved my mind at the time and will relieve it further now, if you confirm it. What do you say?"

"That we want you, not Kuhn." By a gesture, Potter indicated von Steigerwald and himself. "Donovan sent us. We're from the O.S.S.—the Office of Strategic Services. Roosevelt set us up before he was voted out, and he put Colonel Donovan in charge. President Kuhn has found us useful."

Churchill looked thoughtful. "As you hope to find me."

"Exactly. Kuhn and his German-American Bund have been pro-German throughout the war, as you must know. America even sold Germany munitions."

Churchill nodded.

"But now Hitler's the master of Europe, and he's starting to look elsewhere. He has to keep his army busy, after all, and he needs new triumphs." Potter leaned forward, his thin face intense. "Roosevelt, who had been immensely popular just a year before, was removed from office because he opened America to European Jews—"

"Including you," von Steigerwald put in.

"Right, including me and thousands more like me. America was just recovering from the Depression, and people were terrified of us refugees and what we might do to the economy. Fritz Kuhn and his German-American Bund replaced the old, patriotic Republican Party that had freed the slaves. I'm sure that half the people who voted for Kuhn hoped he would send us back to Hitler."

Churchill said, "Which he has declined to do."

"Of course." Potter grinned. "Who would he protect America from if we were gone? He's getting shaky as it is."

Von Steigerwald cleared his throat. "It might be possible to persuade Roosevelt to come out of retirement. Potter here thinks that way. He may be right."

"Or at least to get Roosevelt to endorse some other Democrat," Potter said.

Churchill nodded. "I could suggest half a dozen. No doubt you could add a dozen more. But where do I come into all this? Donovan wants me, you say."

Potter nodded. "He does, but to understand where you come in, Mr. Prime Minister, you have to understand Donovan and his position. He was Roosevelt's man. Roosevelt appointed him, and he's done a wonderful job. The O.S.S. worked hard and selflessly for America when Roosevelt was president, and it's working hard and selflessly for America now that Kuhn and his gang are in the White House."

"Yet he would prefer Roosevelt." Churchill fished a fresh cigar from his pocket.

"We all would," Potter said. "Donovan doesn't think he'll do it—he's a sick man—but that's what all of us would like. We'd like America to go back to nineteen forty and correct the mistake she made then. Above all, we'd like the Bund out of power."

Rolling the cigar between his hands, Churchill nodded.

"But if and when it comes to a war between Hitler and Kuhn, we will be with Kuhn and our country."

"Right or wrong." Churchill smiled.

"Exactly."

Von Steigerwald cleared his throat again. "You're not American, Potter. You're a refugee—you said so. Where were you born?"

"In London," Potter snapped. "But I'm as American as you are. I'm a naturalized United States citizen."

"Thanks to Donovan, I'm sure."

Potter turned back to Churchill. "So far Kuhn hasn't interned us, much less returned us to the Germans. There are quite a few people whose advice and protests have prevented that. Donovan's one of them. We give America a pool of violently anti-Nazi people, many well-educated, who speak every European language. If you've been wondering why so many of us are in the O.S.S. you should understand now."

"I wasn't wondering," Churchill said mildly.

"War with Hitler looks inevitable." Potter paused,

scowling. "Once I told my native-born friend here that England had stood alone against the Axis. He corrected me. America really will stand alone. She won't have a friend in the world except the conquered peoples."

"Which is why we freed you," von Steigerwald added. "If Hitler can be kept busy trying to get a grip on his conquests—on Britain and France, particularly—he won't go after America. It will give President Kuhn time to persuade the die-hard Democrats that we must arm, and give him time to do it. We've taken Iceland, and we'll use it to beam your broadcasts to Britain. We're broadcasting to Occupied Norway already."

Frowning, Churchill returned the cigar to his pocket. "You want me to lead a British underground against the Huns."

"Exactly," Potter said. "To lead them from the safety of America, and to form a government in exile."

"Already I have led the British underground you hope for from London." Churchill was almost whispering. "From the danger of London." Abruptly his voice boomed, filling the tiny cabin. "From the ruins of London I have led the ruins of the British people against an enemy ten times stronger than they. They were a brave people once. Now their brave are dead."

"You," said Potter, "are as brave as any man known to history."

"I," said Churchill, "could not bring myself to take my own life, though I had sworn I would."

"You tried to kill yourself long ago," von Steigerwald reminded him, "in Africa."

"Correct." Churchill's eyes were far away. "I had a revolver. I put it to my temple and pulled the trigger. It would not fire. I pulled the trigger again. It would not fire. I pointed it out the window and pulled the trigger a third time, and it fired."

He chuckled softly. "This time I lacked the courage to pull the trigger at all. They snatched it from me and threw me down, and I knew I should have shot them instead. I would have killed one or two, the rest would have killed me, and it would have been over."

He turned to Potter. "What you propose—what my friend Donovan proposes—will not work. It cannot be done. Let me tell you instead what I can do and will do. Next year, I will run for president."

Von Steigerwald said, "Are you serious?"

"Never more so. I will run, and I will win."

For a moment, hope gleamed in Potter's eyes; but they were dull when he spoke. "You can't become president, Mr. Prime Minister. The president must be a native-born citizen. It's in the Constitution."

"I am native born," Churchill smiled, "and I shall become a citizen, just as you have. It is a little-known fact, but my mother returned to her own country— to the American people she knew and loved so much—so that her son might be born there. I was born in . . ."

Churchill paused, considering. "In Boston, I think. It's a large place, with many births. My friend Donovan will find documentary proof of my nativity. He is a skilful finder of documents, from what I've heard."

"Oh, my God." Potter sounded as if he were praying. "Oh, my God!"

"Kuhn is a Hitler in the egg," Churchill told him. "The nest must be despoiled before the egg can hatch. I collected eggs as a boy. Many of us did. I'll collect this one. As I warned the British people—"

Von Steigerwald had pushed off the safety as his Luger cleared the holster. Churchill was still speaking when von Steigerwald shot him in the head.

"Heil Kuhn!" von Steigerwald muttered.

Potter leaped to his feet and froze, seeing only the faintly smoking muzzle aimed at his face.

"He dies for peace," von Steigerwald snapped. "He would have had America at war in a year. Now pick him up. Not like that! Get your hands under his arms. Drag him out on deck and get one of them to help you throw him overboard. They starved him. He can't be heavy."

As Potter fumbled with the latch of the cabin door, von Steigerwald wondered whether it would be necessary to shoot Potter as well.

Necessary or not, it would certainly be pleasant.

# THE HOLY CITY AND EM'S REPTILE FARM

## Greg van Eekhout
### (With thanks to David Moles)

**E**m and her brother were wrestling an alligator, and nobody was even watching.

"Hey, Em, did ya see the paper this morning? The Garden's giving away a piece of the True Cross."

Judd had a habit of saying outrageous things at the most inconvenient moments. Just now, he was lying atop Ike, a five-footer bred right here on the farm, while Em tried to seal its jaws with tape.

Ike was struggling, Em's bangs were getting in her eyes, and the tape was sticking to itself. "That's nuts," she snarled. "You don't give away a piece of the Cross."

Judd bore down on Ike's head and neck with his elbows. "Well, they're not giving it away, exactly. It's a raffle. Spend $50 on the Temple slots, and they'll deign to let you in the same room with it. Spend $100, and you get entered for a chance to win the splinter."

The alligator finally secured, Em stood up to catch her breath and tried to gauge if her older brother was ribbing her. He had a stupid grin on his face, which meant he was probably being serious.

"Garden's been in trouble for years," he said, trying to sound as if he knew what he was talking about.

"Not enough high rollers, I guess, so they're doing whatever they can to get some attention."

"Raffling off a piece of the Cross? So some retired pilgrim from Florida can hide it in his attic? It ain't right." Em wiped her hands on her apron while Judd used a pole to prod Ike out of the turtle yard he'd escaped to and back to the pond, where he belonged. She looked around the two and a half acres of trees and ponds where she'd spent all fourteen years of her life, thinking that the place had never looked worse. The pumps needed repair, the grass needed resodding, the trees needed a surgeon. Without pilgrims bringing their pilgrim dollars, there was no money for any of it. Except for Judd, and Daddy, still sleeping it off near on noon, it was just her and the critters, as Daddy liked to call the collection of crocs, gators, caymans, turtles and tortoises, rattlesnakes, Bobsey, the two-headed king snake, and Betty, the albino boa.

For years the reptile farm had been a convenient stop in the desert for pilgrims on their way to the Holy City. Here, they could fill their tanks with gas and their stomachs with burgers and slake their thirst with orange soda and milkshakes, and once they were here, they couldn't resist touring the critters, and a lot of the pilgrims would also buy a T-shirt or a shot glass or a postcard with a picture of Bobsey or Betty on it.

Things were different now, since the Templars had built Via-40, bypassing Trail 66 and leaving so many motels and gas stations and roadside attractions, like the Oasis Town Reptile Farm, dying on an obsolete vine.

Most people thought Em was short for Emma or Emily, but Daddy had named her Em for the Mother Road, Steinbeck's name for Trail 66, and she took its loss somewhat personally.

Inside the Snake House, a sagging, chipped-paint barn lined with terrariums, Em dropped a white mouse into Bobsey's tank. The king snake—a pair of Siamese twins, actually, joined two inches below their heads—came out from behind their heated rock and curled toward the terrified mouse.

"Poor Right-e-o," Em cooed. No matter how eagerly he flicked his forked tongue, Right-e-o always lost out to the more aggressive Lefty. Today, even more than usual, Em empathized with the weaker twin.

Inside the house, Daddy was up and stationed before a sea of paper at the kitchen table. With a pencil nub, he scribbled figures in columns, adding and subtracting. He'd been doing this for months.

"You had breakfast yet, Daddy?"

He looked up and smiled at her, but his smile couldn't conceal the stoop of his shoulders. She knew as well as he did that his pencil couldn't hold off the bank from foreclosing.

"Wouldn't say no to a cup of coffee."

The hell with that. He'd eat a proper breakfast. Eggs, and ham, and biscuits, and fried potatoes. But rooting around in the kitchen, she realized it'd have to be just eggs and biscuits. Funds were low, and Ocotillo Grocery, eleven miles down the road, had shut down last month.

She poured flour and water in a bowl and got down to mixing. When she thought about what Judd had told her, about the Garden raffle, her spoon got a little violent.

Giving away a piece of the Cross. She supposed that was sacrilegious. Even worse, it was unfair that some folks had so much while others had so little. It would be like her giving Bobsey away as a door prize because she had a whole crate of six-headed snakes in the attic.

It wasn't right. The Holy City's temples grew fat and fatter while the smaller stations along the traditional pilgrimage route faded away. The least they could do was send some of their spare relics their way.

The mixing spoon flew out of her hand and clanked against the sink.

Daddy called, "You okay in there?"

"Fine," Em said. "I'm fine."

Just struck by a bit of inspiration, was all. Though possibly not divine inspiration.

She came into the Holy City from the desert, sun-burned, dehydrated, and nauseated. She'd walked the last mile, the van—full of pilgrims she'd hitched a ride with—having suffered a burst water pump, and Em had been too impatient to wait with them for repair. In retrospect, walking had been a mistake.

She'd been on the Strip for an hour, stumbling along on the verge of delirium. At least she assumed it was delirium, for what else could explain the obscenely lit spectacle around her? The lesser temples stretched into the distance ahead and behind her, flashing and dancing with neon lights so bright they turned the night sky a dusty orange. She staggered past the neon palm trees and Crosses and fish and halos that fronted the temples of worship and gambling. Her head pounded from the bright lights and from thirst, but as something of a professional in the business of drawing pilgrims, she could only admire the audacity of the Strip.

Her admiration was tinged with envy, for there were more pilgrims in her field of vision than would visit Oasis Town in a year, even before Via-40: parades of flagellants, retirees with white legs and sunburned faces, cripples looking for miracles, pilgrims looking for buffets.

The thirst, the noise, the midnight heat—Em realized with alarm that she was going to faint. And what then? She'd be trampled to death by pilgrims and freaks, right here on the sidewalk. She wished she'd left Daddy and Judd a note before she'd left or had managed to send them a postcard from the road. At least then they might take some comfort knowing she'd died in the Holy City. Though Daddy didn't really go in for that sort of thing.

The world went gray.

There were steel bars digging into her back, and her flesh was burning on a griddle, just like Saladin during the Sixty-fourth English Crusade to take back the Holy Land. Em remembered learning those stories in Sunday school, and she wished she were back in Oasis Town now, with her crayons, coloring Saladin's skin Indian Red.

Cold water splashed on her lips. She sputtered and opened her eyes to find herself staring up at a crinkly brown face.

"Now try drinking some," the man said, putting a bottle of water in her hand. The glass felt deliciously cold, and the water felt even better when she took a good, long swallow.

She wasn't being tortured like Saladin. The bars at her back were the railings of the gate she was leaning against, in front of one of the temples. The griddle was just the sidewalk, hot on her skin, even through her clothes.

She tried to stand, but the man put his hand on her shoulder and gently pushed down. "Don't get up too fast. You got overheated. Desert heat's nothing to take lightly. The Krauts found that out the hard way, didn't they?" He winked and smiled beatifically.

With a wine-red felt tarboosh on his head and a billowing white shirt tucked into baggy sherwals, he looked like a Prohibition-era gangster. "Mark Yiska, from Queen of the City of Angels," he said, holding out a huge, leathery paw.

His hand looked as though it could crush walnuts, but he'd probably saved her life. She gave it a weary shake. "I'm Em . . . from Oasis Town."

She tried to get up again, and this time Mark helped her to her feet, not letting go of her hand until she assured him she wouldn't fall.

"Bless you for your water and kindness," she said, blinking through a wave of dizziness. "I should be going."

Mark shook his head in disapproval. "Miss, you don't look well. Let's find you some shade to rest in. There are some nice palms outside Solomon's Palace—"

"No, no, thank you, but I have to get to the Garden Tomb."

"The Garden will still be there after you rest. What's your rush?"

"I'm entering the raffle," she said, her hand going to her money belt, but instead finding only empty belt loops. Thieves, when she'd passed out. Right here, in front of everybody, on a path full of pilgrims to the Holy City. She would not curse them, not here on the street. She would not cry.

Mark gave her a sad, knowing look. "You're not the first to get robbed in front of the temples, and you won't be the last," he said with a sigh. "Besides, you know the odds on that raffle? You'd be better off playing dice."

"Damn them," Em spat. "Damn them, and may Albion take their souls." And now that she'd gone and cursed them, maybe she could also go back on her intention not to cry. Her eyes filled with precious water. Without money, she didn't know where she'd sleep, or how she'd eat and drink, and worst of all, she wouldn't be able to enter the raffle, and the reptile farm would be buried and forgotten in the desert sands.

Not that she actually thought she would have walked away from the city with a piece of the True Cross in her pocket. Mark was right about the odds. But if she could have at least gotten close to it. Close enough maybe to be able to whittle a credible fake . . .

"Now, don't you despair, miss. Things may not be all as grim as they seem. If you're willing to do a little work for me, I can help you earn some of your money back."

Em braced herself. She'd never been under any illusions that the Holy City was a place of virtue and clean souls. The city of Christ was home to the great, most sacred sites, where Jesus preached and died, but it was also home to the lost and the depraved, and not all favors were acts of kindness. This was where Mark would suggest she sleep with him, or sleep with his friends or business associates, or at least pose for naughty pictures.

He looked at her, deep into her, and what he said was, "Can you drive a truck?"

Even in a city of ostentatious temples, Solomon's Temple impressed. Its high walls blazed with eye-gouging pure white light under blue domes and fiery gold minarets, an island palace in a broad lake of blood. Fountains shot jets of water, dyed and lit red, with arcs and spirals and cascades, as if the giant corpse of Jesus were bleeding under the surface and entertaining the crowds with spurting wounds, all synchronized to blaring Virginian opera. From the center of the temple complex a red neon Cross rose thirty-three stories high, shining a bright crimson beam into the heavens. The temple stated in inarguable terms that the Knights of the Templar were the wealthiest and most powerful men on the continent, and they'd built God's own roadside attraction to prove it.

Em's job was simple enough. Mark had some business inside the temple, and all Em needed to do was stay with his rotten-apple Chevy pickup, parked on the ramp to an underground parking lot, with the engine running.

"I could be five minutes, I could be thirty," Mark said, getting out of the truck. "If I take longer than that . . . Well, just stay with the truck. Don't turn the engine off, because we may not be able to get it started again."

He looked at her very seriously. "Will you be here when I get back, Em?"

He didn't ask her to swear on her immortal soul. At least not in words.

"I'll be here," Em said.

A man approached Mark, full of bluster and officiousness, the red cross on his brown overalls marking him as a Templar squire. After a handshake exchange so smooth Em almost missed it, the sergeant said something sharply and moved off, and Mark withdrew into a service entrance. Em supposed he'd bought himself some parking time.

Em settled in to wait. She was starting to feel nervous about this arrangement.

No, she should be honest with herself. She knew Mark was engaged in some kind of criminal enterprise and that out of desperation, she'd agreed to be his accomplice; what she should do was leave a note thanking him again for giving her water and then climb out of the driver's seat and try to beg and hitchhike her way back to Oasis Town.

Ten minutes passed.

Em opened the glove compartment. It contained a bag of dried dates, a well-worn Navajo Koran, and a girlie magazine. She blushed and slammed the glove box shut.

Fifteen minutes, then twenty. Then thirty, and then, the minutes crawling like a tortoise in the sand, forty.

The Templar squire came back and rapped on her window. "He's got five minutes to get back, and then I'm having this piece of crap towed."

"But he paid for forty-five," Em protested. Of course, she had no idea what Mark had paid for, or why.

"He paid me to look the other way for a while, and his 'while' is up. I'm not a parking meter." Not waiting for her to put up an argument, he hollered something, and in the rearview mirror Em saw a younger squire nod sharply and run off. Moments later a tow truck was backing down the driveway, its fat, rusty hook swaying menacingly.

Should she move the truck, even though Mark had issued strict instructions not to? Leave the truck and try to find Mark inside? Abandon both truck and Mark and try to figure out some other way to raise funds for the Garden Tomb raffle? Maybe she could get a job as a cocktail waitress. She wouldn't be old enough to legally work in bars for four years, but maybe the temple saloons off the Strip wouldn't care.

Mark came sauntering out of the service entrance,

smiling and waving at the tow truck with one hand and swinging a small alligator-hide case, like a doctor's bag, in the other. He settled into the passenger seat, banged the door shut, and through his smiling teeth, said, "Drive."

Em shifted gears and let Mark know exactly what she thought of his tardiness, using language unfit for her own ears; but then she noticed how gray his skin looked and how his smile had tightened into a grimace.

"You're hurt," she said.

Mark carefully shifted to find a more comfortable position in his seat and tucked the alligator-hide bag between his knees. "Some of my friends inside turned out to be not as good friends as I'd thought. Turn left at the Altar of Burnt Offerings—No, no, just go around the cab, we don't have time for traffic lights."

Wiping sweat out of his eyes with his tarboosh, Mark spat staccato driving directions at Em, telling her to cut through the parking lot of the Trumpet Tower, race down an alley behind the Samoans Camp, and wind through the garages at the Road of Horse Entry.

Behind them in traffic, Em heard a squeal of tires and horns blaring, coming ever closer. "Those would be your 'friends' you mentioned?"

"Some of them. My real friends are right now answering some awkward questions back at the temple."

"I see," she said tartly. "So this was an inside job?"

Mark smirked, as though he were about to say something glib, but then his fingers touched the alligator-hide bag, and the smirk disappeared, as though it'd been slapped right off his face. His eyes gleamed. "A job like this can only be arranged on the inside. I was just one link in the chain. I was supposed to carry it from Solomon's to the Fountain and Water Gate, hand if off from there." He swallowed in pain and told Em to go around the Hippodrome, and for God's sake, speed up.

"But the plan's changed," Em said.

"Not really. I was going to backstab my partners and keep it for myself."

Em slammed the brakes, skidding to a stop in front of the flashing, spinning neon stars of the Sepulcher of David, and popped open her door.

Mark reached out and gently touched her hand with his dry old fingers. "I can't drive myself," he said.

"It's the *Templars*, Mark."

Mark smiled, and it reminded Em so much of her Daddy's smile when he was drunk and sad and most vulnerable.

He indicated the bag in his lap with a dip of his chin, a gesture that resembled the bow of a penitent. "What right do they have to possess something like this? The ground Solomon's stands on is sacred to my people, and they took it from us by force, burned our temple, and built their own from the leftover rubble. The thing in the bag was kept safe for hundreds of years before the Templars came along."

"And what do you plan to do with it?"

"I was going to keep it just as safe."

Em would have been less angry if he'd said he were going to sell it. "You mean you were going to lock it up in a vault away from human sight," she said, "like a manacled skeleton in a dungeon, where it can't do anybody any good. It's, it's . . ."

"Bad showmanship?"

Emily crossed her arms over her chest and glared at the steering wheel. "People have a right to see," she said, her voice almost as strong as her conviction.

Mark licked his lips. Em heard them crackle, and she searched the floorboards for water but found none.

"It's not up to me what happens to the thing in the bag any more," he said. "I think that's why I found you in the streets of the Holy City, Em. Because you're going to bring it to a better place."

Em saw the look in his eyes. "You mean *you're* going to bring it. Or we—"

"I'll get you out of the city," he promised. "After that, it's up to you."

Em said another word not fit for her ears and slammed the door shut. She pulled back into traffic and let Mark guide her the wrong way down one-way streets. He told her not to interrupt, and in addition to driving directions, he whispered other things to her as well. He told her things he thought might help her once she got out of the city. He told her things about God, some of which was Sunday school stuff to her, and other things from his people's beliefs, their corrupted faith, as Father Thomas back in Oasis Town would have called it. Mark seemed confused, as if he were trying to work things out for himself but was too tired to do any good thinking. He kept stroking the bag. Em half-hoped and half-dreaded that he would open it up and look inside and that she might catch a glimpse. His speech became more and more interspersed with words of Navajo, until Em could no longer understand what he was saying, but toward the end he asked her in English to bury him before sundown. Em promised she would.

After he died and the sweat on his skin dried, his face still seemed to shine.

The next morning, the Chevy ran out of gas on a hot gravel track in Atomic Golgotha. White earth, lightly tinged with pale green, spread out in dizzying shimmers in all directions. Even with the sun low on the horizon, heat leached through the windshield, cooking the oxygen in Em's lungs. Em grew up knowing the desert around Oasis Town, and she knew her best chance of survival lay in staying with the truck. By noon, it could be 120 degrees, and the truck would provide a little shade and would make her easier to find. But that was the problem. If the Templars tracked her out here, they would take the bag and its contents and torture and rape her, just to make a point. The truck was a bright red spot on the bleached earth, as noticeable from a distance as a bloodstain on a white altar cloth.

In the backseat she found a Navajo tourist blanket that Mark had been using as upholstery. Except for the generations of dust and grime embedded in the fabric, it was identical to the ones she sold in the reptile farm's gift shop. She draped it over her head, and even though it stifled, keeping the sun off her was critical. The blanket hung far enough down that, by threading one of her shoelaces through the handles of the alligator-hide bag and through her belt loops, she could walk with it concealed on her hip.

"This is a lot of trouble for nothing," Em muttered. Within hours she'd be a corpse, anyway.

Perhaps three hours later, Em awoke from a sleep of fever dreams about snakes and alligators and great radioactive lizards stomping the Holy City at the behest of God. Her head pounded with dehydration. Her tongue was wood. She looked up from the sand, where she'd fallen, to find herself surrounded by men in robes colored the blues and greens of the sea. They stood beside llamas bigger than those Em had ever seen at petting zoos, bigger even than any she'd seen in pictures in *National Geographic*. The men wore seashell necklaces and elaborate, spiky wreaths of dried date palm fronds around cloth headcovers. The blades of scrap metal they carried glinted painfully in the sun.

Only when the animals' pungent reek reached her nostrils did Em know the llamas and the men were not a mere vision.

Em swore in a parched whisper that she'd die before she let these Hawaiians take her bag.

For a time, they consulted with each other, their language strange to Em's ears, full of repeated syllables and rhythmic halts, but she recognized an argument when she heard one in any language. Some of the men gestured at the heat mirage on the horizon. Others pointed their weapons at her. If Em had to guess, she would have said the two sides of the dispute could be summed up as "kill her now or take her home and kill her there."

This went on for at least ten minutes. Em couldn't be sure, not only because she wasn't wearing a watch but because she had fainted at least once during the discussion.

When the conversation came to an abrupt halt, one of the men tightened his grip on his axe, the letters "USAF" faded but still visibly stenciled on the blade, and raised it in the air like Daddy about to slaughter a chicken. He came forward.

Em screamed, trying to tell them to wait, but it came out in a choked, inarticulate shriek, not unlike a chicken upon whom the axe has fallen. She tore open the blanket, plunged her hands into the bag, and held its contents aloft, the sun reflecting off the treasure in blinding rays. The man with the axe made a sound almost exactly like the one Em had and threw his forearm across his eyes.

The awed silence that followed lasted perhaps the span of twenty heartbeats.

Then, "Put it back in the bag," one of the men said. "You're coming with us. If you try to run, we'll cut your feet off."

They led her across the sand to a sprawling shanty village of caliche huts and rusted travel trailers, with skeletal corrals for the llamas made of sun-grayed wood. The sand glittered painfully, sprinkled with fragments of greenish glass, fused sand from the bomb blasts that had given Atomic Golgotha its name.

Em had hopes that she'd be brought into the large tent in the center of the village and that there she would be given water; then she would explain that her presence in Atomic Golgotha was not her fault, that the Templars were to blame (surely the Hawaiians spared no love for the Crusaders who'd nuked the Hawaiians' desert), and she would beg for her life. Maybe they would let her return to Oasis Town. Maybe they'd even let her borrow a llama.

Instead, she was left by herself in a pen with two

llamas and their dung. She drank from the same rusty trough the animals did and was grateful for it. The Hawaiians had left her with the alligator-hide bag, seeming unwilling to touch it with their own hands. Fear and attraction were powerful forces, Em well knew. It was the twin engine that generated awe, and as Daddy said, awe was a lever to move men.

The Hawaiians were the poorest people Em had ever seen. Enslaved and persecuted by the Mayans, cheated and exploited by Continentals and Indians, Christians and Muslims alike, the few surviving bands of nomadic Hawaiians occupied niches of America that few others were interested in. Em had seen a film about them at school. The film had emphasized how much Christians and Hawaiians had in common. After all, hadn't Christ been born an islander? In most paintings, Jesus was depicted as a white Continental, even as Christ the Mariner, coming across the Pacific on his balsa raft, to preach and die in the Holy City. But if you thought about it, he must have been brown skinned himself.

One of her guards, the man who'd threatened to cut off her feet, told her to get up and escorted her to the big tent. There, he shoved her to her knees to kneel before a huge, glowering man with a broad face and commanding black eyebrows. He was shirtless, wearing only a long sort of skirt, and he was draped in so many necklaces that Em could only assume he was their chief.

She clutched the bag to her lap.

"Where is home?" the man said.

What kind of question was this? A riddle? Some kind of test, for sure. The Hawaiians had been driven out of every home they'd ever had. The story that Christ had been crucified out here in Atomic Golgotha instead of just outside the City was declared apocryphal by Pope George, but the Church still wanted the Hawaiians gone and had even used hundreds of square miles of desert for atomic testing.

Where was home for a Hawaiian? There could only be one answer to that.

"Hawaii," said Em.

The man frowned, and despite herself, Em winced.

Then he laughed, a huge boom that seemed to make the tent billow. "Miss," he said, "I was asking where you are from."

"Oh." Em's cheeks burned. "I'm from Oasis Town, New Assyria. I live on a reptile farm there with my daddy and brother. My name is Em."

"You are a long way from your home, Em."

And then it all came tumbling out of her, a rapid-fire, half-sobbing torrent of words. She told him about the reptile farm, and Daddy's grim calculations at the kitchen table, about Trail 66 and Via-40 and the raffle at the Garden Tomb. She told him about Mark and Solomon's Temple and how she'd evaded the Templars in the Holy City, and she intended to beg for her life and to be allowed to return home, even if it meant parting with the bag and thing inside.

At least, that was what she had intended to ask for.

Instead, not fully understanding why, she found herself saying, "The bag isn't yours. I have to take it home. It's important."

The chief's eyes were big and dark as charcoal briquettes, and they seemed to express sorrow, amusement, and smoldering anger, all at the same time.

"It is not a small thing to steal from the Templars, girl. They are wealthy as nations and even more dangerous, for their faith is true. When they realize their stolen treasure has come to Atomic Golgotha, my people will be the ones who suffer for it. I am not without compassion for lost souls in the desert, but I can't think of a good enough reason not to present the Templars with their . . . item . . . as well as your head."

Again, Em intended to plea for her life. "The thing in the bag shouldn't be hidden away," she said. "That's what the Templars will do with it. I won't."

The chief nodded, as though he'd reached a firm decision. "We are of different faiths," he said, which was certainly true, because despite baptism and Sunday school, Em wasn't sure she really had any faith at all. "But perhaps our ways are not so dissimilar," the chief continued. "I will allow you to prove your purity by facing an ordeal. Should you please God, I will allow you to go home, and the treasure will remain in your custody."

Em didn't ask what would happen if her faith proved insufficient, though she was certain that would be the outcome.

There were no rattlesnakes on the Pacific islands, but the Hawaiians had lost their homeland ages ago and had adapted their customs to the lands they'd settled and been driven from, from the South American jungles to the North American deserts. They had suffered some of their greatest hardships in their Exodus from Texas, and it was there that they had been subjected to the trials of the snake pits. They'd learned some lessons from that.

Under a cloth canopy, in a deep rectangular hole dug in the sand, the snakes buzzed like a lightning machine in an electric circus. Em had never liked their sweet, musky smell, a little like cucumbers, but now it was so strong it threatened to knock her down into the writhing mass.

The Hawaiians stood around the edge of the pit, which for some reason Em imagined as the rim of a volcano. Had the film at school talked about pushing human sacrifices into lava-filled craters? She couldn't remember now.

The chief looked at her expectantly, and when expectation turned first to impatience and then to unmistakable anger, he said something, and two of the guards rushed at Em.

"I'll go," she said simply, stopping them in their tracks. Better to climb down slowly than to be thrown in and upset the snakes. She clutched the bag to her side and went down the ladder.

They had a snake pit back at the reptile farm, but Em had never done any work in it. That was a job for Judd or Daddy. They had some tricks for surviving a walk across the pit. The first trick was wearing thick

boots with steel reinforced toes. Daddy and Judd also
wore rubber pads fashioned from an old truck tire
under their pants, which made for an awkward gait,
but it had saved their lives and their dignity more than
a few times.

Em had no such protection. Just her dungarees and
her thin canvas sneakers, worn even thinner by her
desert ordeals. She took the last step down the ladder,
and the snakes scorched the air with their rattling.

Snakes don't like to bite folks, Daddy had always
told her. They knew people were too big to eat, and
it could take them weeks to replenish their venom,
and they were vulnerable during that time, so they
much preferred to retreat and hide. Indeed, the snakes
jerked away from her as she gently set her feet down.
But there were a lot of snakes in this pit—four dozen?
a hundred?—and though they scrambled into piles
against the walls, there wasn't much room for them
to hide from this towering, two-legged intrusion in
their midst. And if they were as much an overrated
threat as Daddy insisted, then why wouldn't he ever
let her do work in the pit?

She tried to step lightly, but her feet felt as big as
clown shoes.

People liked to say that snakes could strike faster
than a blink of the eye, but Em knew that to be an
exaggeration. Rattlesnakes only moved about as fast
as a person could throw a punch. That wasn't very
fast, was it? Of course, people got punched all the
time.

She knew the bite was coming before it struck home.

Dusky gray, the rattler was as thick around as
Judd's wrist. It lay straight across her path, not coiled
but stretched out over the bodies of its nest mates,
and it seemed to Em that this one was particularly
angry. It knew Em's faith was weak, it knew that what
she had in the bag wasn't rightfully hers, that any
claim she had on it was driven by greed, and if it was
greed to keep the reptile farm alive, it was still greed,

no better than the Templars', no better than any thief's.

The rattler snapped its body forward, and Em's reflexes took over. She toppled backward and fell, the one thing Daddy said meant certain death in the snake pit.

There was no pain, no sensation of thorns breaking flesh, no ballooning with burning poison. Where she had fallen, there were no snakes.

She dared to open her eyes. The big rattler was wrestling with the bag, which lay on the ground at Em's feet, where she had evidently dropped it.

Thinking profane thoughts about pilgrims and profit, about showing wonders in plain sight, about letting people see whatever they wanted to see, be it albino boa constrictors or miracles, she reached into the bag to remove the cup, then stood, and finished her walk through the serpents.

Climbing up the ladder at the end of the pit, she looked up to face the Hawaiian chief.

"I guess I know what I believe in," Em said.

They fed her and gave her water to drink and to carry with her, and they gave her one of the chief's own llamas, which she rode through Zion and south to Kingman. There she let the llama loose to join the feral herds, and she hitched rides back to Oasis Town, where, upon her return, she submitted herself to Daddy's scolding until he dissolved into tears of relief.

Not until days later did she gather Daddy and Judd at the kitchen table. After finishing a breakfast of chicken eggs and alligator meat, she set the bag on the table. It was dusty and battered, with two prominent punctures that gave Em shivers to think about.

When she displayed what the bag contained, there were more tears.

Then Em told Daddy what they were going to do.

First, they made billboards.

There were still hard months, and Daddy had to sell

the Ford Goliath to keep the bank from repossessing the house and the farm. But things got better as word got out.

The barn got a new roof. The paths around the croc pond were paved. Daddy even paid out of his own pocket to repair the cracks and potholes on Trail 66 for three miles in either direction of the farm. The road brought pilgrims, lots of them, and when the re-opened motor lodge down the way could no longer accommodate them, Daddy built a new motel right next to the reptile farm. It had a swimming pool and a restaurant called Mark's, which served the best burgers in the state, and it also had a separate halal and kosher kitchen.

Pilgrims still loved the critters. They loved to see the Bobsey twins and Betty the albino boa. But the critters were no longer the main draw of Oasis Town. Under Em's direction, the Templar treasure was housed in a little house all its own, set on a small green lawn that never went brown.

The Templars came for it once. They set out from their temple with a great rumbling caravan of trucks and Jeeps and tanks, bristling with guns, and they lost two hundred vehicles and a thousand men in a mighty sandstorm. Not long after, reports started to appear in the papers about the problems they were having within their banking and gaming empire.

Never, not even in jest, not even to impress the pilgrims, would Em ever claim the cup had miraculous properties. She just knew that it made pilgrims happy to see it. For ten dollars, they could have their picture taken with it.

# THE RECEIVERS

*Alastair Reynolds*

With the ambulance sealed and the Rutherford counter ticking nice and slowly, we cleared the hospital checkpoint and sped through the lanes to Sandhurst and Rye, then took the main road east to Walland Marsh and the junction at Brenzett to New Romney. It had been sunny when we departed, but as we neared the coast, the sky turned leaden and overcast, with a silvery-gray mist keeping visibility to a mile or so. The coast road to Dungeness was a patchwork of repairs, with the newest craters either barricaded off or spanned by temporary metal plates. Ralph took it all in his stride, swerving the ambulance this way and that as if he had driven this road a thousand times, never once letting our speed drop under forty miles per hour. I held onto the dashboard as the ambulance lurched from side to side, creaking on its suspension. Ralph wasn't my normal driver, and he took a bit of getting used to.

"Not getting seasick are you, Wally?" he asked, with a big smile.

"In an ambulance, sir?"

"It's just that you look a bit green!"

"I'm fine, sir—right as rain."

"You're in safe hands, don't worry about that."

Between jolts I asked: "Been driving long, have you, sir?"

"Twenty years or so, on and off. Started off a sergeant with the Special Constabulary Unit, then got myself signed up as a private with the London Field Ambulance."

"In France were you, sir, before the retreat?"

"Steady, lad. If the Patriotic League catches you calling it that, they'll have your guts for garters. It's the 'consolidation,' remember. Well, I was there—doing this job. So was Ravel—he was driving for the French, though, and we never met again."

"Ravel, sir?"

"Old teacher of mine. A long time ago now."

I didn't know much about Ralph, truth be told. Mr. Vaughan Williams was his name, but no one ever called him anything other than Ralph, or sometimes Uncle Ralph. He was a familiar face at Cranbrook, always organizing a singsong around the mess piano. They say he used to be a composer, and quite a good one, although I'd never heard of him. Most of the chaps liked him because he didn't have any airs and graces, even though you could tell he was from a good background. I guessed he was about sixty, but strong with it, as if he could go on for a few more years without any trouble. There were plenty like him around: men who had signed up at the start of the war, when they were still in their early forties, and who had hung on ever since. Sometimes when I listened to Mr. Chamberlain's speeches on the wireless, I wondered if I'd still be around in twenty years, with an ambulance mate young enough to be my son.

We passed a gun emplacement that was still in use, two barrels sticking out at an angle, like a pair of fingers telling the Huns where to shove it, and then another one that had been bombed, so that it was just a broken shell, like a concrete-gray hat box that had been stepped on; then we slowed for a checkpoint at a striped kiosk hemmed in with sandbags. The guards had boxes hung around their necks, stuffed with masks in case the gas alarm went off. We were waved through without stopping, and then it was a clear dash along another mile or so of chalky road with barbed wire on both sides. Out of the mist loomed a tall shape, the same gray color as the gun emplacements, and a little further along the road was a similar shape and a third barely visible beyond that. From a distance they looked like tall gray tombstones sticking out of the land. Drawing nearer I saw that the structures were all alike, although I still had no idea of what they were. I couldn't see any doors or windows or gun slits, at least not from the angle we were approaching.

"I don't suppose you have much idea what this is all about," Ralph said. "Never having been to Dungeness, after all. There are some other stations at Hythe and up the coast at Sunderland, but I don't imagine you've been there either."

"No, sir," I admitted.

"What were you doing before you ended up with the Corps?"

"Artillery, sir. Antiaircraft emplacement at Selsey."

"Shoot down much?"

"A few spotter planes. One flying wing and a couple of zeppelins. Then I got wounded in Sevenoaks."

We passed the first shape. Because the road snaked a bit, I was able to see that the front of the object didn't have any doors or windows either, and no sign of gun slits. The main part was a big concrete bowl with a thick rim, tilted almost onto its side so that it faced out to sea like a great curved ear. The bowl was easily fifty or sixty feet across, and its lower rim was about thirty feet off the ground. It was attached—or cast as part of—a heavy supporting wall with sloping sides made of the same dreary gray concrete. A windowless hut was positioned under the rim of the bowl, and rising from the roof of this hut was a metal tower that ended in a pole, sticking up so that it was in front of the middle part of the bowl.

"They've built them big now," Ralph said. "They were only about half the size when I was here last."

"I've no idea what this is all about, sir."

"Really, Wally?"

"Not a clue, sir."

The ambulance slowed a little, and we passed a concrete plinth on which was mounted a curious object, resembling a flattened searchlight on a cradle that could be aimed in various directions. Two men were sitting on chairs attached to either side of the moving part of the cradle. In addition to their gas masks they were wearing heavy black headphones. The men were gripping levers and steering wheels, and as we passed the cradle, it tilted and rotated, making me think of a sleepy dog suddenly waking up to follow a wasp. A third man was standing next to them holding a portable telephone to his ear.

"The name of the game's acoustic location," Ralph said, before looking at me expectantly. "I expect it's all as clear as crystal now?"

"Not really, sir. But you said 'acoustic'—I presume this has something to do with sound?"

"Very good. This is one of the main stations on the south coast. Those chaps we just passed are listening to the sky; that thing they're sitting on can pick up sounds from tens of miles away."

I thought about that for a moment. "Won't they have been deafened by us driving past?"

"No more than you'd be blinded by the sun if you were looking in the opposite direction. The receiver only amplifies the sounds coming into it along the direction it's pointed—nothing else matters. Those chaps steer it around until they pick up the drone of an incoming airplane, and then they nod it back and forth and side to side until they know they've got the strongest possible signal. Then a third chap reads off the elevation and directional angle and telephones that information straight to the coastal defense coordinator, who can then telephone instructions to the big guns or the Flying Corps."

"When we were told to point our guns, sir, I always assumed it was down to spotters."

"Which was undoubtedly what they wanted you think. Not that the Huns didn't have their own stations, but we always reckoned our coordinating system was superior. On a clear day, when the airplanes are within visual range, a spotter will always do a better job than the sound men—it's all a question of wavelengths and the problem of building sound mirrors much bigger than the ones we already have. But when it's dark, or the weather's closed in like this, and the aircraft are a long way out, the fix provided by the sound stations gives us several minutes of advance warning."

The second concrete shape was now to our right. I noticed that the rim of the dish was missing a big chunk and some concrete rubble was lying on the ground under it—it was as if someone had taken a nibble from a biscuit. A man with white gloves and a gas mask was standing by the hut directing us to continue driving.

"Looks like they took a direct hit," I said. "What do you suppose it was?"

Ralph steered for the third shape. "Flying wing or long-range shells. Doesn't make much difference now—the one's as bad as the other."

"Are the concrete things the same as the one the men were steering?"

"Same general idea, just scaled up. The men call them sound mirrors, which is what they are, really— giant mirrors for collecting all that sound and concentrating it on a tiny spot just in front of the dish."

"I don't see how you can steer one of those, sir, let alone nod it back and forth."

"You can't, obviously. But you can move the pickup tube a little, which has a similar effect. The three of them are pointed in slightly different directions, to cover likely angles of approach. On a good day they'll pick up the bombers when they're still grouping over France."

I couldn't see any shapes beyond the third one, so I assumed this was the limit of the Dungeness station. Beyond was a colorless tract of marshy scrub, as far as the mist would allow me to see. The final shape was even more badly damaged than the second one, with two chunks missing from it. A big piece of concrete had even fallen onto the roof of the hut, though the structure appeared undamaged. A guard with a gas mask box around his neck was ushering us to park alongside the hut, gesticulating with some urgency. He had a beetroot-red face and pockmarked cheeks, and he looked thoroughly fed up with his lot.

Ralph brought the ambulance to a halt, and the engine muttered itself into silence. Even through the airtight windows I could hear the slow rise and wail of a siren. The sirens went on for so long and so often that the only thing you could do in the end was pretend not to hear them. If you didn't, you'd go witless with worry.

We got out of the ambulance, collected our gas mask boxes from under the seats, and took two rolled-up stretchers from the rear compartment, carrying one apiece. We didn't know how many injured we would have to deal with, but it always paid to assume the worst—if we had to come back for more stretchers, we would.

"In there," the beetroot-faced guard said, before stalking off in the general direction of the second shape. "Be quick about it—after a shelling like this the flying wings usually come in."

"How many injured?" Ralph called after him, but the man was already fixing his mask into place and appeared not to hear him. A seagull flew overhead and seemed to laugh at us.

"He's having an off day," I said, as we walked over to the hut.

"Your nerves wouldn't be in fine fettle after spending long out here. The Huns have been bombing these listening stations to smithereens for years. Of course, we build 'em up again as soon as they're done—the thing about concrete is it's cheap and quick—but for some odd reason that only encourages them to keep coming back."

"Pardon my asking, but how do you know all about this stuff, sir? Isn't it top secret?"

"It was, although it won't be for much longer. I don't doubt you've noticed those wireless towers that are springing up everywhere?"

"Yes?" I answered cautiously, for I had seen the spindly constructions with my own eyes.

"Rumor mill says they're something that'll put these listening posts out of business in pretty sharp fashion. Pick up planes from hundreds of miles away, not tens. But until they've got 'em strung across the south coast and wired together properly, these acoustic locators are all we've got." Ralph put his hand on the door to the hut. "To answer your first question . . . well, let's attend to the chaps in here first, shall we?"

The door to the hut was stiff with rubberized gas seals, but after a good tug it swung open easily enough. I followed him inside, not quite sure what to expect. Despite the seals, the hut was damp and cold, like a slimy old cave by the sea. Although there were no windows, there was an electric light in the ceiling, a bulb trapped behind a black metal cage, with a red one next to it that wasn't on. The lit bulb gave off a squalid brown glow that it was going to take my good eye a few moments to adjust to. There was some furniture inside: a gray metal desk with a black bakelite telephone, some chairs, some shelves with boxes and technical books, and a lot of secret-looking radio equipment, most of which was also black and bakelite. And a man sitting in one of the chairs at an angle to the desk, with a bandage around his head and another around his forearm, his shirt sleeve rolled up. As we came in, he tugged headphones from his head and put them down on the desk. He also closed a big green log book he had open on the desk, sliding it to the back. I'd only had a glimpse, but I'd seen loose papers stuffed into the log book, with lots of scratchy lines and blotches on them. I noticed there was a fountain pen on the desk next to an inkstand.

The man was a good bit older than me, although I'd still have said he was ten years younger than Ralph—fiftyish, give or take. He still had a moustache even though they weren't in fashion nowadays. He looked at us groggily, as though he'd been half asleep until that moment, and waved us away in a good-natured kind of way. "I'm all right, lads—just a few scratches, that's all. I told 'em it wasn't worth sending out for an ambulance."

"We'll be the judges of that, won't we, Wally?" Ralph said to me, as if we'd been working together for years.

I closed the door behind us.

The man stiffened in his chair and peered at the door with squinty eyes. "Ralph? Good lord, it can't be, can it?"

"George?"

"One and the same, old boy!"

Ralph shook his head in delighted astonishment. "Of all the places!"

A smile spread across the other man's face. "I presume you found out I was working here?"

"Not at all!"

The man laughed. "But it was you that put the word in for me!"

He had quite a posh way of speaking, like Ralph, but there was a bit of Yorkshire in there as well.

I placed my stretcher against the wall, coming to the conclusion I wouldn't be needing it, even though the man would still need to come back to Cranbrook.

"Well, yes," Ralph said. "But that was a while ago, wasn't it? You'll have to make allowances for me, I'm afraid—getting a bit doddery in my old age." He put down his own stretcher and shook his head again, as if he still couldn't quite believe what he was seeing. Slowly he moved to examine the seated man. "Well, what happened? Did you get knocked down in here?"

"No," our patient said. "I was outside, coming down the ladder from the pickup tube, when some shells hit the dish. Got knocked off the ladder by a couple of splinters. Dashed my head on the side of the hut and grazed my arm."

Ralph gave him a severe look. "You were outside during a shelling? You silly old fool, Butterworth."

"The pickup tube needed adjustment. You know how it is—someone had to do it."

"But not you, George—not you of all people. Well, better get you back to Cranbrook, I suppose. The fellow outside said we can expect flying wings. Don't expect you'll be too sorry to miss them, will you?"

"That's always how it happens," George said. "Berthas take out our listening posts, then the planes can come in and pick their targets at leisure. You're right, Ralph, you chaps had best be moving. But you can leave me here—I'll mend."

"Not a chance, old man. Can you stand up?"

"Honestly, I'm fine."

"And we have a duty to look after you, so there's no point in arguing—right, Wally?"

"Right, sir," I said.

Ralph offered him a hand, and the seated man moved to stand up. Seeing that he didn't like having to put weight on his forearm, I wondered if his injury was a bit more serious than just a graze.

Just at that moment there was a distant *whump* that made itself felt more through the ground than the air. It was followed in quick succession by another, a little closer and sharper sounding. Accompanying the sound of the bombs was a mournful droning sound.

"That's your flying wings," George said, standing on his own two feet. "They were quick about it this time—give 'em credit. Probably got U-boats watching the station from the sea."

I heard the boom of our own antiaircraft guns— you can't mistake a seventy-five millimeter cannon for anything else, once you've worked on them. But something told me they were just taking potshots, lobbing shells into the sky in the vain hope of hitting one of those droning, batlike horrors.

"Righty-ho," said Ralph. "Let's get you to the ambulance, shall we?"

I moved to the door and opened it again, just enough to admit a sliver of overcast daylight. At that moment another bomb fell, much closer this time. It was only twenty or thirty yards from the barbed wire on the other side of the road, and the blast launched a fan of sand and soil and rubble into the air. I felt as if someone had whacked a cricket bat against the side of my head—for a moment my good ear went pop, and I couldn't hear anything at all. Suddenly the distance to the ambulance looked immense. My hearing came back in a muffled way, but even so the siren managed to sound more insistent than before, as if it were telling us: *Now you'll believe me, won't you?*

I closed the door hard and looked back at the other two. "I think it's a bit risky, sir. They seem to be concentrating the attack around here."

"We'd best sit tight and hope it passes," George said. "We'll be safe enough in here—the hut's a lot sturdier than it looks."

"I hope you're right about that," Ralph said, sitting down in the other chair. Then he looked at me. "I don't suppose you have the faintest idea what's going on, Wally?"

"Not really, sir. I mean, I gather you two know each other, but beyond that . . ."

Ralph said, "George and I go back a long way, although we haven't clapped eyes on each other in— what? Ten years, easily."

"I should say," George said.

"This is Wally Jenkins, by the way. He's a good sort, although I don't think he much cares for my driving." Ralph leaned toward me with a knowing look in his eye, as if he were about to offer me a sweet. "George and I were both interested in music before the war. Very interested, I suppose you might say."

"I heard you were a composer, sir," I said.

"As was George here. Great things were expected of Butterworth."

I racked my brains, but I didn't think I'd ever heard

of anyone called George Butterworth. But, then again, I'd never heard of Ralph Vaughan Williams, and I'd heard from the men at Cranbrook that he really *was* something, that people used to go to concerts of his music before the war.

"Actually," Ralph went on, "there were three of us back then—George, me, and dear old Gustav."

"Isn't that a German name, sir?"

"Gussie was as English as you or I," George said sternly.

"You did hear what they did to him, didn't you?" asked Ralph. "Locked away by the Patriotic League for having latent Germanic sympathies. They say he hung himself, but I've never been sure about that."

"It was just a name, for heaven's sake. He'd stopped calling himself Von Holst. Wasn't that enough for them?"

"Nothing was ever good enough," Ralph said.

A brooding silence fell across the room, interrupted only by the occasional muffled explosion from somewhere outside. Ralph turned to me again and said, "George and I were both members of the Folk Music Society. Now, I don't imagine that means very much to you now. But back then—this is thirty years ago, remember—George and I took to traveling around the country recording songs. We were quite the double act. We had an Edison Bell disc phonograph, one of the very few in the country at the time. A brute of a machine, but at least it provided a talking point, a way of breaking the ice." He nodded at the equipment on the shelves. "Of course, it meant that we had some basic familiarity with recording apparatus—microphones, cables, that kind of thing." He paused, and for the first time I saw something close to pain in his otherwise boyish face. "In twenty-three I was shellshocked while on ambulance duties in the Salient. I was no good for battlefield work after that, so I was transferred here, to Dungeness. I was one of the operators, listening to the sounds picked up by these dishes, straining to hear the first faint rumble of an incoming airplane. In the end, I was no good for it, and I had to go back to ambulance work; but I got to know some of the names in charge, and when I heard that dear old Butterworth had been shot . . ."

"I was wounded by a sniper," George said. "Not the first time, either—took one in the Somme in sixteen. That second was my ticket out of the war, though. But do you know the funny thing? I didn't want it. What was I going to do—go back to music, with all this still going on?" He shook his head, as if the very idea was as ludicrous as staging a regatta in the English Channel.

"I know how you felt," said Ralph. "I had so many things unfinished when this all began and so many more things I wanted to do. *Lark Ascending*—that needed more work. That opera I keep talking about—I feel as if Falstaff's been standing at my shoulder for twenty years, urging me to get *Sir John* down on paper. And another symphony . . . I've had the skeleton of the *Pastoral* in my head ever since I was in the Somme, all those years ago."

"The bugle player," George said, nodding—he must have heard the story several times.

"They still won't understand it—they'll think it's all lambkins frolicking in meadows."

"Give them time. They'll work it out eventually."

"If I ever write it, old man. That's the clincher. Find myself a spare half hour here, a spare hour there, but if I'm not scribbling letters to Adeline, I'm filling out requisitions for bandages or spare tires, or organizing raucous singsongs around the mess piano. I *have* tried, but nothing good ever comes of it. Most of the time I can hardly hear the music in my head, let alone think about getting it down on paper."

"How is Adeline now?" George asked.

"As well as can be expected, old man."

After a silence George said: "At least we're doing something useful. That's what I keep telling myself. Music was a pleasant dream, but now we've grown up, and there are other things we have to do—proper, serious things, like listening for enemy airplanes or driving ambulances." Something seemed to snap in him then, as if he had been waiting a very long time to unburden himself. "The damage is done, Ralph. Even if you gave me a year off to go and sit in some quiet country cottage and scribble, scribble, scribble, it wouldn't achieve a blessed bit of good. There's too much noise in my head, noise that won't just go away because I'm not in France or not in earshot of the coastal guns. Why, there are times when I think the only place I can concentrate is *here*, in this cold little hut, listening to the noises across the sea."

At that moment the red bulb, which had been dark when we came in, starting flashing on and off. There was a harsh buzzing sound from one of the black boxes on the shelf. Ralph looked at it worriedly.

"That's torn it," George said. "Gas detectors have gone off."

"One of those bombs was carrying gas?" I asked.

"Mustard, phosgene or radium fragments—there's no way of telling from here." George looked at me with narrowed eyes. "Been in a gas attack, Wally?"

"Once, sir. But it's not really gas in the radium shells. It's little particles, but they get carried on the wind just as if they were a gas. They say there are parts of Woolwich no one will be able to live in for years, because that stuff can still get inside you."

"Well, we're better off than they were in Woolwich," George said, with a kind of steely determination that told me he was going to take charge. "Now, the bad news is the seals on this hut aren't going to help us much if the gas drifts our way. They're old and perished, and we couldn't spend long in here anyway before the air got stale."

"What about the ambulance, sir?" I asked.

Ralph shook his head slowly. "No better, I'm afraid."

"But the seals . . ."

"Aren't what they used to be. If we ran into a thick cloud, we wouldn't have much of a chance."

"That's not what they told us in Dorking, sir."

"No, I don't doubt that. But they can't very well have ambulance drivers going around scared out of their wits, can they?"

"I don't suppose so," I said, without much conviction.

"Never you mind about the ambulance anyway," George said. "There's an underground shelter on the other side of the compound, just before the first mirror—you'd have driven past it on your way in. That's safe, and it has its own air supply."

"Will they still let us in?" Ralph asked.

"If we don't dillydally. I see you've both got your masks—that'll save us a jog back to the ambulance." Still not quite steady on his feet, he went to one of the shelves and pulled down a regulation gas mask box. "Now, you two go ahead of me. You'll find the shelter easily enough, and I won't be far behind you."

"You can come with us," Ralph said.

"I can't move very quickly—must have sprained my ankle when I fell off the ladder. Didn't notice until now, what with the head wound and everything."

"We'll carry you," I said. "We can even take you in one of the stretchers—that'll be faster than all three of us hobbling along like a crab." I opened my box and dragged out the gas mask. For some reason I didn't feel as grateful to be carrying it as I usually did. I was wondering if what they had told us in Dorking also applied to the gas masks.

"Open the box, George," Ralph said quietly.

"You two go ahead," George said, as if we hadn't heard him the last time.

"There's no mask in that box, is there?"

George had his back to us, like a boy who didn't want anyone to see his birthday present.

"The box," Ralph said again, with a firmness I hadn't heard before.

"All right, it's empty," George said, turning around slowly. He had the lid open, showing the box's bare interior. "There was a mistake. I took the mask to the compound dressing station, then left it there by accident when I came back to the hut."

"Why did you come back instead of going straight to the shelter?" Ralph asked.

"Because I still wanted to listen, all right? The sound mirror still works, even with those chunks taken out of it. I felt I could still be some use." He gestured helplessly at the headphones. "I still wanted to listen," he said again, more quietly this time.

"You hear it too," Ralph said, wonderingly.

"Hear what?"

"The music. Don't pretend you don't know what I'm talking about, old man. You said this was the only place you could concentrate. You meant more than just that, didn't you? This is the only place where it comes back—the music—as if this war weren't standing between us and everything we ever thought mattered. It's why I couldn't work here any longer, why I had to go back to the ambulance service."

George stared at him without saying anything. So did I.

"I thought I was going insane at first—a delayed effect of the shellshock," Ralph said. "Well, perhaps I was, but that didn't make the music go away. If anything, it just got stronger. It was like hearing someone hum a tune in the next room, a tune you almost recognized—you could pick out just enough of the melody for it to be maddening. I talked to some of the other chaps, thinking there must be some kind of interference on the wires . . . but when I got funny looks, I learned to keep my mouth shut."

"What was the music like?" George asked.

"Beautiful beyond words—what I could hear of it. Enough to break your heart. Well, mine anyway. The *Pastoral*, how I always meant it would sound. I could hear it, as if it were being played to me by an orchestra, as if I were just a listener in the audience. But not just the *Pastoral* . . . there was also the *London*, done differently—I always did mean to take another stab at that one, you know . . . *Lark* . . . and music I don't even recall intending to write but that seems to have *me* all over it."

"It's our music," George said.

"I know, old man. That's what I've been hardly daring to admit to myself, all this time. It's all the music we would have made if this war weren't in the way. I think we *did* write that music, in some weird way, and it's making itself known to us here. No one else hears it, of course. But you and I . . . I think we're like antennae, or microphones, ourselves. I hear the music I would have made, and I suppose you hear your own tunes."

"I hope they're mine. I couldn't bear the idea of them being yours."

"That good, eh?"

"Lovely. Lovely and sad and stirring . . . everything I ever wanted music to be." He closed his eyes for a moment. "But it's so terribly *quiet*. Some days I don't hear it at all. Today it seemed to be coming through stronger than most. If I could only get it down . . ."

"You mean on paper, sir?" I asked. Ralph gave me a blank look, and I said: "It's just that when we came in, I thought I saw some papers in Mr. Butterworth's log book. I didn't make much of it the time, but now that I know about the music, I wondered if you'd been trying to write it down."

George gave a short, weary laugh. "You don't miss much, Wally. I thought I was much too quick for you."

"Can I see?" Ralph asked.

George slid the log book across the desk and opened it again, revealing the loose papers inside. He passed one of them to Ralph. It was a pink form with typewriting on one side. "Never was much good at transcription," he said. "You'd be faster and more accurate. But then it wouldn't be my music you'd be hearing, would it?"

Ralph tapped his finger along the music, making a kind of low tum-te-tum noise. He wasn't exactly singing along with it, but I could tell he was imagining it properly, just as if a band were playing in his head, with all the right instruments. "Well, it's got the Butterworth stamp," he said eventually. "No doubt about that."

George leaned forward a little. "What do you think?"

"I think I'd like to hear the rest of it. This is obviously just a fragment, a few bars of a much larger work."

"I can only write what I hear. As you say, it's as if a chap next door is humming a tune. You can't dictate which tune he'll hum, you just have to go along with him and hope for the best." George paused and looked serious. "Did you ever write any of it down, old boy?"

"Transcribe it, you mean?" Ralph shook his head slowly. "I was too scared to. Scared that if I wrote it down, the music might stop. And that if I put that music down on paper and convinced myself that it really was something I'd come up with, I'd have to admit to myself that I was going quite insane."

"Or that the music's real," George said quietly.

"Now you know why I stopped working here, of course. No use to man nor boy if all I kept hearing was music instead of airplanes."

"I hear the airplanes as well. It's just that the music comes through when they're not there." He turned to me sharply. "Well, Wally, what do you make of it? Are we both for the nuthouse?"

"I don't think so sir," I said.

But in truth I wasn't sure. George might have been younger than Ralph, but they were still old men, and they had both had their share of unpleasant experiences in the war. So had I, in a smaller way, and I still felt that I had my marbles . . . but what kind of condition would my head be in twenty or thirty years from now if the war just kept on the way it had?

Perhaps I would start hearing secret music as well.

"Wally," Ralph said to me, "I want you to listen very carefully. We're Royal Army Medical Corps men. We have a patient here and a duty to protect him. Understood?"

I nodded earnestly, just as if I were still taking ambulance classes in Dorking. "What are we going to do, sir?"

"You're going to take him to the shelter. George will use my gas mask, and you will use your own."

"And you sir?"

"I shall wait here, until you can return with a second mask."

"But the seals, sir . . ."

"Will hold for now. Be sharp about it—we don't have all afternoon."

"No," George said, more to me than Ralph. "He isn't staying here. It's his gas mask, not mine—he should be the one using it."

"And you're thirteen years younger than me, old boy. One of these days, for better or for worse, this war is going to be over. When that day comes, I'm not going to be much good for writing music—I'm worn out as it is. But you've still got some life in you."

"No one'll be writing much music if the Huns take over."

"We thought the world of German music before all this started—Bach, Brahms, Wagner—they all meant so much to me. It seems funny to start hating all that now." Ralph nodded at the still-flashing red light. "But we can discuss this later—provided we keep our voices down. In the meantime, Wally's going to take you to the shelter. Then he'll come back for me, and we can all sit around and joke about our little adventure."

"I'm not sure about this, sir," I said.

"RAMC, lad. Show some spine."

"Sir," I said, swallowing hard. Then I turned my attention to George. "I don't think there's much point arguing, sir. Perhaps it isn't such a bad plan after all, anyway. I can sprint back with another gas mask pretty sharpish."

"Take the mask," Ralph said.

Something passed between them then, some unspoken understanding that was not for me to interpret.

Time weighed heavily and then George took the mask. He said nothing, just fitted it over his head without a word. I put on my own mask, peering at the world through the grubby little windows of the mica eye-pieces.

We left the hut, closing the door quickly behind us. George could not run, but with my bad knee I was not much better. We started making for the first dish, with the promise of the shelter beyond it. Through the mask all the colors looked as yellowy as an old photograph, but George looked back at me and pointed out something, a band of darker yellow lying in the air across our path. Phosgene, I thought—that was the yellow one, not mustard gas. Phosgene didn't get you straight away, but if they mixed it with chlorine, it was a lot quicker. I pressed the mask tighter against my face, as if that were going to make any difference.

It took an age to reach the shelter, with the distance between the sound mirrors seeming to stretch out cruelly. Just when it began to cross my mind that perhaps the shelter did not exist, that it was some figment of George's concussion-damaged imagination, I saw the low concrete entrance, the steps leading down to a metal door that was still partly open. A masked guard, who might have been the same man Ralph and I had spoken to earlier, was urging us down the steps.

When the door was tight behind me, I whipped off my mask and said, "Give me yours, George—it'll do for Ralph."

George nodded and dragged the mask from his face, which was slick with sweat and dirt where the rubber had been pressing against his skin. "Good man, Wally," he said, between breaths. "You're a brave sort."

But the guard would not let me leave the shelter. The red light above the door was telling him that the gas concentration was now too high to risk exposure, even with a mask.

"I have to go!" I said, shouting at him.

The guard shook his head. No arguing from me was going to get him to change his mind. We had been lucky to make it before they locked the shelter from the inside.

Looking back on it now, I'm sure Ralph knew exactly what would happen when I got to the shelter—or he had a pretty shrewd idea. What he said to George kept ringing in my head—about how the younger man would still be able to get some of that music down when the war was over. It was like one runner passing the baton to the other. I don't think he would have said that if he had expected me to come back with another mask.

Because there was no wind that day, the gas alert remained high until the middle of the evening. When it was safe, I went out with two masks and a torch, back to the hut, just in case there was still a chance for Ralph. But when I got to the hut, the door was open and the room empty. Everything was neat and tidy—the box back on the shelf, the headphones back on their hook, the chair set back under the desk.

We didn't find him until morning.

He was sitting in one of the seats attached to the steerable locator we had driven past on our way in. He must have known what to do because he had the headphones on, and one of his hands was still on the wheel that adjusted the angle of the receiver. The other chair was empty. The flattened disk was aimed out to sea, out to France, a few degrees above the horizon.

The thing was, they never did tell me *what* killed him—whether it was the gas, or being out all night in the cold, or whether he just grew tired and decided that was enough war for one lifetime. But what I do know is what I saw on his face when I found him. His eyes were closed, and there was nothing in his expression that said he'd been in pain when the end came.

Now, I know people'll tell you that faces relax when people die, that everyone ends up looking calm and peaceful, and as an ambulance man I won't deny it.

But this was something different. This was the face of a man listening to something very far away, something he had to really concentrate on, and not minding what he heard.

It was only later that we found the thing he had in his hand, the little piece of pink paper folded like an envelope.

Four days later I was able to visit George. He was in bed in one of the wards at Cranbrook. There were about five other men in the ward, most of them awake. George was looking better than when I'd last seen him, all messy and bandaged. He still had bandages on his head and arm, but they were much cleaner and neater now. His hair was combed, and his moustache had been trimmed.

"I'm glad you're still here, sir," I said. "I was frightened you'd be transferred back to Dungeness before I could get to see you. I'm afraid we've been a bit stretched the last few days." I had to raise my voice because Mr. Chamberlain was on the wireless in the corner of the ward doing one of his encouraging "one last push" speeches.

"Pull the screens," George said.

I did as I was told and sat down on the little stool next to his bed. The screens muffled some of Mr. Chamberlain's speech, but every now and then his voice seemed to push through the green curtains as if he were trying to reach me personally, the way a teacher might raise his voice to rouse a daydreaming boy at the back of the class.

"You're looking better, sir," I offered.

"Nothing time won't heal." He touched the side of his head with his good arm, the one that wasn't bandaged. "I'll be up on my feet in a week or two, then I'll get my new posting. No use for me in Dungeness anymore, though—my hearing's no longer tip-top."

"Won't it get better?"

"Perhaps, but that won't make much difference in the long run. They're getting rid of the sound mirrors.

We always knew it was coming, but we thought we'd be good for another year. It turns out that the new system won't need men listening on headphones. The new breed will stare at little screens, watching dots move around."

Mr. Chamberlain said something about "over by Christmas," followed by "looking forward to a bright and prosperous Nineteen Thirty-Six."

"And the music, sir?" I asked.

"There won't be any more music. Wherever it came from, whatever it was that let us hear it . . . it's gone now, or it will be gone by the time they tear down the mirrors. Even if it's still coming through to Dungeness, there won't be anyone there who can hear it. Best to forget about it now, Wally. I've no intention of speaking about it again, and with Ralph gone, that only leaves you. If you've an ounce of common sense— and I think you've rather more than an ounce—you'll say no more of this matter to any living soul."

"I'm sorry about Mr. Vaughan Williams, sir." I'd called him Ralph all the time I had known him, but sitting next to George I found myself coming over all formal. "He was always kind to me, sir, when we were doing our ambulance duties. Always treated me like an equal."

"He was a good man, no doubt about that." George said, nodding to himself. Then he patted the bedsheet. "Well, thank you for coming to visit, Wally. Knowing how busy you ambulance chaps are, I appreciate the gesture."

"There's another reason I came, sir. I mean, I wanted to see that you were all right. But I had something for you as well." I reached into my pocket and withdrew the folded piece of pink paper. "We found this on him. It's one of your transcriptions, I think."

"Let me see." George took the paper and opened it carefully. His eyes scanned the markings he had made on it, the scratchy lines of the staves and the little tadpole shapes of the notes. There were lots of blotches and crossings-out. "Did you see him do this?" he asked, looking at me over the edge of the paper.

"See him do what, sir?"

"He's corrected me! You wouldn't have noticed, but not all of those marks were made by me! The beggar must have sat down and taken the time to correct *my* transcription of *my* music!"

"When we were on our way to the shelter, sir?"

"Must have been, I suppose." George shook his head in what I took to be a mixture of dismay and amusement. "The absolute bare-faced effrontery!" Then he laughed. "He's right, though—that's the galling thing. He's bloody well right!"

"I thought you ought to have it, sir."

He began to fold the paper away. "That's very kind of you, Wally. It means a lot to me."

"There is something else, sir. When we found that sheet of paper on him, he'd folded something into it." I reached into my pocket again and drew out a small brass key. "I don't know what to make of this, sir. But I've a personal effects locker, and my key looks very similar. I think this might be the one to his locker." I felt as if I were about to start stammering. "The thing is, there *is* a locker, and no one's managed to get into it yet."

I passed the key to George.

"Why would he put his key in that piece of paper? Anything personal, he'd have wanted it sent on to Adeline."

"He must have known what he was doing, sir. You being a composer and all that . . . I just wondered . . ." I swallowed hard. "Sir, if there was music in that locker, he'd want you to see it first, wouldn't he?"

"What makes you think there might be music, Wally?"

"When you asked him if he'd written any of it down, he said he hadn't."

"But you wonder if he was telling a fib."

"It's a possibility, sir."

"It is indeed." George's hand closed slowly on the key. "I wonder if him correcting my music was a sign, you know? A way of giving me permission to correct his if I saw something in it I didn't think was right? Or at the very least giving me permission to tidy it up, to put it into some kind of order?"

"I don't know, sir. I suppose the only way of knowing would be to open the locker and see what's in it."

"And you haven't already done so?"

"I thought that would be a bit impertinent, sir, as he'd clearly meant for you to open it."

George passed the key back to me. "I can't wait. Go and see what's inside now, will you? I assume they'll let you?"

"I was his ambulance mate, sir. They'll let me anywhere."

"Then go to the locker. Open it and find his music, and bring it to me. But if you don't find anything . . . I should rather you didn't come back. I wouldn't like to see your face come through that door and then be disappointed. If there's something in there I must have, correspondence or suchlike, then you can have it sent to my bedside by one of the orderlies."

My hand closed on the key. "I hope I'm not wrong about this, sir."

"Me too," George said softly. "Me too."

"I won't be long."

I opened the curtain. The key was hard against my palm, digging into the flesh. Mr. Chamberlain was still going on, but no one seemed to be listening now. They had heard it all before.

# A FAMILY HISTORY

## *Paul Park*

Sailing to Egypt in the spring of 1798, General Bonaparte and his army passed within two miles of the English fleet, northeast of Malta in the middle of the night. What would have happened if Horatio Nelson had set a different course and had captured his enemy at sea?

Of course everything would have changed, instantly and for the better. Its revolution unchecked, France would have become a paradise on Earth, where free men and women raised their eyes from the dirt and stood up straight as if for the first time. Pigs would have learned to speak, donkeys to fly.

Colors would have been brighter, smells sweeter. The weather would improve. God would smile on France and all the French dominions. In June of 1815, gentle breezes would caress the empty fields of Waterloo. A system of high pressure would extend to the New World, and a midsummer hurricane would not rip apart the small, vulnerable French towns of Plaquemines Parish, Louisiana.

It would not destroy the farmhouse of François and Marie Louise de Fontenelle in Pointe à la Hache, a sliver of land between the swamp and the Mississippi River. It would not orphan their children, Amelie and Lucien, and force them to abandon the only home they knew and ride north along the makeshift levees

from which, years before, they had hailed the flotilla
of barges carrying General Bonaparte to New Orleans,
when he took up his duties there as governor.

Disconsolate, the two orphans would not have
found refuge with an aunt and uncle on the Rue des
Dryades in the capital of New France. They would not
grow up sullen and resentful in the grand house of
their relatives, treated like servants' children. At age
sixteen, Lucien would not steal his aunt's jewels and
run away. He would not join the crew of a flatboat
heading north, past the indigo and sugar plantations,
and then the cotton after that, and then the wilderness. Still shy of his seventeenth birthday, he would
not come to rest in the territory of the Omahas, at
Fort St. Jean on the west bank of the Missouri River,
penniless, his money spent.

Two years later, he would not send the following
letter:

"Ma Chere Soeur, my heart bleeds when I think of
you still in the clutches of that madwoman and her
nine-times–cuckolded husband. If there is anything
that mars my current exultation it is that. But let me
tell you what has happened here in this great country
that is as fresh as if God made it yesterday—no, as if
this is still the first morning of creation.

"I think of it that way even as I lie here on my
deathbed, too weak almost to raise my pen."

(In New Orleans, Amelie de Fontenelle would not
wonder at the crude, small, unfamiliar printing on the
envelope, the cherished hand inside. "Ah, is it true?"
she would be spared from thinking.)

"My sister, it is true. I have received a sword's thrust,
but the wound has festered. Yet even so I would change
nothing of that glorious afternoon when Colonel Berna-
dotte broke Jackson's lines, unless it were to spare
you unhappiness or to see my son Logan weaned from
his mother's breast, take his first steps. But like one
of Captain Ney's horse-soldiers at the top of the bluff,
or like a Pawnee warrior with his coup stick in his
hand, my thoughts have ridden far ahead of my story.

"My dear, I beg you to forget your pride and not turn your heart away from my infant son. I assure you, his blood is better than our blood. His grandfather is Big Elk, great chief of the Omahas, and his mother is Bright Sun—Me-um-ban-ne—oh, I would like you to meet her so that you might cherish her as a sister for my sake. Let me explain to you the method of my courtship, for even after everything I can't believe my luck or regret anything that has occurred. You must imagine me friendless and unhappy, hunting deer along the juncture where the Elkhorn meets the Platte. This was when the corn was small, and I came in through the fields of maize and beans. I left my horse and continued, finding the place deserted, or so I thought, because the tribe was hunting in the Sand Hills. I counted three-score lodges, which were mounds of raised earth, thatched with bluestem grass. I wandered among them. All their doors faced east, and all were blocked with an arrangement of dried sticks, so that the men could see if anyone had entered in their absence—all but one, thank God, and it the largest. I entered a low corridor in the earth and soon found myself in a dark space formed by a circle of wooden posts joined overhead by wooden rafters and a cage of willow wands. Light came from an opening in the grass roof, and I could see her sleeping on a raised platform like the princess in the story. Oh, she is so fair! It was in the afternoon, and the air was hot. I learned later she had hurt her foot, which was why she was sleeping in the middle of the day. She was not with the others in the fields, the old women and young children who kept the village while the tribe was hunting buffalo in the west. In this and everything I see the hand of Providence, for she was scarcely awake before we were man and wife, according to the simple ceremonies of her people. We scarcely had a word in common, but even so she begged me to stay, or else she begged me to leave before her mother returned—I would have pursued either course! But I was anxious to find the black-robe at the mission on

Council Bluff and to prepare everything our sainted mother might have asked. And though my wife clung to me, and though she wept, I asked her to be patient, as I would come back the next morning with the priest.

"I wish I had never left her. But even in this tragedy I see Fortune's hand. I would not have been able to prevent, by my presence, what occurred. That night the village was attacked by the vengeful and blood-thirsty Sioux, led by their chief and an American named Benjamin Burgess, also called 'the lion of Missouri.' 'The devil' would have been a better name—Captain Ney had already told me about him, when I saw him at the fort. Burgess was a spy in Jackson's pay. Always he was searching for a means to bring the tribes to warfare on both sides of the river, an excuse for the Americans to intercede. Life and property meant nothing to him. If he could steal away the favorite daughter of Big Elk while the camp was undefended . . .

"Once more I have charged ahead. That afternoon, when the shadows were longest, I reached the mission at Council Bluffs. I was looking for the black-robe, Father de Smet, whom I knew. But he had gone to baptize children in the Ponca villages along the valley of the Wolf River. Instead I found another, a Jesuit named Mylecraine.

"He has given me kindness, and with my wife he is tending to me now, and so I will describe him, a small man, even smaller than Governor Bonaparte when I saw him at the fort with Captain Ney. During the time I have known him, I have never seen him shave his beard, and yet his face is soft, his hands childlike and delicate. I say this to emphasize by contrast the courage he has shown. He is from Brittany, and he studied music before turning to God. Even now he takes his wooden flute and flageolets among the tribes, and I have seen the battle-scarred warriors of the Omaha sit round him in a circle, their faces soft with wonder and delight.

"That evening when I came to him, he packed up his flute first of all. He had seen Bright Sun that winter, when he was a guest in her father's lodge. And though he scolded me for the precipitateness of my wooing, he was smiling as I was, without any notion or thought that at that moment already Bright Sun's mother lay dead, as well as four of the old braves who had not ridden with the others, and several children also, because of the savagery of the Sioux chieftain, Goes-to-War, as well as Burgess the American, whom later I shot down.

"By that time it was dark, and Father Mylecraine and I stayed in the mission. Early the next morning we set off, as joyful as you please. Because he was fluent in all the tongues of the Indians, I was eager, with his help, to explain my wife future to her, how she would accompany us to Bellevue and take up residence. Alas, I was full of plans. Before noon we reached the site of the catastrophe. All was in chaos, and I spent more than an hour helping Father Mylecraine attend to the wounded, while at the same time searching for Bright Sun. There were no horses at the village, so I let one eight-year-old boy take the pony I had brought for my bride and her possessions; he started off along the Platte to discover Big Elk's camp, a distance of a hundred leagues. With the priest's help, another boy told me what I wanted to know, how he had seen Burgess with his fringed coat and beaver hat—the lion, as he called him, but I knew who he was: a huge man with yellow hair down his back, his yellow beard high on his cheeks—there were not two like him in the territory. Even though she could scarcely walk, he had taken Big Elk's daughter across his saddlebow and ridden north into the land of the Oglala Sioux. Anyone could see where the war party had passed. Furious, I rode out after them, following the track, even though Mylecraine begged me to wait while we fetched the soldiers from the fort—there was no time for that! Nor could the captain have left St. Jean to intervene in a dispute between the tribes, not with

General Jackson massing on the other side of the Missouri; beyond question, it was Burgess' plan to drive a wedge between the French and the Omahas, to force Captain Ney to choose between disappointing his allies and abandoning his post.

"I followed the trail of the Oglala, two or three score, it seemed to me. But when I came to the side of the ravine, where the track led downhill toward Sarpy's ford, I saw one horse break away. I was looking for the print of its shoes, a larger horse than any Indian's, and heavily loaded, and shod in the fashion of the United States' Cavalry—I knew what I saw. I thought Burgess would try to remove my wife across the river for safekeeping, perhaps because he thought the Sioux would murder her or worse or otherwise do damage to his schemes. Or else he wanted her for himself. In both cases it made me wild with rage. I pressed my mare forward, and as darkness fell I saw a campfire along the ridge, still on this side of the river, for which I thanked God.

"I loaded my long musket and crept up through the juniper trees. The moon was high and small. With as much stealth as I had, I crept up the ravine outside the glow of the fire, by whose flickering light I saw my wife among the stones, her head bowed, her hands tied in front of her as if in prayer. I can tell you, my heart boiled in my chest. Ben Burgess sprawled beside her, a chunk of roasted deer-meat on the end of his knife. He kept no ceremony with her—his collar was undone, his sleeves rolled up. His yellow beard merged with the hair of his fat chest and shoulders—truly, he was hairy as an animal! And he was no bashful or tongue-tied lover, but spoke freely in the language of the Omahas, laughing and muttering as if all this were a joke! He threw down his knife and lifted up instead a cup of whiskey, which I could determine from the smell. He thrust it into my wife's face. And when she raised her head, and when I saw her expression of despair and passive courage, I thought I could contain myself no longer. I must challenge the lion in his lair, even though I could see Burgess' pistol laid out on the stones, already cocked and primed. But in my rashness I discovered I had climbed into a trap, because no sooner had I stood up and thrust forward into the circle of the light, no sooner had I uttered my first cry, than one of the cursed Indians, his face still painted like a devil's, rose from beneath my feet and knocked my gun aside. He was a brave in his first season, younger than myself, bare chested despite the cold, with broken feathers in his hair. Burgess had not risen to his feet, as politeness or prudence would have required. 'Oho!' he said, still sprawled next to my wife, 'we have a guest. But if it isn't Monsieur Fontenelle!'—he spoke in English. 'What a surprise! But I suppose you're a regular tear-cat, now!'

"How can I describe the expression on my wife's face when she saw me—Bright Sun indeed, but streaked with clouds of anguish and despair. The Indian had his knife at my throat, and he dragged me forward into the firelight. I held out my hand as if to reassure her, but at the same time I saw nothing but blackness ahead of us, as if she and I together had been swallowed up in darkness or the shadow of the pit. I felt darkness overwhelm me, and I raised my hand to push it away, push its shadows from my eyes. The sharp steel was at my throat.

"At that moment, as the darkness threatened to surround me, I heard a noise from away down the hill. I heard a few soft, breathy notes, the low murmur of the black-robe's wooden flute, an air from his native Brittany . . ."

I have seen a photograph of Amelie de Fontenelle, taken when she was in her sixties after the end of the Civil War. She is dressed in mourning. Gray ringlets hang down underneath a white lace cap.

No photograph or painted portrait still exists of her brother Lucien. He was a famous trapper and mountain man, who established a trading post at Bellevue, Nebraska, in the eighteen twenties. His wife was an

Omaha princess named Bright Sun. His only child, Logan, was the chief who bartered the land of the Omahas to the United States government after small-pox had destroyed the tribes. In 1855 he was scalped and murdered by the Dakota Sioux. His father did not live to see it; Lucien Fontenelle was dead from alcohol, or typhus, or suicide by that time, an ugly man, according to letters and journals of various pioneers, with a face like a monkey.

But what if his mother in Pointe à la Hache had not eaten too heavily one evening when she was pregnant, had not dreamed her monkey dream? What if Madame Mercier had been a different kind of woman, one who had taken to heart, perhaps, the great victory off Malta in 1798, when Horatio Nelson's flagship had sunk with all hands? She would have been just a girl, impressionable and easily influenced, perhaps, by the celebrations in the streets. Later on, she might have been overjoyed to take into her home her brother's children after the catastrophe. She might have loaded them with kindness. Stuck in a loveless marriage, she might have felt herself responding to the handsome young Lucien despite the difference in their ages. Generous, open hearted, and naïve, perhaps she could not guard her nephew from the maniacal and sadistic Dr. Mercier, who would have driven the boy not just from the city but from the entire territory of New France—up the Mississippi and then east up the Ohio to the Kentucky wilderness. Several years later he might have sent his sister the following letter:

"Ma Chere Soeur, my heart bleeds when I think of you still in the grip of that madman—I do not speak of my aunt. But I must tell you what has happened in case the worst comes to the worst. I lie here wounded, close to death, shot down by Douglas Sharpe and my erstwhile companions . . ."

(In New Orleans, Amelie de Fontenelle might have wondered at the careful, feminine handwriting on the envelope. "Ah, is it true?" she might have thought.)

"Dear heart, it is true. And so I must leave a record

of what has happened, for you to join together with your memory of our life together in Pointe à la Hache—ah, such times seem a paradise to me. In this way I might feel that my life has a pattern, however fitful and provisional, however much it loops upon itself, as if I were a plaything for an arbitrary and erratic God. I also must inform you of what I most believe: that a war is coming, despite the wisdom of the emperor and his well-known sympathy for the rights of his native subjects, the appeal they have made to his own wild nature. The land is too empty on our side of the river. To the east the land fills up like water in a cup, and the time will come when it will burst its bounds.

"I have seen this at first hand, from the day I left the blessed shore of New France to assume my exile among these Americans. I suppose you must imagine me miserable, bedraggled, without funds, alone in an English-speaking land. Never mind how, but I found myself in a country called the Barrens, in the parish of Edmonson, along the banks of the Green River. This was a terrible desolation, as vast and lonely as the desolation in my heart, a sere expanse of hills and limestone knobs, with dark forests of blackjack trees in the crevices between them. Everywhere were fissures in the earth such as could swallow up a man on horseback—remnants of the earthquake that formed that country in the early days and whose instability can still be felt.

"In this dereliction, though, I found a refuge on a little farm, a few dozen acres and a log cabin chinked with mud, a few rooms to let to travelers. And you will understand what I mean when I suggest that the proprietress of this establishment reminded me of our dear aunt in her kindness toward an orphan far from home. Her name was Madame Mylecraine, but I did not think there was a monsieur, despite the presence of a dark-eyed and dark-skinned boy named Logan on the premises. You see I must describe these things as I first perceived them, not as I learned subsequently. She also had come a long way, because her father was a native of the Island of Man, and she spoke in the Manx language with a hired hand about the place. Oh, there is much for me to tell you. One thing at a time. I pray for strength to reach the end.

"She is small, formed like a woman and a child at the same time, although her hair already holds a silver frost—in this she also reminds me of our dear aunt. She has green eyes, I suppose. On my third night in that house, as I lay sobbing on my bed, she came into my room—these are spaces scarcely large enough to let the door open inward. She stood at the threshold carrying a stick, I thought—the light was behind her and I could not make it out. But I imagined the cudgel in my uncle's hand, as he stood on the landing of the stairs (Oh, I pray that he is dead, and he torments you no longer!), until she moved. Then the light from the hurricane lantern touched her hair and the stick at the same time, revealing it to be a silver flute. She did not blow into it or touch its keys, but she showed it to me only, as if the fact of its existence could be a source of hope. It was outdoors that she played it, as well as a small flageolet or piccolo, a wild, ferocious sound! It was only later that I heard it, after I had revealed to her some news that agitated her in a way I did not understand. In my clumsy English I explained that I had taken employment. I thought she would be pleased! But I was to be a member of the party that would search out and apprehend a highwayman or bandit who preyed on travelers along the road; he always took refuge in one of the huge caves in that area, the largest one, in fact, which stretched many leagues under the earth from the great pit that was its entrance. A Captain Douglas Sharpe had undertaken to search him out.

"This was in the month of October. When I explained it to Madame Mylecraine, in the great room by the fire, I thought she would approve of me, if only because I would be able to pay my way—there were rumors, as always in such places, of buried treasure in the cave.

Instead she was angry and distraught and asked me what I knew of this fellow, Leon Benbourgisse—an uncouth name! I answered what I had been told, that he was a mongrel or half-breed of prodigious strength who had robbed a number of rich gentlemen on horseback and murdered one of them, so that travelers now avoided the entire locality. I thought she would be grateful to dispose of such a one! Instead she said nothing and turned away from me. This was in the evening, when the lamps were lit. She put her kerchief over her head and went out.

"I waited for her to return. When she did not, I went in search of her. In time I followed not her footsteps or the shadow of her passing but a sound at the limit of my hearing, a melody from the Celtic islands, or Brittany, or Acadia, as you and I have heard together from the players in the Place D'Armes. I found her in a seam of sunken rocks below a limestone cliff, a place of evil reputation in that country, if one can judge from the name of Devil's Twist. It was a place where she went to be alone, and I followed the note of her piccolo, which in that amphitheater swelled among the rocks, even though she played quite softly, as I perceived. She had pulled away her kerchief, undone her long hair. When I kicked some stones to alert her to my presence, she turned suddenly, as if from a guilty secret. The music broke as if snapped off. When she saw who it was, she came to me. She took my hand and begged me to consider the extremities of fate that might drive a good man underground, the injustice that might force him to lash out against his tormenters. 'I will not go,' I said. 'Not if you forbid it.' But instead she asked me to continue the next morning to the muster at the gulf of Mammoth Cave so that I could be her eyes in that dark place. So small she was! Almost like a child. I reached to wipe away her tears, to comfort her like a child and a woman— you and I both know that is possible!

"The next morning I rendered myself at the top of the pit, at a distance from the farmhouse of two leagues or else some miles—I will give these measurements in the English fashion, as they were explained to me. We crossed over the stile of fence rails that blocked our way and continued down the ravine at a distance of a hundred feet below the surface of the plain. On each side of the dry streambed we found oak trees and chestnuts, as well as elms and maples and a proliferation of vines and brambles, in all a far greater variety than anything to be found up on the flat. When I remarked on this, my companions first explained to me one of the enduring mysteries of this place, which as we sank down appeared more and more dismal and terrible to me, darker and colder, though it was a bright, hot morning when I left Madame Mylecraine's farm. There is a wind that issues back and forth out of the cave, as if from a bellows or the lips of a stone giant, a breath that is most healthful and bountiful. Consumptive patients, I was told, after all hope was abandoned, could take up residence in the mouth of the Vestibule and be cured in a matter of days. This was first reported in the days of the last war, because the floors of the first galleries are rich in nitre, which is used in the manufacture of gunpowder. Even now we could see the remnants of the abandoned works, while the guides told us stories of their uncles or fathers who had emerged from the pit with their backs straight and their eyes keen, their ponies glossy and well-tempered. I thought at first they were deceiving me.

"But now we stood on a grassy terrace above the entrance, a steep descent to the black arch, choked with planks and timbers, while water dripped down from above. And for the first time I could feel the cold, sepulchral blast, while I watched the swallows dart through the thin water, and at the same time I listened to our commander, Captain Douglas Sharpe, as he explained our tasks. There were twenty-five of us, divided into groups of five.

"Now we also received our iron torches and a bucket of lard among each group. We filled our canteens from the brook and primed our pistols. But we could not light the swinging lanterns in the wind until we had descended beneath the great portal and sixty paces into the cave itself. Here the roof was just a foot above my head. The passage was constricted by a wall built by the miners, leaving only a narrow door. The wind blew like a winter storm, and we must grope forward in the dark. A few feet beyond the wall, the air was calm and still.

"Here we lit our lamps and pressed forward in single file. We stayed in this low, narrow corridor for perhaps a quarter of a mile until it opened out into the Vestibule, a round chamber perhaps two hundred feet across, and the ceiling sixty feet above our heads. Black buttresses of stone jutted from the shadowy walls. Our party of twenty-five had seemed sufficient in the narrow entrance to the cave. But as we pressed forward into the Grand Gallery we seemed small and few. We picked our way among the leaching vats and wooden pipes. We skirted mounds of excavated earth, while for the first time I gave credence to the stories I had heard outside, that the miners in their excavations had disturbed a cemetery of gigantic corpses, ten feet long. It was easy to imagine giants in this place, and to imagine also the ghostly presence of the aboriginal inhabitants of North America, specters from the more recent past.

"As it turned out, this was no idle speculation. Because of it, I was able to find our quarry where the rest failed. For by the light of my swinging torch I descried piles of blackened rushes and abandoned canes, which the Cherokees had used to light their way. As we spread out into the side passages—the Haunted Chambers, as they are called, and the Bridges with their gleaming stalactites—I found myself looking always for these traces that, though ephemeral, seemed more trustworthy (I don't know why!) than the arrows marked in chalk to indicate the correct route or warn me from the brink of some precipice or pit. At the same time it occurred to me what in some fashion I must already have known, that Leon Benbourgisse and his accomplices must have another means of egress from the cave. Else they could not fail to be taken in the Narrows.

"And so as much as I was full of wonder at the dismal choirs of rock, the ghostly chapels with their dripping columns sixty feet above my head, I found myself studying the ground as well, looking for marks of the outlaw's passage. I remembered the way Madame Mylecraine had leaped to his defense and wondered at the connection between them. At the same time I first noticed a shard of broken pottery such as is often found where Cherokees have camped—a distinctive piece, ridges of black on a dull surface. I swung my lantern over one of these, allowing my companions to go ahead. I thought I had seen several of these shards, broken into rough trapezoids, and resolved to look for them. I passed by the Devil's Looking Glass, a sheet of fallen rock. And in a chamber called the Snow Room, where any shout or call brings from the ceiling a shower of crystal flakes, I found what I was looking for—away from the path, where the salt dust was undisturbed, a piece of my broken pot, and beyond a naked footprint.

"I let the torches diminish as the men passed into the Deserted Chamber. I did not call them back. To do so would have dusted me as if with snow. Instead I remembered my promise to Madame Mylecraine, or Kate, as she would have had me call her. With my lantern held in front, I took a few steps forward, around a buttress of the rock. There was a twisting corridor, another piece of pottery. Fifty yards on, I found a hole, a round passage perhaps four feet tall, and in front of it, another footprint.

"Like Robinson Crusoe, I crouched over it. My dear sister, I do not know why I continued, except because there are always choices of this nature in the lives of men, to creep forward in the dark or else fall back. I could feel a wind from the round hole, not enough to threaten my flame. I knelt and pushed up an ascending passage until it opened up into a great space. My light could not reach the ceiling. And I found myself at the edge of a cliff. A spar or promontory of rock protruded thirty feet over the black chasm, ending in a rough point. From the cliff I could see no trace of the far wall, or of the bottom, or of the roof. It was a place at the edge of the world, a strip of rock that passed into the darkness at both sides. I crossed it in five paces, shuffling through the half-burned canes that were as thick here as the saline crystals had been back beyond the hole, piles of them.

"I stretched my lamp over the abyss. Now I could hear at a great distance the rushing of a stream, while some wisps of vapor lifted toward the light. And I could see also the remnants of a painted geometric pattern on the limestone promontory, even on the underside, daubed there by some brave or chief's son as he hung suspended over the depths. On the top I saw three timbers wrapped in bundles of bleached cloth, carved poles or images sacred to the first inhabitants of that place and hidden there, I guessed, from men like me.

"Nor could I keep from my mind the rumors I had heard of buried treasure, purses robbed along the road or the lost gold of these ancient tribes. Even though I understood the foolishness of such tales, I could not stop myself from setting my lantern in a crevice in the rock, carved there, as I saw, for the purpose. On my hands and knees, I climbed out on the base of the promontory, placing my feet in the shallow steps. And I had just promised myself to turn back, to abandon this search or else to call out to my friends, as I still supposed them to be. But then I heard a noise behind me, the chink of an iron chain, while at the same time the light trembled. I turned to see a man against the rock wall behind me, though whether he had followed me out of the hole or had crept toward me from somewhere further on along the ledge, I could not then determine. For a moment I was motionless with horror, because I was convinced that this was Benbourgisse himself, a huge man clad only in leather breeches, with naked legs and a black, naked, hairless chest. He had no beard and no hair on his oiled scalp. He pulled at the swinging torch, and when he turned to me and smiled, his features showed his Cherokee or African parentage. But more horrifying still was what he intended at that moment, as I saw him wrench the iron bar from its crevice in the rocks. Ah, God, he could not leave me here, and so I gathered myself on my stone promontory and leaped at him across the intervening space. In the middle of my jump, he swung the lantern toward me, only high beyond my grasp, launching it out over the abyss, where it fell and was extinguished at once.

"How can I explain to you the terror that I felt, to find myself encased in darkness as I moved? No light, no light at all, darker than night, darker than when you close your eyes, darker, I suppose, than blindness. Every act is an act of faith. I scrambled up toward the wall where I had seen him, guided only by his low chuckle and his soft exhale. But in my desperation I found him and grabbed hold of him, only to feel myself suddenly overpowered, the pistol snatched from my belt, while at the same time I could smell his whiskey-soaked breath and hear his voice muttering as if inside my ear itself, 'Well, ain't you a regular tear-cat, sure enough?'

"Then I could feel his arms tighten around my chest, and it occurred to me that he could crush my bones between his hands or that he could cast me over the lip of the abyss, to follow the light downward forever. He could not be resisted, because he had drunk so deeply from the cave's air. My eyes stared in the darkness, and as I felt the breath crushed out of me, I cried out, 'Please, I have a message from Mistress Mylecraine!'

"Suddenly I was released, flung a little distance onto the stone ground. I saw nothing, smelled nothing, heard nothing, while at the same time I did not dare to move, because I could not guess how far I cowered from the edge of the precipice, or even which direction it lay. I crouched as if at the bottom of my own grave. I raised my face up to the vault above me, imagining at some moment I might hear the strains of a silver flute, an air or melody from the Isle of Man, guiding me upward, always upward into the light of day."

In the big house on the Rue de Dryades, Lucien's lonely and brokenhearted sister might have wiped away a tear.

And though desperate to leave the house of Monsieur and Madame Mercier, still she might not have married at her first opportunity an American lawyer with whom she did not even share a language. Their daughter, Justine Lockett, would not have died in prison waiting for trial after she'd been arrested carrying letters and supplies through the Union lines at Petersburg. A widow, she would not have left young children, one of whom, my great-grandmother, would not have gone north to Virginia to live with her father's family. She would not have married William R. McKenney, a congressman and judge. Her granddaughter would not have met my father, who himself would never have existed for different but related reasons. Sixty years later, a diminutive universe of speculation would have been snuffed out.

# DOG-EARED PAPERBACK OF MY LIFE

## *Lucius Shepard*

My name, Thomas Cradle, is not the most common of names, yet when I chanced upon a book written by another Thomas Cradle while looking up my work on Amazon (a pastime to which I, like many authors, am frequently given), I thought little of it, and my overriding reaction was one of concern that this new and unknown Cradle might prove the superior of the known. I became even more concerned when I learned that the book, *The Tea Forest*, was a contemporary fantasy, this being the genre into which my own books were slotted. Published in 2002, it was ranked 1,478,040 in Amazon sales, a fact that eased my fears somewhat. According to the reader reviews (nine of them in sum, all five stars), the book was a cult item, partly due to its quality and partly because the author had disappeared in Cambodia not long after its publication. I found it odd that I hadn't heard of Cradle and his novel before; out of curiosity, I ordered a used copy and put the incident from mind.

The book arrived ten days later, while I was proofing my new novel, working on a screenplay based on my third novel, for which I was being paid a small fortune, and negotiating to buy a home in the Florida Keys, a property to which some of the screenplay money would be applied. The package lay on my desk unopened for several weeks, buried under papers. By the time I got around to opening it, I had forgotten what it was I ordered. My copy of the *The Tea Forest* turned out to be a dog-eared trade paperback, the pages crimped and highlighted in yellow marker throughout, rife with marginalia. On the cover, framed by green borders, was a murky oil painting depicting a misted swamp with an almost indistinguishable male figure slogging though waist-deep water. I looked on the spine. The publisher was Random House, also my publisher. That made it doubly odd that I hadn't heard of the book. What the hell, I asked myself, were they doing publishing two Thomas Cradles in the same genre? And why hadn't my editor or agent made me aware of this second Cradle?

I turned the book over and glanced at the tiny author photo, which showed a bearded, unkempt man glaring with apparent contempt at the camera. I skimmed the blurbs, the usual glowing overstatement, and read the bio:

"Thomas Cradle was born in Carboro, North Carolina in 1968. He attended the University of Virginia for two years before dropping out and has traveled widely in Asia, working as a teacher of English and martial arts. He currently lives in Phnom Penh. *The Tea Forest* is his first novel."

A crawly sensation moved down my neck and spread to my shoulders. Not only did Cradle and I share a name, we had been born in the same town in the same year and had attended the same university (though I had graduated). I'd also trained in Muay Thai and Shotokan karate during high school—if not for a herniated disc, I might have pursued these interests. I had a closer look at the author photo. Lose the beard, shorten the hair, drop twenty-five pounds and six years, and he might have been my twin. The contemptuous glare alone should have made the likeness apparent.

Someone, I told myself, was playing a practical joke, someone who knew me well enough to predict my reactions. When I opened the book, something would pop out or a bad smell would be released . . . or perhaps it would be a good-natured joke. Kim, my girlfriend, had the wherewithal to doctor an old photograph and dummy up a fake book, but I would not have thought she possessed the requisite whimsy. I dipped into the first chapter, expecting the punchline would be revealed in the text; but after five chapters I recognized that the book could not be the instrument of a prank, and my feeling of unease returned.

The novel documented a trip down the Mekong River taken by four chance acquaintances, beginning in Stung Treng on the Cambodian-Lao border, where the four had purchased a used fishing boat, to Dong Thap Province in the extreme south of Vietnam. It was an unfinished journey fraught with misadventure and illness, infused with a noirish atmosphere of low-level criminality, and culminated with a meditation on suicide that may well have foreshadowed the author's fate.

Judging by the wealth and authenticity of the background detail and by the precisely nuanced record of the first-person narrator's emotional and mental life, the novel was thinly disguised autobiography; and the configuration of the narrator's thoughts and perceptions seemed familiar, as did the style in which the novel was written: It was my style. Not the style in which I currently wrote, but the style I had demonstrated at the start of my career, prior to being told by an editor that long, elliptical sentences and dense prose would be an impediment to sales (she counseled the use of "short sentences, less navel-gazing, more plot," advice I took to heart). Cradle Two's novel was no mere pastiche; it was that old style perfected, carried off with greater expertise than I had ever displayed. It was as if he had become the writer I had chosen not to be.

I went to Amazon again, intending to have another

look at the webpage devoted to *The Tea Forest* and perhaps find the author's contact information; but I could not locate the page, and there was no evidence anywhere on the Internet of a second Thomas Cradle or his novel. I tried dozens of searches, all to no avail. I emailed the seller, Overdog Books, asking for any information they might have on the author; they denied having sold me the book. I sent them a scan of the packing slip, along with a note that accused them of being in collusion with one of my enemies, most likely another writer who, envious of my success, was mocking me. They did not respond. I riffled through the pages of the novel, half-expecting it to dematerialize along with the proof of its existence. I had often made the comment that if ever I were presented with incontrovertible evidence of the fantastic, I would quit writing and become a priest. Though I was not yet prepared to don the cassock, the book in my hands seemed evidence of the kind I had demanded.

The narrative of the *The Tea Forest* was episodic, heavy on the descriptive passages, many of them violent or explicitly sexual; and these episodes were strung together on a flimsy plotline that essentially consisted of a series of revelations, all leading the narrator (TC by name, thereby firmly establishing that Cradle Two had not overstrained his imagination during this portion of the creative process) to conclude that our universe and those adjoining it were interpenetrating. He likened this circumstance to countless strips of wet rice paper hung side by side in a circle and blown together by breezes that issued from every quarter of the compass, allowing even strips on opposite points of the circle to stick to each other for a moment and, in some instances, for much longer; thus, he concluded, we commonly spent portions of each day in places far stranger than we were aware (although the universes appeared virtually identical). This, he declared, explained why people in rural circumstances experienced paranormal events more often than urban dwellers: They were likely to notice unusual events, whereas city folk might mistake a ghost for a new form of advertising, or attribute the sighting of an enormous shadow in the Hudson River to chemicals in the air, or pay no attention to the fact that household objects were disappearing around them. It also might explain, I realized, why I was no longer able to unearth any record of the novel.

I had the book copied and bound and FedExed the copy to my agent. The cover letter explained how I had obtained it and asked him to find out whatever he could. He called two mornings later to congratulate me on a stroke of marketing genius, saying that *The Tea Forest* could be another Blair Witch and that this hoax concerning a second Thomas Cradle was a brilliant way of preparing the market for the debut of my "new" style. When I told him it wasn't a hoax, as far as I knew, he said not to worry, he'd never tell, and declared that if Random House wouldn't go for the book, he'd take me over to Knopf. At this juncture, I began to acknowledge that the universe might be as Cradle Two described, and, since there would be no one around to charge me with plagiarism, I saw no reason not to profit from the book; but I told him to hold off on doing anything, that I needed to think it through and, before all else, I might be traveling to Cambodia and Vietnam.

The idea for the trip was little more than a whim, inspired by my envy of Cradle Two and the lush deviance of his life, as evidenced by *The Tea Forest*; but over the ensuing two months, as I reread sections of the novel, committing many of them to memory, the richness of the prose infected me with Cradle Two's obsessiveness (which, after all, was a cousin to my own), and I came to speculate that if I retraced his steps (even if they were steps taken in another universe), I might derive some vital benefit. There was a mystery here that wanted unraveling, and there was no one more qualified than I to investigate it. While I hadn't entirely accepted his rice paper model of the universe, I believed that if his analogy held water, I might be able to perceive its operations more clearly through the simple lens of a river culture. However, one portion of the novel gave me reason for concern. The narrator, TC, had learned during the course of his journey that in one alternate universe he was a secretive figure of immense power, evil in nature, and that his innumerable analogs were, to some degree or another, men of debased character. The final section of the book suggested that he had undergone a radical transformation, and that idea was supported by a transformation in the prose. Under other circumstances, I would have perceived this to be a typical genre resolution, but Cradle Two's sentences uncoiled like vipers waking under the reader's eye, spitting out a black stream of venom from which the next serpent would slither, dark and supple, sleekly malformed, governed by an insidious sonority that got into my head and stained my dreams and my work for days thereafter. Eventually I convinced myself that Cradle Two's gift alone was responsible for this dubious magic and that it had been done for dramatic effect and was in no way a reflection of reality.

The book, the actual object, became an article of my obsession. I liked touching it. The slickness of the cover; the tacky spot on the back where a clerk or prior owner had spilled something sticky or parked a wad of chewing gum; the neat yet uninspired marginalia; the handwritten inscription, "To Tracy," and the anonymity of the dedication, "For you"; the faintly yellowed paper; the tear on page 19. All its mundane imperfections seemed proofs of its otherworldliness, that another world existed beyond the enclosure of my own, and I began carrying the book with me wherever I went, treating it as though it were a lover, fondling it, riffling its pages, fingering it while I drove, thinking about it to the point of distraction, until the idea of the trip evolved from a whim into a project I seriously considered, and then into something more. Though was ordinarily a cynical type, dismissive of any opinion arguing the thesis that life was anything other than a cruel and random process, my affair with the book persuaded me that destiny had taken a hand in my life, and I would be a fool not to heed it (I think every cynic's brassbound principles can be as easily overthrown). And so, tentatively to begin with, yet with growing enthusiasm, I started to make plans. As a writer, I delighted in planning, in charting the course of a story, in assembling the elements of a fiction into a schematic, and I plotted the trip as though it were a novel that hewed to (but was not limited by) the picaresque flow of Cradle Two's voyage along the Mekong. There would be a woman, of course—perhaps two or three women—and here a dash of adventure, here a time for rest and reflection, here the opportunity for misadventure, here a chance for love, and here a chance for disappointment. I laid in detail with the care of a master craftsman attempting a delicate mosaic, leaving only one portion undone: the ending. That would be produced by the alchemy of the writing or, in this instance, the traveling.

I intended to hew closely in spirit to the debauched tenor of Cradle Two/TC's journey, and I hoped that by setting up similar conditions, I might have illuminations similar to his; but I saw no purpose in duplicating its every detail—I expected my journey to be a conflation of his experience. The lion's share of his troubles on the trip had stemmed from his choice of boats, so rather than buying a leaky fishing craft with an unreliable engine for cheap, I arranged to have a houseboat built in Stung Treng. The cost was negligible, four thousand dollars, half up front, for a shallow-draft boat capable of sleeping four with a fully equipped galley and a new engine. Once I completed the trip, I intended to donate it to charity, a Christian act that, given the boat's value in U.S. dollars, would allow me to take a tax write-off of several times that amount. I informed Kim that I'd be going away for six to eight weeks, roughing it (she considered any activity that occurred partially outdoors to be roughing it) on the Mekong, far from five-star hotels and haute cuisine, and that she was welcome to hook up with me in Saigon, where suitable amenities were available. However, I cautioned her that I would be attempting to recreate the mood described in *The Tea Forest*, and this meant I would be seeing other women. Perhaps, I suggested, she should seize the opportunity to spread her wings.

Kim, a tall, striking brunette, had an excellent mind, a background in microbiology, and a scientist's dispassionate view of human interactions. We had discussed marriage and discussed rather more the possibility of having children, but until we reached that pass, she was comfortable with maintaining an open relationship. She told me to be careful, a reference both to safe sex and to the problems I'd had in compartmentalizing my emotional life, and gave me her blessing. I then contacted my agent and instructed him to sell *The Tea Forest* while I was gone. These formalities out of the way, I had little left to do except lose some weight for the trip and cultivate a beard—I thought this would help get me into character—and wait for the end of the fall monsoon.

I flew to Bangkok and there took passage on the Ubon Ratchatani Express toward the Lao border, berthed in an old-fashioned sleeping car with curtained fold-down beds on both sides of the aisle. I spent a goodly portion of the evening in the bar car, which reeked of garlic and chilis and frying basil, drinking bad Thai beer, trying to acclimate myself to the heat that poured through the lowered windows. From Ubon, I traveled by bus to Stung Treng, a dismal town of about twenty-five thousand at the confluence of the Mekong, the Sesan, and the Sekong Rivers. It was a transit point for backpackers, a steady trickle of them, the majority remaining in town no more than a couple of hours, the length of time it took for the next river taxi to arrive. I had thought to pick up a companion in one of the larger Cambodian towns downriver, but as I would be trapped in Stung

Treng for three days while the boat was being fitted
and provisioned, I posted signs at the border, in the
open-air market, and around town, advertising a cruise
aboard the *Undine* (the name of my houseboat) in
exchange for personal services. Women only. See the
bartender at the Sekong Hotel.

I was heading back to the hotel, passing through
the market when a mural painted on a noodle stall
caught my eye. Abstract in form, a yellowish white
mass of cells or chambers, spreading over the front
and both sides of the stall—though crudely rendered,
I had the idea that it was the depiction of microscopic
life, one of those multicelled monstrosities that you
become overly familiar with in Biology 101. It was
such an oddity (most of the stalls were unadorned, a
handful decorated with religious iconography), I stopped
to look and immediately drew a gathering of young
men, curious to see what had made me curious and
taking the opportunity to offer themselves as guides,
procurers, and so forth. The stallkeeper, an elderly
Laotian man, grew annoyed with these loiterers, but
I gave him a handful of Cambodian riels, enough to
purchase noodles for my new pals, and asked (through
the agency of an interpreter—one of the men spoke
English) what the mural represented.

"He don't know," said the interpreter. "He say it
make peaceful to look at. It make him think of Nirvana. You know Nirvana?"

"Just their first couple of albums," I said. "Ask him
who painted it."

This question stimulated a brief exchange, and the
interpreter reported that the artist had been an American. Big like me. More hair. A bad man. I asked him
to inquire in what way the man had been bad, but the
stallkeeper would only say (or the interpreter could
only manage to interpret) that the man was "very
bad." I had only skimmed the last half of *The Tea
Forest*, but I seemed to recall a mention of a creature
like that depicted by the mural, and I suspected that

the mural and the bad man who had created it might be evidence supporting Cradle Two's theories.

That afternoon I staked out a table in the Sekong's bar and was amazed by how many women volunteered for my inspection. Two balked at the sexual aspects of the position, and others were merely curious; but eleven were serious applicants, willing and, in some cases, eager to trade their favors for a boat ride and whatever experiences it might afford them. I rejected all but four out of hand for being too young or insufficiently attractive. The first day's interviews yielded one maybe, a thirty-four-year-old Swedish schoolteacher who was making her way around the world and had been traveling for almost five years; but she seemed to be looking for a place to rest, and rest was the last thing on my mind.

The bar was a pleasant enough space—walls of split, lacquered bamboo decorated with travel posters, Cambodian pop flowing from hidden speakers, and a river view through screen windows. A standing floor fan buzzed and whirred in one corner, yet it was so humid that the chair stuck to my back, and the smells drifting up from the water grew less enticing as the hours wore on. Late on the second day, I was almost ready to give up, when a slender, long-legged woman with dyed black hair (self-barbered, apparently, into a ragged pageboy cut), camo parachute pants, and an oft-laundered Olivia Tremor Control T-shirt approached the bar. She unshouldered her backpack and spoke to the bartender. I signaled to him that she passed muster. He pointed me out, and she came toward my table but pulled up short a couple of feet away.

"Oh, gosh!" she said. "You're Thomas Cradle, aren't you?"

Flattered at being recognized, I said that I was.

"This is fantastic!" She came forward again, dragging the backpack. "I shall have to tell my old boyfriend. He's a devoted fan of yours, and he'll be terribly impressed. Of course, that would make it necessary to speak with him again, wouldn't it?"

She was more interesting-looking than pretty, yet pretty enough, with lively topaz eyes and one of those superprecise British accents that linger over each and every syllable, delicately tonguing the consonants, as if giving the language a blowjob.

"It's hellish outside," she said. "I must have a cold drink. Would you care for something?"

Her face, which I'd initially thought too young, mistaking her for a gangly teenager, had a waiflike quality; a white scar over one eyebrow and small indentations along her jaw, perhaps resulting from adolescent acne, added a decade to my estimate.

"I'll take a Green Star, thanks," I said. "No ice."

"Gin for me. Tons of ice." Her mouth, bracketed when she smiled by finely etched lines, was extraordinarily wide and expressive, appearing to have an extra hinge that enabled her crooked grin. "I'll just fetch them, shall I?"

She brought the drinks, had a sip, closed her eyes, and sighed. Then she extended a hand, shook mine, and said, "I'm Lucy McQuillen, and I loved your last book. At least I think it's your last." She frowned. "Didn't I hear that you'd stopped writing . . . or were giving it up or something? Not that your presence in Cambodia would refute that in any way."

"I have got a new novel coming out next spring," I said.

"Well, if it's as good as the last, you'll have my ten quid."

"The critics will probably say it's exactly the same as the last."

We teetered on the brink of an awkward silence, and then she said, "Shall I tell you about myself? Would that be helpful?"

"That's why I'm here."

"Okay. I'm thirty-one . . . thirty-two next month, actually. I've lived in London all my life. I graduated from the Chelsea School of Design and worked at a firm in the city for a while. Five years ago I started my own firm, specializing in urban landscape design. We were doing spectacularly well for a new business . . ."

A foursome of prosperous-looking Cambodian men entered the bar, laughing and talking; they acknowledged us, inclining their heads and pressing their hands together in a prayerful gesture, a gesture that Lucy returned, and they took seats at a table against the back wall.

"To put it succinctly," Lucy went on, "I'm a victim of multiculturalism. My East Indian accountant stole from me, quite a large sum, and fled to India. I couldn't recover. It was an absolute disaster. I'm afraid I was a mess for some time thereafter. I had a little money left in personal accounts, and I started out for India, planning some pitiful revenge. I'm not certain what I had in mind. Some sort of Kaliesque scenario, I suppose. Gobbets of blood. His wife screaming in horror. Of course, I didn't go through with it. I bypassed India completely, and I've been bumming around Southeast Asia for a couple of years. My money's running low, and, to be frank, this voyage would extend my trip and give me the time and leisure to write a new business plan."

"You must be good at what you do," I said. "To be so successful at such a young age."

"I've won awards," she said, grinning broadly.

"I would have thought, then, you could have found investors to bail you out."

"As I said, I was a mess. Certifiably a mess. Once they noticed, investors wouldn't touch me. I've calmed down a great deal since, and I'm ready to have at it again."

She fit into the "too eager" category, yet I found her appealing. The Cambodian men burst into applause, celebrating something one of them had done or said. The light was fading on the river, the far bank darkened by cloud shadow. I asked Lucy if she understood the requirements of the position.

"Your sign was somewhat vague," she said. "I may

be misreading it, but I assume 'companion' is another word for girlfriend?"

"That's right."

"May I ask a question?"

"Go for it."

"Surely a man of your accomplishment must have a number of admirers. You're not bad looking, and you obviously have money. I don't understand why you would be in the market."

"It's in the nature of an experiment," I said. "I can assure you that you won't be harmed or humiliated in any way."

"A literary experiment?"

"You might say."

"You know, I didn't intend to seek the position," she said. "I was just . . . intrigued. But I must admit, having Thomas Cradle on my resumé would do wonders for my self-esteem." She had a deep drink of her gin-and-tonic. "If the position is offered, I do have two conditions. One you've already spoken to—I'm not into pain. Short of sea urchins and safety pins, I'm your girl. I believe you can expect me, given a modicum of compatibility, to perform my duties with relish."

"And the second condition?"

"Instead of leaping into the fire, as it were, I'd prefer we took some time to become comfortable with one another. Give it a day or two. Will that be a problem?"

"Not at all."

One of the Cambodian men bought us fresh drinks. He spoke no English, but Lucy chatted him up in his own tongue and then explained that his friend had received a promotion, and he would like us to join them in a toast. We complied, and, after bows and prayerful gestures all around, I asked if she had studied Cambodian.

"I pick up languages quickly. One of my many gifts." She gave another lopsided smile. "I do have some bad habits I should mention. I tend to run on about things. Talk too much. Just tell me to stuff it. People have been telling me that since I was a child. And I'm a vegetarian, though I have been known to eat fish. I'm picky about what I consume."

"My cook's big on veggies," I said. "Too much so for my tastes."

"You have a cook?"

"A Vietnamese kid. Deng. He's crew and cook. The pilot's an old guy in his sixties. Lan. He speaks decent American, but he doesn't talk to me much . . . not so far, anyway."

"La-de-da!" said Lucy. "Next you'll be telling me you have your own private ocean."

A breeze stirred the placid surface of the river, but it had no effect on the humidity in the restaurant.

"There's one thing more," Lucy said. "I'm afraid it may erase whatever good opinion you've formed of me, but I can't compromise. I smoke two pipes of opium a day. One at noon, and one before sleeping. Sometimes more, if the quality's not good." She paused and, a glum note in her voice, said, "The quality is usually good in these parts."

"You have an adequate supply on hand?"

She seemed surprised by this response, unaware that her confession had put her into the lead for the job. "I've enough for the week, I think."

"Is opium the actual reason you want to extend your trip?" I asked.

"It's part of it. I won't lie to you. I recognize I'll have to quit before I return to London. But it's not the main reason."

Another backpacker, a short woman with frizzy blond hair, entered and, after peering about, approached the bartender. I signaled him to send her away. Lucy pretended not to notice.

"Would you like to see the boat?" I asked.

An alarmed look crossed her face, and I thought that this must be a major step for her, that despite her worldliness she was not accustomed to giving her trust so freely. But then she smiled and nodded vigorously.

"Yes, please," she said.

The sun was beginning to set as I rowed out to the *Undine*, moored some thirty yards from shore. A high bank of solid-looking bluish gray cloud rose from the eastern horizon, its leading edge ruffled and fluted like that of an immense seashell, a godly mollusk dominating the sky; fragments of dirty pink cloud drifted beneath, resembling frayed morsels of flesh that might have been torn from the creature that once inhabited the shell, floating in an aqua medium. The river had turned slate colored, and the houseboat, with its cabin of varnished, unpainted boards and the devilish eyes painted on the bow to keep spirits at bay, looked surreal from a distance, like a new home uprooted and set adrift on a native barge, its perfect, watery reflection an impressionist trick. Lan sat cross-legged in the bow. So unchanging was his expression, his wizened features appeared carved from tawny wood, his gray thatch of hair lifting in the breeze. Deng, a cheerful, handsome teenager clad in a pair of shorts, scrambled to assist us and lashed the dinghy to the rail. He exchanged a few words in Vietnamese with Lucy and then asked if we were hungry.

The same breeze that had not had the slightest effect at the bar here drove off the mosquitoes and refreshed the air. We sat in the stern, watching the sunset spread pinks and mauves and reds across the enormous sky, staining hierarchies of cumulus that passed to the south. The lights of Stung Treng, white and yellow, beaded the dusky shore. I heard strains of music, the revving of an engine. Deng brought plates of fish and a kind of ratatouille, and we ate and talked about the French in Southeast Asia, about America's benighted president ("A grocer's clerk run amok," Lucy said of him), about writing and idiot urban planners and Borneo, where she had recently been. She had an edge to her personality, this perhaps due to working with wealthy and eccentric clients, rock stars and actors and such; yet there was a softness underlying that edge, a genteel quality I responded to, possibly because it reminded me of Kim . . . though this quality in Lucy seemed less a product of repression.

Deng took our plates, and Lucy asked if I had anyone back in the States, a wife or girlfriend. I told her about Kim and said she might meet me in Saigon.

"I suppose that's where I would leave you," she said. "Assuming you deem me suitable." Her mouth thinned. "I probably shouldn't put this out there, because whenever I show enthusiasm, you become reticent. But this is so wonderful." Lucy's gesture embraced the world as seen from the deck of the *Undine*. "In order to get rid of me, you may have to throw me overboard." She sat forward in the deck chair. "What are you thinking about?"

I saw no reason to delay—the prospect of spending another day at the Sekong was not an engaging one. "Welcome aboard," I said.

"Oh, gosh!" She pushed up from the chair and gave me a peck on the lips. "That's marvelous. Thanks so much."

We went inside, and I showed her the shower, the galley, and the king-size bed; then I left her to wash up and stood looking out over the river, listening to the loopy cries of lizards, alerted now and again by the plop of a fish. Night had swallowed all but the lights on the shore, and I could no longer make out Lan in the bow. Deng sat on the roof, legs dangling, reading a comic by lantern light. I felt on the brink of something ineluctable and strange, and I suspected it had to do more with Lucy than with the voyage. Kim's caution notwithstanding, I anticipated losing a piece of my soul to this forthright, tomboyish, opium woman. When I went back down, I found her on the bed, her legs stretched out, toweling her hair, wearing only a pair of panties. It looked as if two-thirds of her length were in her legs. Bikini lines demarked her small, pale breasts. A brass box of some antiquity rested on the sheets beside her.

She came out from beneath the towel and caught me staring. "I know," she said. "I'm revoltingly thin. I look better when I've put on five or six pounds, but I can't keep weight on when I'm traveling."

"You know that's bullshit," I said. "You look great. Beautiful."

"I'm scarcely beautiful, but I do have good legs. At least so I've been told." She stared at her legs, pursed her lips as if reappraising them; then she said, "I came all the way from Vientiane today, and I'm exhausted. So if you don't mind, I'll indulge my filthy habit earlier than usual this evening." She patted the box. "It's awfully bright in here. Can something be done?"

I joined her on the bed, switched on a reading lamp, and cut the overheads.

"Much better," she said.

She opened the box, removed a long pipe of wood and brass, and unwrapped yellowish paper from a pressed cake of black opium.

"I'll be completely useless once I've smoked," she said. "However, you may touch me if you like. I enjoy being touched when I'm high."

I asked if she would be aware of what was going on.

"Mmm-hmm. I may act as though I'm not, but I know."

"Where do you like to be touched?"

"Wherever you wish. My breasts, my ass." She glanced up from her preparations. "My pussy. Go lightly there, if you will. Too much stimulation confuses things in here." She tapped her temple.

She pinched off a fragment of opium and began rolling it into a pellet, frowning in concentration; her hands and wrists were fully illuminated, but the rest of her body was sheathed in dimness; she might have been a trim young witch up to no good purpose, drenched in the shadow cast by her spell, preparing a special poison that required a measure of light for efficacy. She plumped the pillows, making a nest, and lay on her side.

"Kiss, please," she said.

Her lips parted and her tongue flirted with mine. She settled into the pillows and lit the pipe, her cheeks hollowing as she sucked in smoke. She relit the pipe three times, and after the last time, she could barely hold it. After watching her drowse a minute, I stripped off my clothes and lay facing her, caressing her hip, tasting the chewy plug of a nipple. Her eyes were slitted, and I couldn't tell if she was focusing on me, yet when my erection prodded her thigh, she made an approving noise. I slipped a hand under her panties, rested the heel of it on her pubic bone, thatched with dark hair, and let the weight of one finger come down onto her labia. The intimacy of the touch seemed to distress her, so I reluctantly withdrew the finger, but I continued to touch her intimately. Holding her that way became torture.

"Lucy?" I whispered.

She didn't appear to be at home. Her breathing was shallow; a faint sheen of sweat polished her brow. I had no choice but to relieve the torment as best I could.

I hadn't thought that I could take such pleasure from fondling a nearly comatose woman. The thought that she was submitting to me had been exciting. I had walled off such practices from my sexual life, yet I now found myself imagining variations on the act, and I believed that Lucy would be a willing partner to my fantasies. The woman I'd met in the bar had, over the course of a few hours, been transformed into a practicing submissive. I had known other women to exhibit a manner markedly different from that they later presented, women who, upon feeling secure in the situation, had changed as abruptly as Lucy. But Cradle Two's rice-paper model was in my head, people shunting back and forth between universes without realizing it, and I thought if I could see those women now, I would view their sudden transformation in a new light, and I speculated that this Lucy might not be the same who had climbed into the dinghy with me. One way or another, I had presumed her to be a normal, bright woman who had survived a shattering blow, but it was evident that she had picked up a kink or two along the road to recovery.

In the morning I woke to a drowned gray light, the cabin windows spotted with rain. Lucy was sitting up in bed, inspecting her stomach.

"I'm all sticky," she said, and gave me a sly smile. "You were wicked, weren't you?"

"Don't you remember?"

She gave the matter some study, screwing up her face, as might a child, into a mask of exaggerated perplexity. "It's a little hazy. I definitely remember you touching me." She scooted down beneath the sheets, snuggling close. "It made for a decent icebreaker, don't you think? There'll be less reason for nerves when we make love."

"Now you mention it, I doubt there'll be any." I clasped my hands behind my neck. "Last night was surprising to me."

"A sophisticate like you? I wouldn't have believed it possible to surprise you."

I caught her by the hair and pulled her head away from my chest, irritated by the remark. Judging by her calm face, she didn't mind the rough treatment, and I tightened my grip.

"I wasn't mocking you," she said. "I'm your admirer. Honest. Cross my heart and spit on the pope."

I released her, astonished by the behavior she had brought out in me. She flung a leg across my waist, rubbing against me, letting me feel the heated damp of her.

"Would you care to see another of my tricks?" she asked.

"What do you have?"

"Oh, I've got scads." She folded her arms on my chest, rested her chin upon them, and gazed at me soberly. "You'd be surprised, I mean really, really . . . *really* surprised, how wicked I can be."

Travel has always served to inspire me, as it has many writers, as it apparently did my alter ego; yet the farther we proceeded down the Mekong, the more I came to realize that there was a blighted sameness to the world and its various cultures. Strip away their trappings and you found that every tribe was moved by the same passions, and this was true not only in the present but also, I suspected, in ages past. Erase from your mind the images of the kings and exotic courtesans and maniacal monks that people the legends of Southeast Asia, and look to a patch of ground away from the temples and palaces of Angkor Wat—there you will find the average planetary citizen, a child eating the Khmer equivalent of a Happy Meal and longing for the invention of television.

The landscape, too, bored me. Like every river, the Mekong was a mighty water dragon, its scales shifting in hue from blue to green to brown, sometimes overflowing its banks, and along the shore were floating markets, assemblies of weathered gray shanties resting upon leaky bottoms that were not much different from shacks on the Mississippi or huts along the Nile or the disastrous slums of Quito spilling into the Guayas, fouling it with their wastes . . . and so I did not delight, as travelers will, in the scenting of an unfamiliar odor, because I suspected it to be the register of spoilage, and I derived no great pleasure from the dull green uniformity sliding past or in the sentinel presence of coconut palms, their fronds drooping against a yellow morning sky, or the toil of farmers (though one morning, when we passed a village where people were washing their cows in the river, I felt a twinge of interest, remarking on the possible linkage between this practice and the Saturday morning ritual of washing one's car in a suburban driveway). Neither did I have the urge to scribble excitedly in my journal about the quaint old fart who sold Lucy a bauble in a floating market and told a story in pidgin English about demons and witches, oh my! Nor did I, as might an ecotourist in his blog for true believers, fly my aquatic mammal flag at half-mast and rant about the plight of the Irrawaddy dolphins (yet another dying species) that surfaced from muddy pools near the town of Kratie. And I did not exult, like some daft birder, in the soaring river terns and kingfishers that dive-bombed the waters farther south. I was solely interested in Lucy, and my interest in her was limited.

Within a week we had developed an extensive sexual vocabulary, and though it stopped short of sea urchins and safety pins, we were depraved in our invention—that was how I might have characterized it before embarking upon the relationship, though I came to hold a more liberated view. Depravity always incorporates obsession, but our obsession had a scholarly air. We were less possessed lovers than anthropologists studying one another's culture, and because we made no emotional commitment, our passion manifested as a scientific voyeurism that allowed us to explore the scope of actual perversity with greater freedom than would have been the case if our hearts were at risk. We approached each other with coolness and calculation. "Do you like this?" one of us would ask, and if the answer was no, we would move on without injured feelings to a new pleasurable possibility. Apart from badinage, we talked rarely, and when not physically involved, we went away from each other, she to craft her business plan, sketching and writing lists, and I to sit in the stern and indulge in a bout of self-loathing and meditate on passages from *The Tea Forest* that reflected upon my situation. Five days on the Mekong had worked a change in me that I could not comprehend except in terms of Cradle Two's novel. Indeed, I lost much of the urge to comprehend it, satisfied to brood and fuck my way south. I felt something festering inside me, some old bitterness metastasizing, sprouting black claws that dug into my vitals, encouraging me to lash out; yet I had no suitable target. I yelled at Deng on occasion, at Lan less frequently (I had grown to appreciate his indifference to me); but these were petty irritations that didn't qualify for a full release, and so I lashed out against myself.

Of my many failings, the most galling was that I had wasted my gifts on genre fiction. I could have achieved much more, I believed, had I not gone for the easy money but, like Cradle Two, had been faithful to my muse. Typically, I didn't count myself to blame but assigned blame to the editors and agents who had counseled me, to the marketers and bean counters who had delimited me, and to the people with whom I had surrounded myself—wives and girlfriends, my fans, my friends. They had dragged me down to their level, seduced me into becoming a populist. I saw them in my mind's eye overflowing the chambers of my life, the many rooms of my mansion, all the rooms in fantasy and science fiction, all the crowded, half-imaginary party rooms clotted with people who didn't know how to party, who failed miserably at it and frowned at those few who could and did, and yearned with their whole hearts to lose control, yet lacked the necessary passionate disposition; all the corridors of convention hotels packed with damaged, overstuffed women, their breasts cantilevered and contoured into shelf-like projections upon which you could rest your beer glass, women who chirped about Wicca, the Tarot, and the Goddess and took the part of concubine or altar-slut in their online role-playing games; all the semibeautiful, equally damaged, semiprofessional women who believed they themselves were goddesses and concealed dangerous vibrators powered by rats' brains in their purses and believed that heaven could be ascended to from the tenth floor of the Hyatt Regency in Boston, yet rejected permanent residence there as being unrealistic; all the mad, portly men with their bald heads and beards and their eyeballs in their trouser pockets, whose wives caught cancer from living with them; all the dull hustlers who blogged ceaselessly and had MacGyvered a career out of two ounces of talent, a jackknife, and a predilection for wearing funny hats, and humped the legs of their idols, who blogged ceaselessly and wore the latest fashion in emperor's new clothes and talked about Art as if he were a personal friend they had met through networking, networking, networking, building a fan base one reader at a time; all the lesser fantasists with their fantasies of one day becoming a famous corpse like Andre Breton and whose latest publications came to us courtesy of Squalling Hammertoe Woo Hoo Press and who squeezed out pretentious drivel from the jerk-off rags wadded into their skulls that one or two Internet critics had declared works of genius, remarking on their verisimilitude, saying how much they smelled like stale ejaculate, so raw and potent, the stuff of life itself; all the ultrasuccessful commercial novelists (I numbered myself among them) whose arrogance cast shadows more substantial than anything they had written and could afford, literally, to treat people like dirt; all the great men and women of the field (certain of them, anyway), the lifetime achievers who, in effect, pursed their lips as if about to say "Percy" or "piquant" when in public, fostering the impression that they squeezed their asscheeks together extra hard to produce work of such unsurpassed grandiloquence . . . Many of these people were my friends and, as a group, when judged against the entirety of the human mob, were no pettier, no more disagreeable or daft or reprehensible. We all have such thoughts; we find solace in diminishing those close to us, though usually not with so much relish. And while I kept on vilifying them, spewing my venom, I recognized they were not to blame for my deficiencies and that I was the worst of them all. I had all their faults, their neuroses, their foibles, and then some—I knew myself to be a borderline personality with sociopathic tendencies, subject to emotional and moral disconnects, yet lacking the conviction of a true sociopath. The longer I contemplated the notion, the

more persuaded I was to embrace the opinion es-
poused in *The Tea Forest* that Thomas Cradles everywhere were men of debased character. The peculiar
thing was, I no longer took this judgment for an insult.

Our fifth day on the river, Lucy scored a fresh supply of opium from a floating market, and that night,
a dead-still night, hot and humid as the inside of an
animal's throat, once she had prepared a pipe, she
held it out to me and said, "I believe the time is
right."

"No, thanks," I said.

She continued to offer the pipe, her clever face ordered by a bemused expression, like a mother forcing
her infant son to try a new food, one she knows he
will enjoy.

"I've smoked pot," I said. "But I don't know
about this."

"I promise you, you'll have a grand old time. And
it'll help with the heat."

I took the pipe. "What do I do?"

"When I light the pipe, draw gently on it. You
mustn't inhale deeply, just enough to guide the smoke."

It was as she said. Once guided, the smoke seemed
to find its own way, plating my throat and lungs with
coolness and enforcing a dizzy, drifty feeling. I lost
track of what Lucy was doing, but I think she, too,
smoked. We lay facing one another, and I became
fascinated by the skin on her lower abdomen, pale
and, due to shaving, more coarsely grained than the
rest. My limbs were heavy, but I managed to extend
a forefinger and touch her. The contact was so profound, I had to close my eyes in order to absorb the
sensations of warmth and softness and muscularity.
With effort, because I had little strength and not much
volition, I succeeded in slitting my eyes, focusing on
an inch of skin higher up, a tanned, curving place. My
focus narrowed until I appeared to be looking at a
minute fraction of her whole, a single tanned atom,
and then I penetrated that atom and was immersed in
a dream, something to do with a lady swimming in a

pool floored by a huge white lotus, its petals lifted by
gentle currents, and an anthropomorphic beast with
the head of a mastiff who ate cockroaches, pinching
off their heads, draining them of a minim of syrupy
fluid that he chased with diamonds, grabbing a handful
from a bowl at his elbow and crunching them like
peanuts, a fabulous adventure that was interrupted,
cut off as if the channel had been switched, and replaced by the image of a night sky into which I was
ascending.

The lights in the sky appeared scattered at first but
grew brighter and increasingly unified, proving to be
the visible effulgence of a single creature. It was
golden-white in color and many chambered, reminding
me of those spectacular, luminous phantoms that
range the Mindanao Trench, frail complexities surviving at depths that would crush a man in an instant;
yet it was so vast, I could not have described its shape,
only that it was huge and golden-white and many
chambered. Its movements were slow and oceanic, a
segment of the creature lifting, as though upon a tide,
and then an adjacent segment lifting as the first fell,
creating a rippling effect that spread across its length
and breadth. All around me, black splinters were rising toward the thing, sinister forms marked by a
crookedness, like hooked thorns. Dark patches formed
on its surface, composed of thousands of these splinters, and it began to shrink, its chambers collapsing
one into the other like the folds of an accordion being
compressed. Unnerved, I tried to slow my ascent, and
as I twisted and turned, flinging myself about, I
glimpsed what lay behind me: a black, depthless void
picked out by a single, irregular gray shape, roughly
circular and, from my perspective, about the size of a
throw rug. The gray thing made me nervous. I looked
away, but that did nothing to ease my anxiety, and
for the duration of my dream—hours, it seemed—I
continued my ascent, desperate to stop, my mind
clenched with fear. When I woke near first light, my
heart hammered and I was covered in sweat. I recalled

the mural in Stung Treng, noting the crude resemblance it bore to the glowing creature, but a more pressing matter was foremost in my thoughts.

I put my hand on Lucy's throat and shook her. She felt the pressure of my grip. Her eyes fluttered open, widened; then she said, "Is this to be something new?"

"What did you give me last night?" I asked. "It wasn't opium."

"Yes, it was!"

"I've never seen a record of anything like what I experienced."

"Not everything is written down, Tom." She moved my hand from her throat. "You're so very excitable. Tell me about it."

I summarized my evening and she said, "You may have had some sort of reaction. I doubt it will reoccur."

"I'm not smoking that shit again."

"Of course you won't." She sat up. "But to more pressing business. I may get my period today—I'm feeling crampy. So, if you want to get one in before the curse is upon me, this morning would be the time."

Lan had his work cut out for him. North of Kampong Cham, the Mekong was more than a mile wide, but massive dry-season sandbars rendered the river almost impassable. Often there was a single navigable channel and that had to be located, so we went more slowly than usual, with Deng going on ahead of the *Undine* in the dinghy, taking soundings. To break the monotony, we camped one night on an island where we found driftwood caught in the limbs of trees fifteen and twenty feet high, pointing up the dramatic difference in water level between the rainy season and the dry. We erected a tentlike structure of mosquito netting and lounged beneath it, drinking gin and watching a strangely monochromatic sunset bronze the western sky, resolving into a pageantry of yellows and browns. Deng cooked over an open fire on the beach, prepar-

ing a curry. As darkness closed down around us, there
was an explosion of moths, nearly hiding him from
view (we glimpsed him squatting by the fire, a sha-
manic figure occulted by flurrying wings), and when
he brought the curry to us, what was supposed to be
a vegetarian dish had been thickened by uncountable
numbers of moths. Lucy had a nibble and declared it
to be: "Not bad. They give it kind of a meaty flavor."
I had been incredibly careful about food since arriving
in Asia, wanting to spare myself the misery of stomach
problems, but I was hungry and stuffed myself.

The following morning I was stricken with severe
diarrhea. I blamed the moths and Deng. He kept out
of my way for the next two days. On the third day,
while resting in the stern, I caught sight of him on
the island helping Lucy fly a kite, and then, later that
afternoon, I saw him sneaking into our cabin. Thinking he might be stealing, hoping for it, in fact (I was
feeling better and wanted an excuse to exercise my
temper), I went inside. Lucy was sitting on the bed,
leaning toward Deng, whose back was to me. He appeared to be fumbling with his shorts. I shouted, and
after tossing me a terrified glance over his shoulder,
he bolted for the door.

"What the fuck's going on?" I asked.

"For God's sake," Lucy said. "Don't act so wronged."

I was taken aback by her mild reaction—I had expected a denial.

"I took pity on him," she said. "There's no reason
for you to be upset."

"You felt bad, so you were going to blow him?"

She frowned. "If you must know, I was going to
manipulate him."

"A hand job? Oh, well. If I'd known that's all it
was . . . Shit. My mom used to give the paperboy hand
jobs. Dad would look on and beam."

She gave me a defiant look.

"Are you serious?" I asked. "You don't see you
did anything wrong?"

We held a staring contest, and then she said, "Can

you imagine being sixteen, trapped on a boat with people who're having sex as much as we do? He was pathetic, really."

"So he came to you and asked for a hand job? And you said, 'Oh, Deng, soulful child of the Third World . . . ' "

"He asked for considerably more than that. I told him it was all I could manage." She crossed her legs and gazed out at the river. "Since we've been going at it, I've had an almost ecumenical attitude toward sex. It's not as though we're in love, yet that's the feeling I get when I'm in love. It makes me wonder if I've ever been in love."

"Ecumenical? You mean like you want to spread it around?"

"That's one way of putting it," she said frostily.

"I don't want you to feel that way. I'm territorial in the extreme."

"Yes, I'm beginning to grasp that." She stretched out on the bed, placed her hand on a paperback that lay open beside her. "It won't happen again."

I sat next to her on the edge of the bed. "Is that all you have to say?"

"Do you want an apology? I apologize. I should have known it would distress you." She waited for me to respond and then said, "Should I leave? I'd rather not, but it's your boat. If you're determined to view what I've done as a betrayal . . ."

"No, I'm just confused."

"About what?"

"About your attitude . . . and mine. I don't understand why I'm not angrier."

"Look," she said. "Do you really believe I'm seeking another sexual outlet? That I'm not getting enough? Nymphomaniacs don't get this much."

"Yeah, okay," I said, still dubious.

"So, are we going to move past this?"

If she was lying, she deserved a pass on the basis of poise alone. I grudgingly said, "It might take me a while."

"How long would you reckon 'a while' to be? Long enough for you to feel horny again?"

To get her off the subject, I asked what she was reading.

She showed me the cover of *The Tea Forest* and said, "I'd forgotten how brilliant this was."

It took me a second or two to process her remark. "You've read *The Tea Forest*? Before this trip, I mean?"

"Didn't I tell you?"

"You said you'd read one of my books, but you never said which."

"This was the only one I could find. The clerk in the bookstore mentioned that you'd gone off writing . . . or something to that effect. I guess he wasn't aware of your recent work."

I told her I was feeling queasy and, taking the satellite phone, went into the stern and called my agent. I asked if he had turned over every stone in hunting for a book called *The Tea Forest* by Thomas Cradle. He was concerned for my well-being and asked if I wasn't carrying this a little too far; he told me that they had begun publicizing the hoax, and hundreds of fans (including librarians, collectors, and so forth) had written in to my website claiming to have done exhaustive searches, none yielding a result. That left me with the proposition, however preposterous, that Lucy was not of this universe . . . not this particular Lucy, at any rate. I had no idea when the current incarnation had come aboard or when she might disembark, and then I realized something that, if I hadn't been flattered by her recognition of me at the Sekong Hotel, might have alerted me to her origin much earlier. I had grown a beard and let my hair grow long, drastically altering my appearance. It was Cradle Two whom she had recognized, probably from his author photograph, and this helped establish that she, the Lucy of the Sekong Hotel, had shifted over from an adjoining universe. Or perhaps I had been the one who shifted. According to Cradle Two, so many people and things were constantly shifting back and forth, that such distinctions scarcely mattered.

Picking through this snarl of possibility, I thought that Lucy and I might have shifted many times during the previous two weeks and that the Lucy of the Sekong might not be the Lucy of this moment—*The Tea Forest* must exist in more than one universe—and it occurred to me that the novel presented a means of crudely defining the situation. Every hour or so for the remainder of the day, I asked Lucy a question pertaining to *The Tea Forest*. She answered each to my satisfaction, which proved nothing; but the next morning, while she trimmed her toenails in the stern, I asked if she found the ending anticlimactic, and she said crossly, "Are you mad? You know I haven't had time to read it."

"The ending?" I asked. "You haven't read the ending?"

"I haven't even begun the book! Must I repeat that information every half-hour?"

Two hours later I asked her a variation on the question, and she replied that the ending had been her favorite part of the novel and followed this by saying that it would have been out of character for TC to complete the journey. He was a coward, and his cowardice was its own resolution. To end the book any other way would have been dramatically false and artistically dishonest. I (Cradle Two) was a modernist author, she said, prowling at the edges of the genre, and had I taken TC into the tea forest, I would have had to lapse into full-blown fantasy, something she doubted I could write well. She went on to dismiss much of postmodernism as having "an overengineered archness" and, except for a few exemplary authors, being a refuge for those writers whose "disregard for traditional narrative (was) an attempt to disguise either their laziness or their inability to master it." She concluded with a none-too-brief lecture on cleverness as a literary eidolon, a quality "too frequently given the stamp of genius during this postmillennial slump."

After listening to her ramble on for the better part of an hour, I was disinclined to ask further questions, and truthfully there was no need—I had proved to my satisfaction that Cradle Two's model of the universe was accurate in some degree, and I wanted Wicked Lucy back, not this pretentious windbag. I went outside and paced the length of the *Undine*, sending Deng scuttering away, and tried to make sense out of what was going on, overwhelmed by feelings of helplessness brought on by my new understanding of the human condition, a condition to which I had paid lip service, yet now was forced to accept as an article of faith. "The river was change," Cradle Two (and perhaps Cradles 3, 4, 5, ad infinitum) had written. "It flowed through the less mutable landscape, carrying change like a plague, defoliating places that once were green, greening places that once were barren, mutating the awareness of the people who dwelled along it, infecting them with a horrid inconstancy, doing so with such subtlety that few remembered those places as having ever been different." It had been my intention to shoot straight down the Mekong to the delta and spend most of the six weeks there; but now, recalling this passage, I felt a vibration in my flesh and panicked, fearing that the vibration, my fixation on the delta, and, indeed, every thought in my head, might reflect the inconstancy cited by Cradle Two. I had begun to feel a pull, a sense of being summoned to the delta that alarmed me; I sloughed this off as being the product of an overwrought imagination, but nonetheless it troubled me. For these reasons, I decided to break the trip, as Cradle Two's narrator had done, hoping to find stability away from the river, a spot where change occurred less frequently, and stop for a week, or perhaps longer, in what once had been the capitol of evil on earth, Phnom Penh.

In the future I expect there to be systems that will allow a boy on a bicycle, balancing a block of ice on his handlebars, to pedal directly from Phnom Penh into the heart of Manhattan, where thousands will applaud and toss coins, which will stick to his skin, covering him like the scales of a pangolin, and he will bring with him wet heat and palm shadow and a sudden, fleeting touch of coolness in the air, and there will follow the smells of moto exhaust, of a street stall selling rice porridge sweetened with cinnamon and soup whose chief ingredient is cow entrails, the dry odor of skulls at Tuol Sieng prison, marijuana smoke, all the essences of place and moment, every potential answer to the Cambodian riddle fractionated and laid out for our inspection. Until then, it will be necessary to travel, to not drink the water, to snap poorly composed pictures, to be hustled by small brown men, to get sick and rent unsatisfactory hotel rooms. I yearned for that future. I wanted to live in the illusion that persuades us that true-life experience can be obtained on the Internet. Barring that, I wanted to find lodgings as anti-Cambodian as possible, one of the big American-style hotels, an edifice that I felt would be resistant to the processes of change. Wicked Lucy, however, insisted we take a room at the Hotel Radar 99, where she had stayed on a previous visit.

The hotel was situated in an old quarter of the city, well away from modernity of the kind I favored, and no element of the place seemed to have the least relation to the concepts of either radar or ninety-nine. The building was three stories of decrepit stone that had been worn to an indefinite salmon hue—it might originally have been orange or pink (impossible to say which)—and had green French doors that opened onto precarious balconies with ironwork railings. Faded, sagging awnings skirted that section of the block, overhanging restaurants and shops of various kinds; and parked along the curb at every hour of day or night were between ten and twenty motos, the owners of which, according to Lucy, provided the guests, mostly expats, with drugs, women, and whatever else they might want in the way of perversity. You entered through a narrow door (the glass portion painted over with indigo) and came into a dark green-as-a-twilit-jungle foyer, throttled with ferns and fleshy-leaved plants. There was never anyone behind the reception desk. You were compelled to shout, and then maybe Mama-san (the elderly Japanese woman who owned the place) would respond, or maybe not. Beyond lay a tiny court-yard where two clipped parrots squabbled on their perch. Our room was on the second floor, facing back toward the entrance, the metal number 4 turned side-ways on the door. Apart from lizards clinging to the wall, its decor was purely utilitarian: a handful of wooden chairs; a writing desk that may once have had value as an antique; three double beds about which mosquito netting could be lowered, all producing ghastly groans and squeaks whenever we sat on them and playing a cacophonous avant-garde freakout each time we made love. The bathroom was also an an-tique, with a claw-footed bathtub, a chain-pull toilet, and venerable tile floors. Stains memorializing lizard and insect death bespotted the cream-colored walls and high ceilings. Everything smelled of cleaning agents, a good sign in those latitudes.

I spent five days rooted to the room, trying to deny and resist change, infrequently stepping out onto the balcony to survey the street or going into the corridor overlooking the courtyard to observe the tranquil life of the hotel. I could detect no change in my surroundings—proof of nothing, but I grew calmer nonetheless. A Ger-man couple was staying in the room on our left, two Italian girls on our right. Farther along: Room 2 was home to a pair of twenty-somethings: a thin, long-haired man with a pinched, bony face and a Canadian flag embroidered on his jeans and a gorgeous gray-eyed blonde with full breasts and steatopygian but-tocks. She was the palest person I had met in Cambo-dia, her skin whiter than the bathroom tiles (covered, as they were, by a grayish film). I never saw her leave the room, not completely. She would open the door and, without letting loose of it, as if it were all that kept her from drifting away, offer a frail, zoned, "Hi," then hover for a while, looking as though she were going to make some further comment, before fluttering her fingers and vanishing inside. Once at noon, when the sunlight brightened the courtyard floor, casting a lace of shadow from a jacaranda tree onto the stone floor, she performed this ritual emergence half-nude, dressed in a tank top, her pubic hair a shade darker than that on her head, yet firmly within the blonde spectrum. It became evident that she was distressed about her boyfriend—he was overdue, probably off buying drugs (heroin or opium, I guessed), and she hoped these appearances at the door would hurry him along.

After five days Lucy tired of indulging me, of bringing me food, and coaxed me outside. I began taking walks around the immediate neighborhood, but I had no desire to explore farther afield. I had been to Phnom Penh twenty years before, and I had snapped pictures of the temples of Angkor Wat, skulls, the Killing Fields, crypts overgrown by the enormous roots of trees, and I had slept with expat girls and taxi girls, and I had partied heartily in this terrible place where death was a tourist attraction, getting kicked out of bars for fighting and out of one of the grand old colonial hotels along the river for public drunkenness. I needed no further experience of the country and was content to inhabit a few square blocks, reconciling myself to the idea that things had always changed around me, and how were you to distinguish between normal change and a change promulgated by a transition from one universe to the other? Did such a thing as normal change even exist? People, for example, were so predictable in their unpredictability. Amazing, how they could do a one-eighty on you at the drop of a hat, how their moods varied from moment to moment. Perhaps this was all due to physics, to universes like strips of rice paper blown by a breeze and touching each other, exchanging people and insects and corners of rooms for almost identical replicas; perhaps without this universal interaction people would be ultrareliable and their behavior would not defy analysis, and every relationship would be a model of logic and consistency, and peace could be negotiated, and problems, great and small alike, could be easily solved or would never have existed. Perhaps the breeze that blew the strips of rice paper together was the single consequential problem, and that problem was insoluble. I understood that what had panicked me was a fundamental condition of existence, one that a mistaken apprehension of consensus reality had caused me to overlook. I further understood that I could adapt to my recently altered perception of this condition and found consolation in the idea that I could train myself to be as blind as anyone.

Around the corner from the hotel was a restaurant that sold fruit shakes. A young girl tended it. She stood behind a table that supported a glass display case in which there were finger bananas, papayas and several fruits I could not identify, bottled milk and various sweeteners in plastic tubs. She spent much of her day cleaning up after a puppy that wandered among a forest of table legs, sniffing for food, pausing now and again to piss and shit—thus the fecal odor that undercut the sugary smell of the place. In the darkened interior were blue wooden chairs and tables draped in checkered plastic cloths and poster ads featuring Cambodian pop stars stapled to the walls. On the fourth day after I started going out, Lucy and I were having fruit shakes when the blonde girl from the hotel wandered in, clutching a large straw bag of the sort used for shopping. She sat against the back wall, staring out at the street, where a couple of moto cowboys were attempting wheelies, the *brraaap* of their engines overriding the restaurant's radio. Lucy waved to her, but the blonde gave no reaction. Her skin was faintly luminous, like ghost skin, and her expression vacant.

"I'm going to see what's wrong," Lucy said.

"Nothing's wrong," I said. "She wants a shake."

Lucy pitied me with a stare. "I'll be back shortly." She joined the blonde at her table, and they spoke together in muted voices. With their heads together, one light and one dark, they posed a yin-yang juxtaposition, and as I sipped my shake, I thought about having them both, a fleeting thought that had no more weight than would the notion of taking a shot at Cate Blanchett. One of the moto cowboys pulled up facing the restaurant and shouted—he wore what looked to be a fishing hat with a turned-up brim, the word LOVE spelled out in beads on the crown, and he appeared to aim his shout at the blonde. She paid him no mind, busy conferring with Lucy. He shrugged, spoke to someone on the sidewalk I couldn't see, and rode off. The puppy bumped into my foot. I nudged him aside and concentrated on sucking a piece of papaya through my straw. When I looked up, Lucy had taken the blonde by an elbow and was steering her toward our table.

"This is Riel," Lucy said. "Riel, this is Thomas."

Her eyes lowered, the blonde whispered, "Hi."

"That's an interesting name," I said. "It's spelled the same as the currency?"

The question perplexed her, and I said, "Cambodian money. The riel? Is it spelled the same?"

"I guess." At Lucy's prompting, she took a seat. "It's French. Like Louis Riel."

"Who?" I asked.

"A famous Canadian. The Father of Manitoba."

"I didn't know Manitoba had a father," said Lucy pertly.

"Tell me about him," I said.

"People say he was a madman," Riel said. "He prayed obsessively. They hanged him for treason."

"And yet he fathered Manitoba." Lucy grinned.

"Mitch says they must have named the money over here for him, too," Riel said.

The counter girl, who had ignored her to this point, came over and asked if she wanted something.

"Make her a banana shake," Lucy said, surprising me that she would know what Riel wanted.

I asked Riel if she was from Manitoba, and she said,

"Yes. Winnipeg." Then she asked Lucy if she could have custard apple instead of banana.

I inquired as to who Mitch was, and Lucy said, "The ass who was with her. He ran off with their money. I told her she should stay with us until she figures out what to do."

This snatch of conversation summed Riel up—she saw her beauty as a type of currency and was, perhaps, mad—and summed up our relationship with her as well. It seemed Lucy had found someone more submissive than she herself was. She sent messages with her eyes saying that she wanted this to happen.

"Yeah, sure," I said.

Riel greedily drank her shake, eschewing a straw. She was, if you overlooked her drug abuse, a sublime creature possessed by a serene absence.

Once she finished her shake, Lucy went off with her, saying that they were going to "get something" for Riel. I went back to the hotel and read and stared out the window. The sky was almost cloudless, a few puffs drifting high, but then it flickered, the entire blue expanse appearing to wink out, like a television image undergoing a momentary loss of power, and a large cloud roughly resembling a canoe appeared in the lower sky; the roofline above which it floated also seemed different, though I couldn't have told you how. But the canoe-shaped cloud . . . I was certain it had not been there seconds before. I expected another flicker, and when none came, I was relieved; and yet I felt again that that summoning toward the south. A longing pervaded me, a desire to be on the move, and that longing intensified, faded, intensified . . . It was as if, having risen to the bait of *The Tea Forest,* something was tugging gently on the line, trying to set the hook deep before reeling me in.

After an hour the women returned and went into the bathroom, where they remained for twenty-five minutes. When they emerged, Riel was topless and wobbly. A trickle of blood ran down her arm—it might have been a scarlet accessory designed to contrast with her milky skin. With an arm about her waist, Lucy helped her to lie on the bed next to ours, cleaned away the blood, and wrangled off her jeans. Riel fell into a light sleep. Lucy started to disrobe.

"What was all that in the bathroom?" I asked, putting down my book.

"She had trouble getting a vein." Lucy skinned out of her panties. "I assisted."

"And now?"

She put a finger to her lips and stretched out beside Riel and began to caress her. This male fantasy held no particular appeal for me in the abstract, yet now I was captivated by Lucy's tenderness and thoroughness. She left no area of Riel's skin unexplored, licking and rubbing against her with the delicacy of a cat. The bed played an oriental music of squeaks and *sproings* when she went down on her, a lengthy symphony with prolonged, hushed spaces between the notes, reflecting discrete movements of Lucy's fingers and tongue. They achieved a simultaneous climax, Lucy digging between her own legs with her left hand, letting forth a gasp, and Riel, becoming active at the end, crying out while holding Lucy's head in place.

Lucy wiped her mouth dry on the sheet. She crossed to the bed upon which I lay and took my hand, saying she wanted to watch me make love to Riel. I needed no urging, but her eagerness made me self-conscious and briefly reinstituted a morality that viewed the world through prim spectacles and characterized such behavior as degenerate and vile. I said something to the effect that I didn't know or I wasn't sure, a delaying action; but Lucy pressed a condom into my hand.

"Hurry," she said. "While she's still wet."

I liked how Riel, a sleepy heroin girl, would coast in sex, gliding, billowing, alone on her white ocean when I was joined to her. That first time, though, when she gazed up at me with Chinese eyes, those gray irises and shrunken pupils gazing out from a beautiful porcelain mask, old eyes weary of something, perhaps of everything, she seemed the embodiment of a Zen wisdom—by sinking to the bottom of the world, surrendering herself to its flood, she had gained infinite knowledge through the rejection of knowledge. I turned her onto her stomach in order to avoid her eyes, wishing to remain ignorant of whatever she might know about me in her Buddha ignorance, and soon roused a clanking, violent music from the bed.

Riel was all about appetite. When she ate, she ate wholeheartedly, and when she drank, she drank single-mindedly, and when she was inspired to talk, she talked a blue streak, and when she fucked, although stoned, never as active as Lucy, she gave it her all. I asked her if heroin didn't muffle the sexual drive, and she said, "Yes . . . but once you get started, it's kind of cool." She and Lucy and I deployed our bodies in every possible permutation, and over the span of several days, I learned there was a qualitative difference between their addictions, one that defined their drugs of choice. Compared to Lucy's elaborate ritual with the pipe, Riel's affair with the needle had a decidedly American character (stick it in and get off). This distinction carried over into their attitudes toward sex, and I was led to generalize that whereas opium women might prefer to grill thin slices of your heart, skewering each with a toothpick, devouring it over a period of years, heroin girls will, if given the chance, swallow it in three quick bites. Riel became increasingly needy—needy for food, alcohol, drugs, and orgasms. I could empathize with her boyfriend. Had we been alone together, I would have dumped her myself. Beauty is not sufficient compensation for a demanding nature. But with Lucy to share the load, her demands were acceptable.

I discovered that a threesome required more drama to sustain it than did a twosome, and at first we manufactured drama. Games became the order of the day. Often Lucy and Riel would get high, leaving me to orchestrate these exercises. I enjoyed having two women, limp as dolls, whom I could exploit however I chose. When that became boring, I let Lucy take the lead. One afternoon she insisted I read a passage from *The Tea Forest* before having sex with Riel. The passage involved Cradle Two's narrator speaking to a German girl he had picked up in a Phnom Penh bar during the break in his trip. He had just finished helping her fix and was dictating the terms of their relationship. In speaking the lines, I felt an absolute conviction, as if my voice and Cradle Two's had merged:

" 'If you have to puke again,' I said, 'go outside, okay?'

"The girl tried to focus, but she gave it up; her head lolled, and an arm slipped off the sofa, her fingers trailing in the vomit.

" 'I'm not your pimp,' I told her. 'I'm not going to be your pimp. What I'm going to do is use you to attract a certain class of man. You want to fuck for money, okay, I'll pay you. Don't let the men I set you up with pay you. You'll probably have to do two or three tricks. For now, though, I'll be the only one fucking you. I need to make sure you can do the things they like. I'll keep you in dope and give you a place to live. I'll regulate your drugs . . . that way you won't get too big a habit. You have to learn to manage your habit. You can't do that, you're on your own.' "

Prior to this, I had, of course, recognized the resonance between the addition of Riel to our union and Cradle Two's novel—indeed, I had done little other than recognize such resonances since beginning the trip. More to the point, reading the passage brought home to me how much of the veneer of the civilized man had worn off. I was a long walk from becoming an unregenerate criminal like the narrator of *The Tea Forest*, and perhaps I would never achieve that level of criminality; but I was headed down the path he had trod. At one point I considered calling Kim and mak-

ing a stab at redemption, hoping that her rational
voice would reorient me; but Lucy and Riel stared at
me with dull opiated expectancy from a nipple-to-
nipple embrace, and I decided that the call could wait.

We started going out at night into the neon-braided
streets of central Phnom Penh, putting on one-act
plays in the thick, hothouse air, treating that city of a
million souls as if its mad traffic and buzzing motos,
its brutal history and doleful present, were merely a
backdrop for our entertainments. We, or rather Lucy
and Riel, sought out fortune-tellers, those who lined
the riverbank by day, when the parks were thronged
with tai chi practitioners and tourists and badminton
players, and by night, when the poor gathered with
their children to squat along the embankment eating
boiled eggs and fried beetles, and the prosperous
fortune-tellers with fancy booths at Wat Phnom, their
altars adorned with strings of Christmas tree lights,
candles, incense, and bowls of fruit, and cluttered with
porcelain sages, Ramayana monkeys, Buddhas with
holographic halos sheltering beneath gilt parasols . . .
A more generous writer might have inferred that this
profusion of seers and charlatans was but a veneer
masking the rich spiritual life of the populace, always
in communion with the city of ghosts that interpene-
trated with and cast a pall over the city of blood and
stone; and yet it meant nothing to me, or, to be accurate, it might someday provide the background detail
for a story, and if a host of sad phantoms had materialized before me, creatures with bleak, negative eyes
and bodies of lacy ectoplasm, I would have taken due
notice and then done my best to ignore them, being
consumed by other mysteries. We shooed away beautiful lady-boys and Cambodian kids with dyed Mohawks
who were trying to prove something by bumming cigarettes from Americans, and we discouraged the taxi
girls who came at platoon strength from alley mouths
and bars, girls in their teens and maybe younger,
chirping slogans from the hookers' English phrase
book and then retreating in sullen disarray, chiding

one another in singsong Khmer for being too aggressive or not aggressive enough. We disregarded the entreaties of ragged amputees and blind men with bowls, and we ate hallucinatory food from stalls, bugs and guts and whatnot, and inspected vendors' wares—the arms dealers were of especial interest to me. They commonly operated on street corners (some nights, in certain quarters, there seemed to be one on almost every corner) and offered a wide selection of handguns and ammo, the odd assault weapon—hardly surprising in a country where you could, I'd been told, blow away a cow with a rocket launcher for a fee of two hundred dollars, less if you were prepared to haggle. I saw in them the future of my own country, where death was celebrated with equal enthusiasm, although candy-coated by Technicolor and video games and television news. When the coating finally wore off, as it threatened to do, there we would all be, in Cambodia.

As we strolled along Street 51 one night, after a late supper at a grand old colonial hotel on the riverfront near Wat Phnom hill, we happened upon a blue wall bearing the painted silhouette of a girl flying a kite, a Beardsley-like illustration; beside it were the words HEART OF DARKNESS BAR. In addition, there was a painting on the door very much like the mural on the market stall in Stung Treng. I wanted to check the place out, intrigued by the mural, by the name of the bar and the juxtaposed irony of the sign, but Lucy said it was dangerous, that the Coconut Gang hung out there, and someone had recently been murdered on the premises.

"What's a Coconut Gang?" I asked.

"Rich assholes. Khmer punks and their bodyguards. Please! Let's go somewhere else."

"All I want is to have a quick look."

"This is no place to play tourist."

"I'm not playing at anything. I'm a writer. I can use shit like this."

"Yes, I imagine being shot could prove an invaluable resource. Silly me."

"Nothing like that's going to happen."

"Do you have the slightest idea of where you are? Haven't you noticed this is a hostile environment? They don't care if you're a bloody writer. They don't discriminate to that degree. To them, you're simply an idiot American poking his nose in where it's not wanted."

A smattering of Cambodians had paused in their promenade to kibbitz, amused by our argument. Feeling exposed, I said, "All right. Fine . . . whatever. Let's just go, okay?"

Lucy looked around. "Where's Riel?"

We found her in the entryway of the club, staring at a stuffed green adder in a bottle and being stared at by two security men. Mounted on walls throughout the main room were dozens of bottles, some containing snakes, other objects less readily identifiable, and bizarre floral arrangements, someone's flawed conception of the Japanese form. Riel evaded Lucy's attempt to corral her and went deeper into the club, which was also a misconception, an Asian version of a western bar with a big dance floor and booths but with the details, the accents, all wrong. The dance floor was packed with Cambodian men and taxi girls and young expats working out to "Smells Like Teen Spirit." As we proceeded through the club, every couple of feet we crossed into a zone dominated by a new perfume or cologne.

We located a niche in the crowd at the bar, and when the harried bartender deigned to notice us, we ordered drinks. The clamor and the loud music oppressed me, and the young Khmer men in body-hugging silk shirts and gold watches and Italian shoes who eyed Riel made me uneasy. I wasn't disturbed by the possibility of her straying—my attitude toward her was devoid of possessiveness—but I presumed she might be a source of trouble; though the place did not seem dangerous, just another drunken revel in post-millennial Southeast Asia, expressing the relief Asians felt on having survived the worst life had to offer, or so they believed . . . or so I thought they believed. I realize now that it was the same party, more or less, that has been going on for as long as there have been party people.

One drink, I estimated, would be the limit of my tolerance for the Heart of Darkness; but a college-age American kid pushing through the press, Dan Something, muscular and patchily bearded, a frat type on holiday, was brought up short by the sight of Riel. He struck up a shouted conversation with her, bought her a second drink, and invited us to join him and his friends in one of the many private rooms that opened off the main space; there we could talk more comfortably. Riel turned him down, but Marilyn Manson's "Tainted Love" started to play, a song that made me want to break things, particularly Marilyn Manson, and I accepted.

Inside the private room (black walls; furnished with a grouping of easy chairs and a sofa; centered by a coffee table upon which lay a pack of cigarettes, cigarette papers, and a heap of marijuana), Dan introduced us to Sean, a hulking, three-hundred pound, shaven-headed version of himself, his lap occupied by a teenage taxi girl in T-shirt and knock-off designer jeans, tiny as a pet monkey by comparison, and Mike, also accessorized by a taxi girl, a lean, saturnine guy with evil-Elvis sideburns, multiple facial piercings, and tats, the most prominent being a full sleeve on his right arm, a gaudy jungle scene that was home to tigers, temples, and fantastic lizards. Dan, Riel, Lucy, and I squeezed onto the sofa; I was all but pushed out of the conversation, and had to lean forward to see what was happening at the opposite end, where Dan had isolated Riel, sitting between her and Lucy. Air conditioning iced the room, and the din of the dance floor was reduced to a thumping rumor.

Dan and Sean (Sean was a little man's name—in a perfect world, he would have been named Lothar) had recently arrived from Thailand and spoke rapturously of Khao San Road, the backpacker street in Bangkok.

This identified them, if they had not already been so identified, as a familiar species of idiot. Khao San was a strip of guesthouses, internet cafés, bars, tattoo joints, travel agents, etc., where each night, indulging in the distillation of the backpacker experience, hundreds of drunken expats assembled to gobble deep fried scorpions and buy sarongs and wooden bracelets at the stalls lining the street, and—their faces growing solemn—to swap stories about the spiritual insights they had received while whizzing past some temple or another in a VIP bus. They had hooked up with Mike, a college bud, in Phnom Penh. He had been in-country for less than three weeks yet talked about Cambodia with the jaded air of a long-term resident. I guessed him to be the brains of the outfit.

Dan held forth at some length about his hour-and-a-half tour of the Killing Fields, explaining to the ever-so-blitzed Riel (she had added three drinks and the better part of two joints to her chemical constituency) how it had been majorly depressing, yet life affirming and life changing. The Cambodian people were awesome, and his respect for them was so heartfelt, I mean like totally, that he managed to work up a tear, a trick that foretold a future in show biz and may have achieved the desired response among the inebriated breeding stock back in Champaign-Urbana, where he attended school, inducing them to roll over and spread, overborne by the sensitive depths of his soul; but it zipped right past Riel. Listening to him gave me a feeling of superiority, and I could have kept on listening for quite some time; but Lucy was unhappy, pinched between me and Dan, and I thought it appropriate to drop a roach into the conversational soup.

Leaning forward, I asked, "Why don't you have a taxi girl like your pals here?"

Dimly, Dan seemed to perceive this as a threat to his ambitions toward Riel. A notch appeared in his brow, and he squinted at me meanly. Then inspiration struck, perhaps an illumination akin to his moral awakening at the Killing Fields. He acquired an expression of noble forbearance and said, "I don't do whores."

Sean loosed a doltish chuckle; the faces of the taxi girls went blank.

"Seriously," Dan said, addressing first me, then Riel. "I revere women too much to want to just use their bodies."

"Shit, man," Mike said, and he burst out laughing. This set everyone to laughing, with the exception of Riel. Our laughter drowned out Dan's earnest protests, and once it had subsided, Mike confided to us that Dan's girl had fled the room. "She was one psycho bitch," he said. "One second she's grabbing his junk, the next she's talking a fucking mile a minute, pointing at shit."

"What was she pointing to?" Lucy asked.

"Fuck if I know. I was too wasted, and she was talking Cambodian, anyway."

Lucy inquired of the taxi girls in Khmer and, following a back-and-forth, gave her report. "She said the room was different."

"Huh?" said Sean.

"That's what they told me."

"I like being used," Riel said out of the blue.

This alerted even Dan, who had been sulking.

"It makes me feel, you know . . ." Riel spaced on the thought.

"How *does* it make you feel?" asked Mike.

Riel deliberated and said at last, "When Tom comes inside me, it's like I'm being venerated." She turned her calm face to me. "I wish you'd come in me without a rubber, so when I walk around I could feel it running down my thigh. It'd be like a reminder of what you felt. Of what I felt." She looked to Lucy. "You know what I mean? Isn't it that way for you?"

Lucy's head twitched—it might have been a nod— and she compressed her lips. The college boys stared at me in wonderment. They had, I thought, taken me for a relative or some kind of neutered loser. The taxi girls were transfixed, hanging on Riel's every word.

"It's because I'm beautiful, I feel that way, I think. Mitch always told me I was beautiful. Lately he wasn't being honest, but he believed it once upon a time. Now, with you guys . . ." She smiled at Lucy and me. "I'm this exotic country you've traveled to. Like Cambodia. I'm a lot like Cambodia. The land of beautiful women." She waved at the taxi girls. "You're absolutely perfect. You are. You've got these perfect titties. So firm, I don't have to touch them to know."

Sean's girl blushed; he gaped at Riel.

"Mine are too soft." She glanced at her breasts. "Don't you think?"

Lucy and I answered at the same time, her saying, "No," and me saying, "They're fine."

This, the implication that the three of us were in a relationship, provoked Mike to say delightedly, "Fuck!"

"Could I have another drink?" asked Riel, and, turning to Dan: "Maybe you could bring me a drink?"

He hesitated, but Mike said, "Yeah, get us all one, man," and he went off with our drink order; the door opening allowed a gust of music inside.

Lucy started to speak, but Riel cut in line and said to me, "Mitch wanted to sell me to other men, but I wouldn't let him. I wonder if that's why he left."

"Beats me," I said.

"You wouldn't sell me, would you, Tom?"

I had a pretty fair buzz going, but nevertheless I noted that this was another disturbing resonance between my life and *The Tea Forest*. "There's no need," I said. "I'm rich."

With a finger, Riel broke the circle of moisture her glass had made on the table. "I don't guess it matters. Someone's always using you."

"Oh, for heaven's sake! I am fed up with your dreary pronouncements!" Lucy put the back of one hand against her brow, a move suitable to an actress in a silent film, and imitated Riel's fey voice: "It's all so morbidly banal!" She dropped the impersonation and said angrily, "If you reduced your drug intake, you might have a sunnier outlook."

Unruffled, Riel said, "You're not where I am yet. You'll have to increase your drug intake to catch up."

Sean and Mike glanced at each other. I could almost see a word balloon with two downward spikes above their heads, saying in thought italics: *This is way cool!* The taxi girls lost interest and idly fondled their new best friends; but their interest was restored when Riel asked Mike if he planned to have sex with his girl there in the room.

"If you'll have sex with Tom and Lucy," he said.

"No," I said.

"Why not, man? We're all friends."

"Little orgy action. Yeah," said Sean, and had a toke off a joint that his taxi girl held to his lips.

"You haven't even introduced us to your dates," I said to Mike. "That's not very friendly."

"Hey, fuck yourself, dude," said Sean, suddenly gone surly, no doubt due to some critical level of THC having been surpassed.

Mike said, "Oh-oh! You don't want to be getting Sean upset. My man's third team All American. He's a beast."

Sean glared at him. "Fuck you, too."

"Really?" I leaned back and crossed my legs. "What position do you play? No, let me guess. You're an *offensive* lineman, right?"

Lucy put a cautioning hand on my knee.

"Nose guard," said Sean, unmindful of the emphasis I'd placed on the word *offensive*.

Riel started singing, a breathy, wordless tune that drew everyone's notice, and then broke it off to say, "Your friend's been gone a long time."

"It's nuts out there," said Mike. "He's probably still trying to get served."

"Or hooking up with another whore." Sean extended a hand to Mike, who slapped him five but did so listlessly, as though out of obligation.

The door flew inward, and a diminutive Cambodian, one of the gold watch/silk shirt crowd, with a high polish to his hair and an inconsequential mustache, burst into the room, along with the pumping beat of a Madonna song. He shouted at the taxi girls. Behind him was an older man whose eyes ranged the room. Lucy caught at my hand. The taxi girls, too, shouted; their shrill voices mixed incoherently with that of the younger man. Sean dumped his taxi girl onto the floor and stood, his face a beefy caricature of disdain. The older man produced an automatic pistol from behind his back, aimed it at Sean, and spoke to him sharply in Khmer.

"Get down!" Lucy said. "He's telling you to get on your knees!"

Looking dumfounded, Sean obeyed. The taxi girl scrambled up, confronting the young man. They both began to yell, and then he punched her flush in the face, knocking her to the floor. Sean said something, I wasn't sure what. The older man butt-ended him, and he slumped across the taxi girl's legs. She sat against the wall, dazed and bleeding from the mouth. The other taxi girl was still shouting, but the shouts seemed remote, as did the sight of Mike frozen in his chair. The shock I had felt when the incident began had evolved into the kind of fright that grips you when your car spins out of control on an icy road; everything slowed to a crawl. Lucy sheltering against my arm, Riel gazing with mild interest at the gun, Sean moaning and clutching his head—all that was in focus, remarkably clear, yet it was like a child's puzzle with a very few pieces that I couldn't solve. I had the knowledge that whatever was going to happen would happen, and I would die in that little icy black room with Madonna woodling about love and a hooting, armwaving, hip-shaking crowd attempting to cover up the unappetizing facts of their existence with celebration.

The young man (he couldn't have been more than eighteen or nineteen) strode to the center of the room. I was half-hidden behind Lucy, pressed back into the cushions, and until then I don't think he had been able to see me unimpeded. He did not look my way at first—he plainly wanted to strut, to bask in his dominance; but when his eyes fell on me, his prideful expression dissolved. He put his hands together, fingers and palms touching as if in prayer, and inclined his head and jabbered in Khmer.

Bewildered, Lucy said, "He's apologizing to you. He's begging you not to tell his father and asking your forgiveness."

I gawked at her.

"Say something," she said sotto voce. "Act in control."

It had been years since I smoked, but I needed a cigarette to marshal my wits. I reached for the pack on the table and lit one. "How can I forgive him when this animal is holding a gun on us? Ask him that."

Lucy spoke to the young man, and he snapped at the bodyguard, who lowered the gun and withdrew. The young man then reassumed his prayerful posture.

"Tell him he can go," I said. "If he leaves immediately, I won't tell his father."

She relayed the message, and the young man backed toward the door, bowing all the while.

"Wait!" I said, and Lucy echoed me in Khmer.

The young man stopped, holding his pose. I let him stew in his own juices, and his hands began to tremble—his fright increased my spirits more than was natural.

"Tell him to take care of our bill before he goes," I said. "And have them turn the music down."

"Jesus fuck!" Mike said once he had gone. "I thought we were dead! What the fuck just happened?"

Sean struggled up into a sitting position. His taxi girl tried to minister to him, but he brushed her away.

"Shit!" said Mike, and then repeated the word.

The other taxi girl kneeled beside her friend and mopped blood from her mouth and chin.

Lucy, regaining her poise and said to me, "He must have mistaken you for someone else."

"Who the fuck are you, guy?" Mike asked. "Some kind of fucking . . . ?" His imagination failed him and he said again, "Shit!"

"Tom's a hero," said Riel, smiling goofily.

"Apparently so." Lucy picked up her drink and saluted me with an ironic toast. "A hero to villains, at any rate. Could there be something you haven't told us?"

With a groan, Sean heaved up from the floor and flopped into the chair—he was one unhappy nose guard. "That guy like to bust my fucking skull."

"Have a drink," said Mike.

The volume of the music was cut in half. I asked Riel to close the door, and, reaching out languidly, she pushed it shut, putting an end to Madonna. I butted my cigarette, yet it had tasted good, and I lit another. The smoke was hitting me like opium fumes, making my head swim. "Maybe we should go."

"Oh, do you think so?" asked Lucy nastily. "We might as well stay now. What more could happen?"

"I'd like to have my drink," said Riel. "Where's . . . you know, your friend?"

"Dan," said Mike. "Yeah, where the fuck is he?"

The taxi girls went to hover beside their men. Lucy's eyes pried at me, trying to see whatever it was she had overlooked in me. She knew something wasn't kosher. I was on my third cigarette when Dan reentered, carrying a tray of drinks.

"You missed out, man," said Mike. "Tom saved our fucking ass."

He delivered an exaggerated play by play of the assault and my "heroics," and Sean, pressing an iced drink to his head, provided color commentary. "That was one cold dude, man" and "I didn't know what the fuck he was talking about" were exemplary of his contribution. In response to this last, I asked Lucy what had been the young Khmer's problem.

"He accused Nary . . ." She indicated Sean's girl. "Of giving the third girl—the one who left—drugs."

"Why? Because she freaked out about the room?"

Lucy spoke to the girls and then said, "The girl has a fondness for Ecstasy. Dith, the young guy, had forbidden her to use any more. They have a relationship, though I can't quite gather what it is, and he believed that these two slipped her some in a drink. They claim she just started behaving oddly. She said a mirror vanished off the wall."

"Crazy bitch," said Dan.

"Let's go." I stood, followed in short order by Lucy. "You coming, Riel?"

She held up a forefinger, addressed herself to her drink, and chugged it in two swallows.

Dan put on a woebegone look. "Hey, come on! You guys don't have to go."

But Riel was already at the door. She paused to flutter a ditsy wave. " 'Bye, Danny," she said.

The *Undine* was moored at the port facility on the Tonle Sap, a short distance from where it joined the Mekong and close by a huge multistory barge, its paint weathered to the grayish white of old bone. In years past this had housed a dance hall, a brothel by any other name, and now the top floor was home to the offices of the Cambodian Sex Workers Union and other such organizations. Womyn's Agenda For Change, the sign above one door spelled out in English. The following morning, sitting in the stern of the *Undine*, I watched streams of taxi girls trundling along the balconies, passing in and out of rooms where their sisters had once slaved, busy being empowered, fighting the good fight against the corporate giants that sought to use them as guinea pigs to test experimental AIDS vaccines. I supposed their sisterhood boosted morale and saved lives, and I knew it was dangerous work. Lucy compared them to the Wobblies back in the 1920s and said many girls had been murdered for their efforts. Yet to my eyes they might as well have been streams of ants plucking a few last shreds of tissue off a carcass—they had no conception of the forces mounted against them, no clue how absurd and redundant a name was Womyn's Agenda For Change.

Since my arrival in Phnom Penh, the changes (flickerings in the sky, subtle alterations in urban geography, etc.) had grown more frequent or, due to an increased sensitivity on my part, more observable. The episode with the taxi girl and the vanishing mirror was the first evidence I'd had that anyone else noticed them, though the evidence was impugned by the possible use of drugs. If the changes were observable by others, if this were other than a localized effect, and if it occurred in a place less disorderly than Phnom Penh, it would be the lead story on the news. I expected that when I reached Dong Thap the changes might be even more drastic. The prospect unnerved me, yet it held a potent allure. Like the narrator of *The Tea Forest*, I was being drawn to complete the journey and I wanted to complete it. The previous night's incident had convinced me that I was undergoing a transformation like the one documented by Cradle Two in the novel. I had taken undue pleasure in the exercise of control over the young Khmer in the Heart of Darkness, and I wondered if the person for whom he had mistaken me could have been the alpha-Cradle, that secretive, powerful figure, the Platonic ideal of Cradles everywhere. The notion that I was evolving into such a ruthless and decisive figure was exhilarating. I had never possessed either quality in great measure, and the proportions of the man, the fear he inspired, were impressive. Yet I was being pulled in another direction as well, and that was why I had returned to the *Undine* and sat in the stern, the satellite phone in my lap, ignoring the faint, sweetish reek of sewage, gazing at the barge and at eddies in the brown water.

When I called Kim, she answered on the third ring and told me this wasn't a good time. I asked if she had company. She was noncommittal, a sure sign that one of my colleagues, or one of hers, was lying in bed beside her. I said it was important, and she said, "Hang on."

I pictured her slipping into a robe, soothing the ruffled sensibilities of her lover, and carrying the phone into the living room. When she spoke again, her tone was exasperated.

"You don't call for three weeks, and now you just have to speak to me?" she said. "I got so worried I called Andy [my agent], and of course you'd called him. This is so typical of you."

I apologized.

"Are you in trouble?" she asked. "Do you want to run off to Bali with some teenage nymph and jeopardize everything we've built together?"

"It's not that."

"Because if that's the case, I'm sick and tired of having to coax you back. I'm ready to give you my blessing."

"It's not that! Okay? I want you to do me a favor. Andy was going to make copies of *The Tea Forest*. Did he send one to me?"

"I don't know. You have a package from him. I put it with the rest of your mail."

"That's probably it. Could you take a look?"

While she checked, my eyes returned to the barge. A number of women were kneeling on the foredeck, painting signs for a protest, and others had gathered in the bow, listening to a speaker who was talking into a hand-held megaphone, doing a bit of consciousness-raising. Now and then her high-pitched voice blatted out and there was a squeal of feedback.

"It's here," Kim said. "Do you want me to express it?"

"I want you to read it."

"Thomas, I don't have the time."

"Please. Read it . . . as soon as possible. I can't talk to you about what's happening until you've read it."

There was a silence, and then she said, "Andy told me you were developing some worrisome obsessions about the book."

"You know I'm a . . ."

"Just a second."

A man said something in the background; after that

I heard nothing. When Kim came back on, she said with anger in her voice, "You have my undivided attention."

"Sorry."

"It's not important. You were saying?"

I'd lost the thread, and it took me a second to pick it up.

"I'm not the kind of guy who's likely to lose it," I said. "You know that."

"Are you doing a lot of drugs?"

"Did Andy say he thought I was?"

"Not in so many words, but . . . yeah."

"Well, I'm not. There are some strange correspondences, very strange, between the book and what's going on here. I need another point of view."

"All right. I'll read it Wednesday night. I can't until then. Tomorrow's a nightmare."

A drop of sweat trickled into my eye, and I wiped it away. Not even eight-thirty, and the temperature was already into the nineties. I felt a sudden upsurge of emotion and realized how much I missed Kim. Though I had tried to throw my heart in a new direction, though Lucy was an interesting woman and, without doubt, more sexually adventurous than Kim, I was ready for some home cooking, and I asked Kim if she was planning to meet me in Saigon.

"If you still want me to," she said.

We discussed when she would come, at which hotel she should stay, and spent some time repairing the rift in the relationship. I was so consoled by the familiarity of her voice, so excited by the predictable promise it conveyed, I suggested that we could marry in Saigon, a suggestion she did not reject out of hand, saying we should table the matter until she arrived. I thought we both had concluded that these adventures, these dalliances no longer served a purpose—they had become interruptions in our lives, and it was time we moved on. Yet when I hung up, it was as though I had cut myself off from her. I felt a total lack of connection and regretted having mentioned marriage. I

went into the bow and asked Lan if we could head
south in the morning. He sat facing the river and its
farther shore, his legs dangling over the side of the
houseboat, wearing a grease-stained pink T-shirt and
shorts; he pushed a shock of gray hair from his eyes
and peered up at me like an old turtle, blinking, cran-
ing his stiff neck.

"Anytime," he said. "Need provisions."

"Send Deng into town."

He chuckled, showing his gapped yellow teeth.
"Deng."

"What's so funny?" I asked.

"Gone. You scare him. He tells me you are a bad
man. He says a bad man is unlucky for people
around him."

I thought Deng's leaving probably had more to do
with Lucy than with his perception of my character.
"You don't believe that, do you?"

"Maybe," said Lan.

"Then why haven't you deserted?"

"No reason." He fixed his eyes on a barge loaded
with crates chugging upstream, crapping an oil slick
and black fumes. "Need provisions," he said.

That afternoon, under an overcast sky, we visited a
market on the outskirts of the city, a place where the
pavement ended and green countryside could be seen
off along the main road; the streets widened to form
an open area—a square, if you will—of tapioca-
colored dirt amid dilapidated buildings, none more
than two stories tall. Infirm-looking, vertically compro-
mised stalls of weathered wood were clumped alongside the buildings, pitched at eccentric angles. If you
squinted and let your eyes slide out of focus, they
resembled old, hobbling, gray-skirted women, some
leaning together, who had paused for breath during a
constitutional and never stirred again. The majority of
the stalls were the offices of fortune-tellers, and this
was the reason for our visit: Lucy's favorite fortune-
teller could be found there. Why she picked him out

of all the fortune-tellers in Phnom Penh, I hadn't a clue. He offered no complicated graphs and charts to demark your fate, as did many. His method was to rub dirt into her palm to make the lines stand out and mutter abstractions about her future until she was satisfied. Perhaps appearance played a part in her choice. Iron-gray hair hair fell in tangles over his chest and shoulders, and tattoos, faded to intricate blue scratchings, wrote an illegible legend on his arms, chest, neck, and forehead. He had a wispy goatee, wore a wraparound that covered his loins, and could usually be found smoking a cigar-sized spliff, which may have accounted for his benign gaze. His colleagues, most neatly dressed in western-style clothing, free of tattoos and spliffs, gave him a wide berth.

While Lucy consulted her wizard and Riel dawdled at a stall that sold cheap jewelry, I walked through thin crowds along one of the market streets leading off the square and, after a bout of token haggling, bought a U.S. army-issue Colt .45 and six clips of ammo from an arms dealer. Though old, the weapon appeared to be in good working order. The dealer encouraged me to test fire it, but I was afraid that I might be reported—I had no conception of the legalities attendant upon buying a gun. I tucked the pistol into my waist, beneath my shirt, and hustled back toward the square. A block along from the arms dealer, I stopped dead in my tracks. Standing in the doorway of a building on the corner was a bearded man dressed identically to me—shorts, sandals, a black T-shirt—and with an identical (as far as I could determine from a distance of forty feet) face and build. I imagined that we wore the identical stunned expression. We locked gazes for a moment, and as I hurried toward him, he ducked into the interior of the building. I raced after him, through the door and into the midst of twenty or thirty people slurping noodles at wooden tables, nearly knocking over a waitress who carried a load of dirty dishes. Her irritation gave way to confusion. She glanced toward the kitchen, then at

me, and that told me all I needed to know. I ran through
the kitchen and out onto the street behind the restaurant. There was scant pedestrian traffic—some kids
kicking around a soccer ball, two women talking, a
man looking under the hood of a beat-up yellow
Toyota—and no sign of my double. I walked along in
the direction of the square, peering into doorways, my
excitement draining. What could we have said to each
other, anyway? We could have compared notes on
Cradleness, on what it meant to be a Cradle, for all
the good that would do. Possibly I could have learned
something new about the delta, but nothing, I thought,
that would have greatly illuminated its central mystery. It had been a strange thing to see myself, yet
now, at a remove from the moment, I questioned
whether he had actually been my double. A bearded
man in shorts and a black T-shirt at a distance of forty
feet who had fled when approached by a stranger on
the run: I told myself he might have been anyone.

In my absence, the center of the square had been
taken over by an elephant. It was kneeling, a heap of
fresh dung close by its hindquarters, and Riel stood
at its side, like a princess beside a weathered castle
wall, talking to a boy in shorts, twelve or thirteen,
mounted behind the animal's neck. A farmer's son, I
thought, who had ridden the family tractor into town
to show it off. I found a stall adjacent to Lucy's wizard
that sold coffee sweetened with condensed milk and
sat on a rickety folding chair and watched Riel trying
to entice the boy into giving her a ride (he kept wag-
ging his finger no, and scowling), while the elephant
flexed its trunk and blinked away flies, presenting an
image of stuporous discontent.

The crowds were thinner in the square than they
had been on the side streets, so Riel was the object
of much attention, especially from the male stallkeep-
ers. I sipped my coffee and thought about the gun
pushing against my pelvic bone, imagining it had been
snatched from the hand of a dead officer during the
Vietnam conflict and wondering how many lives it had

snuffed out. It had been an impulse buy, although the
impulse was informed by a lifelong fear of and fascination with guns and was given a quasi-rational basis by
the idea that I might need it once we reached the
delta. It was a steel phallus, a social ill, all those things
that left-wing politics said it was; yet its cold touch
warmed me and added weight to my purpose, enabling
the fantasy that my mission there was important.

Lucy finished her consultation and joined me for
coffee. "It's going to rain," she said.

The clouds had gone from a nickel color to dark
gray brushed with charcoal; the muggy heat and the
smell of the elephant's dung had thickened. I laid an
envelope on the table by Lucy's hand.

"What's this?" she asked, fingering it.

"Severance pay," I said.

She met my eyes steadily, and I thought she would
object or demand an explanation; but she only looked
away, her face neutral.

"So what did he tell you, your guy? What's in your
stars?" I asked, breaking a silence.

"Obviously not a trip south," she said. "Oh, well.
Like they say, all good things . . ."

"I hope it's been good."

She appeared to rebound. "It's been an adventure . . .
and good." She grinned. "No complaints on this end."

"It's about time you went home and kick-started
that career, don't you think?"

"Advice? And from someone who should know better?" she said merrily. "I shall have to reevaluate my
impression of you."

"Just a thought."

The stallkeeper switched on a radio and tuned into
a station playing reggae—Peter Tosh and elephants,
the essence of globalization. Lucy inspected the contents of the envelope. "This is a lot of money," she
said. "It's too much, really."

"I was hoping you'd see to Riel."

She nudged the envelope over to my side of the
table. "I don't want to be responsible."

"I thought you fancied her."

"The lesbian thing . . . it's my exhibitionist side coming out. It works for me when the right guy is around. Otherwise . . ." She wrinkled her nose.

"Look, I'm not expecting you to spend much time on this. Give it a week or so, and try to pass her off to someone decent. That shouldn't be much of a problem. Maybe you can trick her onto a plane back to Winnipeg. If she stays here, she's bound to run into someone who'll fuck her up worse than she already is."

"All right. I'll do my best for her, but . . . I'll do my best."

I took her hand, letting my fingers mix with hers. "I'm going to be in London next spring. I'll give you a call, see how you're doing."

"I'm likely to be busy," she said after a pause. "But, yes. Do call, please."

We held hands for ten or fifteen seconds, reestablishing the limits of our limited affection, and then Lucy said, "Oh, my gosh. Look what she's doing now."

Riel had stepped around to the front of the elephant, facing it, and was dancing, a slow, eloquent, seductive temple-girl dance, arms raised above her head, hips swaying, as if trying to charm the beast. The elephant appeared unaffected, but everyone in the square had stopped what they were doing to watch. A livid stroke of lightning fractured the eastern sky, its witchy shape holding against the sullen moil of clouds, and was followed by a peal of thunder that rolled across green fields into the city. As it passed, the sky flickered, the clouds shifted in their conformation; but such phenomena had grown so commonplace, I would not have noticed except that it added a mysterious accent to the scene.

"Do you think she's in any danger?" Lucy asked.

"From the elephant? Probably not," I said. "The boy seems calm."

"We should fetch her, anyway. It's time we went

back." She tucked the envelope into her bag, yet made no move to stand. "Whatever comes, I think we've helped her."

"We provided a place where she didn't have to worry about survival. But I don't think we can claim to have helped."

"What should we have done? Put her in a clinic? She wouldn't last a day. We're not her parents . . . and it's not as if she cares a fig about us. She'd be off in a flash if something better happened along."

"Maybe something better will come along. That's why I gave you the money."

Lucy acknowledged this gloomily.

"She may care about us more than you think," I said. "Her attachment to the world is flimsy, but we became her world for a few weeks. Flimsy or not, she formed an attachment."

"Isolate one moment, if you can, when she demonstrated genuine affection."

"That little speech she gave at the Heart of Darkness. I . . ."

"I knew you'd bring that up."

"I realize it was done for shock value. But it was inspired by a kernel of affection."

Lucy's fortune-teller scurried out from his stall and made a playful run at Riel—his shoulders were hunched and arms dangling, as though he were pretending to be a monkey tempted by a piece of fruit yet afraid to touch it. She continued to dance, and he wove a path about her, feinting, lunging at her, and scooting away; whenever he came near, he scattered some sort of powder at her feet. The scene held a curious potency, like a picture on a card, the representation of an archetype in a Cambodian Tarot, an image that seemed easily interpretable at first glance, but then, in the way of many Asian scenes, came to seem an impenetrable riddle: the wizard scuttling forward and retreating and the mystery void girl, the blonde sacrifice, lost in abandon, in holy, slow dementia, dancing before the massive, dim-witted, iconic beast. Lucy mentioned again that we should be going. Another peal of thunder, an erratic rumbling, hinted at something souring in the darkened belly of the sky. Vendors hastened to cover their merchandise, unrolling cloths and makeshift awnings. A sprinkle of rain fell, yet still we sat there.

"Snake country. That is what my daddy called Vietnam whenever he'd had a few, referring not only to his service in the delta, but to the country at large. He'd reach a garrulous stage in his drunk and deliver himself of some bloody, doleful tale, staring into his glass as if relating his wartime experiences to gnats that had drowned in a half-inch of Jim Beam. I think these stories were intended as self-justification, explaining in advance why he was probably going to kick the crap out of me later on, capping off his evening with a spot of exercise; but I heard them not as apology or warnings about the world's savagery—they had for me the windy lilt of pirate stories, and I loved to hear him lying his ass off, boasting of his prowess with a fifty-millimeter machine gun, blowing away gooks from the stern of a swift boat, dealing death while his comrades were shot to pieces around him . . . and, oh, watching them die had ripped the heart from his chest—the survivor's guilt he felt, the nightly visitations from torn, shattered corpses. Yet he couldn't help that he had been made of sterner stuff than they, and, when you got right down to it, he had relished his days in Vietnam. He had been called, he said, and not by love of country. If he had it to do over, he wouldn't so much as step on a bug for a country that hadn't done squat for him. No, he was convinced that he had been summoned to an unguessable purpose that he could never put a name to, that had nothing to do with war. That was the sole element of his narrative that rang true, the part about being summoned, and this was likely due to the fact that I could relate to such a summons. He hated the Vietnamese, but he was a natural-born hater, and I doubt now that he ever went to Vietnam. He showed me no mementos or photos of him and his buddies, and the stories lacked detail, though as the years wore on, he added detail (whether his memory improved or he was polishing a fictional history, his stories caused me to become fixated on guns and violence, and this led me to do a crime that earned me a nickel in the prison camp at Butner). His war record was the only thing he took pride in, yet it may all have been a drunken fantasy. 'The goddamn gooks make wine out of snake's blood,' he muttered once before passing out, and the conjuration of that image, red-like-pomegranate wine that beaded on the lip of a glass in a yellow-claw hand, the drops congealing thick as liquefied Jell-O, sliding down the throat in clots, slimy and narcotic—that said it all for me about snake country.

"Unlike my daddy, who came with guns blazing and the ace of death in his eye, I had the shits when I entered Vietnam, and several degrees of fever. I lay in the bottom of the boat, trying to hold in my guts, and avoided looking at the sky, which was playing its usual tricks, only with greater frequency—to look at it intensified my fever. We had some trouble at the border post. The Vietnamese run a tighter ship than does Cambodia, and since we didn't have enough money for a respectable bribe, the officials threatened to confiscate our boat; but then Jordan helped them get an overloaded pick-up unstuck from a muddy ditch, and after that they were all smiles and stamped our passports and waved us through into a portion of the Mekong renowned for its whirlpools. We were cautioned that much larger craft than ours had been sucked under, but we negotiated this treacherous stretch without incident and, below the town of Chau Doc, entered an area known as the Nine Dragons, where the river split into nine major channels, and there were as well minor channels, islands, and a maze of man-made canals spider-webbing an enormous area. At a riverside gas station, we received directions to the Kinh Dong Tien, the canal that would carry us toward the tea forest.

"The boating life on the canals was more lively than we had yet encountered, even in the vicinity of Phnom Penh, and was so dense that signs on the riverbank directed traffic, warning when not to pass on the left and such. There were mobile floating rice mills, boats loaded with construction supplies, with coconuts, plumbing fixtures, furniture, watermelons, and so forth, and the banks were crowded with shacks, and beyond them were fields reeking of DDT. People stared open-mouthed at us and laughed at our wretched condition—covered with insect bites and sores, putting along in that wreck of a boat, the rudder held on with adhesive tape, the engine sputtering. Some of them, moved by charitable impulse, offered assistance, and others offered produce and drinking water, but I was in no mood to accept their charity. My fever had worsened, and the spiritual darkness that afflicted me had deepened to the point that I saw everything through a lens of distaste and loathing. Every smile seemed mocking, every friendly gesture masked an inimical intent, and I wanted nothing to do with this infestation of small brown people who swarmed over the delta, polluting it with their pesticides, with their shitting, squalling babies, and their brute insignificance. 'You don't go hunting termites with a rifle,' Daddy once told me. 'You poison their fucking nest.' Recalling that comment, I thought maybe he had gone to Vietnam after all . . .''

Not long after the events described in this passage, Cradle Two's narrator (and, I would guess, Cradle Two himself) grew too ill go on, or, as the narrator implies, he used illness as an excuse for quitting because his fear of what lay ahead came to outweigh the pull he felt to complete the journey. After being treated at a local clinic, he recuperated in Phnom Penh and there wrote the ending to the book, claiming to be in mental communion with a multiplicity of Thomas Cradles, several of whom managed to enter the tea forest; yet even if you accepted this to be true, it was not a true resolution—he lost contact with the various Cradles once they passed beyond the edge of the forest, and so he contrived an ending based on clues and extrapolation.

I had been wise not to emulate Cradle Two's journey to the letter, I realized. As I've mentioned, the lifestyle he was forced to adopt due to lack of funds left him prone to disease and injury, whereas I, traveling in comfort aboard the *Undine*, had maintained my health. I had no doubt that I would see journey's end; but now that I was on the final leg, I debated whether or not I wanted to see it. The spiritual darkness remarked on by Cradle Two's narrator had descended upon me in full, though it might be more accurate to say that my social veneer had been worn away by the passage along the river and my dark nature revealed. I understood my essential character to be cold and grasping, violent and cowardly, courageous enough should my welfare demand it, yet terrified of everything, and I was, for the most part, comfortable with that recognition. (All men possessed these qualities, although I—and, I assumed, my fellow Cradles—must have them in spades.) When Kim called, presumably to report on her reading of *The Tea Forest*, I refused to answer. She rang and rang, calling every half hour; I switched off the satellite phone, not wishing to be distracted from steeping in my own poisonous spirit, basking amid thoughts that uncoiled lazily, turgidly, like serpents waking from a long sleep . . . like Cradle Two's ornate sentences. Yet as my bleakness grew, so did my fear. I wanted to retreat from the delta, to return to my old secure life. The fear was due in large measure to what I saw whenever I set foot out of the cabin. As we drew near Phu Tho, the hamlet that served as the jumping-off place for the tea forest, the changes that twitched and reconfigured the clouds, that caused mirrors to vanish from walls and rooftops to assume new outlines, became constant, and I felt myself to be the only solid thing in the landscape. It was like watching time-lapse photography. A village glided past, and I saw tin roofs rippling with change, acquiring rust, brightening with strips of new tin, dimpling with dents that would the next second be smoothed out, and a group of people coming from their houses to stare and wave would shift in number and alignment, vanishing and reappearing, wearing shabbier or more splendid clothes, and the sky would darken with running clouds, lighten and clear, the clouds then reoccurring, assuming different shapes, and the green of the fields would vary from a pale yellow-green to a deep viridian, and every shade in between; and Lan at his post in the prow, he would change, too, his skull narrowing and elongating, stubble sprouting from his chin, one leg withering, a cane materializing by his hand—yet before long he was hale once again. I sequestered myself in the cabin, doing my best to ignore disappearing pots and suddenly manifesting piles of dirty clothing. I had nothing to guide me through this leg of the journey—I had gone farther along the path than Cradle Two, and his novel made no mention of this phenomenon. On half a dozen occasions, I was on the verge of ordering Deng to turn the boat and make for Phnom Penh, but I persevered, though my heart fluttered in my chest, itself registering (or so I feared) the process of change as we slipped back and forth between universes, approaching an unearthly nexus. And then, less than five miles from Phu Tho, either the changes ceased or they became unobservable. We had reached a place where all things flowed into one, the calm at the heart of the storm.

Phu Tho itself was unremarkable, a collection of small concrete-block houses, painted in pastel shades, gathered about a landing and a ranger station (a mosquito-infested tin hut) where you gained admission to the national park beyond, a wetlands that contained the tea forest. But the canal and its embankment in the vicinity of Phu Tho was a graveyard of boats: motor launches, rafts, dinghies, sailboats of every size, barges. Thousands had been dragged onto land and an un-

countable number of others scuttled—in order to clear
a channel, I conjectured, though that reason no longer
applied, for the channel had been blocked with submerged and partially submerged craft, and our progress was halted more than a mile from the hamlet. To
reach it, I would have to pick my way on foot across
the drowned hulks of a myriad boats.

We arrived at our stopping point in early morning,
when drifts of whitish fog lay over all, ghosting the
forest of prows and masts emerging from the water
and the wreckage of crushed and capsized hulls spilling over the shore as if a tsunami had driven them to
ruin. The majority (like the *Undine*) were adorned
with painted eyes to drive away evil spirits, and these
could be seen peering at us through the gauzy cover,
seeming to blink as the fog thickened and thinned—
it was an eerie and disconcerting sight, its effect ampli-
fied by the funereal silence that held sway, accented
by the slop of the tide against the houseboat, an unsa-
vory sound that reminded me in its erratic rhythm of
an injured cur licking a wound. The people we had
talked to along the canals would surely have told us
of this obstruction, and it followed, then, that Phu
Tho, this Phu Tho, must be a singular place designed
to mark journey's end for every Thomas Cradle (ex-
cepting those who failed to complete their journeys),
and that in other Phu Thos, life went on as always,
the canal busy with its usual traffic, and that I was,
despite Lan's presence, for all intents and purposes,
alone.

I packed a rucksack with a change of clothes, pro-
tein bars, water, the gun, binoculars, a coiled length
of rope, the Colt, a first-aid kit, an English-Vietnamese
pocket dictionary, repellent, and my dog-eared copy
of Cradle Two's novel, thinking that his ruminations
about the tea forest might be of value. Lan was waiting on deck, dour as ever; before I could instruct him,
he said, "I stay here three days. Then I go. Bring
police." Phu Tho spooked him, though you couldn't
have determined this from his expression. I felt oddly

sentimental about leaving him behind, and as I began
my trek to shore, negotiating a path of slippery, tilted
decks and slick hulls, tightroping along submerged
railings, I speculated about his past and why he had
stuck it out with me. I decided that it must have to do
with habits cultivated during the Vietnam conflict—he
may have been an army scout or ARVN and thus had
developed a love-hate relationship with Americans.
Before long, however, the exigencies of the crossing
demanded my full attention. Twice I had to retrace
my steps and seek a new route, and once, when I was
up to my neck in water, I nudged something soft, and
a bloated, eyeless face emerged from the murk and
bobbed to the surface. I kicked the body away in revulsion, but I had the impression that the face had
belonged to a man of about my size and weight. This
was more than a graveyard for boats. I imagined that
many more Cradles might be asleep in that deep.

A third of the way to shore, I stopped to rest atop
the roof of a sunken launch. The sun was high, showing intermittently between leaden clouds; the fog had
burned off, and though the heat was intense, I was
grateful for it. I felt a chill that could not be explained
by my immersion in water. The stillness and the silence, the corpse I had disturbed, the regatta of dead
ships, looking more ruinous absent its ghostly dress
and stretching, I saw now, for miles along the canal,
a veritable boat holocaust: It was such a surreal scene,
its scope so tremendous, I quailed before it; yet as
always something drove me on. I was around fifty,
sixty yards from shore, taking another rest, when
music kicked in from one of the houses. It carried
faintly across the water, but I could make out Little
Richard telling Miss Molly it was all right to ball. The
song finished, and after an interval, Sly Stone's "Everyday People" began to play. That sunny jingle served
to heighten Phu Tho's desolate air. I wiped sweat from
my eyes and scanned the houses, trying to find the
source of the music. No people, no dogs or pigs or
chickens. Banana fronds lifted in a breeze, but no

movement otherwise. I took a look through my binoculars. On the façade of a pale green house was a mural like the one I'd seen in Stung Treng, and again in Phnom Penh, depicting a yellowish, many-chambered form. The next song was Neal Diamond's "Girl, You'll Be a Woman Soon." Whoever was selecting the music had begun to piss me off.

The boats close in to the hamlet were relatively undamaged, still afloat, and this made the going easier. I scrambled ashore to the tune of "Low Rider" and rested on an overturned dinghy, the moisture steaming out of my clothing. I took the gun from my pack, tucked it into my waist, and headed for the pale green house, walking across a patch of mucky ground bristling with weeds and, apart from butterflies and some unseen buzzing insects, devoid of life. The vibe I received from Phu Tho was not so much one of abandonment (though it clearly had been abandoned), but of its impermanence, of the tautness to which its colors and shape were stretched over an inscrutable frame. It was as if at any moment my foot would punch through the rice paper illusion of earth into the void below; yet I had a firm confidence that this would not happen, that its frailty, its temporality, was something I simply hadn't noticed before but that had always been there to notice—frailty was an essential condition of life—and that I noticed it now spoke to the fact that I had come to a place less distant (in some incomprehensible way) from the source of the feeling. This was a complex and improbable understanding to have reached in the space of a hundred-foot walk, with music blasting and all the while worrying about what was inside the house and whether it had been wise to swim in water as foul as that in the vicinity of the hamlet; yet reach it I did, for all the benefit it bestowed.

The song faded, and the *put-put* of a generator surfaced from the funk, the singer advising his listeners to take a little trip, take a little trip with him, and an enormous man stepped from the door. He was well over three hundred pounds (closer to four, I reckoned), and stood a full head taller than I, clad in shorts and sandals and a collarless, sweat-stained shirt sewn of flour sacking. His arms and legs were speckled with inflamed insect bites, and his complexion was a sunburned pink, burst capillaries reddening his cheeks and nose; but for these variances, his bearded face, couched in an amused expression, was the porcine equivalent of my own.

"You're late to the party, cuz," he said in a voice rougher than mine, a smoker's voice with a country twang.

I was slow to respond, daunted by him.

"Better come on in," he said. "Looks like you could use a sit-down."

The floors of the house were of packed dirt carpeted with straw mats, and the mats were filthy with fruit rinds, empty bottles, crumbs, magazines (porn and celebrity rags), and all manner of paper trash. Centerfolds were taped to the walls. A bare, queen-sized mattress took up one end of the room; at the opposite end was a mildewed easy chair without legs and two card tables with folding chairs arranged beside them; a small TV-DVD player sat on one of the tables, DVDs scattered around it, and there was also a record player of the sort high school girls used to own in the sixties to play 45s. Sitting by the record player, holding a stack of 45s in her lap, was a slim, worn-looking Vietnamese woman of about thirty wearing a print smock. The man introduced her as Bian, but he didn't bother to introduce himself. He wedged himself into the easy chair—it was a tight fit—and sighed expansively. The sigh seemed to enrich the sickening organic staleness that prevailed in the house, and I pictured the individual molecules of the scent as having the man's pinkish coloration and blobby shape.

"Want a beer?" He spoke to Bian in Vietnamese. "She'll bring us a couple."

She went into the back room, a thin silver chain attached to her ankle slithering behind her, anchored to a stone half-buried in the floor. The man saw me staring at it and said, rather unnecessarily, "I didn't keep her on a leash, the bitch would be gone."

"No doubt," I said.

Bian brought the beers and stationed herself once again by the record player—taped to the wall above her head, like a dream she was having, an airbrushed redhead with pendulous breasts gazed at a porn star's erection delightedly and with a trace of wild surmise, as if it were just the bestest thing ever.

My initial take on the fat man, that he might be the powerful Ur-Cradle, had waned. He was a gargantuan redneck idiot, and my astonishment at his presence, at having this sorry proof of what I had previously only supposed, was neutralized by his enslavement of Bian and his repellent physical condition. On the face of things, he was a step or three farther along the path to the true Cradle than I was, a distillation of the Cradle essence. I didn't trust him, and I let my beer sit untasted. Yet at the same time I had a sympathetic reaction to him, as if I understood the deficits that had contributed to his character.

I asked where he had gotten the beer, and he said, "Some of the boys hijacked supply barges to get here. Hell, with what's on them barges, a man could survive for years. I been here must be four, five months and I hardly put a dent in it."

"By 'the boys,' you mean men like us? Thomas Cradles?"

"Yeah." He groped for something on the floor beside his chair, found it—a rag—and mopped sweat from his face. "Not all of them look like us. I guess their daddies slept with somebody different. But they all got the same name, least the ones I talked to did. Most push on through without stopping, they're so damn eager to get into the tea forest."

"Apparently you weren't that eager."

"Look at me." He indicated his massive belly. "A man my size, I'm lucky I made it this far, what with the heat and all. I was about half dead when I got here. Took me a while to recover, and by the time I did, the urge wasn't on me no more. That was strange, you know, 'cause I was flat-out desperate to get here. But hey, maybe the animal can't use fat junkies. Anyhow, I figured me and Bian would squat a while and make a home for the boys. You know, give them a place to rest up, drink a few beers . . . get laid." He shifted about in his chair, raising a dust. "Speaking of which, twenty bucks'll buy you a ride on Bian. She might not look it, but she got a whole lot of move in that skinny ass."

Bian cast a forlorn glance my way.

"I'll pass," I said. "What can you tell me about the tea forest?"

"Probably nothing you don't know. Some boys been coming back through lately, ones that didn't make it all the way to wherever. They're saying the animal don't need us no more. Whatever use it had for us, it's about over with . . . Least that's the feeling they got."

"The animal?"

"Man, you don't know much, do you? The animal. The creature-feature. It's painted on the wall outside. You telling me you never seen it before?"

I told him what I had seen, the murals, the creature in my opium dream, and that I had sworn off drugs for fear of seeing it again.

"Well, there's your problem, dude," he said, and gave a sodden laugh. "I mean, shit! How you expect to pierce the veil of Maya, you don't use drugs? You sure you're a Cradle? 'Cause from what I can make out, most of us stayed stoned the whole damn trip."

It was in my mind to tell him that if he was any example, most of us were serious fuck-ups; but instead I asked what he thought was going on.

"'Pears we all see it a little different," he said. "This one ol' boy, he told me he figured what we saw wasn't exactly what was happening. It was like a symbol or a . . . I don't know. Something."

"A metaphor?"

He didn't appear familiar with the word, but he said, "Yeah . . . like that. Everyone I've talked to pretty much agrees the animal needs us to protect it from something." His brow furrowed. "Those splinters you saw when you were high? I reckon they're like these stick figures I saw. Every time I did up, I'd see them standing around parts of the animal, guarding it like. Fucking weird, man. Scared the shit out of me. But I kept on seeing them 'cause I couldn't do without ol' Aunt Hazel."

The reference eluded me.

"Heroin," he said. "I had a monster habit. First week after I kicked, it was like I caught the superflu." He had a swallow of beer, wiped his mouth with the back of his hand. "Now the next question you're going to ask is, How come it chose us? Everybody's got a theory. Some I've heard are fucking insane, but they all boil down to basically the same thing. Something about us Cradle boys is pure badass."

His prideful grin told me that he was satisfied with this explanation and would be unlikely to have anything more intelligent to say on the subject. "You said some of them came back? Are they still here?"

He shook his head. "They couldn't get shut of this place fast enough. If you're after another opinion . . . way I hear it, some boys are still wandering around the fringe of the forest. They didn't feel the urge strong enough, I guess. Or they were too weak and gave out. You could talk to them. The ones that come back used park boats, so getting to the forest ain't nothing."

Bian said something in Vietnamese, and the man said, "She wants to know if you're going to fuck her."

"I don't think so," I said.

He relayed this information to Bian, who appeared relieved. "You can always change your mind. Bian don't care. She's a regular scout . . . ain't you, darling?" He reached out and chucked her under the chin. "You don't know what you're missing. She's got a real educated pussy." He settled back in the chair and gave me a canny look. "I bet you're a writer."

Surprised, I said, "Yeah," and asked how he knew.

"I didn't *know*. Us Cradles tend to be literary types more often than not. And seems like the boys who ain't interested in Bian are mostly writers . . . though there's been a couple like to wore her out. But what I was getting at, seeing how you're a writer, maybe you can make sense of their scribbles. I got a whole bunch of their notebooks."

"You have their journals?"

"Journals . . . notebooks. Whatever. I got a bunch. The boys that stop in, they figure they're going to need food and water more than anything else. They buy provisions and leave their stuff for me to hold. If you want to check it out, it's in the back room there."

It took him two tries to lever himself out of the chair. Going with a rolling, stiff-ankled walk, he preceded me into the room and pointed out the possessions of other Cradles scattered willy-nilly among crates of canned goods and stacks of bottled water and beer: discarded packs, clothing, notebooks, and the usual personal items. Copies of *The Tea Forest* could be seen poking out from this mess, as ubiquitous as Lonely Planet guides in a backpacker hotel. I squatted and began leafing through one of the notebooks. The handwriting was an approximation of my own, and the words . . . The notebooks were a potential gold mine, I realized. If this one were typical of the rest, I could crib dozens of stories from them, possibly a couple of novels. It struck me anew how odd all this was, to be seeking clues to a mystery by poring over journals that you yourself had written . . . or if not quite you, then those so close to you in flesh and spirit, they were more than brothers. Intending to make a comment along these lines, I half-turned to the fat man and caught a blow on the head that drove splinters of light into my eyes and sent me pitching forward on my stomach into a pile of clothing. If I lost consciousness, it was for a second or two, no more. Woozy, my face planted in a smelly T-shirt, I felt him patting down my pockets, pulling out my wallet, and heard his labored wheezing. My right hand was pinned

beneath me, but I was able to slide my fingers down
until I could grip the Colt and, when he flipped me
onto my back, I aimed the gun at the blur of his
torso—my vision had gone out of whack—and pulled
the trigger. Nothing happened. My finger was outside
the trigger guard. He grabbed the barrel, tugging and
jerking at the Colt, grunting with effort, dragging me
about, while I hung on doggedly, trying to fit my finger
into the guard.

Everything moved slowly, as if I were trapped beneath the surface of a dream. I recall thinking what a
dumb son of a bitch he was not to knock my arm
aside and use his weight against me; and I had other
thoughts as well, groggy, fearful thoughts, a dull wash
of regrets and recriminations. And I realized I should
have known from the disorderly state of the various
Cradles' possessions that the fat man was not holding
them in safekeeping, that he had simply emptied their
packs on the floor while going through them, and the
men whose lives they represented were probably adrift
in the canal . . . and then my finger slipped inside the
guard. There was a blast of noise and heat and light,
a searing pain in my hand, and two screams, one of
them mine.

My eyes squeezed shut, clutching my wrist; it was
all I could do at first to manage the pain. I knew the
Colt had exploded, and my sole concern was the extent of my injuries. Though it bled profusely, the
wound seemed minor—the explosion had sliced a
chunk out of the webbing of skin between my forefinger and thumb. My ears rang, but I soon became
aware of a breathy, flutelike sound and glanced at
the fat man. He lay sprawled among his victims' dirty
laundry, head and shoulders propped against a crate,
staring at me or, more likely, at nothing, for his eyes
did not track me when I came to a knee; he continued
to stare at the same point in space, whimpering softly,
his pinkish complexion undercut by a pasty tone. He,
too, was clutching his wrist. His hand was a ruin, the
fingers missing, except for a shred of the thumb. With

its scorched stumps and flaps of skin, it resembled a strange tuber excavated from the red soil of his belly. His lower abdomen was a porridge of blood and flesh, glistening and shuddering with his shallow breaths—it appeared that swollen round mass was preparing to expel an even greater abomination from a dark red cavity in which were nested coils of intestine. I'd never seen anyone's guts before, and though it was a horrid sight, the writer in me took time to record detail. Then his sphincter let go, and revulsion overwhelmed me.

I staggered to my feet and spotted Bian frozen in the doorway, watching the fat man die with a look of consternation, as if she had no idea how to handle this new development. Dizzy, my head throbbing, I stepped over the fat man's legs. I could do nothing for him; even had there been something, I wouldn't have done it. Bian had retaken her chair in the front room and was fingering her 45s, the image of distraction. I sat opposite her, removed the first-aid kit from my pack, and cleaned my wound with alcohol. A thought occurred to me. I pulled out my English-Vietnamese dictionary and found the word for key.

*"Danh tu?"* I said, pointing to her chain. I went through several variant pronunciations before she grasped my meaning. She said something in Vietnamese and mimed plucking something from a hip pocket.

"Okay, I get." She made a keep-cool gesture. "I get."

I bandaged my hand, and as I secured the bandage with tape, the fat man, emerging from the safe harbor of shock, began pleading for God's help, babbling curses, lapsing now and again into a fuming noise. Bian selected a record, fitted it onto the spindle, and his outcries were buried beneath the strings and faux-pomp of "MacArthur Park." The music started my head to pounding, but it was preferable to hearing the fat man groan.

The sky had opened up, and rain was falling, a steady downpour that would last a while. I saw no reason to hang around. I repacked my rucksack and

nodded to Bian, who responded in kind and gazed out
the door, tapping a finger in time to the beat. As I
walked down a weedy slope toward the park ranger's
shack, I could find in myself no hint of the profound
emotion that was supposed to come with taking a life,
with having violated this most sacrosanct and oft-
breached of taboos, and I pondered the question of
whether I would feel the same if I had killed a non-
Cradle. I'd had a bond of sorts with the fat man, yet
I had a minimal reaction to his death, as if the life I'd
taken were mine by rights, thus negligible . . . though
he might not be dead. Another song, "Nights In White
Satin," began to play, presumably to drown out his
cries; yet I thought Bian might be unmindful of his
condition and was simply luxuriating in the lush, syrupy music that she had taken refuge in during her
months of enslavement. I marveled at the calmness
she displayed upon exchanging captivity for freedom.
Perhaps it was an Asian thing, a less narcotized appreciation of what Riel had known: Someone was always using you, and thus freedom and captivity were
colors we applied to the basic human condition. Perhaps what was a cliché in our culture bespoke a poi-
gnant truth in hers.

Writers tend to romanticize the sordid. They like to
depict a junkie's world, say, as edgy, a scraped-to-the-
bone existence that permits the soul of an artist to
feel life in his marrow and allows him to peer into the
abyss. Many of them believe, as did Rimbaud, or at
least tout the belief, that derangement of the senses
can lead one to experience the sublime; but for every
Rimbaud there are countless millions whose senses
have been deranged to purely loutish ends, and I am
inclined to wonder if *le poete maudit* achieved what
he did in spite of drugs and debauchery, not because
of them. Whatever the case, I was convinced, thanks
in part to the example set by my gargantuan pod
brother, that the sordid was merely sordid. I might be
disagreeable and sarcastic, but my efforts to bring

forth my inner Cradle had been pretty feeble: kinky sex and a smattering of mean-spirited thoughts. Those were minor flaws compared to murder and enslavement. If the trait for which the "animal" needed us had anything to do with our innate repulsiveness, that might explain why I felt its call less profoundly than the others.

It was midafternoon when I set out for the tea forest in a motor launch left by (if the fat man were to be believed) one or another returning Cradle, with the rain falling hard, drenching my clothes, and the sky as dark as dusk. Rain pattered on the launch, hissed in the reeds, and had driven to roost the birds that—so my guidebook attested—normally stalked the wetlands. I followed a meandering watercourse through marshes toward a dark jumbled line in the distance. My head was bothering me. I felt cloudy, vague, gripped by a morose detachment, and assumed I had suffered a mild concussion. Images of Kim, of Lucy and Riel (most of them erotic in nature), were swapped about in my head, as were concerns about the new novel, about my health, about what would happen now that the end of the journey was at hand, and a belated worry that Bian would report me for killing her captor. However, as I drew near the forest, a feeling of glory swept over me. I was on the brink of doing something noble and essential and demanding self-sacrifice. The feeling seemed to come from outside myself, as if—like mist—it surrounded the forest in drifts through which I was passing, emerging now and again, returning to my confused state.

At the verge of the forest, I cut the motor and glided in, catching hold of a trunk to stop myself. The melaleuca tea trees (there must have been thousands, their lovely fan-shaped crowns thick with leaves, extending as far as the eye could see) were between twenty and thirty feet high, and I estimated the depth of the water to be about four feet, lapping gently at the trunks. They cast an ashen shade and formed a canopy that shielded me from the worst of the rain.

A smell of decomposition fouled the air—I wrapped a T-shirt about the lower half of my face to reduce the stench. Peering through the gloom, I spotted other boats, all empty, and bodies floating here and there, bulking up from the dark gray water, their shirts ballooned taut with gasses. The trees segmented my view, offering avenues of sight that were in every direction more or less the same, as if I were trapped in some sort of prison maze.

I restarted the motor and had gone approximately two hundred yards into the forest when I noticed a thinning of the trees ahead and a paling of the light that might signal a clearing; but I could not discern its extent or anything else about it. The bodies that islanded the water near the boundary of the forest were absent here, and this gave me; pause. I cut the engine again and surveyed the area, I could discern no particular menace, yet I had an apprehension of menace and reacted to every sound, jerking my head this way and that. Unable to shake the feeling, I decided a retreat was in order. I swung the boat around and was about to restart the engine, when I spotted a gaunt, bearded man sitting in the crotch of a tree.

At first I wasn't sure the figure was not a deformity of the wood, for his hair and clothing were as gray as the bark of the tree, and his skin, too, held a grayish cast; but then he lifted his hand in a feeble salute. He was lashed in place by an intricately knotted system of rags that allowed him a limited range of motion. His features were those of a Cradle, yet whereas the Cradles I had met with previously were of the same approximate age as me, he appeared older, though this might have been the result of ill usage. "How's it going?" he asked. His voice, too, was feeble, a scratchy croak. I asked why he had lashed himself to the tree.

"If I were you I'd do the same," he said. "Unless you're just going to turn around and leave."

I let the boat come to rest against the trunk of a tree close to his.

"Seems a waste," he said. "Coming all this way and then not sticking around for the show."

"What show?"

He made an elaborate gesture, like a magician introducing a trick. "I don't believe I could do it justice. It's something you have to see for yourself." He worked at something caught in his teeth. "I think this'll be my last night. I need to get back to Phnom Penh."

Nonplussed, I asked why he hadn't gone farther into the forest.

"I'm not a big believer in an afterlife."

"So you're saying the ones who continue on past this point, they die?"

"Questions of life and death are always open to interpretation. But yeah . . . that's what I'm saying. There's two or three hundred of us left in the forest. Some cross over every day. They're half-crazy from being here, from eating bugs and diseased birds. Stuff that makes your insides itch. They finally snap." He glanced toward the clearing. "It's due to start up again. You'd better find something to tie yourself up with. What I did was strip clothes off the corpses."

"I've got something."

I secured the launch to the trunk. The crotch of the melaleuca was no more than a foot above water level and, once I had made myself as comfortable as possible, I removed the coil of rope from my pack. The man advised me to fashion knots that would be difficult to untie and, when I asked why, he replied that I might be tempted to untie them. His affable manner seemed sincere, but we were no more than fifteen feet apart, and my visit with the fat man had made me wary. I kept the knots loose. Once I settled, I asked the man how long he had been in the forest.

"This'll be my fifth night," he said. "I was going to stay longer, but I'm almost out of food, and my underwear's starting to mildew. I want to leave while I'm still strong enough to top off that fat fuck in Phu Tho."

"I wouldn't worry about him."

"Oh, yeah?"

"I dealt with him," I said, wanting to give the impression of being a dangerous man.

"He tried something with you?"

"I didn't give him the opportunity."

I asked if he lived in Phnom Penh, and as the light faded, he told me he operated a small business that offered tours catering to adventure travelers interested in experiencing Cambodia off the beaten path. He went into detail about the business, and although his delivery was smooth, it seemed a rehearsed speech, a story manufactured to cover a more sinister function. I let on that I was also a businessman but left the nature of the business unclear. Our conversation stalled out—it was as if we knew that we had few surprises for the other.

The rain stopped at dusk, and mosquitoes came out in force. I hoped that my faith in malaria medication was not misplaced. With darkness, a salting of stars showed through the canopy, yet their light was insufficient to reveal my neighbor in his tree. I could tell he was still there by the sound of his curses and mosquito-killing slaps. I grew sleepy and had to struggle to keep awake; then, after a couple of hours, I began to cramp, and that woke me up. I asked how much longer we had to wait.

"Don't know," the man said. "I thought it would be coming earlier, but maybe it won't be coming at all. Maybe it's done with us."

Irritated, I said, "Why the hell won't you tell me what's going on?"

"I don't know what's going on. I've got some ideas, but they're pretty damn crazy. You seem stable, a lot more so than most of the pitiful bastards left out here. What I was hoping was for you to give me your take on things and see if it lines up with mine. I don't want to predispose you to thinking about it one way of the other. Okay?"

"The fat guy, he said he thought that whatever it

is—the animal, he called it. He thought the animal wanted our help because the Cradles were badasses."

"Could be. Though I wouldn't say badass. Just plain bad. Rotten." I heard him shifting about. "Wait and see, all right? It shouldn't be much longer."

I spent the next hour or thereabouts hydrating and rubbing cramps out of my legs. One night of this, I told myself, was all I was going to take. The cramps abated, and I began to feel better. However, my mind still wasn't right. I alternated between alertness and periods during which my thoughts wandered away from the forest, wishing I had never left home, wishing Kim was there to steady me with her cool rationality, wishing that we could make a real family and have babies, wondering if I would see her again, not because I felt imperiled and believed I might not survive the tea forest but because of my commitment-phobic character and faithless heart. It was in the midst of this reverie that the man in the tree beside me said, "Here it comes."

I could see no sign of "it," only darkness and dim stars, and asked in which direction he was looking and what he saw.

"Don't you feel that?" he asked.

"Feel what?"

The next moment I experienced a drowsy, stoned sensation, as if I had taken a Valium and knocked back a drink or two. The sensation did not intensify but rather seemed to serve as a platform for a feeling of groggy awe. I saw nothing awe-inspiring in my immediate surrounding, but I noticed that the darkness was not so deep as before (I could just make out my neighbor in his tree), and then I realized that this increased luminosity, which I had assumed was due to a thinning of mist overhead, was being generated from every quarter, even from under the water—a faint golden-white radiance was visible beneath the surface. The light continued to brighten at a rapid rate. In the direction of the clearing, the trees stood out sharply against a curdled mass of incandescence and cast shad-

ows across the water. I began to have some inner ear
discomfort, as if the air pressure were undergoing
rapid changes, but nothing could have greatly dimin-
ished my concentration on the matter at hand. It appeared the forest was a bubble of reality encysted in
light—light streamed from above, from below, from
all the compass points—and, as its magnitude increased, we were about to be engulfed by our confining medium, by the fierce light that burned in the
clearing, a weak point in the walls of the bubble that
threatened to collapse. Filamentous shapes that might
have been many-jointed limbs materialized there and
then faded from view; bulkier forms also emerged,
vanishing before I could fully grasp their outlines or
guess at their function . . . and then, on my left, I
heard a splashing and spotted someone slogging
through the chest-deep water, moving toward the
clearing at an angle that would bring him to within
twenty or twenty-five feet of my tree, reminding me
of the man portrayed on the cover of *The Tea Forest*.
As the figure came abreast of the tree, I saw it was
not a man but a woman wearing a rag of a shirt that
did little to hide her breasts and with hair hanging
in wet strings across features that, although decidedly
feminine, bore the distinct Cradle stamp. She passed
without catching sight of me.

What prompted me to attempt her rescue, I can't
say. Perhaps a fragment of valorous principle surfaced
from the recesses of my brain and sparked sufficiently
to disrupt my increasingly beatific mood. More likely,
it was the desire to learn what it would be like to
(essentially) fuck myself—would I prove to be a screamer
or make little moans? Or perhaps it was the beatific
mood itself that provided motivation, for it seemed to
embody the concept of sacrifice, of giving oneself over
to a higher purpose. I undid the knots that bound me
to the tree and jumped down and went splashing after
her. She heard me and wheeled about, and we stared
at one another. The light had grown so intense that
she was nearly cast in silhouette. Dirt was smeared

across her brow and cheeks and neck. She had a wild, termagant look.

"I won't hurt you," I said, hoping to gentle her. "I promise. Okay?"

Her expression softened.

"Okay?" I came a step forward. "I want to help. You understand?"

She brought her right hand up from beneath the water and lunged toward me, slashing at my throat with a knife. She had me cold, though I saw it at the last second and tried to duck . . . but she must have slipped. She fell sideways, and I toppled backward. The next I knew, we were both floundering in the water. I locked onto her right wrist, and we grappled, managing to stand. Turned toward the source of that uncanny light, she hissed at me. Droplets of water beaded her hair and skin. They glowed like weird, translucent gems, making her face seem barbarous and feral. Her naked breasts, asway in the struggle, were emblems of savagery. She kneed me and clawed and, whenever our heads came together, she snapped at my cheek, my lip; but I gained the advantage and drew back my fist to finish her . . . and slipped. I went under, completely submerged, and swallowed a mouthful of that stew of filth and decomposition. When I bobbed back up, I found her standing above me, poised to deliver a killing stroke. And then there was a flat detonation, *blam*, like a door slamming in an empty room. Blood sprayed from her elbow, and she was spun to the side. She staggered and screamed and clutched her arm, staring up into the tree to which the gaunt man was secured—he was aiming a snub-nosed pistol. Cradling her arm, the woman began to plough her way toward the clearing, hurrying now, glancing back every so often. I clung to a trunk and watched her go. The man made some comment, but my ears were still blocked by the changes in air pressure, and I was too disoriented to care what he said.

The forest brightened further, and the light around me gained the unearthly luster favored by artists of

the late Italian Renaissance that you sometimes get
when the afternoon sun breaks through storm clouds,
and the break widens and holds, and it appears that
everything in the landscape has become a radiant
source and is releasing a rich, spectral energy. Close
by what I presumed to be the edge of the clearing,
the trees—both their crowns and trunks—had gone
transparent, as if they were being irradiated, shifted
out of existence. As the woman approached these
trees, a tiny dark figure incised against the body of
light, she suddenly attenuated and came apart, dissolv-
ing into a particulate mass that flew toward the center
of the light. I could see her for the longest time, dwindling and dwindling, and this caused me to realize that
I had no idea of the perspective involved. I had known
it was vast, but now I recognized it to be cosmically
vast. I was gazing into the depths of a creature that
might well envelop galaxies and minnows, black holes,
Chomolungma, earth and air and absence, all things,
in the same way it enveloped the tea forest, seeming
to have created it out of its substance, nurturing it as
an oyster does a pearl. And this led me to a supposition
that would explain the purpose of my journey: Like
pearls, the Cradles were necessary to its health . . .
and it may have been that the whole of mankind was
necessary to cure it of or protect it from a variety of
disorders; but for this particular disorder, only Cradles
would serve.

I did not reach this conclusion at once but over
the course of an interminable night, watching other
deracinated Cradles—twenty or more—cross the
drowned forest to meet their fate, repeating the transition that the woman had made. The druggy reverence
I had earlier felt reinstituted itself, though not as
strongly as before, and I felt a compulsion to join
them, to sacrifice my life in hopes of some undefined
reward, a notion allied with that now-familiar sense of
glorious promise. I believe my fight with the woman,
however, had put me out of that head enough so that
I was able to resist—or else, having nearly run out of

Cradles, the thing, the animal, God, the All, whatever you wished to call it, needed survivors to breed and replenish its medicine cabinet (giving the Biblical instruction "Be fruitful and multiply" a new spin) and thus had dialed back the urgency of its summons.

Toward dawn, the light dimmed, and I was able to see deeper into the thing. I noticed what might have been cellular walls within it and more of the ephemeral, limblike structures that I had previously observed. At one point I saw what appeared to be a grayish cloud fluttering above a dark object—it looked as if one of the lesser internal structures had been coated with something, for nowhere else did I see a hint of darkness, and there was an unevenness of coloration that suggested erosion or careless application. The fluttering of the cloud had something of an animal character—agitated, frustrated—that brought to mind the approach-avoidance behavior of a mouse to a trap baited with cheese, sensing danger yet lusting after the morsel. I recalled my opiated vision aboard the *Undine*, the gray patch that had been chasing after the luminous void-dweller, and I thought the coating must be the blood and bones of countless Cradles reduced to a shield that protected it from the depredations of the cloud. Soon it passed from view, seeming to circulate away, as though the creature were shifting or an internal tide were carrying it off.

A deep blue sky pricked with stars showed among the leaves overhead, the last of the light faded, and I continued to squat neck-deep in the water, staring after it, trying to find some accommodation between what I thought I had known of the world and what I had seen. While I was not a religious man, I was dismayed to have learned that the religious impulse was nothing more than a twitch of evolutionary biology. I could place no other interpretation on the event that I had witnessed. The parallels to the peak Christian experience were inescapable. I was dazed and frightened, more so than I had been in the presence of the creature. My fear had been suppressed by the concomitant feelings of awe and glory, and though I knew it had not truly gone anywhere, that it still enclosed all I saw and would ever see, now that it was no longer visible, I feared it would return . . . and yet I was plagued by another feeling, less potent but no less palpable. I felt bereft by its absence and longed to see it again. These emotions gradually ebbed, and I became eager to put that oppressive place behind me. I splashed over to the tree where I had tied up the boat and began fumbling with the line.

"Hey, brother," said the man in the tree adjacent to mine. "Take me with you."

Anxiety floored the superficial nonchalance of his tone. He still held the pistol, though not aiming it at me. I told him to find his own boat—there were plenty around.

"I don't have the will to leave," he said. "And if I don't leave, that thing's going to get me." He offered me the pistol. "You have to help me. I won't try anything." He laughed weakly. "The shape I'm in, it wouldn't matter if I did."

I knew he had been playing me, that his every word and action had been designed toward this end; but he *had* saved my life. I took the gun and told him to bind his hands as tightly as he could manage. When this was done, I helped him down from the tree and into the boat. He was frail, his skin loose on his bones, and I guessed that he had lied to me, that he had been in the forest far longer than five nights. I checked his bonds, settled him into the bow, and climbed in. The man seemed greatly relieved. He pressed his fists to his forehead, as if fighting back tears. When he had recovered, he asked what I thought about things now that I had seen the show. I summarized my reactions and he nodded.

"You didn't carry out the metaphor as far as I did," he said. "But yeah, that pretty much says it."

I asked him to explain what he meant by carrying out the metaphor.

"If you accept that our bad character is what makes

us useful to it . . . or at least is symptomatic of the quality that makes us useful. Our psychic reek or something." He broke off, apparently searching for the right words. "You saw that gray, swarming thing? How it seemed reluctant to come near the part that was treated? Coated, as you said."

"Yeah. So?"

"Well, given that we were the element holding off the gray thing, and that our one outstanding characteristic is our essential crumminess, my idea is that the animal used us for repellent."

I stared at him.

"You know," he said. "Like mosquito repellent. Shark repellent."

"I got it."

"It's just a theory." He obviously assumed that I disagreed with him and became a bit defensive. "I realize it trivializes us even more than how you figured it."

I unscrewed the gas cap and peered inside the tank—we had enough fuel for the return trip.

The man chuckled and said, "It's kind of funny when you think about it, you know."

All journeys end in disappointment if for no other reason than that they end. Life disappoints us. Love fails to last. This has always been so, but the disappointment I felt at the end of my journey may relate more to a condition of our age of video games and event movies. To have come all this way and found only God—there should have been pirates, explosions, cities in ruins, armies slinking from the field of battle, not merely this doleful scene with a handful of Cradles and a glowing bug.

A better writer than I, the author of *The Tea Forest*, once said, "After you understand everything, all that's left to do is to forget it." I doubted my understanding was complete, but I saw his point. I could return home and lash myself to a tree and never leave again; I could make babies with Kim and subsume my compre-

hension of the world, the universe, in the trivial bustle
of life. Perhaps I would be successful in this, but I
knew I'd have to work at it, and I worried that the
images I retained from my night in the forest would
fatally weaken my resolution.

During the ride back, the man became boastful. I
empathized with this—it gave you a heady feeling to
have abandoned God, to have left Him in His Holy
Swamp, trolling for Cradles, and though you knew this
wasn't actually the case, that He was still big in your
life, you had to go with that feeling in order to main-
tain some dignity. When we reached Phnom Penh, the
man said, I'd be treated like a king. Anything I
wanted, be it women, drugs, or money, he'd see I got
more than my share, a never-ending bout of decadent
pleasures. Could he be, I wondered, the Ur-Cradle,
the evil genius at the center of an Asiatic empire, the
crime lord before whom lesser crime lords quailed? It
was possible. Evil required no real genius, only power,
a lack of conscience, and an acquisitive nature such
as I had seen at work in the tea forest. Men were,
indeed, made in Its Image . . . at least writers and
criminals were. Whatever, I planned to put the man
ashore at the nearest inhabited village and then head
for Saigon and, hopefully, Kim.

Another passage from *The Tea Forest* occurred
to me:

". . . He had tried to make an architectural statement of his life after the tea forest, to isolate a geometric volume of air within a confine whose firm
foundations and soaring walls and sculptural conceits
reflected an internal ideal, a refinement of function, a
purity of intent. Though partially successful in this,
though he had buried his memories of the forest beneath the process of his art, he became aware that the
task was impossible. One journey begat another. Even
if you were to remain in a single place, the mind traveled. His resolves would fray, and, eventually, everything he had accomplished and accumulated—the swan

of leaded crystal keeping watch from the windowsill, the books, the Indonesian shadow puppets that haunted his study, the women, his friends, the framed Tibetan paintings, the madras curtains that gaudily colored the bedroom light, his habit of taking morning tea and reading the Post at Damrey's stall in the Russian Market, the very idea of having possessions and being possessed—these things would ultimately become meaningless, and he would escape the prison he had fashioned of them into the larger yet no less confining prison of his nature, and he would begin to wonder, What now? When would the monster next appear and for what purpose? How could he, who had been granted the opportunity to understand so much, know so little?"

It was a dreary prospect that Cradle Two painted, one I chose to deny. Unlike him, I had performed a redemptive act by saving the man—that signaled hope for improvement, surely—and I believed that, with Kim's help, I could shape a world that would contain more than my ego and ambition. I would learn to make do with life's pleasures no matter how illegitimate they were. And if I thought too much about the forest, why then I could write about it. *The Tea Forest* need not be a stand-alone book. A sequel might be in order, one that further explored the nature of the animal; perhaps a trilogy, a spiritual odyssey with a well-defined and exalting ending. I smelled awards, large advances. Small things, yet they delighted me.

The sun was up and the air steamy, baking the weeds and the little houses, when we came to Phu Tho. A putrid stench proceeded from the pale green house where the fat Cradle had died, and the innumerable ruined and stranded boats looked almost festive in the morning light, like the remnants of a regatta at which too good a time had been had by all. We had reached the banks of the canal when I remembered something. I told the man to wait, that I had left certain of my possessions in the fat man's house. He sank to the grass, grateful to have a rest. I walked back to the house and peeked in the door. Bian had fled and taken her records. I tied my T-shirt about my nose and mouth to cut the smell and steeled myself. It promised to be a disgusting business, retrieving the notebooks of my dead brothers, but I had my career to think of.

# NINE ALTERNATE
# ALTERNATE HISTORIES

## *Benjamin Rosenbaum*

1. The point of convergence. If any given event may have two subtly different alternate causes, perhaps both may obtain. If history books from two alternate timelines that arrive at the same place have different reasons to tell the same lies, convergence is possible, maybe inevitable.

2. The point of convergence, theological. Perhaps we evolved from apes, from shambling lichen molds, were molded out of corn after the destruction of our elder mud siblings, coalesced out of wishes, lost our way in the unused back service hallways of the fifth floor of a metadepartment store in the dreamlands and took the wrong elevator, were created by a loving god, were trapped here by an evil demiurge, were banished here to unlearn false ideas, are dreams in the mind of the Red King, made up this game and forgot we were playing it. Or all these at once, and this is the point of convergence, the point at which the histories become indistinguishable, and, as of today, it no longer matters what story we tell.

3. The point of divergence, personal. It's raining now in Freie Strasse. Without moving my head, I see five hundred new white explosions every instant: rain-

drops punishing the dark sidewalk, the dark street, five hundred tiny fists, and then five hundred more. Had I left Starbucks fifteen minutes ago, I would be at the office now. Dry.

We humor ourselves that these decisions matter.

Or else we console ourselves that they don't.

4. The point of convergence, personal. Instead of asking, "Had I but . . . ?" or "Had I not . . . ?" ask "Did I really?"

You broke his doll. He cried. And then there are stories as to why. You maintained your innocence; you thought you had a right to play with this doll in this way. You were accused of insensitivity. He argued for malice. Secretly you suspected yourself of an irrepressible caprice, a wild demonic hunger for the world to go bang. Like a beast inside you that was beyond your control. But maybe that was not how it was at all.

You know the one you kissed when you shouldn't have? You had a headache. There was not really time. Also, it was too early, not right. And it ended badly. Did you really want that kiss? What were you thinking? Maybe you were showing off. Maybe you were about to cry, and the kiss stopped it. Maybe you would have done anything just to feel something. Maybe you were giddy. Maybe you were angry. It's hard to recall. Was it really you who broke the doll? Sometimes you take an old photograph out of a box, or compare two dates in your mind, and suddenly fall into a new history.

Maybe you have an army of pasts, crowding around each of those moments. Maybe an army of ghost-yous were cheated, tricked into sharing a future, when they could have lived so many different lives.

5. The pandemonic history. You made every decision, you took every choice. You kissed and killed and greeted meekly and ignored everyone you ever saw. You ate rocks, tossed babies out of windows. Broke

and mended every doll. At every moment you were conscious of a choice, you made all choices. At every moment when you thought you had no choice, that circumstances forced your hand, you chose everything then too, you kept and broke and ignored and reinvented every promise, incurred and evaded every consequence. At every moment your memory elides, because you were sunk into habitual action, just getting from point A to point B, you did every possible thing then too—crashed the car, stopped and stared out at the marsh, sang country songs in languages you don't even know.

In fact, you speak every language, even languages that don't exist, because right now, right this moment, you are in the midst of using your tongue and throat in every possible way. It makes a huge howl filling the space of all those yous.

And every person and pigeon and raindrop makes all choices too, filling the space. Filling the possible space.

The history of all this destroys narrative; it is a sculpture, a thick fabric, each instant a knot exploding into a flower of threads.

And you are tracing your finger over one thread, choosing a life. But you could stop right now.

Isn't that restful?

Isn't that a restful thing to think?


6. The alternate history is here, it is just not evenly distributed. There are places the South won the war. There are places the Nazis won the war. There are places the Revolution succeeded and lapsed into the everyday. There are places the rightful king was restored. There are stacks of skulls. There are clusters of adobe buildings in the sun, where water runs, cold and clear, in secret shaded places, and the women's hands sift the grains of corns and there is peace. There is just government and technical brilliance and magic. There are those who heal with their hands, and there are places where superstition was banished by the light

of Reason. There are lithe, furry, upright creatures with heads the size of softballs who carry spears, running among the vines.

7. The definite history.

We love choice. Choice is liberty, choice is the bounty of the common man. When we tell ourselves alternate histories, we are reassuring ourselves of the profaneness of events. We might have lost the war, we tell ourselves. We might have lost. And then everything would be different. There was a point of divergence. For want of a nail.

(If you had kissed the other one, instead . . .)

And so too in this moment: For want of will, for want of clarity, for want of love, we could lose this moment, this war, this choice. We stand at a fork in the road, and one road leads down into darkness and the other up into light. Choose, choose, choose, choose, choose wisely.

We stand in the supermarket aisle and read ingredients. These cookies have partially hydrogenated vegetable oil; these do not. Plus they are made with organic flour. This stock has a P/E of 15. This browser has better security. This job is nearer to my house. This one loves me best.

But perhaps this cry of "choose" is like the hooting of an owl. Perhaps choice is limited to the Planck radius, and damping effects make of our macroscopic world a clockwork machine. Perhaps God guides the nail from the shoe, dropping the horse, grounding the king, losing the battle, because God wants the war lost. Perhaps this is all overdetermined by historical inevitability. Perhaps the date of your death is written already in the pages of the Book of the Norns, partially hydrogenated vegetable oil or no.

Perhaps this history is the only history, perhaps it is a series of equations with definite solutions, perhaps it commands our obedience. And this is to say that it is sacred, that there are secret numbers behind apparent choices, that if we could see the world finally, we would not see choices but only things. And then when we wrote alternate history, we would only write: No.

8. The provisional history. Conceivably, the world is a machine designed to solve some problem. Perhaps it is a problem that cannot be solved analytically or intuitively; it requires a world, it requires a sequence of events. The solution cannot be apprehended from afar, all at once; instead, a tree of possibilities must be exhaustively traversed. Moments must be gone through, one after the other, each moment the startling, unpredictable result of the last, a chain of events followed until it becomes clear that the chain is not approaching a solution. Then the machine must backtrack, erasing the events, resetting the state, and then embarking down a different path.

So this time you are living in now, perhaps it has no durability. Unless it yields results, it will be erased. Your choices are provisional; if they work out, they will be retained. Otherwise, you will choose again. We may say, adjusting the framing of our narration to the bounds of your phenomenological experience: You will have the chance to choose again.

You will have a chance to unbreak the doll, unkiss the kiss. On the other hand, all this will be lost.

What is it like, then, to tell such a tale, to tell a story that turns out to have no consequences? A story of a draft universe, a narrative transaction that is rolled back and eliminated, of deaths postponed, shadow lives swirling and then clearing, as a mist, until the final, the correct life is found?

(If the machine ever even halts; some problems are insoluble).

Restful, restful.

9. The provisional history, theological. I am crying for you, Beloved. I am killing you, and I am crying. And then you are here again. And on and on, until you have done your duty. Until I have understood. Thank you. Thank you. I am sorry. Thank you.

# About the Authors

**Robert Charles Wilson** is the author of more than a dozen novels, including the Hugo Award-winning *Spin* and its sequel, *Axis*, as well as *A Bridge of Years*, *Darwinia*, *Mysterium*, *Blind Lake*, and *Bios*. His next novel will be *Julian Comstock: A Story of the 22nd Century*. Born in California, he currently lives near Toronto.

Award-winning novelist **Jeff VanderMeer** is the author of the best-selling *City of Saints & Madmen*, set in his signature creation, the imaginary city of Ambergris, in addition to several other novels from Bantam, Tor, and Pan Macmillan. He has won two World Fantasy Awards, an NEA-funded Florida Individual Writers' Fellowship, and, most recently, the Le Cafard Cosmique Award in France and the Tähtifantasia Award in Finland, both for *City of Saints & Madmen*. He has also been a finalist for the Hugo Award, Bram Stoker Award, IHG Award, Philip K. Dick Award, and many others. Other novels such as *Veniss Underground* and *Shriek: An Afterword* have made the year's best lists of Amazon.com, *The Austin Chronicle*, *The San Francisco Chronicle*, and *Publishers Weekly*, among others. His work, both novels and short stories, has been translated into over twenty languages. *The Thackery T. Lambshead Pocket Guide to Eccentric & Discred-*

*ited Diseases* may be his most famous anthology and is considered a cult classic, still in print along with his Leviathan original fiction series.

**Stephen Baxter** was born in Liverpool. He holds degrees in mathematics and engineering and has worked as a teacher of math and physics and in information technology. He is also a Chartered Engineer. In 1991, Baxter applied to become a cosmonaut, aiming for the guest slot on *Mir* eventually taken by Helen Sharman, but fell at an early hurdle. His first professionally published short story appeared in 1987 and his first novel in 1991. Baxter has been a full-time author since 1995, with over forty science fiction novels published around the world. He is the President of the British Science Fiction Association, a Vice President of the H.G. Wells Society, and Fellow of the British Interplanetary Society. Baxter and his family moved to Northumberland in 2004. His current project is a pair of books describing a catastrophic inundation of the Earth: *Flood* and *Ark*.

**Gene Wolfe** grew up in Houston, Texas, where he attended Edgar Allan Poe Elementary School. He dropped out of Texas A&M and got a CIB in Korea. In 1956, he graduated from the University of Houston. He and his wife, Rosemary, were married that year; they have two sons and two daughters, three granddaughters, a step-granddaughter and a step-grandson. Wolfe has written *The Fifth Head of Cerberus*, *Peace*, *The Devil in a Forest*, *The Book of the New Sun*, *Castleview*, *There Are Doors*, *Soldier of the Mist*, *Soldier of Arete*, *Soldier of Sidon*, *The Book of the Long Sun*, *The Book of the Short Sun*, and others. His work has won two Nebula Awards, three World Fantasy Awards, the Deathrealm Award, the British Science Fiction Award, the British Fantasy Award, and others. His short fiction is collected in *The Island of Doctor Death And Other Stories*, *Castle of Days*, *Endangered Species*, *Storeys From the Old Hotel*, *Strange Travel-*

*ers*, **Innocents Aboard**, and **Starwater Strains**. A two-volume fantasy, The Wizard Knight, is complete with the publication of **The Wizard**. He's been the Guest of Honor at a Worldcon, a World Horror Convention, and a World Fantasy Convention. His latest novel is **An Evil Guest**.

**Liz Williams'** mother is a Gothic novelist, and her father was a part-time conjuror, so she didn't have a hope. She's been a science fiction fan since the age of ten, and she started writing seriously about ten years ago. Jack Vance's Planet of Adventure series was responsible, and she's still a huge fan of Vance. Other favorites include Ursula K. Le Guin, Ray Bradbury, Mary Gentle, George R.R. Martin, C.J. Cherryh, Tanith Lee, and Marion Zimmer Bradley. She now writes full time, but she has had various incarnations. Her background is in history and philosophy of science; having done degrees in philosophy and artificial intelligence at the Universities of Manchester and Sussex, she did a doctorate at Cambridge, graduating in 1993. She held a variety of part-time jobs, including a now-infamous stint on Brighton's pier as a tarot reader, before full-time work in Kazakhstan. She also spent a year running an IT program at Brighton Women's Centre, then became a full time writer in 2002.

**Theodora Goss** was born in Hungary and spent her childhood in various European countries before her family moved to the United States. Although she grew up on the classics of English literature, her writing has been influenced by an Eastern European literary tradition in which the boundaries between realism and the fantastic are often ambiguous. She lives in Boston, where she is completing a Ph.D. in English literature. Her short story collection, **In the Forest of Forgetting**, which includes World Fantasy Award nominee "The Wings of Meister Wilhelm" and Nebula Award nominee "Pip and the Fairies," was published in 2006. **Interfictions**, an anthology she coedited with Delia

Sherman, was published in 2007. Her short stories and poems have been reprinted in a number of Year's Best anthologies, including *Year's Best Fantasy*, *The Year's Best Fantasy and Horror*, and *The Year's Best Science Fiction and Fantasy for Teens*. Visit her website at www.theodoragoss.com.

**Greg van Eekhout**'s stories have appeared in places such as *Year's Best Science Fiction*, *Year's Best Fantasy & Horror*, *Asimov's Science Fiction*, *Magazine of Fantasy and Science Fiction*, and *Realms of Fantasy*. His debut novel, *Norse Code*, will be released in May 2009. Greg lives in San Diego and blogs at http://www.writingandsnacks.com.

**Alastair Reynolds** was born in Barry, South Wales, in 1966. After getting a Ph.D. in astronomy he moved to the Netherlands to work for the European Space Agency. He turned full-time writer in 2004. He and his wife have returned to South Wales, near Cardiff. His first fiction sale appeared in *Interzone* in 1990, and he published his first novel, *Revelation Space*, in 2000. *Revelation Space* was shortlisted for the BSFA and Clarke awards, and his second novel, *Chasm City*, went on to win the BSFA. Subsequent works include another six novels, of which the most recent are *Pushing Ice* (2005), *The Prefect* (2007), and the far-future space opera *House of Suns* (2008), as well as the linked novellas "Diamond Dogs," "Turquoise Days" (2003), and two collections of short fiction, *Galactic North* and *Zima Blue* (2006). Forthcoming are stories in *Galactic Empires* and *The Starry Rift*. His story in *Other Earths* stems from a long fascination and love affair with the music of Ralph Vaughan Williams and his contemporaries.

**Paul Park** lives in Massachusetts with his family and occasionally teaches at Williams College. Since finishing four novels set in an alternate version of eastern Europe (the Roumania Quartet—*A Princess of Roumania*, *The*

*Tourmaline*, *The White Tyger*, *The Hidden World*), he has been writing short fiction. "A Family History" came out of a fundraiser for the Clarion West workshops, during which he auctioned off on eBay certain elements of an as yet unwritten story—the theme, the title, the various locations, the characters, the genre, etc. The winners would provide these things, and he would write a story that incorporated them. "A Family History" is the result.

**Lucius Shepard** was born in Lynchburg, Virginia, grew up in Daytona Beach, Florida, and lives in Vancouver, Washington. His short fiction has won the Nebula Award, the Hugo Award, The International Horror Writers Award, the National Magazine Award, the Locus Award, the Theodore Sturgeon Award, and the World Fantasy Award. His latest works are a short novel, *Softspoken*, a career retrospective, *The Best of Lucius Shepard*, and *Viator Plus*, a collection of newer work from PS Publishing in Britain.

**Benjamin Rosenbaum** grew up in Arlington, Virginia. He wanted to be either a superhero, a scientist, or a writer. He didn't want to be the kind of scientist who carefully studies and contemplates natural phenomena, however; he wanted to be the kind who builds giant ray guns. As for being a superhero, while he does have superpowers, he reports that they are not very impressive, and he could never design a costume to his liking. He therefore decided to be a writer. He says, "Typically, when you ask writers why they write, they look at you dourly and say, 'I have to. I am driven to do so. If you do not absolutely have to write, spare yourself this misery.' Not me. I don't have to write. I write because I love it. I'm grateful for every minute I get to do it. It's like being a superhero, but you don't need a costume."

# CJ Cherryh

## *Complete Classic Novels in Omnibus Editions*

**THE DREAMING TREE**
*The Dreamstone* and *The Tree of Swords and Jewels*
0-88677-782-8

**THE FADED SUN TRILOGY**
*Kesrith*, *Shon'jir*, and *Kutath*.            0-88677-836-0

**THE MORGAINE SAGA**
*Gate of Ivrel*, *Well of Shiuan*, and *Fires of Azeroth*.
0-88677-877-8

**THE CHANUR SAGA**
*The Pride of Chanur*, *Chanur's Venture* and
*The Kif Strike Back*.            0-88677-930-8

**ALTERNATE REALITIES**
*Port Eterntiy*, *Voyager in Night*, and *Wave Without a Shore*
0-88677-946-4

**AT THE EDGE OF SPACE**
*Brothers of Earth* and *Hunter of Worlds*.    0-7564-0160-7

**THE DEEP BEYOND**
*Serpent's Reach* and *Cuckoo's Egg*.    0-7564-0311-1

**ALLIANCE SPACE**
*Merchanter's Luck* and *40,000 in Gehenna*    0-7564-0494-9

To Order Call: 1-800-788-6262
www.dawbooks.com

# C.S. Friedman

*The Best in Science Fiction*

# RM Meluch

## *The Tour of the Merrimack*

"An action-packed space opera. For readers who like romps through outer space, lots of battles with gooey horrific insects, and character sexplotation, *The Myriad* delivers..."     —*SciFi.com*

"Like *The Myriad*, this one is grand space opera. You will enjoy it."     —*Analog*

"This is grand old-fashioned space opera, so toss your disbelief out the nearest airlock and dive in."
                    —*Publishers Weekly* (Starred Review)

**THE MYRIAD**          0-7564-0320-1
**WOLF STAR**          0-7564-0383-6
**THE SAGITTARIUS COMMAND**
                    978-0-7564-0490-1
and now in hardcover:
**STRENGTH AND HONOR**
          978-0-7564-0527-4

To Order Call: 1-800-788-6262
www.dawbooks.com

DAW 48